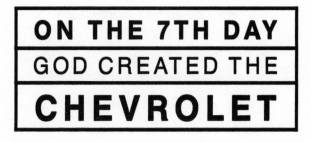

ON THE 7TH DAY
GOD CREATED THE
CHEVROLET

Also by Sylvia Wilkinson

Fiction

Moss on the North Side

A Killing Frost

Cale

Shadow of the Mountain

Bone of My Bones

Nonfiction

The Stainless Steel Carrot: An Auto Racing Odyssey

Dirt Tracks to Glory

Juvenile

The True Book of Automobiles

I Can Be a Race Car Driver

World of Racing series (10 titles)

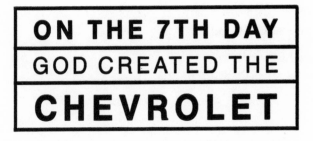

ON THE 7TH DAY
GOD CREATED THE
CHEVROLET

BY SYLVIA WILKINSON

Algonquin Books of Chapel Hill
1993

Published by

Algonquin Books of Chapel Hill

Post Office Box 2225

Chapel Hill, North Carolina 27515-2225

a division of

Workman Publishing Company

708 Broadway

New York, New York 10003

© 1993 by Sylvia Wilkinson. All rights reserved.

Printed in the United States of America.

Library of Congress Cataloging-in-Publication Data

Wilkinson, Sylvia, 1940–

   On the 7th Day, God Created the Chevrolet /

by Sylvia Wilkinson. — 1st ed.

   p. cm.

   ISBN 0-945575-13-0

   1. Vietnamese Conflict, 1961–1975—Veterans—North Carolina—

Fiction.   2. Automobile racing—North Carolina—Fiction.

3. Brothers—North Carolina—Fiction.   I. Title.   II. Title: On

the 7th Day, God Created the Chevrolet.

PS3573.I4426A83   1993

813'.54—dc20   93-13727

                                                   CIP

10 9 8 7 6 5 4 3 2 1

First Edition

for John Morton

Acknowledgments

The author is grateful to the following people for their help with this book: John Morton, Joe Tobin, David Vance, Lanky Foushee, Mike Barto, Freddie Lorenzen, Humpy Wheeler, Richard Howard, Tim Flock, Ralph Moody, Banjo Matthews, Linda Vaughn, Richard and Lee Petty, Wendell Scott, Darel Bennett, Johnny Woods, Mike Ferrari, Andy Bondio, Ashley Page, Raymond Williams, Crawfish Crider, Rick Knoop, Charlie Eddy, John Christie, Dan Baker, Bill Bennett, Turkey Ford, Willy T. Ribbs, Thurman George, Cravon George, Jeff Wasserman, Dave Rosenblum, David Pearson, Jimmy Jones, Ralph Murphy, Joe Littlejohn, Leonard Villette, Ray Morton, Ned Jarrett, Tommy Wilkinson, Jeff Kline, Gerald Searles, John Kalagian, Dave Kent, Bill Libby, Ryan Falconer, Jerry Bledsoe, Lyman Morton, Joey Cavaglieri, Shaylor Duncan, Dennis Aase, Alex Umstead, Pete Feistmann, Bobby York, Erv Houston, Rocky Moran, Bill France, Sr., Jim Hunter, William Neely, Bobby Isaac, Charlie Selix, Bud Moore, Soapy Castles, Clayton Cunningham, Darren Snyder, Jimmy D. Brown, and Gene Hingert.

Those guys who came up from bootleg running were tough and they raced hard. The first thing I learned when I went down there thinking I was hot stuff was the North was not race country. The South didn't have baseball and football then; racing was it. The first thing I did was get my doors blown off.

—FREDDIE LORENZEN

ON THE 7TH DAY
GOD CREATED THE
CHEVROLET

I

"Doggone it, Tom. You go just as fast the wrong way as you go the right way."

After Tom hit seventeen, using money that emerged from his pocket like magic, he bought his dream car, a '55 Chevy Bel Air. With his little brother Zack beside him, the familiar road to town branched out into an expanding labyrinth of pavement and dirt. Zack's unspoken job was to figure out everything but the driving. If left up to Tom, they would just leave their farm, forgetting half of what they needed to carry. Or run out of gas. Or they would get lost and Tom would get mad. He would drive by road signs too fast for Zack to see them.

But Tom only had one speed—as fast as he could go. He drove his Chevy even faster at night than he did in daylight. A barrier of fur, flesh, and bone with silver orbs set in its face frozen in his headlights—Tom reasoned it stood in his path to prove he was fast enough to dodge it. And he did.

"I never killed anything," he claimed, "not even a stupid old possum."

Although Tom Pate got accused of a lot, Zack's memory also says this is true. But even Tom can't deny he hit a wall or two.

Tom's big one happens in 1968 at Martinsville, the half-mile paved oval where he had broken his arm the year before. The race is two hundred and fifty miles long, five hundred trips in a circle, but before four hundred revolutions, Tom's motor blows in a big way, catching fire on its own oil. His rear tires lose their grip as oil finds its way between the rubber and the pavement. He crashes straight in, his right foot hard on the

1

brake of Bullfrog Embers' red Chevrolet, the impact shoving the engine into the front of the cockpit. When his forward motion stops, he tugs on his right foot but it stays on the pedal. Flames off the burning oil come up past his knees, blackening the air he is trapped in.

Tom holds his breath, turning his face toward the window and reaching down into the flames until he feels his ankle. Then he pulls apart the twisted metal that grips his foot, an act he never could have accomplished in the shop. When he yanks open the window net and reaches through to lift his body clear, skin slides away from his hands; his gloves have melted. He drops to his knees on the track. The noise around him seems awful, worse than the engine explosion.

Maynard Peyton, his silver-haired crew chief, runs to the car with the bucket of water he had planned to dump over the radiator during the next pit stop and shoves both of Tom's burned hands under the water. They sizzle like steak on a grill.

The awful noise passes again as the field of cars threads single file behind the pace car, snaking around his wreck.

"Only had one bucket," Maynard grunts. "Get that foot in there too."

Tom twists his body around trying to get his foot in the bucket, but now the emergency crew takes over. When Tom's melted goggles are lifted from his eyes in the ambulance, he sees his hands and his foot and knows there should be pain, but there is none. The last pain he felt was in his ears when the engine let go.

Later, in the hospital, he hears Maynard talking but not to him. Then he hears a stranger's voice: "Second degree, some third on the tips. May need a graft, but he's young and healthy. His face looks bad, but it's superficial. Just a bad sunburn. The goggles melted, but they saved his eyes."

"Maynard!" Tom shouts. "You and that doctor get in here where I can see you."

Maynard sticks his face around the corner and smiles. "You're going to get well, Pate, okay? We're just deciding how long he has to put up with you. Boy, are you ugly!"

The doctor walks across the room and picks up Tom's chart from the foot of the bed. He seems too young. Tom doesn't like that. And he isn't Southern. Tom's face itches. He lifts his right hand to scratch his nose, but to his surprise, his hand is a large white basketball on the end of his arm. The other one matches.

"The danger of infection must be past before he is released," the doctor says.

As soon as the doctor leaves the room, Maynard says, "Hey Pate, you're famous."

"How's that?" Tom replied.

"You know how they call Richard Petty, King Richard? You're King of Turn Three at Martinsville. From now on they're calling it Pole Cat Corner."

"Are you going to let somebody else drive my car, Maynard?"

"Sure, I already hired him."

"Not funny."

"Take a couple of weeks before you've got a car again. And if anybody drives it, it'll be me."

"What if it had been my fault?"

"New guy in there for the next race, buddy. We don't allow mistakes in this business. Tell that to the genius who built that engine."

"You built it."

"Right. And you busted it."

After Maynard leaves, Tom tries to go over his words in his head. He can't remember what they talked about. They must have given him something. He feels goofy.

He knows where he is. In the hospital, the same damn place in Martinsville. He sees a nurse pass his door, the same nurse

3

he had after his last crash. "Hey," he calls. She looks in with a smile: auburn hair, a turned-up nose, and a shape that refuses to hide under the stiff uniform. "Hey, yourself," she replies and disappears. The last time she was his nurse, he'd just had a broken arm; he'd only pretended to be helpless.

He tries to push the covers back with his hands. He feels like he is in a straitjacket. He kicks at the sheet with his one good foot and sits up, dropping both feet to the floor. As he stumbles to the door of his room, he feels a draft. He looks down; he is wearing a skirt and his legs are bare from the knees down. There are bandages on his right foot and it hurts when he puts his weight on it. He makes his way slowly to the tiny bathroom. A black, greasy face with broken, peeling skin, skin that resembles an old coat of paint being attacked by stripper, fills the tiny mirror over the sink.

He tips his head from one side to the other; the black face tips at the same time. Maybe his nurse didn't recognize him.

He goes back to his doorway and waits until she passes again.

"I bet you didn't recognize me, huh?"

"You're the same driver who got hurt here before."

"I don't do it all the time, really. Just here." She starts to move on. "Wait a minute," he says. "I want you to dial the phone for me." He holds up hands that resemble giant white boxing gloves. "I need to call my mother."

"Long distance?"

"Yeah."

"We'll have to use the pay phone at the end of the hall. I'll get some change. Can you walk without assistance?"

"I'll meet you at the phone," he answers as he walks sideways down the hall, his back to the wall. The nurse places the phone on his shoulder and lifts his white mitt to steady it. He tries to smell her perfume while she dials the numbers that he calls out, but his nose doesn't seem to work. She hurries away when she is done.

Gladys answers on the first ring. She sounds frightened.

"Hey, Mama. It's me."

"Tom. You've hurt yourself again. We heard it on the radio."

"Yeah, Mama. I'm going to be okay, though, don't worry."

"Oh, thank the Lord. Did you break your arm again?"

"No, Mama. Just got a little hot in there is all. But look, right now I need some help if you know what I mean. I mean, I've got these big bandages on my hands and I can't do anything for myself. I couldn't even dial the phone. I can't hold a spoon or do a button, or a zipper. I have these itches all over me I can't scratch. It's kind of embarrassing, Mama. I mean there's some things I've got to do, like soon."

"Tom, don't they have someone there who can do that for you, a nurse?"

"Yeah, I've got a nurse. But I was kind of hoping you could come up here . . ."

"Oh, Tom, I can't possibly leave right now. It's your daddy. I can't leave him alone a minute. He goes walking off and we have to go out looking for him. I'm scared to death he's going to wander off and we won't be able to find him. His mind isn't all there anymore. You knew he had another stroke? No, I guess you didn't," she answers her own question. "If you would come home, Tom, I could take care of both of you just fine. If you'd get one of your friends to bring you or I could send Zack. He took everybody to the beach for the weekend, but when they get back . . ."

The operator interrupts. "Your three minutes are up, sir. Deposit fifty cents more, please."

"Tom, what shall I do?" Gladys pleads.

"I can't get my hands in my pockets, operator. I don't have

5

my wallet," he talks as fast as he can. "Mama, never mind. I hope Daddy is feeling better, okay? I'll work it out. I've got to go now. I . . ."

The phone goes dead. Tom lets it roll off his shoulder. It bangs against the wall. He kicks at it with his bad foot, but stops short of letting it hit. He sees a woman at a desk at the end of the hall, so he edges up there, addressing her from across the hall, his bare backside to the wall.

"I left the phone off the hook," he tells her.

"I can't hear you," the woman says without looking up.

He moves toward her, crossing his bandaged hands behind him. "I couldn't hang the phone up."

When she sees his face, she grimaces. "I'm sure the next person past will see that."

"How do I go about getting a different nurse?"

"Who is your nurse?"

"Sally."

"Sally! You don't like Sally? Everyone likes Sally."

"I don't like her. I want the one I saw go in the room across the hall. The big one with the red nose and short gray hair."

"Mildred."

"Yeah, Mildred. I want Mildred to be my nurse."

"I'm sorry, young man, but without a legitimate complaint, you don't get to change nurses. Besides, Sally is in charge of this floor. Mildred is just a scrub nurse."

"Okay, okay. Here's my complaint." He leans over, but she backs away as if he smells bad. "Sally's a personal friend," he presses on. "I mean we went out a few times, okay? What I really meant to say is she kind of has the hots for me. It's sort of embarrassing, but. . . ." He leans over farther to whisper and the woman rolls her chair backways. "I . . . never mind."

He turns to leave, forgetting his bare backside for a moment before he spins around again on his good foot, sidewinding back down the hall. His burned foot is starting to hurt. He checks the corridor before he backs across the hall into his room.

There are voices outside, but no nurses pass. He kicks his wastebasket over, dumping the ugly contents of cotton and gauze. His face is stinging. He goes into his bathroom. Hot tears run through the grooves on his face. When he presses the giant ball of gauze on his hand to his face, it grabs at his loose flesh. He can't even tell if there is a hand inside the white ball. He can't move it.

He can't hold it much longer. He tries steadying his penis between his two bandaged hands. No good; it slips away from him. He leans against the wall, shifting the weight to his good foot and lifting the bandaged one. That doesn't work either. He can't hold his balance on the bad leg. He straddles the toilet, trying to gather up the cloth of his gown, when suddenly he feels a cold hand on his organ.

"Hurry up, okay, buddy? I got work to do."

He turns to face her, seeing her through his stinging eyes. She doesn't recoil from his damaged face.

"Mildred?"

"Yeah?"

"Okay, I'll hurry. Just let me think about it a second. Maybe if you turned on the water in the sink and I could hear it running, that would make it come faster. Don't go and leave me, okay, please? I know I can do it. It's just different is all. I really appreciate this, Mildred. You're okay. Finally I meet the woman of my dreams and she's rushing me."

Before the end of the season, Tom Pate is racing again. The stiffness in his hands when he shaves or buttons his clothes is forgotten when he drives Bullfrog's race car. There isn't even a dent in his confidence, though he jumps out of the car a little faster when one of the crew guys yells fire while working on his overheated engine. He shivers when Fireball Roberts's niece tells him that after her uncle died in a fiery crash the funeral home sent the family a smoked ham. Now Tom has to wear a cap because the skin on his face sunburns easily. But he loses nothing on the race track.

"Do you really feel that good or are you trying to convince me?" Maynard asks during a practice break at Waverly, Tennessee.

"Just look at my laptimes. What do they say?"

Maynard smiles. He tells Tom a story. "I had this old dog once back on the farm. He lost one of his hind legs, tore it off in a muskrat trap. Old Cottonpicker would go up to a tree and lift that leg like he needed to. And he'd set down and kick fleas on the back of his head with the foot that wasn't even there. Smiled just as contented."

"Save that story for my brother. That's the kind of stuff I've had to put up with from him all my life."

Maynard frowns and shakes his head. "I'll save it to tell to you again when you've learned enough to understand it. When do I get to meet Zack? I want to meet the Pate who has some sense."

"Not for a while."

"You know, I can't figure what's the matter with you young guys. Why don't you get that war won and get it over with? I hate to even think it, but I've got a feeling you're losing this one."

"I didn't lose," Tom defends. "I just went over there and did what a bunch of old guys like you told me to do."

"General Patton said we have never lost a war," Maynard adds with a smile, "but his grandfather fought with Lee in Virginia. Guess it's all in how you want to see things."

"I can't tell what you're talking about half the time, Maynard."

"I know you can't. And you don't even bother to listen if I'm not talking about racing. But that's the way drivers are, even the good ones. Lorenzen couldn't have found his way around a cornfield on a tractor if it hadn't been for Ralph Moody coaching him."

"I thought Lorenzen was a carpenter."

"That's exactly what I mean, smart guy. But he was a hell of a race driver while he lasted."

"I'm a hell of a driver too," Tom answers, ducking Maynard's playful punch.

"I know it. I know it. You tell me every day. And every now and then, you show me."

During the next session, Maynard's good mood begins to fade. Tom's laptimes have ceased to improve. Maynard tells him where to drive coming out of the turns, but he fails to change his line. He isn't running close enough to the wall.

"It's too loose," Tom complains when he pits.

"I'm not telling you again, Pate!" he shouts. "Quit bitching about the car. It ain't the car's fault. The wall's just sitting there. It ain't jumping out in front of you." Maynard empties his pockets of tools and approaches the driver's window. "If you can't do as I say, then maybe you will do as I do. Get your ass out of my car," he orders.

Maynard climbs in, throwing out the seat padding. He takes one warmup lap before putting the car where he wants it. He keeps going for two straight laps, obviously enjoying himself and delighting his crew. When he pits, Tom is gone.

"You want me to go find him?" one of the mechanics asks.

"Naw. Let him stomp off and have his tantrum. I bet he stuck around long enough to see me do it right."

Tom comes back and, following Maynard's path out of the turns, puts the car on the pole.

"Well, Pole Cat," Maynard snorts. "At least you're not so big for your britches that you can't learn something."

Tom keeps his thoughts to himself. When he was a little boy, his uncle Vernon had told him that Little Joe Weatherly

9

and Curtis Turner put their britches on one leg at a time like everybody else, so Tom started lying on his back to put both legs in at once.

Tom Pate finally wins his first Grand National that Sunday in the Labor Day Clash at Waverly.

"I think I could have beaten Petty," he tells Maynard when they are loading his trophy into the truck, "even if he hadn't broken."

"Yeah, then why weren't you beating him before he broke?"

Tom smiles and leans against the truck. "You know what Petty says: the last quarter mile is the only lap that counts. You just run the others for exercise."

This time Maynard keeps quiet. He sees that all it takes is one trip to the victory circle for Tom Pate to feel that he belongs there.

2

When the Pate boys were little, their mother sent them on an errand in Summit, handing Tom the exact change to pick up a package at the dry goods store. After old lady Brunswick mistook a nickel for a quarter and gave him two dimes change, Tom bought two double scoop cones—one for himself and one for his little brother, Zack.

"If she'd just given you one dime too much," Zack questioned in his customary way, "would you have gotten two single scoops or one double scoop?"

"I'd have given you a lick," Tom laughed.

Tom Pate was ten when he discovered that rivers only run just one way. Zack could only watch as his brother spun out of sight. Tom's naked body in the tractor tube looked like a white cup in a fat black saucer. He rode the Yellow River almost to Raleigh. He tossed his tube over a post on a private dock and walked to a gas station, where he talked a pretty lady into a quarter for a Tru-Ade and an oatmeal cookie. "I forgot my wallet," he said, and shrugged. She handed him the money with her hands over her eyes. Then Tom offered a Merita bread driver five dollars he didn't have for a ride back to Summit, negotiating as naked as a jaybird while his mother sobbed over his empty clothes back home on the riverbank.

Hershel Pate got a call from the Wake County sheriff to come get his son, and during the ride back home, Tom described his close calls on the river—bouncing down the paddle wheel at the old mill, speeding past a dozen sleeping water moccasins. Zack asked his daddy to stop the truck, got out, and rode home in the inner tube in the back of the pickup, clutching his glasses in his hand, the wind drying his tears as fast as they fell from his eyes.

Two years later on a Saturday in June, Tom hatched secret plans for Zack to join him on another journey away from the confines of North Carolina farm life. A skywriter glided over Goose Bottom community in a red and white Piper Super Cruiser, dancing through smoke letters with the grace of a swift chasing a mayfly over the pond. After the pilot finished his words, COCA-COLA, the COCA broken into scattered puffs before he shut off his COLA smoke, he dove to an unknown place to the west of the Pate farm. The Pate boys watched him disappear, as if he rode down a rainbow to a pot of gold.

"Where you reckon he goes to, Tom?" Zack puzzled.

Tom didn't answer. He was set on greeting the pilot after he landed on the grass strip near the Summit city limits. He planned to beg a ride. He jumped on his bike, the one he had recently ridden into a tree while admiring the smoke from an iron pipe stuffed with gasoline-soaked cotton on his rear hub. Tom pedaled the wobbly bike with the bent front wheel out the driveway and on down the road.

The next Saturday, Tom rushed Zack through their chores without explanation, shucking corn in the crib with the speed of a machine. A gust of wind grabbed their attention—the devil's breath—and the crib door slammed and caught on the new latch their daddy had installed. Tom jumped at the door, fighting it like a dog with its head stuck between two railings, kicking it so hard the whole structure rattled.

"That's not going to make it come open," Zack said. "You're just wasting your time."

Tom swung around on his haunches, diving after Zack, who scrambled up the pile of corn. The ears rolled out from under the smaller boy's feet, sending him sprawling down onto Tom's brogans. Tom kicked Zack until the younger boy gasped for air. Then Tom crouched down by the door, his face buried in his arms. Zack crawled over slowly and sat beside him. As Zack lifted his shirt, Tom glanced at the raw red spots on his little brother's stomach and shivered. He had left the red imprint of the star off the bottom of his brogan in three places.

Their silence was broken by the airplane. Tom rolled onto his side and looked upward through the slats. Then he pounded the corn until his knuckles were raw while he listened to the stops and starts of the skywriter writing words he couldn't see in the plane they could have been in.

When Tom Pate was twelve, he'd got a tickle when he shinnied up the pole on the monkey bars in the Summit Park playground. Zack had tried it and said he felt the tickle too, but he really didn't. By now, a year later, Tom didn't think about the tickle on the monkey bars; it was there all the time.

One day that summer when he saw a flash from the sky and felt the first sharp drops, Tom started to get the whole picture. He dropped his hoe in the backfield. Next he pedaled to Parsons' Garage to watch them put together a flathead for the jalopy race, with thunder in the distance like airplanes heading into the sky. Then he rode by the high school to watch Holly Lee Pedigrew practice her twirling alone, until she ran to the bus stop, carrying her baton like a lightning rod as the sky over the ball field blackened with storm clouds. Something was stirring in him; looking at wrenches turn and Holly Lee twirl made it churn faster. He rode back to their pond, stripped down and jumped into the water.

Zack saw him diving repeatedly into the pond, pulling himself up to the pier with just his arms. Each splash back into the water ripped through Zack's ears like an unmendable tear. His brother had a farmer's body: two halves sewn together at the waist, the top half brown, the bottom half white flesh that only saw the light of day when he swam. Zack put his fists over his eyes to shut out the vision of Tom's two-toned body frying in front of him like a strip of bacon. He couldn't believe it; Tom was swimming in a lightning storm.

"Come on in, sissy britches," Tom called when he spotted Zack. He slid his hands down his white legs, setting the mud loose from the hairs like brown blood.

"Tom, it's not just some dumb rule that Mama made, okay?"

Yet because Tom had told him to, Zack slowly pushed his shoes off, undid the straps on his overalls, then rolled his glasses up inside. He shoved a red frog with his toe and as it hit the water, Tom shot up from underneath, spurting a stream from his mouth. His brown chest glowed white from the flash and the thunder hit hard, before the light had faded.

Zack began to sob because he knew he wasn't going in, "Please, Tom, get out!" He ran up the hill to their house, falling in the slick manure on the path and crunching his glasses inside his clothes. He yelled one more thing but Tom didn't hear him over the thunder: "You're going to die, Tom Pate!"

Before supper Tom came inside, soaking wet. His mother met him with dry clothes and a towel she had warmed in the oven. "It started raining when I was in the lower field," he said, which wasn't a lie. He spotted Zack watching him from the stairway as he peeled down his wet underpants. He crossed his hands over his organ and pressed his knees together, doing what they called "Mickey Mouse at six-thirty." Zack squinted.

"Where're your glasses, four-eyes?"

"Where *are* your glasses?" their mother repeated from the kitchen. "Not another pair broken!"

That night when they were talking in bed, Tom explained his revelation to Zack: "Are you starting to get the picture around here, Zack?"

"What picture?"

"Listen, I got it figured out. See, this is what farming is all about. You watch your calf get born. Here's the picture that goes on the 4-H poster: this little kid in a clean pair of bibs and a fat calf with the crap washed off his tail. But you know that baby calf gets ugly and turns into a cow and gets eaten. Same with seeds. You plant seeds and it's supposed to be really neat when they come up, only you know you got to chop out the grass and there's always going to be too much squash and they'll make you eat it till it runs out your ears. Either there's no watermelons or so many of them you lose your craving. Then you get old and fall off your tractor and die in the dirt. That's what it means to be a farmer."

3

Tom drove his '55 Chevy Bel Air up his driveway, horn blasting for the family to run out to see his new paint job, the color shimmering in the sun like a creek running with fool's gold, two-toned, red with pearl white trim.

Everybody liked it but Hershel. Even Rachel, his big sister, who thought red nail polish was gaudy. "It's a little loud," she said flatly, "but it's pretty."

"*I* wouldn't have picked it," Gladys said, "but it does suit you, Tom."

"Good enough to eat, like the candy apple you got me at the fair, Tommy." Annie, the baby, shouted. She tugged on her big brother's hand. "I wanna go for a ride."

"It's the same old car, Annie," Rachel said.

"Well, it looks different."

"Red hot," Zack said, with his thumbs up the way Tom did.

"Yeah!" Tom gave him a big smile and thumbed him back.

Hershel turned to go back into the barn, but Tom sprang in front of him. "What do you think?" Hershel stopped, balling his fists that were black with engine oil from his broken tractor, but not looking Tom in the eye. "What was wrong with the blue it come in?"

"Everybody's is turquoise blue, Daddy."

Hershel stared at the barn door; for a minute he didn't move. Then he swung around and pointed an oily finger at Tom, inches from his nose. "You really want to know what I think? I'll tell you what I think. I think the day that car come in this driveway, I got the last lick of work out of you. I think you're a speed demon. And as for that color, I don't know where my son got his colored blood."

"Hershel!" Gladys cried.

"I wanna go for a ride," Annie repeated hopelessly.

"Not today," her mother answered. Zack was already in the front seat beside Tom.

"Where we headed?" Zack asked as they turned onto Highway 43. He hung on as Tom peeled rubber for forty feet.

"The Blue Moon," Tom replied. "Screw him." Then he smiled slightly and added, "I know who's gonna *love* my paint job."

Soon after he had financed his Chevy at the Cut-Rate lot in Butner, Tom became a regular at the Blue Moon Drive-In, where girls skated up to the car door and hooked a tray on the window. When he drove in that Saturday, three carhops drifted around the lot, appearing as aimless as butterflies, yet with their eyes set on the window of his glistening red Chevy as though it was the only flower there with any honey. Then they went into formation and headed to Tom's window. Zack dreamed of those girls at the Blue Moon with half moons of flesh slipping out the backs of their too-short short-shorts and their fronts rising like his mama's yeast rolls. When one of them rested her elbows on the sill, twelve-and-a-half-year-old Zack slid up in the seat so he could see down the front of her tight uniform.

In Summit there was one place to go. One station to listen to. One car to covet. And one girl to desire: Holly Lee. At first Zack thought her name was Meatloaf, which was what the tag said that rested over where he imagined her left nipple was, but when she leaned in the window, he saw it said in smaller letters: TODAY'S SPECIAL.

"I love it," Holly Lee acclaimed. "My favorite color." Zack saw that she wore a lace bra with a piece of curved wire that had worked out of the cloth, pressing a dimple in her left breast.

"Thanks. I wanted you to be the first to see it."

"Root beer float, right?" Holly Lee asked Tom as she elbowed the other carhops away. Her hair clustered in golden curls around a round red cap cocked to one side with a chin strap, the crown of the chief carhop. Her waist, wrapped in a black cummerbund, was small enough for a set of man's hands to encircle. Her face was beautiful except for one flaw: one of her front teeth wasn't white, like a piece of wood in a fence that needed painting. "That your little brother?" she asked.

Zack's face heated up as he turned away, wondering if she was thinking that he was looking at her dark tooth or down her blouse, or both. Tom nodded with a smile, not looking directly at her, but at the space between the steering wheel and the outside mirror.

"Cute little guy," she commented. "Too bad he's got to wear big old glasses to cover up them pretty eyes."

Holly Lee brought the floats, one large and one medium, hooking the tray to the window.

"Careful. Don't scratch the paint," Tom cautioned. He unhooked the tray and took it inside. He didn't reach for his pocket, so Zack began counting out his change, figuring he'd have to pay for Tom's, too.

"Put it up, Zack," Tom ordered and shoved back his brother's hand full of change. "Or, give it to Holly Lee to bet on me tonight. I'll quadruple your money for you." Tom gave Zack's thirty-five cents to Holly Lee, who dropped it into her apron pocket.

Every Saturday night after the sheriff was in bed, on a quarter mile of pavement outside of town, the Night Owls gathered at midnight with their cars. They met in the old parking lot by Solomon's abandoned mill. The start line was worn slick and plastered with rubber. If you were to accept the gospel according to Hershel Pate, the downfall of his son was more than the Blue Moon's pink flesh and blond hair dunked in beer and peroxide, darkening near the scalp like the center of a black-eyed Susan. The downfall of Tom Pate was candy-apple metal-flake red with glass packs screaming horsepower so loud that the pavement throbbed, with covers on its chrome lake pipes that Tom pulled off his '55 Bel Air two-door hard-top V-8 before he took on every male in Goose Bottom who wore the Night Owl Car Club jacket. Tonight, Holly Lee's round bottom was clad in red pedal pushers and perched on somebody else's fender.

"Hey, baby, you might scratch my paint, you know?" Tom had reminded her that night. "It's fresh."

"Shit, man," Lanky Fowler mumbled, "her britches is so tight they musta come out of a spray can."

Buck Herndon showed up with blue lights under his fenders that in the dark made his whitewalls into neon circles. When he drove up and got out, no one said anything; they just stared. Finally Lanky looked at Tom, then the other heads started turning. Tom felt their eyes on him. He put on a half smile as he crossed his arms against his chest. Buck waited.

"Kinda niggerish, Buck, don'tcha think?" Tom asked.

Buck got in his car without answering and left. In an hour or so he was back, blue lights gone, but no one said anything. He just moved in line, waiting for his turn to run and his turn to speak.

"They got this cool thing down at Parsons' that sits up on your dash and you can watch the stoplight in it without look-ing up. Can get right up on the light before you put your foot down."

"You need all the head start you can get, Bubba."

"My old man says to me, 'I b'lieve you been making your bends too fast, son,'" Lanky related. "'You wore out a set of good Sears Roebucks in two weeks,' he tells me."

"Mine gives me this," Slick pitched in: "'Them glass packs

fill up with soot and make so much racket, you're just asking to be pulled.'"

"Don't you listen to this one, Holly Lee." She studied her fingernails as if she was reading a Burma Shave message on each one. "Tell 'em what he said about the rubber, Slick."

"My old man pulled out a used rubber from under the seat and said, 'Son, I b'lieve you been poking that Rigsbee girl.'"

A hoot went over the crowd, followed by a hush. Tom Pate was ready to take a run. He warmed his engine. Lanky took a rag and brushed the pebbles off his tires. Tom pulled beside a new turquoise Bel Air. Holly Lee walked between the cars. She held the red flashlight high, then swung it down, spinning her body around to watch the cars. The run was over in seconds, a squeal and a roar that sent the pigeons flapping out of their night nests in the deserted mill. Jigger Carmichael, the grandson of Carmichael Yarn and Hosiery, took second place in the two-man contest in his new 283.

Jigger added to the pot and tried again; Holly Lee was the banker with the greenbacks spread out in her hand like an ever-growing fan. On his fifth run against Tom, Jigger swerved in the gravel at the end of the strip, peppering the side of the mill that his family had put out of business.

"Jigger buys a 283 and still can't touch Pate's 265."

"Jigger thinks buying eighteen more cubic inches puts an inch on his dick."

"He thinks pulling on it adds five."

"Not big around, but it sure is short."

Buck broke his silence. "You seen that ugly piece of shit Harris Carmichael number three traded his Jag for?"

"That ugly piece of shit is a Porsche, you dumb fuck, Buck."

"Well, I may be a dumb fuck, Lanky, and that may be a Porch, whatever that is, but Pate could leave that washtub blowing smoke at Main and Cedar."

Jigger got out of his car. The engine ticked and hissing sounds came from under the hood. He slammed his door so hard that Holly Lee slid off the fender of Lanky Fowler's Chevy two cars away. Tom turned to him and said, "You tell your cousin Harris I'll race him for his car. Yeah, that's what I'll do."

Tom Pate crept home at dawn on Sunday, sixty dollars in his pocket, enough to cover his paint job and two car payments, plus the dollar seventy-five he owed Zack, who had been asleep for hours. Tom had his lake pipe covers back on, purring up the driveway, holding his horses now. His balls ached from parking with Holly Lee. She had popped her bra undone for him again like the top off a Coke, as far as she let him go. He tried to keep the Chevy from scraping bottom when his wheels dropped in the tractor ruts, but because of the lowering blocks stuffed between his rear axles and springs the gas tank dragged the big rock near the well. He prayed it wouldn't wake up his old man. He parked near the hose so he could wash the Chevy first thing when he got up, too late to go to church on Sunday, his day of rest.

Three hours after Tom fell asleep, Hershel Pate walked out for a smoke before driving to Sunday school, before having to tighten his tie that chafed his Adam's apple. Gladys had scrubbed his blackened fingers with an old toothbrush the night before so that now they left no smudges on his cigarette. He looked at Tom's car like it was something that had come down out of the sky and parked in his yard in the night, letting out a bunch of little Martians instead of his eldest son. All that chrome and color flashed and teased him like the women on McMannon Street when he was a young man and didn't have money for their favors. When he was Tom's age, his family had to worry about their next meal.

Hershel tried to convince himself that Tom's having that car wasn't what irked him that day, the Lord's day, that what really irked him the most that Sunday morning was Tom's rewrite of the Bible, pasted on the back bumper of a car that he bought with money no one knew how he got, a sticker lettered black on a yellow background: ON THE 7TH DAY, GOD CREATED THE CHEVROLET.

Hershel walked to the car and kicked at the bumper sticker until he skinned off the message.

During Tom's evening conversation in bed with his little brother, he allowed he no longer planned to be champion of the world in one of those open-wheel cars like Harris Carmichael, Sr., the richest man in Summit, had in his car collection. That was pretty much for rich foreigners. The boys had seen a movie, *The Crash Helmet,* about racing in Europe. Every time they saw it, Tom disliked the heroine a little more. No sooner than she got the race driver to marry her, she started whining for him to quit racing. After the fourth time they saw it, Tom decided he wouldn't give up one trip around a race track in that car for ten women like her.

And Tom was no longer interested in being an inventor. Years ago, he had stitched his big sister Rachel's stockings to her underpants; it would have made them millionaires if he'd been the first to show it to Harris Carmichael. Now Harris Sr. was cranking out panty hose by the millions. And *Car Craft* magazine pictured men racing a thing called a go-kart that looked just like the Speed Seat Tom had invented, powered by a kick-start Maytag washing machine motor he got at the junkyard. But now Tom had put together a whole different picture about what he was going to be.

Soho the palmist lived in a rusty house trailer that sat in the middle of a pig lot near Summit. As Tom and Zack approached, she threw a pan of slops to the pigs so they snorted away from the doorway toward their food. Once inside, Zack, who was known to be tight as a drum with his money, wouldn't pay a nickel to see his future. The boys didn't tell Soho, but Tom had put down his dollar to find out if he was really going to be a stock car driver.

Soho read great things ahead for Tom, the standard fortune-teller fare: adventure, fame, beautiful women, he was going on a long journey, far away from Summit, with a dark and beautiful woman who was very rich and loved him dearly. Every time Soho mentioned a new fact, Tom rabbit-punched Zack's arm and laughed. So far she hadn't mentioned cars.

"Night owl," she surprised him. "Night owl eats the crow at night," she went on, "but the crow eats the owl by day. The common crow tricks the owl into turning its head till it wrings its own neck," she began to cluck. Tom squirmed in his chair. "Blue racer," she grinned, wiggling her finger. "So black, it's blue. Blue snake slivering into the night. Ain't got no venom. Gets away by being fast."

Then suddenly Soho frowned, her ugly brown face like a peach seed with eyes. She pointed into his hand with her yellow hook of a fingernail.

"What? What?" Tom said. "Hurry up."

"The life line stops. There is a hole."

She had found a blank spot. A nothing. A big hole in his life that extended to his death.

"A hole? When does the hole come?" Tom asked weakly.

"Soon. With the start of the new year. Very bad. Very bad," she said sincerely.

Tom didn't punch Zack again. On the way home, Zack tried to make him feel better. "She was just trying to get you to come back and give her a dollar again."

But Tom worried over that blank spot until he went back to see her, after Christmas. He was eighteen now, the time when he figured the hole was to come into his life. He borrowed all the money Zack had on him—fifty-three cents—to put gas in his car.

On the way over, Zack attempted to entertain him with his latest *Tales from the Crypt*: "Mr. Bigsby, who was a rich man, thought this medium was a fake so he decided to trick her. He went to a seance and told the medium he wanted to talk to his dead wife. See, his wife wasn't really dead because he just left her at home. Then when the medium talked to her, he said, 'See, she's a phony,' and when he got home, guess what?"

Tom wasn't in the mood for games: "Dead as a doornail, right?"

"You musta read it."

"That wasn't too tough, Zack. What did being rich have to do with anything?"

Zack thought a minute. He didn't remember any souls for sale in that one.

"I don't think the Crypt Keeper likes rich people."

"That makes two of us," Tom answered.

Soho's Palmist sign was leaning against the outside, the fingers pointing at the ground. A colored man came to the door. Zack stood behind his brother while he talked to the man, tipping his head to read the writing on the upside-down hand: JOB 37:7: HE SEALETH UP THE HAND OF EVERY MAN, THAT ALL MAN MAY KNOW HIS WORTH.

"Where is Soho?"

"Pigs eat her," the man mumbled.

Zack shivered. "Why?" Tom asked.

"'Cause she dead."

While they were driving home, Zack chattered. "Listen to this, Tom. There's this fortuneteller, see, and she makes a fortune reading palms, always telling everybody how rich they're going to be. She's making so much money that she just keeps buying hogs and fattening them up and eating a pig a

24

week. Ham every day and not just Sunday. Then one day when she goes out the door to carry all her money to the bank, she falls down and breaks her leg, right in the hog lot. And every day those pigs keep getting hungrier and hungrier. And they keep oinking for her to go get their food and she keeps beating on their snouts and saying leave me alone, you rotten old hogs, I've got a broken leg. Guess what happened?"

"It wasn't my dark hole she was looking into last time I talked to her, Zack. The reason Soho saw my life go into a dark hole was that was where she was going."

"I like my story better. I think it's even better than the one about a man who got accidentally locked in a mausoleum and was forced to eat the body of his embalmed girlfriend and pickled himself."

Tom laughed and hit the steering wheel with his fist and said something Zack spent the rest of the ride home pondering: "I don't have anything to be afraid of, here or in hell. I won a race against the devil, Zack. Everybody else is just second best."

4

"How can a man with good sense risk his neck to go running in a circle like some harebrained dog that can't find a scent?" Tom was bending over to get the garbage out for his mother. He froze as if waiting for Zack to kick him into motion.

"Daddy's just reading the paper," Zack whispered in his ear.

"Dumbest thing I've ever heard of," Hershel Pate went on, "a grown man driving a car as fast as he can go in a circle so small he can't help but run into everybody else's cars. That's not what a car's meant for. What's the point of it?"

"I'm sure I don't know, Hershel," Gladys replied from behind a pile of envelopes that she was stuffing for Summit Savings and Loan. "Some men like to do things for the sport of it, I suppose. I have never seen why there'd be any sport in going out and shooting a gun, just to be killing, myself."

"Hum. Says here the fellow who took first place up at Greenmont Raceway got two hundred eighty-six dollars." He paused, then repeated it: "Two hundred eighty-six dollars. Must be a lot of fools paying to see it."

Tom winked at Zack before he went out the back door.

For Tom Pate, stock car racing started a year before at the red clay oval burned into the ground in front of a stack of weathered bleachers, the first racetrack he ever saw: the Yellow County Speedway outside of Summit. Cars were jalopies, a ratty collection of discarded Fords, bouncing over the rutted, oil-stained clay, wrecked again and again, but coming back from the dead for one more shot at glory, a fresh heart beating under the hoods of their battered old bodies. Tom heard stories about Red Vogt, the great stock car engine builder down in Atlanta who built bootleggers' engines on one side of his shop and revenuers' on the other. And these outlaw men, chased by government cars as fast as theirs, were the best race car drivers of their day. As for drivers, he didn't know any real ones yet.

The Yellow County Speedway drivers raced at night, since during the summer days people had to work and the air was so dry that cars and people would choke on the dust. At first Tom and Zack went to the Speedway on Friday nights to watch from the bleachers. When he finished his chores, Zack rode his bike down to Parsons' Garage where Tom worked. He told their mother he was going to the show in Summit.

The brothers would rush into the empty seats in the turns. Flying mud balls would pelt them, and when they undressed for bed after the races, clods fell out of their clothes. They swept them up—Tom called them track turds—to flush down the commode before their mother saw them.

"How come that red car got to start up front again this week?" Zack asked Tom. "Doesn't seem fair to always give him a head start."

"He's the fastest guy, that's why. That's why they qualify, so the fast guys don't run over the slow guys at the start."

At turn one all the cars slid in together and their drivers threw them sideways so they would be heading straight on the way out. The whole pack appeared poised to crash at once, creating total bedlam out of their sportsmanlike order. There was the sense of the impossible about to occur: twenty cars making that first turn in a seething mass. From every direction, men flocked to turn one for the start, waiting like self-appointed eyewitnesses for one man to make a mistake that could not be isolated because of his close quarters: Samuels crossed it up or Hopkins leaned too hard on Smith. They always found someone to point the finger at after the metal crunching was done. Some nights the pack made it like they were driving on rails; some nights the result was chaos.

That, Tom understood and explained to Zack, was the challenge of circle track driving. "You're trying to keep all that power stuck to the ground, see, pedaling as hard as you can." Tom knew the only vehicle his younger brother had powered in a circle was his bicycle. "Imagine you've got a fence around the outside of your circle. When you run in a circle, which is really more like an oval, the turns are there to slow you down after each one of the straightaways, and if the fence is there, you don't have any choice. If you don't slow down at all, you don't make it through the turn. But if the guy beside you doesn't let up, then you can't let up either, even if you have to take a chance. The guy who wins is the last one to back off." Then he paused and added, "Unless he's the one who runs out of talent and goes into the fence."

Zack's lesson on the art of driving came before Tom had learned lesson number two himself: that all the talent in the world wasn't going to win races if he didn't have a race car to drive.

After Tom graduated from Summit High, his job at Parsons' Garage as a mechanic went from part time to full time. He drove to work in his Chevy, the neat round gauges in front of him. When he got to Parsons', he sometimes crawled into the abandoned race car that had been sitting in the weeds since Clyde Henry ran out of money two summers before, the vacant sockets in its dash like eye holes in a skull. He would grasp the giant steering wheel of the '34 Ford with his left hand and the nonexistent shifter with the right. Zeb Parsons saw the boy daydreaming in the race car. "Old man Henry is over the hill," he offered, "if you know what I mean. Don't say I told you, but I believe that race car's yours for the asking.

See if you can talk him into building you a motor. That he can still do."

Tom gave his mother ten dollars a week out of his fifty-four take-home pay. "We can hire a colored boy for half that to do farm work," she told Hershel after Tom went full time. The forty-four dollars Tom had left each week went into his cars.

He worked nights on the Ford. And Zack got off the bus at Parsons' every day after school instead of going home. One afternoon at Parsons' when Tom was pulling the bottom end of the engine apart, and Zack was sitting on the floor with a pan of solvent between his legs, scrubbing parts with a wire brush, Clyde Henry and Zeb Parsons leaned against the work bench, watching the boys work. Clyde had been telling about the time he'd won the feature at Statesville in 1947; it was the second time that week they had heard it. His voice stopped in his throat as though someone had hit a switch. Holly Lee was standing at the door.

"Tom Pate, I been waiting for you to pick me up for an hour."

Tom jumped to his feet. "Holly Lee. I forgot. You got off early today, huh?"

"I get off early every Tuesday, if it is any concern of yours, which it don't seem to be. If it hadn't been for Buck Herndon, who give me a ride over here, I'd be standing there till the cows come. . . . Tom Pate, that is the ugliest old junk pile I ever seen!" she exclaimed.

Tom stopped what he was doing and stepped backwards, squinting at the car as though his eyes had lost their focus. Clyde and Zeb were struck dumb.

"Don't you tell me," she went on, "that this is the reason we don't ever go to the show anymore? This is a race car?"

Holly Lee stepped inside the shop and walked over to the car, her hands on her hips. Zack had never seen her move

29

without her skates; her movements looked jerky and it seemed to take her a long time to get to the car. She tipped her head sideways, staring at Tom as if he were a crazy man. Tom grabbed for the words in his throat because he had to stop her from saying anything else in front of Clyde and Zeb. "It's—it's a different kind of racing, Holly Lee," he stammered. "It's not like drag racing where people don't ever run into each other. You get hit a lot so you get a bunch of dents. No need to waste your time beating them out . . ."

"Get hit! You mean you wreck?" She crossed her arms and stepped back, a pink bubble rising out of her mouth, popping and getting sucked back inside as she snapped, "This thing looks like it's done got wrecked one time too many already."

Clyde Henry could take no more. "Get that woman out of here. Can't have no woman hanging around a race car. Bad luck."

"She doesn't mean any harm, Clyde," Tom put in quickly. "You know how women are. She just doesn't know any better."

"What do you mean I don't know no better? I got two eyes same as a man, don't I? I been to the movies. I know what a race car looks like. And I betcha I know a lot better than a bunch of men when I'm looking at something the cat wouldn't drag in."

"Heard of a man got kilt up at Hickory," Clyde insisted. "Some woman hanging 'round his car let one of them bobba pins fall outta her hair. Right in his carburetor. Stuck it wide open." Clyde's mouth stayed wide open too when he finished talking, tobacco juice running out one corner and stopping in the stubble on his chin.

"I think you better go, Holly Lee," Tom said.

"Woman got no business 'round a car," Clyde went on. "Man don't keep his mind on his work when a woman hangs around. He's the one who pays for it."

"I don't even use bobby pins," she snapped. "Bobby pins is for tacky hicks."

"Woman eating peanuts down at Cowpens. Shells got sucked right in a fellow's engine. Ruint it."

"Tom Pate's the one who eats peanuts with shells," she retorted, "not me. I don't even like 'em, except the salted in the can."

"Joe Weatherly and Curtis Turner love their doll babies much as the next man," Clyde went on as though Holly Lee didn't exist, "but they'd be the first to tell you, they got their place. And it ain't around a race car. They keep a count, them two. Hundreds of them."

"That's what you got in mind, Tom Pate? A hundred women?"

Zack looked at Tom. His brother couldn't find any words. Finally he mumbled, "I don't even know a hundred women, Holly Lee. Don't know a dozen pretty ones."

She put her hands back on her hips and popped her gum again. Tom froze like a man trying to fend off a striking snake.

"I *know* how to handle another pretty woman," Holly Lee said flatly, and spun around to leave as though her feet had sprouted their own wheels.

To hear the engine they were working on rev up in the back of Parsons' Garage, making a few hot runs down 43, then ducking back behind the building before the state man came to check it out—or even dragging his Chevy over in the Solomon's Mill parking lot—that was one thing. But the first time Clyde's flathead started up at Yellow County Speedway with the sound bouncing back down off the bleachers was like the first time Tom heard Elvis sing. Nothing else was ever going to compare, except maybe going to Darlington to the big one.

Tom let the engine warm up slowly the way Clyde had told

him. Clyde kept the carburetor in the refrigerator. He wouldn't tell anybody why, but they believed he knew what he was doing.

The old driver had promised to give Tom a lesson before he let him run the car, but he arrived at the track hunched over with aching kidneys. Zeb and Tom had to help him through the window. After he took the Ford around for a few laps, they pulled him back out. Clyde stood bent in the same position as when he'd sat at the wheel. "If a car don't bust up your top half, it'll get you on the bottom end," he moaned. "When your hotshot days is done, remember I told you that. My guts is ruint." That was the last time Clyde sat in the driver's seat.

Tom grabbed the door posts and swung through the window like a gymnast. He waited for Clyde's instructions, but the old driver ambled away towards the outhouse.

"Take her out," Zeb suggested. "Get the feel of it."

Tom headed for the track before the words were out of Zeb's mouth. On his first lap around, he drove in the center of the road. Then he tried giving the engine more throttle, feeling the car slide sideways. The Ford bounced across the ruts left from the last race, and yanked the steering wheel from his grip.

Since the track hadn't been wet down yet, the dry clods off his wheels hit the board fence like bullets. Each lap he came around, he caught up to his own dust. The cloud thickened until he was driving half-blind. But each lap he went faster.

"Your brother is going to be a talent to be reckoned with," Zeb Parsons told Zack. "He's already fast as the guy on the pole last week. He's got a feel for it that you just have to get born with. And don't tell your daddy I said that. He'll tack my hide to the smokehouse wall. Lord knows why, but his kid's a natural."

Each time Tom revved the engine higher, cleaning it out,

looking for traction as he threw the Ford into the turns, a feeling went through him, making him want to run faster. His speed increased until the pedal was on the floor. Suddenly he felt the car lean into the wall, and heard a scraping sound on his right side. Tom had slid up too high; the race car rattled along the outside fence, adding another body crease.

Clyde walked out of the outhouse. "He'll really get going as soon as he finds some decent equipment," Zeb whispered to Zack. "He ain't scared to hang it out a little already."

Tom drove until the engine sputtered, low on fuel. As he pulled down into the infield, he saw Clyde and Zeb coming to meet him. He was smiling as Zeb pounded on the roof.

"Whatcha think, Pole Cat?" Zeb asked.

"Fill 'er up," he answered. "And check the oil and water. How did I look? Did I look fast?"

Zack ran for the gas can.

"Hold your horses, boy," Clyde said, grabbing Zack by the back of his shirt. "There's some pretty impatient fellows wanting to get across that track that figure they get to race too. Pole Cat has to stay off the track for a while." The infield started to fill up with spectators as the other racers streamed across the track into the pit area. The water truck went out to prepare the surface.

Zack caught a sad look in Clyde's eyes as Tom pulled himself out through the window and dropped to the ground. Then Clyde straightened his body and took Tom's shoulders in both hands. "Hot damn," he said, "we got us a racer."

The Night Owls drag racing out at Solomon's Mill were left to fight among themselves when Tom Pate and his '55 Chevy Bel Air moved on. Buck Herndon and Jigger Carmichael shared the rewards. Holly Lee gave up waiting for Tom to pick her up at the Blue Moon; Buck seemed to always be there when she needed a ride. Tom still kept his Chevy clean and running smoothly. If Zack's clothes were greasy, Tom made him ride sitting on a towel, sweeping the dirt from his feet off the floor mat with a whisk broom.

But the race car was a different story. When Clyde hosed the Ford down after every trip to the speedway, the dirt dropped from under it like cowpiles. Tom added so many more dents that he quit trying to pound them out. Number 7 looked as if it had been painted with a broom dipped in white paint. Yet inside that engine went every extra cent Tom earned and every dollar he won when he finished in the money.

By the time Clyde allowed Tom to write his name over the door that summer—he carefully lettered his nickname "Pole Cat"—Tom knew a race car fit him like a new skin on a seven-year bug that left its old shell stuck on a tree. In fact, he knew from the first lap he took around the Yellow County Speedway that if life was in colors, then racing was candy-apple red and everything else was a pale shade of pink.

Tom ran the car without his parents' knowledge every Saturday night for two months until, one Sunday, Marvin Simmons said to Hershel at church, "That boy of yours is getting to be a real hotshoe."

"How's that?" he asked, not understanding what Marvin meant.

"Down at Yellow County. He'll win a race before summer's over, you can count on it."

"Is that so?" Hershel replied, never admitting he'd known nothing about it.

Zack ran out to tell Tom, who was washing his car. "Tom! Daddy knows. Marvin Simmons blew the whistle on us at church."

For a moment, Tom stood motionless, then he began to twist his chamois between his hands. "What'd Daddy say?"

"Nothing. He acted like he already knew."

Tom swept the chamois across the hood of the Chevy, shaking his head. "If he didn't say anything, he didn't even know what Marvin was talking about."

The boys waited all week for their daddy to confront them, but he never did. On Friday Tom had the motor running in the Chevy, ready to head to Parsons' to help Clyde load the car on the trailer. When Zack started out the back door, his mother stopped him in the kitchen.

"Where are you headed off to so fast, young man?"

"I'm done. I've got to go help Tom with something over at Parsons'."

"I don't think it's a good idea for you to spend all your weekends hanging around a filling station with grown men."

"I'm not hanging around the station."

"Oh, you aren't. Well, where are you hanging around?"

"Uh," he stammered, "Zeb wants Tom and me to take this car out for somebody."

"Out to where?"

"Out to Yellow County Speedway," he blurted out.

"The race track! Zachary, those fast cars are too dangerous for you to be around."

"I've been around them already with Tom and lived to tell about it, Mama." He started backing towards the door. The horn blasted on the Chevy. "Tom's getting mad at me for holding him up, Mama."

"Those cars might blow up or run you down. You just haven't heard all the awful things that have happened at that terrible place. The Perkins family lost their oldest son when a car turned over and mashed his head and . . ."

"Mama, that was five years ago."

Zack was afraid she was going to tell him about the guy who got scalded when a radiator broke and the one who got his arm ripped off. He hadn't known his mother read that part

35

of the *Summit News*. The horn blew again. Gladys wound her hands in her apron and no more horror stories came out. Instead, she said, "Well, just so long as you and Tom don't even *think* of driving one of them." Her voice was like a child who has just asked for the moon for Christmas and is smart enough to know it isn't going to be in her stocking.

Gladys Pate held on to Annie's shirttail to keep her from running across the bleachers after the man selling boiled peanuts. Annie wore her favorite yellow shirt with the front and the rear of a rabbit on her front and rear. Rachel hadn't changed since she got home from work at Simon's Department Store. Gladys had recombed her hair, which was smoothly rolled into a bun. She had on the blue dress she wore to go shopping in town and a sweater over her shoulders, latched by the pearl strand with a clip on each end that Rachel had bought her at Simon's. Hershel wore his bibs. The cloth from the knees down was red with mud, the way his pants always were, except on Sunday. Once, when the hogs got out on Sunday morning and he'd had to run them down in his suit pants, he'd gone to church that way.

When Gladys realized she was dressed too nice, she whispered to Rachel, "This is a rough crowd," and pulled Annie close. She trembled when she first saw Zack facing them from the pit area, then Tom's back as he bent over a car.

Annie jumped up on the seat. Zack could see her face, her buttonhole mouth and her eyes little dots under her bangs. When she found him, she started bouncing up and down on the bleacher bench and waving. He waved back.

Gladys grabbed Annie's shirttail again, this time because the little girl wanted to go down where her brothers were and didn't understand why she couldn't. First Gladys told her it was because she was a child, then Annie saw a little boy in the pits, holding his father's hand. Then Gladys told her it was because she was a little girl. Annie had to believe her then because she couldn't find a single girl, little or big, among the cars.

"Look at that clodhopper up there," Tom remarked to Zack without turning his head.

"You mean Daddy?"

"You know who the hell I mean."

"Yeah, I didn't know he was a racing fan."

"Why didn't he stay the hell home? Marvin Simmons oughta learn how to keep his big mouth shut. Daddy didn't even bother to show up when I graduated from high school. So he comes to see me race looking like he just slopped through the hog lot."

"You think he's going to come down and say you can't race?"

"Let him try."

The boys got caught up in the action of the night, and Tom didn't mention the family again. Zack didn't look again either, after the stand filled with people, their family melting into the crowd.

Something was wrong with the engine. It ran rough at first, which wasn't unusual, but the way Clyde listened, stopped, and turned screws indicated that the carburetor that had come out of the icebox with frost on its sides wasn't right. Tom went out for a practice lap, but drove back to the pits immediately. When he came towards them, the engine made small explosions out the short pipes underneath. Clyde mumbled a cuss word before walking back to his tool box.

When Clyde lifted the hood, Tom shook his head. He began banging his fist on the steering wheel.

"Stop that, will you?" Clyde growled. "I can't think."

The practice speeds picked up with engines snarling around them as the cars went sideways into the turns, fighting for traction. The evening was hot so the track dried out fast. The thud of mud balls on the fence died down as the air filled with dust and exhaust. Before they could get Tom back on the track, the rest of the cars lumbered back into the pit area to line up for qualifying.

"Damn it, Clyde," Tom finally blurted, "if you don't get this thing going soon, we might as well go home."

When Clyde heard that, he decided to take a breather. With his face flushed and his hair stuck to his forehead with sweat, he looked too old to ever have been a driver. "If you think you can do it better, get your lazy ass out here and try," he spit out. "You sit in there like you're too high and mighty to get your hands dirty anymore."

Zack had never heard Clyde, or anyone except their daddy, talk to Tom like that. Tom slid down in the seat, took a pack of cigarettes from his sleeve and lit one up.

"Go draw a qualifying number," Tom ordered Zack. When Zack returned, he showed Clyde the number thirteen, earning a disgusted look.

The other cars shut down their engines. When a preacher started talking on the loudspeaker, all the men took off their caps except Clyde, who kept working. Tom didn't bow his head. Zack half-bowed so he could keep watching. A scratchy recording of the "Star-Spangled Banner" made it halfway through before the needle skipped over to the end. People in the stands looked around and sat down slowly, not sure if the song was finished or if they were going to try again. Nobody had remembered to put up the flag. When a few men started yelling and clapping, the crowd dropped to the bleachers to wait for qualifying to begin.

The first car went out. The number thirteen slot was reached and passed and Tom lost his place in line. Clyde, Zack, and Zeb Parsons pushed the car aside. Tom climbed out and went to watch beside the track. Drivers were setting times that he had beaten before easily.

After Tom walked away, Clyde asked Zack to get in the car

in his place and turn the engine over. It wouldn't fire at all, the battery was worn down. Zack could smell gas. He had sat in the car before and pretended to be a driver, turning the wheel and making engine sounds. His imagination wouldn't work now. He felt sad, like the game was over.

Soon Clyde stepped back and crossed his arms. He didn't tell Zack to get out. Other mechanics began to gather around the car, pointing, making suggestions. Zeb drove his wrecker over and hooked jumper cables to the battery. Then he reached behind his wrecker seat and pulled out a spray can. For the first time, Clyde looked interested. After he lifted his eyebrows and nodded, Zeb bent over. When everyone jumped back from the engine, Zack felt panicky, wondering if he should dive out the window and roll away from the car before it blew up. Then Clyde spoke. "Try her again, Zack."

He cranked the motor over and, to everyone's surprise, it started. Clyde disappeared beneath the hood and Zack felt the gas pedal under his foot moving on its own.

"Hop out," Clyde told him. As soon as he did, Tom climbed in again, the engine sound having called him back to the car like his mother's supper bell. A strange smell hung in the air, not just exhaust, or raw gas from the flooded engine. It smelled like somewhere else, a hospital or the vet's office. Zack felt a little dizzy. "Ether," Zeb said, answering Zack's unspoken question.

Tom rushed to the staging line. Clyde ran behind him and began to check the tire pressures, hooking up a bicycle pump and pumping frantically. He tossed Zack the gauge and waved him to the other side. When Tom's turn came, he took off, the pump ripping from Clyde's hand. "Hold your horses, goddammit," Clyde swore.

A man at the pit exit held up his hand, and Tom was forced to wait while Clyde stumbled over to unscrew the pump from the tire. Tom took off again before he could screw on the cap.

"Asshole," Clyde mumbled. "Your brother is a asshole,"

he told Zack, but watched intently as Tom took his warmup lap. "Don't sound right yet. Goddammit. The best motor I ever built and some chickenshit little thing is messed up. . . . You got the watch?"

Zack had forgotten it. He turned to get it, but Clyde said, "Never mind," and walked over to Marvin Simmons, who was already clocking Tom.

Tom qualified tenth that night, his worst for the summer. He felt too surly to talk to anyone before the race started, and walked away or backed up every time anyone came up to him. He never liked to talk much before a race, but tonight he was unapproachable, trying to concentrate his anger in his hands and feet, to make him drive faster. Clyde worked over the engine until time to roll the car to the grid.

When the green flag waved, Tom was already on the gas, passing two cars before they crossed the starting line. The starter didn't flag him out for jumping the start. Up ahead a car went sideways in the second turn, sliding towards the wall. By the time Tom got there, the car had moved back down into the groove, so he passed under him, so low that people jumped back from the corner. The track was so rough down low, Tom's teeth jarred.

Clyde cheered when he passed. Tom had made it safely through the traffic, popping out at the end of the first lap, already in fifth place. By that time, everyone was watching one car, number 7, Tom Pate's, the Pole Cat. Zack thought that maybe this day, the worst beginning for a race they had ever had, was going to be the day that Tom won for the first time.

Then the roar began to subside. The cars were slowing; there was a crash up ahead. A man stood beside the track, holding the yellow caution flag to keep the cars from passing each other until the wrecked cars could be cleared off the track. Tom's number 7 went past, its white paint peppered with mud dots. Zack and Clyde waved at him, but he wasn't looking. Zeb took his wrecker out and headed for the back side of the track. He rode down on the apron against the flow of traffic. They ran slowly now, single file, bouncing along the ruts.

"That sonavabitch Groggins thinks Tom passed him after the accident," Clyde said.

"I b'lieve he did, Clyde," Marvin Simmons replied.

"I'll be goddamned. He was clear of Groggins before those assholes even thought of crashing."

"You can't even see the back side from here, Clyde."

"You don't have the slightest notion of what I can see," Clyde snapped.

Marvin laughed and turned to another man, who laughed with him. "Naw, Clyde, I guess not."

Clyde, determined to have the last word, let his words turn to mumbles about not letting that sonavabitch get around. A mechanic from Groggins' team went up to the flagman, and started talking, pointing angrily at Tom each time he came by. The flagman began pointing the flag stick at Tom, signaling for him to let Groggins around. Clyde walked over and started talking into the flagman's other ear, but he shook his head, his mind made up. He wasn't going to restart until Tom got back into fifth position. Zeb brought the wrecked car zigzagging into the pits, its rear wheels frozen.

Tom watched the flag stick. With each pass the starter got angrier at him for holding up the restart. He knew he was long around that car before the crash, but the starter wasn't going to back down.

When Tom dropped back, Clyde stamped his foot.

"Forget it, Clyde," Zeb said. "Either he falls back or we stand here all night."

"Put that sonavabitch in the fence!" Clyde shouted.

When the green waved, Clyde's anger was instantly replaced by excitement. Tom easily repassed Groggins on the first lap and began to press on third place. But as he let up for the first turn, Zack noticed a little puff of blue smoke. "Clyde, the engine's smoking," he said.

Clyde gave Zack such a mean look that he wished he'd kept his mouth shut. "I didn't see nothing," Clyde said. "Just loaded up from running all them slow laps. Clean your glasses, boy." On the next pass, the rear view of the car was lost in the traffic, but Zack kept watching for the smoke.

"How many more laps?" Clyde asked him.

"I don't know. I forgot to count."

"You're useless as tits on a boar, boy."

Clyde walked over to ask Marvin and Zeb, getting two sets of answers: anywhere from five to ten more laps.

"Now you count them, boy," he said to Zack, "and let me know when there's. . . . Oh my god!"

Tom's car was wrapped in blue smoke, pouring from around the wheels. As he came off the last turn before the pit entrance, there was an explosion under his feet. The steering wheel ripped from his hands. Before he could grip it again, the car snapped around. He saw the two cars coming at him. Then they vanished and he saw the fence. He was spinning. Fence boards filled his vision before the impact.

Zack and Clyde watched the field split to go around Tom as he bounced back off the wall into their path. The field didn't split soon enough. The first hit was hard and in the passenger side, tipping Tom's car up on two wheels then shoving it sideways into the wall again. When he came down on all fours and was struck the second time from the rear, the Ford shot forward like a bumper car at the carnival.

Tom felt each blow harder than the last as he groped for something to grab. The car was hit again and again, spinning one way then the other, out of control. When he grabbed for the steering wheel, trying to brace his arms against it to stop the lashing movement of his upper body, his shoulder hit the door. The car steered itself as the wheel ripped out of his hands again. His chest struck the wheel and one of his arms buckled and was slung out the window like a rag doll's.

People ran away from the inside edge of the track as the rest of the pack dropped down to miss the crashed cars. Clyde shoved Zack backwards and he sat down hard, then scrambled to his feet. He was sure he'd seen Tom's arm fly out of the window. It was as if his brother was a magnet drawing every car there; all the cars he had passed were hitting him now. By the time Zack got to his feet, the track was blocked; the terrible movement stopped. One car trickled around the pileup. The flagman threw down his yellow flag and grabbed a red one, waving it frantically even though no one was passing the start-finish line. The last running cars coasted into the pits and shut down their motors.

Men went running to the pileup, tugging drivers out of the windows. One driver crawled across a hood—he wore an old Air Force helmet with a star with wings. Tom didn't wear a helmet. Zack ran to the wreckage. Crew men were pushing and shoving, all trying to get to their drivers. A wide ooze of oil was coming down the track; two men slipped and fell on their hands and knees in the black stream. When the siren blasted on the Summit volunteer fire department pickup, everyone ran away from the track. Zack smelled the gasoline then. Instead of trying to get away, he ran towards the cars, climbing up on fenders, across hoods and tops, trying to get to Tom. He snagged his jeans on something that cut through to the skin. Finally he saw the hood of number 7; it was shorter, stuffed like ham in a biscuit. He crawled on top and hung off the roof, looking inside. The seat was empty.

"Zack, get your ass out of there!"

He turned around. It was Tom. He was standing beside the track. How could he have been in the accident if he was standing over there? Zack scrambled back over the cars, even faster than he'd come in. When his feet hit the sticky track, Tom grabbed his arm and pulled him away, back from the pile of twisted cars. The fire truck shot water on the steaming cars, diluting the gasoline that splattered on the clay. As Tom kept pulling him, Zack felt as though they were running away, trying to escape from the scene of the crime before someone grabbed them and blamed them. But Tom was leading Zack to a spigot. "Here," he said, "wash your knee off before Mama sees it."

Zack pulled up the leg of his jeans. His kneecap was brown with blood and oil. The cut stung when Tom washed it out with an oil rag. After Tom pulled the pant leg back down, blood trickled inside Zack's jeans, soaking into his sock. Tom rubbed his wrists and stared at the pile of cars. His shoulders were hunched forward, making him seem shorter.

The wreckage never caught fire. Zeb Parsons cautiously approached the outside car in the pileup, like a cat sticking out his paw and tapping a mouse he had killed. When he decided it was safe, he hooked up his wrecker cable to the outside car, a '36 Plymouth, and began yanking it away from the others. Five cars were finished for the night. A man on a tractor came out and began dragging a harrow over the ruts. The wrecks were dragged outside the speedway into the parking lot. Tom's car was the worst.

"Your engine let go," Tom began to explain to Clyde as the car passed through the gate, swinging on the wrecker hook with its rear wheels buckled. "I didn't do anything wrong. It just spun around on its own. I was going to win that damn race. I know I was. Nobody in the world could've beat me tonight. Fireball Roberts couldn't have beat me tonight."

Clyde didn't respond for a while, just kept packing up his tools. Then he looked up at Tom. "Go tell Zeb to set it down on the trailer. It sure ain't gonna roll up the ramps."

Tom and Zack walked to the parking lot. Zeb had already deposited the car on the trailer. Listening to the cheers and roar as the engines restarted inside the speedway, Tom felt a flash of anger. What right did they have to go on without him? Zack stared at the car; it sat sideways, hanging over the edge of the trailer. When he looked inside, he saw that the seat he had padded with cotton was shoved up against the door.

"Tom, don't you think you ought to get one of those helmets?" a familiar voice spoke behind them.

Both boys turned around in surprise. Until they heard their mother's voice, they'd forgotten the family was there. She stood in the muddy lot, her black Sunday shoes stuck with clay, but her blue dress as crisp as when she went shopping. Rachel and Annie weren't with her, but Hershel walked over to look at the car on the trailer.

"What did you say, Mother?" Tom asked, as if he were talking to a stranger.

"I said, you should get one of those helmets. A lot of the boys have them on." Her eyes were shiny in the weak light.

Tom shook his head, so she stepped back and brought her purse around and pressed it to her stomach, her fingertips making dents in the patent leather.

"Why don't you give me one for Christmas?" Tom finally said. Zack had tried to get him to wear an old football helmet that Coach Beal had given him at school, but he'd refused because it looked chicken.

"Hello, Clyde," Gladys said, undaunted by Tom.

"Howdy, Mrs. Pate. Surprised to see you here," he said dumbly.

"Yes, me too," Gladys answered.

Hershel was walking around the car, studying it. In his muddy bibs, he looked like the one who was properly dressed. Gladys was out of place, her heels sinking in the mud. Zack tugged on her arm.

"Mama, you're messing up your shoes."

She looked down at them and back at him with no surprise on her face. "Yes, I know." She hesitated, then took Zack's arm. "I told the girls to go on home with Mrs. Spencer's son," she said. "They need to get their dresses ironed for Sunday school." Zack led her towards a patch of grass. She slipped a little walking there, tightening her grip on his arm. "Your britches are going to need a patch," she said to him, not noticing the blood. Zack glanced down and saw that it had blackened like oil in the faded blue of his jeans. She frowned at the car on the trailer. Oil dropped out and splattered on the trailer bed. "Imagine how I felt when I saw you get in that car, Zachary."

"Me?"

"Yes, when Tom got out. Before it all started."

"Oh, then. Well, I wasn't planning on driving it. Not yet, anyway."

"Oh, Zachary," she said and looked up at the dark sky. "What did I do wrong?"

"You didn't have anything to do with it, Mama. The engine blew up."

Tom watched his father's moves as if he were watching a thief. Hershel was walking around the wreck as though it were a cow he might want to buy.

Clyde was the first person to speak to Hershel. "We had us a good one going there, Hershel, until the damn engine let go." He looked at Gladys. "Excuse me, Mrs. Pate," he added.

Gladys didn't flinch. She wasn't responsible for Clyde's language.

"Spun in my own oil," Tom put in, relieved that Clyde had understood what had happened. Zack remembered the ominous blue whiff out the pipe that Clyde hadn't wanted to see.

Finally Hershel walked away from the car towards his wife,

who waited to be led like a dance partner in any direction he chose to go, even if it was back into the mud. He still hadn't spoken. He took her by the arm. When it looked as though he were going to leave without saying a word, Tom moved quickly, jumping in front of them. Hershel stopped suddenly, steadying his wife beside him. Face to face, Hershel was still bigger than Tom, even with his hat in his hand.

Tom stood there like a child who has gotten everyone's attention but has forgotten what he wanted to say. He started to speak, weakly. "Well, what did you think?"

His daddy stared at him. Zack moved so he could see his father's face. Hershel looked puzzled, as if he were trying to figure out how to make something work without reading the instructions. He started to leave again, but Tom stood his ground, moving into his path again. Tom's eyes flitted around nervously.

When it was clear to Hershel that his wife wasn't going to answer the question for him, he regarded the car again, slowly. For a few seconds Zack felt sorry for his daddy, the way he did for a dumb kid in school who got called on but couldn't answer the teacher's question. The race car groaned, settling into place on its oil-splattered trailer that Zack had painted red. Hershel turned back to look Tom squarely in the eyes.

"I guess you ain't gonna get killed today," he said, and smiled the kind of smile you know won't get returned. Then he led his wife away.

After the crash, Tom no longer spent his nights getting the race car in shape. It would never run again. Tom never went back to Solomon's Mill, where Jigger Carmichael's new 283 cubic inch '58 Chevy Biscayne had become the car to beat. Tom's '55 Chevy had bald tires and there was no money to replace them. No matter how much better he was than Jigger,

Tom would have been left at the start, spinning his wheels. On his way to the Blue Moon, Tom passed the statue of the Big Boy who used to hold a hamburger. Big Boy wore a nightshirt and instead of his hamburger he now offered a tire: TIME TO RETIRE the sign said. Tom's new set still rested on the layaway shelf in the storage room.

Mud spattered around his Chevy undercarriage from potholes in the driveway, but he quit bothering to wash it off. The paint lost its sheen like a bruised apple. After work one Saturday evening, Tom parked on the back side of the Blue Moon lot and waited for Holly Lee to get off work. He pounded his fist on the steering wheel until she showed up. He hadn't seen her or been to the Blue Moon since before Clyde's engine blew and ended the Ford's racing life.

Holly Lee spotted his car and walked over to his window. She stood shorter, her skates tied together by their laces and thrown over her shoulder.

"Hey," Tom greeted.

"Hey, yourself." When she rested her elbows on his window, her skates hit his door. She jumped back. "Oh, I'm sorry. I hope it didn't scratch."

Tom answered, "No big deal."

"Where you been lately? You look kinda down in the dumps."

"Yeah, kinda. Buck coming by?"

"I don't know. I don't care if he is. I don't have to go nowhere with him. Not if you want to go somewhere."

"I'm busted. Flat busted."

"I heard something. Don't know if it was true, but I heard you had a big wreck."

"Yeah, it was pretty big."

"Why didn't you call me and tell me? You didn't hurt anything, did you? Buck said he saw you get out and you were walking okay."

"Car's hurt pretty bad. But you don't care about that."

"I care. I mean I don't care much about the car, but I care if it bothers you. And I know it does."

He shrugged and slid down in the seat.

"Mama's working graveyard," she said. "We can go to my house to watch television." Tom reached across the seat and opened the door on the passenger side.

With Holly Lee beside him, he headed without thinking to Flycatcher Road, a winding back road where drivers liked to test their skill. As he started his run, the Chevy skidded over onto the shoulder once as his right rear hit a pile of horse manure. Holly Lee didn't flinch or cry out, riding with blind confidence in his ability. He reached over and put his right hand over her left as he slowed. She smiled at him and squeezed his fingers.

"I guess we better go to your house," he offered. "I'm running on empty."

"Yeah," she replied. "I been missing riding with you. Buck's not as good as he thinks he is."

Tom and Holly Lee watched TV with her two little sisters, Noel and Belle, until their bedtime.

"How come your sisters have such funny names?" he asked after they went to bed.

"They're named after Christmas same as me. Mama says Christmas is the only time of the year worth living."

Tom stared at the TV. A cowboy show was on; he couldn't remember the guy's name. He looked too sissy to be a real cowboy, but Holly Lee said he was cute.

"What's going on with you and Buck?" Tom said. "I heard he was your boyfriend now."

"He is not. Who told you that?"

"He did. Well, not exactly. He told Lanky and Lanky told me. He said he did it with you."

"He did not. He is a lying son of a bitch. He did it, but I didn't do it with him."

She stopped talking. Her face burned red; it looked like anger, but she didn't seem mad. She sat with her hands on her knees, staring straight ahead. One of the little girls called her name from the back room.

"Go to sleep, Noel. You hear me?"

Noel went silent.

"Noel has nightmares," Holly Lee said.

"Buck ever come over here?"

"No!"

"You don't have to get upset. I just wondered."

"I never asked him over. I wouldn't have given him the time of day, Tom Pate, if you hadn't forgotten I was alive even." The old Holly Lee began to come back. "You know you used to make me real mad sometimes. When you wouldn't talk to me or when we'd be on a date and you'd stop in a gas station and start talking to a bunch of guys like I wasn't even alive. I'd get so mad, I could spit."

She stood up, bending over to pull down the legs of her pants that fit snugly around the muscles in her calves. She walked to the doorway of her mother's bedroom.

"Come in here," she said. "I've got something I've been saving for you."

Her expression didn't match her words; it was as if she'd practiced them, but wasn't sure if she meant what she said.

Tom followed her into her mother's bedroom where the bed was piled with stuffed animals and a silk pillow with Oriental designs on it. Holly Lee opened a drawer in the table beside her mother's bed. Then she spun around to face Tom and handed him a rubber.

5

The Ford lay over on its side in the kudzu behind Parsons' where the mechanics dumped old oil. Everything worth anything was gone: the transmission and rear end, the two wheels that weren't bent. Clyde had even pulled his engine and put the carburetor back into his refrigerator. Tom sold his twenty-dollar racing tires for eight to make a car payment on the Chevy; he was three payments behind. One of the tires blew out as soon as it was inflated because of a cut from the accident, so he had to give two dollars back.

Zack told Tom the vine that reached for the words POLE CAT over the door looked like a green hand coming out of a grave.

"You know, Zack, sometimes I get pretty sick and tired of the way you make stories out of everything," he snapped.

It was true that number 7 was dead and he was just Tom Pate again. For a while, he went to the Yellow County Speedway and stood in the pits, waiting for a car to need a driver. But he gave that up.

One Sunday morning in August, he walked straight into his mother's kitchen from outside, squinting in the morning light as if the sun had come up to spite him. Except for Hershel, who was slopping the hogs, the whole family was eating breakfast by the time Tom got home, including his uncle Vernon and great aunt B.B., who had moved in with them.

Tom carried a pack of cigarettes rolled in his T-shirt sleeve, the Lucky Strike circle showing through the cloth. Each morning he combed his hair into a ducktail, and that's where it stayed after the water dried, but this morning it fell loose over his ears with one Dagwood Bumstead cowlick protruding

51

as though he had been hit on the back of the head with a board.

"If you need the money for a haircut, why don't you ask?" Vernon said. "I'll give you the money." Tom knew Uncle Vernon, the bank teller, wasn't really offering him money; it was his way of saying his hair was too long. He didn't glance in his uncle's direction, dunking his face under the kitchen spigot instead of going into the bathroom to wash up. Then he wiped his face and hands on the towel that Rachel had embroidered, the one that was just for show. Rachel gasped as if he had broken something.

Gladys led her son to his chair as though he were a stranger in her kitchen, putting all the leftover food in front of him in a semicircle on the table. The previous afternoon he had eaten a hamburger at the Blue Moon with the last change he had. Holly Lee had gotten caught giving him free root beers and had her pay docked for a month. There was no folding money left in his wallet. All he and Holly Lee had found in her refrigerator was milk that smelled sour and a bottle of sweet gherkins, which they emptied.

While he ate the eggs, bacon, and gravy biscuits, holding his face low and shoving things into his mouth, his mother turned her back. He pulled up the bottom of his T-shirt to wipe his chin, ignoring the paper towel that she had put beside his plate. Then he stopped eating for a moment to let the food settle, his stomach swollen with gas. When he belched, Rachel acted offended and left the table.

"I can't believe you didn't have any more sense than to get that done," Uncle Vernon told him.

Gladys turned from rinsing the fancy towel out in the sink and hanging an old one in its place. "What are you talking about, Vernon?" she said. "Can't you leave the boy alone until he finishes eating? I can tell just as good that you missed supper, Tom."

"I'm talking about that tattoo on his arm," Vernon insisted.

"Tattoo!" She swung around, grabbing both of her son's arms so hard he dropped his knife and fork. She slung his right arm against his body as if it had bitten her when she saw the drawing. "Oh, good heavens, Tom. What have you done to yourself!"

On his right bicep, the face of a wildcat spread out gray, the outline of the cat's face as smeared as an ink drawing on wet paper. Gladys began to rub at the tattoo with the wet towel in her hands. "Ouch, Mama. Be careful. It's pretty sore."

"Oh my gracious, Tom. It won't come off. It's real." Her voice faded to a squeak, then came back like air into a bellows. "Young man, you tell me who did this to you."

"This friend of Holly Lee's, Mama. Her aunt, actually."

"You mean a grown woman did that?"

"She's not grown. Well, not grown like you are. She's about twenty-five, I guess. All I have to do is tune up her '54 Ford Custom."

"She thinks you ought to pay for that? I think she ought to go to jail for doing that to a boy who doesn't know any better."

"Mark my words," Vernon put in, "someday when you're not the same foolhardy person you were when you were young and stupid, there it is, in broad daylight telling everybody you ain't got the sense to plan ahead."

"Yeah," Tom retorted, "and what's that on your arm, an Easter egg decal?"

Vernon rubbed his own arm that was covered by his long-sleeved white Sunday shirt. "That's exactly what I mean," he replied. During World War II, he'd gotten a serpent with wings tattoo that lay snarled in the hair of his forearm like a snake in the grass. "I always thought it hurt me at the bank," he said.

Annie jumped up from her chair and ran to see. "Is that a

wolf, Tommy?" she asked, pressing her index finger between the wildcat's eyes.

"No. It's a wildcat," he told her, flexing his muscle. "A jaguar."

"Sure looks like a wolf," Zack said as he walked behind Tom to see the design. "I just learned something about wolves, Tom. Wolf packs have a leader, but if you're not the leader, it's better to be a little weak wolf than a strong wolf. You see, when the leader gets mad, the weak wolf turns up his throat and makes it easy for the strong wolf to grab him and kill him."

"What's so great about getting killed?" Tom asked.

"He doesn't get killed. The strong one just gets bored and walks off. At least that's what this book said."

Gladys turned her back to them, sending the water into the sink full force, the spigot venting her anger.

"That sure looks more like a wolf than a cat to me, Tommy," Annie giggled. "Tell him about the wolf we saw yesterday at the Farmers Exchange, Zack."

Zack waited for Tom to ask him to tell the story, but instead Tom rolled his arm around to study his tattoo again. He had taken the Jaguar emblem from a magazine for Holly's aunt to copy and she'd kept it beside her on the table as she dipped the needles into the colors with the machine strapped to the back of her hand. She had shown him her book of stencils. She was used to following a pattern she transferred to a person's skin, drilling in a black outline, then filling the colors in, like in a child's coloring book. The edges of Tom's tattoo weren't sharp; it looked as though the cat had been drawn on a blotter. It hadn't come out like he had hoped.

"Does it hurt when they do that?" Zack asked.

Tom nodded, tapping a cigarette out of the pack he took from his sleeve. "Yeah, it hurts a lot. A lot worse than they let on." He lit the cigarette with his other hand, his eyes on the tattoo while he struck a match on the side of his boot, then cupped his single hand around the flame. "I tell you what it feels like. Like I took a hot cigarette and stuck it on your skin. Then it goes numb."

"Is that what happened to the hair on your arm? It burned off?"

"She shaved it off. Then she put on Vaseline. She said it wouldn't bleed, but it bled like a . . ."

"Can you erase it and let me do it over?" Annie asked. "I can draw a lot better than that. Want me to show you?"

Tom didn't answer her. He stared at his mother's back. She lifted her hand to her face—to wipe away a tear, he could tell. Her shoulders jerked. He stood up, trying to think of something to say to her, but nothing came, so he climbed up the stairs to his room.

"Tom," Zack called after him, "I wanted to tell you about the half wolf this man had down at the Exchange. When I tried to pet him, he growled and tucked his tail between his legs." Zack started up the stairs. "Then the man who owned him told me you couldn't pet him like a dog . . ."

As Tom turned into their bedroom and shut the door, Zack glimpsed the animal smeared on his arm like a dark bruise. He ran to the top of the stairs.

"Where are you going, young man?" Gladys called. "We leave for Sunday school as soon as your father gets back."

"I've got to tell Tom something."

Zack opened the door to their room. Tom lay face down on the bed, pushing his feet out of his boots and letting them drop off the edge of the bed as Zack entered.

"Tom, you should have seen this wolf. He might still be there. If you want to, we can go down after I get home from church. The man told me when you're training a dog, you knock him in the head once and he never forgets who's boss. But even if his wolf lets him boss him just a little bit, you never can tell when he might come back growling and go for the jugular. I'd still like to have one though, wouldn't you?"

Tom rolled over and stared at his brother as if he were speaking a foreign language.

"I bet you could do it, Tom. Me and you could. We could train him if he knew we were his friends."

Tom shook his head slowly. "Naw, you don't train a wolf, Zack," he said with a yawn, closing his eyes and belching again. "You'll just spend your life with a big stick, reeducating him."

Tom fell asleep in front of Zack, seconds after he stopped talking, his breath coming out in the half snore that Zack heard at night when their talks would stop. Their mother called him from the base of the stairs, so he backed out of the room, closing the door softly.

Later that afternoon, Tom awoke to a tickling on his arm. When he swatted at it, thinking it was an insect, he felt his hand hit something solid. He rolled over and opened his eyes to Annie's wide-eyed look, her fingers covering her bottom lip. She had a paintbrush in her other hand. Her leftover paint-by-numbers colors were spread out on Zack's bed. She lifted her fingers away from her lip. The tips were dotted with blood. Two crimson drops reached over her bottom lip and chased each other into the dimple on her chin.

"Annie, for god's sake."

Tom sat up and took the little girl into his arms and held her face against his chest. "Annie, I wouldn't have hit you on purpose for anything in the world."

She nodded into his chest and didn't cry.

His eyes found the sore spot the tattoo had made on his arm. It was stiff now, the wildcat transformed as in a dream: its fur gray and soft as a kitten, its eyes bright green.

The next afternoon the family was mowing in the lower field. Hershel drove his tractor. He patted the back pocket of his bibs, then jabbed the tractor brakes, stopping so fast that Zack fell out of the mower seat. He shut off the engine.

"It's gone," he said into the silence.

Gladys walked to the front of the tractor. Zack climbed to his feet and joined her. The girls moved towards them with their pitchforks.

"My wallet's gone," he told his wife. He turned to look over his shoulder at the expanse of the field of fallen hay. "It must have worked out of my pocket."

Gladys dropped her face in silence as if she were praying for a few moments, then she said, "We will all just stop doing what we were doing and find it."

She divided the field into five sections for them to begin their search. They combed the field for hours with rakes and pitchforks, looking for the wallet that held the money from the first load of tobacco. Zack ran back to the house to check the pickup seat and his daddy's chairs at the table and on the porch, but it wasn't there. At first it seemed like a game to the children, but when it appeared no reward was going to be found, they began to slow, complaining to each other.

Gladys' initial resolve wore down also. "Honestly, Hershel," she said as the light got thin, "why didn't you leave that money in the drawer? Then all this would be for a dollar-fifty wallet."

"Because I wasn't in the house when I got it," Hershel snapped. "Don't start into me with your whining. I never lost my wallet before in my life. It's here on our property somewhere. I'm sure of it. I remember distinctly counting it out as I set in the truck down at the warehouse."

After Hershel went back to the barn to get a flashlight and the women went in to prepare supper, he sat for a moment in the tractor seat. He felt his empty pocket again. Then he ran his hands under the seat and around the shifter in the dark. When he climbed down and reached between the seat and the frame, his shoulder touched the hot exhaust pipe and he recoiled, backing into the wall. Without another thought, he spun around and drove his fist into the door frame, skinning the knuckles so deep he felt as though his arm was scalded. He struck his forehead against the same rough wood four times before he stepped outside. He stood a moment, getting his balance and placing his other palm over his sticky knuckles. The pain inside his head was still worse than his bruised forehead.

He walked outside, slowly moving towards the lighted kitchen of his house. He stopped, squinting in the thin moonlight. He saw the dark outline of a tall man coming up the driveway. He walked to meet him. His troubles were over. Someone was bringing his lost wallet to him.

"Howdy," Hershel called.

The figure stopped.

Hershel kept walking until he was within ten feet of the man. Then he froze, anger sweeping through his body.

"How come you walking?" Hershel demanded.

Tom didn't answer.

Hershel took two steps closer.

"How come you stole my wallet?"

Tom shook his head and turned towards the house.

"Answer me, goddammit. You sonavabitching common thief." Tom heard growling sounds from his father's throat as if he were confronting an animal who was guarding his turf.

"You're acting crazy, old man," he replied, keeping his distance. "What's the matter with you?"

"You did it, didn't you?" Hershel insisted. "I don't know why I didn't think of it until now."

"I didn't take your wallet," Tom countered before he went up the steps into the house. "And I didn't make it rain too much or your pig die either."

Tom's mother carried his supper up to his room. He found the tray when he came in to dress after his bath. It was stew with too many potatoes and not enough meat, but he ate every scrap and sopped up the pot licker with the three biscuits she had wrapped in wax paper. Then he left on foot.

Tom didn't come back that night. The next day he left work at noon, pushing an old Military 45 Harley that had stood against Parsons' back wall for years. He was soaked with sweat when he reached home. Hershel saw him from the lunch table. Tom leaned against the barn, taking a cigarette from the pack in his sleeve.

"That sonavabitch's not eating at my table tonight," Hershel snorted, his forehead and hand were spotted with dark red scabs that he couldn't remember how he got.

"He said he didn't take your money, Hershel," she replied.

"He says a lot of things," Hershel retorted. "What happened to his fancy car? Did you ask him that? Zeb Parsons told me the finance company come and got it. When was the last time he give you his rent? His back is against the wall, if you ask me. He'll take anything that ain't nailed down."

Gladys watched Tom walk into the barn, then come out with his hands filled with tools. He spent the afternoon and evening working on the Harley. Near dusk, after he had kicked the starter until his leg muscle ached, the engine rumbled to life once, then died for another hour. By the time the rest of the family sat down to supper, the Harley was running fitfully, the air hanging with blue smoke. Hershel got up from his seat while the motor thumped outside and took the fresh plate and silverware from Tom's place. Gladys trembled when they clattered into the kitchen sink.

When her husband sat back down, she said grace quickly. Soon they heard Tom ride the Harley out the driveway, its sound battering through the trees on Highway 43 until it faded into silence.

That night Tom came into his and Zack's room, stopping in the doorway. Zack hadn't heard the Harley come back. The hall light shone behind Tom, making his face too dark for

Zack to read. At first the shadows made him look scary, but the longer Zack looked at him, the more he knew Tom was the frightened one. He didn't understand why he hadn't spoken.

Then Zack heard him cuss. Aunt B.B.'s globe had fallen off the top shelf of the closet and hit him in the forehead, but he caught it before it hit the floor. Tom stood in the moonlight, holding the globe in one hand like a basketball player studying to make a foul shot. His other arm curled around the rolled-up bundle of Zack's sleeping bag.

"If I told you to do something," Tom asked finally, "would you do it?"

Zack's legs drew up under the covers. "Yes," he answered. His blood shot through his veins like ice water and covered his body with goose pimples. What if it was something he was too chicken to do and he let Tom down?

"Come with me to Greenmont, Zack." He drew into a ball. Then Tom tried to yank his legs back straight, but he didn't uncoil.

Zack fell back asleep and dreamed Tom was holding his head in his hands. "You're too short to be on my team," Tom told him. "I take back asking you to come with me." When Tom bent over to pat him on the shoulder one last time before he left, he dropped his head and it rolled down the steps and smashed like a melon at the bottom.

The next morning when Gladys pulled back the covers to wake Tom, she found three rolled-up quilts with Aunt B.B.'s globe on the pillow. B.B. followed Gladys in and gathered up her globe.

"So that's who took my globe without asking," she said. "I should have known."

The thighs of Tom's jeans and the shoulders of his shirt were still wet from the rain the night before when he tried to escape the storm by huddling under an overpass. He'd slept sitting up against the bike, its heat drying his backside. The lightning's flash had caught the pigeons walking the underpass ledge like ducks in a shooting gallery.

His Harley thumped into his first night away from home, sputtered into the second as cars and trucks sailed past him, and split like a blistered tomato before the third. When it rolled to a stop, he pushed it onto the dirt shoulder, its oil pouring over innards sticking out through its side like a mortally wounded animal. It had been on its last legs when he left, but he would have jumped on anything that would carry him yelling distance away.

He had packed his things in the cracked leather saddlebags, strapping them under the army surplus sleeping bag he'd taken from Zack's side of the closet, and putting his dirty socks and underwear in the ammunition box on the front of the motorcycle. His good shoes and a towel were stuffed into the leather gun holder beside the right handlebar.

Tom rolled the Harley towards the woods, trailing oil black and thick as tar. After the back wheel jammed and oil puked on his right boot, he cursed the bike and shoved it over. Pine twigs snapped beneath it as it dropped, and he heard a popping sound from the saddlebag. His shaving lotion.

Tom leaned against a tree and closed his eyes, the smell of Aqua Velva flooding his nostrils and the wet bark soaking through his pants. A quick shiver went through his body, but his chill left when he opened his eyes. He tied the laces of his good shoes together and hung them over his shoulder, pulled his laundry from the ammunition box and crammed it in beside his clean clothes. He buckled the saddlebags around the sleeping bag, forming an awkward pack for his back.

As he started to walk down the highway, watching his feet and sensing that the trees beside him were not moving, he felt as if he were on a treadmill. He couldn't remember what the last highway sign said; when he'd passed it, he hadn't expected it to be the last one he'd see. This was country he'd planned to move through; stopping here hadn't entered his mind.

He turned and looked back. The white star on the tank of the army drab Harley shone from the woods. That tank had forty cents worth of gas he wished he hadn't bought about four miles before. He walked some more, looked back again. The letters on the rear fender—U.S. CAV 103—were now too small to read. He walked backwards until the star was lost in the undergrowth, then stood still a moment to be sure that the sight of it was gone, drowning into the green trees. The sound of the Harley played in his head like a song he couldn't identify, thudding at his temples, but soon that was gone too and there was only the slow crunch of gravel under his boots.

He cut through the woods to the back of a Pure Oil station, going in the restroom that had FOR CUSTOMERS ONLY lettered on the door. He locked the door, dumping his clothes from his pack onto the floor, shards of the broken Aqua Velva bottle clinking onto the tile. There was no soap or paper towels so he dry shaved with the razor he had remembered to bring. He shook the glass from his dark blue shirt and put it on, feeling the wet spot of aftershave on his back. Enough rested in the cap to splash on his face; it burned in the cuts across his chin. He dabbed them with toilet paper to stop the bleeding. Before he walked out, he kicked part of the glass up against the wall. Someone in his mind scolded him about barefoot children. Mama. He had to get something to eat soon before he went crazy. He rolled down his sleeves, hiding the wildcat tattoo with Annie's paint cracking on top of the scab.

Tom had enough money for a few days if he played it carefully, but he walked to a restaurant and spent it all on one steak dinner. The restaurant was dark. While his eyes adjusted to the gloom he could barely see two waitresses moving around the tables, their white aprons glowing as though they were lighted. One was old and shapeless and the other was pretty, with thick black hair that muscled its way out of the heavy braid down her back. There was enough sash left from the apron to make a giant bow on her backside. He walked to a table on her side, shoving his belongings beneath. He could smell his shaving lotion in the smoky room. She did too.

"You smell very nice," she smiled, putting down a place setting rolled in a napkin beside his hand. He pulled his hand off the table when he saw a smudge that he had missed. He cleaned it with the napkin before she came back for his order. She didn't seem to notice. She had an accent that was foreign. Her black and white uniform with a short skirt like a French maid made her seem more like a dancing girl than a waitress.

After he finished his steak, which was a little tougher than what he was used to, he ate all the bread and crackers in the basket she brought. Then he ate the potato, skin and all, and the parsley and spiced apple ring. He drank countless cups of coffee; she kept refilling until his ears began to buzz. He would only have thirty cents left—dessert or a tip for Aurora, her name scrawled in a childlike handwriting on the check she brought.

"Aurora," Tom said, and she smiled when he used her name. "What kind of pie do you have?"

"Pecan. Key Lime. Apple. Maybe berry. Blue or black, I don't know." Her hands moved when she talked as if she were drawing pictures of what she was saying.

"Which is the biggest?"

She laughed aloud. "You are hungry man. I cut for you. Make big."

"Apple."

After she left, he felt the stare of the man at the table beside him, a ruddy man who had come down to a table from a bar stool. He also called Aurora by name. Tom had heard the whining sound of his diesel shutting down before he walked in. He had parked its bulk between the restaurant and the neon sign, blocking the colored lights that had bounced across Tom's table.

The pie arrived, filling the plate. She had heated it and topped it with ice cream. Now he was sorry he had spent her tip. He ate the good part first, then chewed at the rubbery scraps of stale crust. Aurora was talking to the red-faced man, who said he had a load to haul to Memphis. He asked her if she'd like to ride with him. She shook her head.

"Anytime you change your mind, all you have to do is ask," he said and pushed his chair back to leave. After he was out the door and Tom felt his truck move away, sending the colored lights back across his table, he got up to go to the john. As he passed the man's table, he plucked up the dollar tip and wadded it into his pocket. When he returned to his seat, he smoothed the bill, putting it under his glass before Aurora returned.

"May I clean your table?" she asked. "I leave soon."

"Sure," he replied and pushed back his chair, watching the dollar go into her apron pocket.

"Muchos graçias, señor."

"Going to Memphis?"

She looked at Tom in surprise. "Memphis?" Then she understood. "No, not Memphis. Dwayne, he always ask me to ride in his truck. I know what he after."

"Do you like him?"

"Not much. No. He leave me good tip." She looked at the table and frowned. "Tonight I think he mad at me. Too bad." She laughed. As she stacked the dishes, she looked at Tom. "Do you have a truck too?"

He grimaced and shook his head.

"Car?"

He shook his head again. She tipped her head to the side.

"I have a motorcycle," he answered. "But it broke."

"You will fix mañana."

"No. I mean really broke. Gone. Dead."

"That is too bad," she replied as if he had lost a relative. "I am sorry for you." Before she picked up the stack of dishes, she asked, "Where are you going?"

"Greenmont," came out of his mouth. "I've got a job waiting up there to drive a race car for a guy."

"Greenmont. I believe that is twenty miles. Or more maybe."

"Is it? I better start walking," he replied, but didn't budge.

"Walk! You cannot walk to Greenmont. You could have ridden with Dwayne, but he gone now."

"Guess I'm out of luck," he smiled. She smiled back and walked into the kitchen.

There were four small trailers behind the restaurant where the waitresses lived and one large one for the owner-cook and his wife, who operated the cash register. Though his body was exhausted, Tom lay awake, his brain alive with coffee. Aurora's thick black hair spread across his right shoulder. He had untwisted her braid that felt as dense and heavy as another appendage. She had fallen asleep like an exhausted child after they made love. She wasn't feminine and soft like Holly Lee; she moved as though her whole body was a muscle. Her olive skin was filled out as far as it should go, with one tiny flaw near her navel, a puncture wound covered with tissue-paper skin. When he asked, she said she had left home, Puerto Rico, with her mother when she was seven to live in Norfolk. Her drunken stepfather, a sailor, had stuck his knife there two years ago, mistaking her for her mother, she thought. But her mother believed he hated Aurora. Her mother packed Aurora's things to send her to New York where her aunt lived, but the trucker she hitched a ride with from Norfolk lied to her and went the wrong way. She jumped from his truck and hid from him. She'd found a job in the restaurant. She had no people in this town, Crescent City.

The next morning she brought Tom food from the restaurant, running across the gravel driveway to the trailer with a plate of eggs and bacon.

"The woman who order this leave without eating. It will go to waste," she explained, then ran back inside. Tom watched her through the window. In broad daylight her waitress dress seemed more like the outgrown clothing of a child. After he ate, he left with the saddlebag and sleeping bag over his shoulder, walking behind the restaurant so she would not see him through the front window.

In the center of town, men waited on the street corners for pickup work. He walked down the railroad tracks and watched a man with a long stick run hoboes out of the boxcars like animals. He asked if there was a race track nearby; there was one ten miles away at Raneyville, but was shut down until spring.

At dark, Tom walked back to the restaurant. He stood in front of the front window, waiting until she saw him. When she smiled, he walked back to the trailer, dropped into her bed, and fell asleep.

Everything Aurora cooked, all the leftover meat she brought from the restaurant, she chopped into bits and mixed with rice. Tom picked out the meat and shoved the rice to the side of his plate. After he found a job loading trucks at the cigarette factory, he bought hamburgers at the drive-in on his walk to her trailer. She worked long hours, never complaining, handing Tom her money as soon as he moved in, even the tips from her apron pocket.

The first time he showered in the tiny trailer, he tried to wash around the paint Annie had put on his arm, but it cracked away later on while he worked. One day as he sat on the front step, he noticed the last chip was gone, leaving only the smudged face of the wildcat looking through the hair on his arm. When he had walked outside the trailer to smoke, Aurora followed him like a dog. He ignored her, reaching into his wallet and taking out a grammar school photo. It was the first time he had looked at it since he left.

"Wish before that swift is out of sight," she interrupted his thoughts, pointing at a fast moving bird. "Oh, you are too slow. Who is that?" she asked him, pointing now to the picture.

"Annie, my sister."

"She look like you. What is Summit Elementary?"

Tom held the picture closer for a moment. "Summit is the town I came from."

"Where were you going, Tom Pate? When you come here?"

He didn't answer. Nothing formed in his head but a pain behind his eyes.

"Why do you follow me everywhere?" he answered instead. "I'm not going anywhere."

She sat down beside him on the steps. "In Puerto Rico, I go out with my brother to smoke," she explained. "Sometimes he give me cigarette."

Tom held the pack out to her, but she shook her head. He didn't know what she wanted; she didn't seem to want much at all except to be with him.

"See the birds coming from the mud?" she asked.

He nodded as his eyes found the swallows in the wet area where the gutter ran over behind the restaurant.

"Those birds," she went on, "live the winter under the mud with the frogs and turtles and come out for spring time. They must be going under now."

"They don't live under the mud, Aurora. They're just getting it for nests or something. Birds don't do that."

"Yes, they do. In Puerto Rico I saw the fishermen lift their nests and they were filled with muddy birds."

"You were just a little kid. You thought that was what you saw."

"It was."

"I don't think you are eighteen," he said.

She looked surprised. "How you know?"

"Because all you have that's eighteen is your body. How old are you really?"

She didn't look at him, but held up her hand, opening and closing it three times. Tom dropped his head and wheezed, shoving the picture of Annie back into his wallet.

He stayed with Aurora past Christmas, his first one away from home. He had the flu for a week and lay sweating in the narrow bed while she slept in Zack's old sleeping bag in the corner. One morning he woke to find a dead pigeon on his chest. When he flung it into the floor, she scooped up the wet mass of feathers.

"A dead dove on the chest will take the sickness away." She stood with her offering cupped in her hands.

"That's a goddamn rotten pigeon that got hit by a truck. You're fucking nuts sometimes, you know. Leave me alone!"

When she brought him water, he took the glass and threw it hard, shattering it on the front of the cabinet.

"I'm going nuts in this little place," he said, his voice muffled in the pillow. She picked her way through the glass, her brown toes gripping her flip-flops, and put a cool washcloth on his forehead.

"There is a fortuneteller down the street. She will tell our fortune if I carry her dinner. We will find if we will leave here soon for a big house."

"Yeah, great. The last one told me about you. Dark, beautiful, a long way from home. Only she said you'd be rich. She sure missed there."

Aurora lifted Tom's hand. "I read your hand."

She studied it briefly, then squeezed it shut without speaking.

"What?" he asked.

"Not good. The line of life stops very soon."

He yanked his hand from her. "I killed the last fortuneteller who told me that."

On Christmas Day the restaurant was closed so they slept late and ate cold pizza for every meal. The parking lot filled with sleeping truckers who couldn't make it home for Christmas. A little boy rode around the trucks on a bicycle that was too big for him.

"Look at that little colored," Aurora said as she peeked through a hole in the curtain. "He has stolen a bicycle."

Tom rolled over in the bed and lifted the curtain. The boy wobbled past on a tall bike, then fell over. Tom shook his head. "No. He has parents like mine who buy everything too big for you. You end up wearing it out before you outgrow it." The child got under way again, then stopped beside the fire hydrant in front of the restaurant to climb down to the ground.

By New Year's Day, 1959, Aurora had taken down the tree in the restaurant window to head off bad luck. When she dragged the cedar to the trash, small strips of silver tinsel snagged on dead weeds in the vacant lot beside the trailer. An old colored woman with strings of popcorn tied around her waist stopped in the alley to pry the stand off the tree with a forked metal rod. She rested for a moment, dropping her bulk onto a garbage can while she picked the gumdrops off a thorn tree, ate a few, then dropped the rest into her apron pocket.

Tom watched the old woman from the open door of the trailer. He had robbed the gumdrops off Annie's thorn tree the Christmas before, leaving only the black ones. Annie had put her hands on her hips in mock anger and said to him, "Caught you good. I know who doesn't like black gumdrops." Annie had laughed loudly as she put down the food offering for Santa Claus and then ran up the steps.

Before the old woman moved on, she took the paper angel with a perfect, cone-shaped skirt that Aurora had made. The angel had reminded Tom of Annie in her nightgown, except that Annie's hem would be hanging out on one side, and she would have chocolate cake icing on her chin. Tom took out Annie's picture.

"She look just like you," Aurora observed.

"You said that before."

"I have no pictures of me as a little girl. I do not know what I looked like. There were no mirrors," she babbled. "I wish I had brought one of my sisters with me, one of the babies."

"A baby. You're talking nuts again. How would you work and look after a baby?" he asked.

"I would find a husband to look after me and I would pick the vegetables he raised in his garden. We would buy a little farm." She began to pout, her fingers spreading over her stomach. "He would build me and the baby a little house." Then she began to speak in Spanish. Aurora spoke English only when she was happy, all her anger spurting out in Spanish. But that day when she talked of the baby, when she pretended

70

she wanted something she knew was already to be, Tom's anger took over.

He began to gather up his things, his socks and clothes from the floor, stuffing them into the saddlebags. When they were full, he grabbed a grocery bag and dumped in his things from the bathroom. He picked up the glass ball he'd bought for Aurora for Christmas with snow inside that fell on a little house. He didn't know why he picked it up.

She let out a shriek when he touched the ball. He put it back where it sat, placing it exactly over the round clean spot on the dusty table. Aurora dropped back onto the bed. He hurried as fast as he could. He had to get out the door because if she touched him, his anger had only one direction to go. As he opened the door, she lunged forward, digging her fingers through a belt loop on his jeans. Her tug was firm, an anchor dropping from a boat. He swung randomly with open palms and didn't turn to see where his blows struck. Finally she let go, putting her hands over her face. When he was out the door, she scratched her own nails down the face she had saved.

Tom climbed into the seat of a truck that stopped for him by the side of the highway. The door was shut before the anger drained from his hands.

"Moving on, eh, buddy?"

Tom looked up and saw the driver's face for the first time: Dwayne, the trucker who had tried to get Aurora to ride to Memphis, smiling straight ahead. When the truck lunged forward with Tom inside, he felt like he was back in the giant tractor tube the day he rode to Raleigh by mistake, swept down the Yellow River the only way the river could go.

7

"Maa-a-a!" Rachel's scream shot between the pines as sharp as the cry of a dying peacock. She was at the trash pile, where she had dragged a burlap bag filled with roots and broken plow pieces, carrying her hoe across her shoulder like a rifle.

Gladys, Annie, and Zack all knew that Rachel was prone to crying wolf. Gladys straightened up, taking Zack's bean basket from him. "Zack, you go see about Rachel."

"She's got her hoe, Mama. Probably just a black snake."

"Don't you argue with me. If something has got your sister, you'll regret it till your grave for being lazy."

He shrugged and walked slowly towards the path.

"You pick your feet up, young man. You're intentionally being pokey."

He found Rachel on her knees in the center of the trash pile beside the curved porcelain halves of their old toilet, a pose that suggested she had vomited and somehow split the appliance in two. She had dropped her hoe, which Zack stepped on, the handle banging him squarely between the eyes, driving his glasses frames into his forehead.

"Zack, look!" she bellowed.

He held his hand under his bloody nose and waded into the trash pile. His blood spotted the porcelain as he bent over; Rachel saw it and stepped backwards with a gasp. She wet her handkerchief in water collected in an old tin can and jammed it under his nose.

"Look, I said!"

His eyes finally focused on what she was waving in her other hand: a mangled chunk of leather, his daddy's wallet hatched from the giant porcelain egg. The money was still there, green as a ripe bean in a rotten hull. The wallet had caught in the hidden curve of porcelain.

Before supper a joyful Gladys carefully peeled the wet bills apart and warmed them on her biscuit pan. Annie wanted to make a money sandwich to put on his plate.

"You just hand it to him this evening, honey. Your daddy doesn't have much of a funny bone about his money."

"I was the one who found it," Rachel put in.

"And tell him Rachel found it and you dried it for him."

"Annie didn't dry it, Mama. You dried it."

"I know, Rachel dear," she replied softly. "And I want you to get full credit for finding it. You were the one who found Daddy's long lost money."

"I don't even want to hand it to him," Annie pouted.

Gladys shushed them, waving her hand like a wand. "I did think he left with a little something to tide him over until he found work," she said softly to no one, shaking her head while the two wrinkles between her eyes deepened. "He left not knowing where his next meal was coming from . . ." Tom had been gone now more than a year.

"What are you talking about?" Rachel asked.

"Tom, dear."

"I don't think he starved to death, Mama," Rachel said flatly. "As long as there are women in the world, one of them will take care of my darling, handsome brother. Why do you still care so much about him? He didn't care a hoot about us. Why would you rather he'd stolen Daddy's money?"

Gladys regarded her as if she had spoken in an unknown tongue, then turned away without answering.

"I know how to solve our problem," Zack blurted, his voice pinched through his swollen nose. "Let's get Tom to hand it to him since he was the one who stole it."

"You thought he stole it too!" Rachel shouted. "Don't act so holier-than-thou, Mr. Goody Two-Shoes."

To everyone's surprise, when Rachel handed her father his money, he took it from her and put it in his wallet like she was paying an overdue bill.

"Where'd you find this?" he asked.

"It was in the commode, the one you threw on the trash pile. Somebody broke it in two."

"Me and Junior Parsons," Zack confessed, hoping for some credit for finding the money. "Him, actually. He was shooting spiders and there was a big one in the hole."

"I found it," Rachel inserted.

"Hershel took the money back out of his wallet and looked at it again. "Yep, that figures," he said as he slid the wallet back into his overalls. He reached to pull a leg off the chicken in front of him.

"What figures?" Rachel asked.

"That's why I thought that commode was no good. Kept plugging up." Then he turned slowly to look at Zack as he reached for a biscuit. "You busted up a perfectly good commode, boy."

8

At seventeen, after a wet winter reduced his mail-order harmonica to silent rust, Zack took a big step: he bought a seven-dollar guitar from Percy's Pawn-It. His fingertips were sore from practicing, the steel strings having cut his flesh instead of building calluses like it said in *Learn to Play the Guitar at Home*. He listened to a twelve-year-old blind girl from Morganton at the Wednesday night fellowship slide her tiny hands up and down strings that had met his fingers like razors. He shut his eyes while she played, and for a moment stole the blind girl's music, including the applause that always followed when the song wasn't religious.

"You ought to listen instead of sleeping," Rachel scolded as they left the church, "and you might learn something."

"I was so listening."

"Anyway, I think someone ought to tell you, in a friendly way, that you don't seem to have an ounce of natural talent."

Zack felt like shaking Rachel until her tear-shaped glasses with the rhinestones across the top fell off.

The family gathered around Hershel as he talked with Marvin Simmons, known behind his back as The Mouth of Summit. Marvin nodded at Zack as he said to Hershel, "Hear that boy of yours done bought him a ticket to ride."

"How's that?" Hershel asked.

"Bought him a geetar down at Percy's. Next thing you know he'll be off to the Opry and you won't have a man left to get the crops in," Marvin chided. "Or maybe it's that rolling and rocking he's got on his mind."

"Rock and rolling," Rachel corrected without looking at Marvin.

"I got some rocking and rolling on my mind too," Hershel replied. "Putting *rocks* in the mud hole on the back road after he *rolls* them up out of the bottom."

Marvin laughed loudly.

"Daddy's a real comedian," Zack said to no one as he climbed into the back of the pickup.

That evening after supper Zack waited motionless at the bottom of the stairs, watching his father. Hershel stood in the living room, his back to Zack, turning in his hands the guitar that Zack had left on the settee. Suddenly Hershel dropped the instrument, like a bird of prey who has lost his appetite, and was out the door before the flat note from the fallen guitar reached Zack's ears.

Zack sat in the pickup beside Highway 43, his guitar in his lap. He sipped on a fifth of Southern Comfort left over from the previous Saturday night. Snatches of music from the Stallion Club whispered up the pavement, as sweet in the summer night as whiffs of perfume from a girl dancing around him in the dark. His girlfriend Laurie wouldn't go out tonight; she was mad because he'd driven by her house last night with a truck load of guys, blowing the horn and yelling obscenities, and her daddy had recognized him hanging out the window. Zack was sure the real reason was that Laurie had decided they had gone as far as they were going to go, until he committed to marrying her. He thought her skin was too thin, her eyes too pale, her coloring not meant to be looked at in bright light; she had a transparent look like a pond fish in a jar.

Zack took one more swallow. That was enough. He had his nerve up now. He drove to the Stallion Club. He parked the pickup near the garbage cans and walked past the row of freshly washed cars with all the latest speed equipment—the same cars that used to frequent the Blue Moon Drive-In before it shut down.

He spotted Holly Lee across the room while she waited on tables, her blond curls gathered into a pile on top of her head with single curls breaking away like petals on an overripe rose. The chief carhop hat no longer rested on the side of her head; without it she seemed more a woman than a girl. Rumor had it that Holly Lee left the Blue Moon because the fry cook there kept after her for a date. When she refused, he cooked her orders last, making her customers angry. The Blue Moon had other troubles too before it closed: the young kids liked the fast food at the new McDonald's. The Blue Moon regulars had staged a brief protest when McDonald's first opened, parking in front and blowing their horns, before they drove to the Stallion Club for good.

When Holly Lee smiled at the Stallion Club customers, her teeth glistened, the lone dark tooth hiding in the dim light, missed by men who never knew her in the light of day. Beneath her short white cowgirl skirt with red stars, Zack saw that her long legs were wrapped in black fishnet panty hose.

"What'll you have?"

He almost sang back "Pabst Blue Ribbon," but instead he said, "Did you know that my brother, Tom, invented panty hose?"

She looked at him as if nothing any of the men in that room said would register on her brain unless it were the choice of draft or bottled beer.

"Hurry up, mister. Drink or leave. Draft or bottle. I got thirsty guys waiting on me."

"Bottle. Tom says a glass doesn't hold as much as a bottle and you get gypped."

"Eighteen?"

"No, one will do for now."

"I mean your age, funny guy."

"They carded me at the door."

"Law says I got to ask again before I serve you."

"Yeah, just turned. I'll show you if you want to see. My brother, Tom, is twenty-two now. He's a stock car driver."

She had walked away before he finished talking. Zack watched her draw the beers, a circle of amber-filled glasses around his one brown bottle. Carrying them back through the crowd to the customers, her head bobbed like a pigeon.

"Bet you miss your skates, huh?" he said as the bottle was planted with a clunk in front of him.

"Fifty cents, buddy, small change if you've got it."

He dug into his pocket, producing three quarters, but squeezed them a moment, knowing as soon as they hit her tray, she'd spin out of his reach until he emptied his beer.

"I don't have a red Chevy Bel Air with a candy-apple paint job like Tom did. I've got a pickup, a blue one. Kind of an old blue junky pickup."

Finally her eyes stayed level with his.

"Tom who?" she asked.

He grew so excited with success that he could hardly control himself. "Tom Pate," he said brightly.

"How do you know him? He's been gone four years."

"He's my brother. He's my brother," he repeated.

"Jack?"

"No, Zack."

"I remember you. You were a little kid. You still don't look a spit like him. You in touch with Tom?" She began to wipe the counter in front of Zack with a rag she had on her tray. A man called her name but, to Zack's pleasure, she ignored the man as decisively as she had ignored him earlier. Her face moved closer and he could see her dark tooth. He grew uneasy under her stare, but his eyes fell on a part of her anatomy that made it even more difficult to hold his composure. "Maybe," he replied, a little too cute-sounding, like Annie playing a game. He grew panicky, afraid he had chased her back into her silence, but she said, "You hang around. I got to get back to work, but you hang around. I want to talk to you."

"Are you singing tonight?"

"Maybe," she said, mocking him.

"I've got my guitar out in the truck. I'll back you up if you like."

She was gone into the crowd, with only the top of her blond pigeon head keeping her from being lost to his sight.

"I don't know if you made me sound better or worst."

Zack didn't answer. He didn't care. He had Holly Lee beside him in his daddy's blue pickup parked in front of her house, his guitar in his lap with its neck sticking out the window.

"I mean you don't really play none too good, like just a bunch of chords and stuff. You play like you're just learning out of some how-to-play book."

"Yep. *Learn to Play the Guitar at Home in Only Fifteen Hours.*" He carefully played a C-chord.

"And tonight was about your tenth hour, right?" She laughed, so he replied, "Nope. Eighth."

"They don't pay me," Holly Lee said. "Did you know that? They put my picture out front and half the guys in there come to hear me sing. By the time I get let off serving to do my singing, most of them are so plastered they don't know if I'm on key or not." Talking easily now that she was off work, Holly Lee confided, "Tom never even knew I could sing."

"He never mentioned it," Zack agreed. He began to strum the same soft chord, over and over.

"He never even asked me what I knew how to do. Probably

figured all's I knew how to do was roller-skate." Then she laughed again. It seemed a knowing laugh. "I got married. You tell him that. Two years ago Easter. You tell him that if he ever calls."

"I didn't know you were married." Zack straightened up and glanced around the dark street, taking his hand off the guitar and touching the key in the switch before he slumped back down.

"I'm not married anymore, anyway. Separated, I guess you call it. Dumbest thing I ever did, thinking Tom Pate's left me so the world come to an end. He would of laughed at who I married anyway. Buck Herndon. Sorry piece of shit. Excuse me. You don't seem like a person I ought to talk like that in front of."

"I talk like that. My sister, Rachel, says I f-word everything."

"F-word? Oh, I get it. She a teacher or something?"

"No. Well, yes, she is. Worst kind. A Sunday school teacher."

"Figures."

"Rachel says I'm f-word crazy." He placed his fingers on the frets and resumed strumming the strings.

"Maybe you are more like your brother than you act. He sure was fucking crazy. I sure am sick and tired of hearing you play them chords, if you know what I mean."

"Sorry." Zack's hands dropped off his guitar. First he tried to stuff it between his legs, then between him and Holly. Then he thought better of that and shifted it between him and his door, moving closer to her. It would have been easier if that harmonica had been what it was cracked up to be. "Do you remember what the cowboy stars in the movies do with their guitars after they sing their love songs?" he asked. "I guess they're sitting in a wagon or something instead of a damn '52 GMC pickup."

Holly smiled and said, "I'd suggest Percy's Pawn-It."

"How'd you know that was where I got it?"

"I didn't." Then she paused. "What are you after, Zack Pate, as if I didn't know?"

His stomach went weak and he bent over on himself like a rag doll. "Yeah," he said softly, then somehow found the words: "Tom said never to settle for second best."

She was silent. Maybe for once he had said the right thing.

"He said that," she said finally, "Tom Pate said that?"

"Yeah, all the time."

"And he wasn't just talking about his car?"

"No. I don't think so. I mean, I know so," he stammered. Zack was digging into his memory. What had Tom really said about Holly Lee? Not much he could repeat.

"Then how come he left me without a word? Without one lousy word?" Her voice was shrill. He expected lights to flash on in the dark houses on her street. She banged her fist on the dash.

"Don't do that," he said finally and took her hand in his. "You're going to hurt yourself." He thought he heard a little sob. He didn't know what he was going to do if she started crying.

"I'm not going to hurt myself, dammit," she said. "If I hurt anybody, it is going to be somebody else, not me."

"Atta girl," he said stupidly.

Finally he thought he heard her start to giggle. He wasn't sure she wasn't crying.

"Let's go in," she said suddenly.

"In your house?"

"Yeah, Ma's at work and my sisters are asleep. It's my house too. I pay more than half the rent."

Zack reached for the throat of his guitar, but before he had gripped it, she added, "And leave that damn thing out here."

She got out on her side and he followed, unable to take his

eyes off her long enough to lock the truck door. The door ahead of them was dark, darker than the house. It reminded him of Holly Lee's tooth luring him inside. When she pushed it open, he went behind that dark tooth door that he'd first seen, six years ago, on the day Tom took him along to show Holly Lee his paint job. That was the night he'd had his first wet dream.

Later, Zack stood in front of her house. He felt as if he had been thrown out naked with the world laughing and pointing. He looked down to see if he had his clothes on. He did. No one was there; it was completely quiet except for an over-turned garbage can that rolled while an animal rummaged through its contents. He put his hand on his back pocket and felt the hard shape of his empty wallet. Holly Lee had charged him twenty dollars.

So it was a night of losses for Zack: his virginity, twenty dollars, and finally, his guitar. No one stole it from his pickup, though they could have just lifted it through the open window. But by dawn it was lost to him. Hershel Pate, after tossing and turning through two predawn hours of *Learn to Play the Guitar at Home in Only Fifteen Hours,* plucked the instrument and the empty Southern Comfort bottle from beside Zack's bed be-fore the sun rose, threw the bottle into the living room waste-basket for everyone to see and, gripping the guitar by the throat like a chickenhouse snake, dismembered it on the first hard object he met: the kitchen stove.

The cars going into town had pounded a possum flat as a bathmat. Zack dozed off in the bushes, then woke up shiv-ering at dusk, his clothes damp with the dew. At first he thought of going back home for dry clothes, of sleeping one more night in his soft, warm bed, delaying leaving one more time.

Before he left home he had decided he would eat when he

wanted to, not by his mother's schedule, at the same time every day. But his stomach was still obeying her, telling him it was hungry three times a day as if he'd accidentally brought a little piece of her along. Instead of packing food, he had used the last space in his backpack to stuff in his aunt B.B.'s globe, Tom's only inheritance from the old lady who had died a year after he left.

Zack had combed the newspapers in the Summit Public Library, searching for some mention of Tom as a stock car driver. In his four years of looking, he found only dead men—one killed each year—and men who won. "You know the only way to get your name in the newspaper?" Tom had told him four years ago, "Win or screw up." One of the dead was estimated to be nineteen, three years younger than Tom would be now. The boy wasn't named Tom Pate or nicknamed Pole Cat; he had no name. The accident had happened in Greenmont, home of Greenmont Raceway, the town Tom always said he would pick to start his racing career. Zack had to admit the information was unsettling. By now it would be stranger for Tom to be there in Greenmont than it would be for him to be gone.

His last view of Summit from the Trailways bus was the site of the Blue Moon Drive-In with pavement cracks sprouting grass and the drive-up speaker posts stripped like harvested tobacco stalks. A new arrival in town might think it was an abandoned field. Zack searched for the place that used to be the first slot, reserved for Tom's red Chevy that drew Holly Lee skating to the window with free root beers.

Then the bus lurched forward and the scenery he knew was gone; an unfamiliar Burma Shave sequence popped up: DON'T STICK / YOUR ELBOW / OUT SO FAR. / IT MIGHT GO HOME / IN ANOTHER CAR. Even his elbow couldn't go home; the windows of the air-conditioned bus were sealed shut.

At that moment all Zack knew for sure was which direction to go if he didn't want to end up home.

9

Three nights after Zack left, a young woman with a child came to Summit, got off the bus in town, not knowing it stopped later at the Gulf Station in Goose Bottom. The dark woman asked directions to the Pate place and, carrying the child over her shoulder, made her way on foot in a cold spring rain.

Gladys Pate's eyes were sore that night from crying. She had been remembering her boys, the rainy evening almost ten years before when she'd sent them out to find nine baby chicks that her best hen had lost in a sudden shower. Zack brought home two wet chicks, zipped inside the front of his windbreaker. Tom reached into his coat pocket, stacking five balls of wet, yellow feathers on her kitchen table.

That night Gladys opened the door to a knock without peering through the curtain and switching on the porch light as Hershel had warned her to do. She let the pair in without hesitation and dried them off as though she had finally found two of her long lost baby chicks alive.

A few months after the second Pate son left Goose Bottom, Tillie and Mallard Justice, a colored couple, moved into Aunt B.B. Pate's abandoned house to work the fields. Everybody in Goose Bottom knew the Pate boys had upped and left and that the eldest one had sown some wild oats on the road—one oat in particular—that had come back home without him. One Saturday, Gladys Pate and her grandson met Tillie as they were walking back up to the house with the newspaper. "Good morning, Aunt Tillie. Going to town?"

"Yessum. That your new grandbaby I heared so much about?"

"Yes, this is Tommy. Speak to Aunt Tillie, Tommy."

The dark little boy jammed to a stop and faced the ground in silence. "He's a bit bashful yet." The black hair on the back of his head shimmered like a crow's feathers.

"I declare, Mrs. Pate," Tillie exclaimed, "that baby's dark as a nut!"

Gladys, a bit taken aback by the remark, replied, "Yes, his mother is Spanish. Tommy knows two words for everything," she said proudly.

"I know his mama," Tillie said. "Don't know as I ever seen her tending to her baby, though. Seen her out working like a man."

"Men are what we're short of around here, aren't they, Tillie?"

"Yessum." Tillie looked at the same ground Tommy stared at. Her husband, Mallard, had been missing for a week on a bender.

"I like to believe the good Lord sent us Aurora," Gladys added, lifting her face skyward instead of across the field where Hershel and Aurora each carried an end of a bag of fertilizer, "to replace what the man down under took away."

10

In Greenmont Zack got a job at Maurice's Pure Oil. After a couple of paychecks, he lost his fear of having nothing to eat, but he still hoarded every leftover nickel like a hamster stuffing his jaws with sunflower seeds. He reckoned that growing up on a farm did this: without a pantry full of canning, a couple of pigs in the smokehouse, and enough wood to last till spring, a country man nourished fears of starving and freezing to death. In his family, one of the seven deadly sins was to pay cash money for something that you could make or grow yourself.

During his lunch hour, Zack went to all the auto parts stores asking about Tom. He had found three Tom Pates in the phonebook who weren't his brother and one T. C. Pate. *C* wasn't Tom's middle initial, but he called anyway. The man who answered said his name was Tobias.

Then Zack rode a bus to the local track. No one was there but a truck driver in a Greenmont Cemetery and Mortuary truck dumping red clay in the potholes. The truck had the same green mountain painted on the door as was on the race track sign at the entrance. Every time a grave was dug, the driver told him, the extra clay went to the race track, and every time the cars raced, they took some of the clay home with them. The man had never heard of Tom Pate. Zack felt like Sergeant Friday on "Dragnet," trying to solve a murder that hadn't happened.

After he stopped at Auntie's Bar and Grill on his block, he hurried in the front door of his boarding house and up the staircase with his dinner of hamburgers and fries under his jacket. Although his landlady offered meals, he refused to become one of the family of misfits around her table.

He sat on the windowsill as he did every night, glancing down now and then, in case Tom might be walking by below. It was like trying to pin the tail on a donkey that wasn't even there when he took off the blindfold. He'd never expected any surprises outside his window back home, but he couldn't stop looking out in Greenmont to marvel that what was out there was not home. And since it wasn't home, maybe it could have Tom walking through it.

He had been thinking about going to a movie. He had never been to a movie by himself. In the movies he used to see with Tom, there was always a sidekick, Mexican or Indian: Pancho, Tonto, Little Beaver. That was the part he played to Tom. He had trouble imagining what Pancho, Tonto, or Little Beaver would do by themselves.

Then all of a sudden one rainy evening he saw him.

Zack went running down the stairs and out onto the porch. Tom had been walking down the sidewalk, right in front of the boarding house. But when Zack got down the steps, there was no one there. He ran down the sidewalk and looked in all the parked cars. No one. All the old men sitting on the porch were watching him. He slowly climbed the porch stairs and dropped into one of the chairs in the row of geezers. The rain fell from his hair to his face, sizzling on his skin.

"Looking for somebody?" one asked.

Zack shook his head. Finally he found his voice. "No. I thought I saw somebody I knew."

He climbed back up to his room and sat on the bed, ready to dive under the covers at the first noise. What was wrong with him? He felt like a wild rabbit raised in a shoebox, who'd been dumped into a world that all the other rabbits knew about naturally. But it was starting to come clear what he was really afraid of. It was like when he'd found the star imprint from Tom's brogan frozen in the mud months after he'd gone. Tom was the only living person he knew who left a ghost behind. Zack had been running down a trail for a long time, following the tracks of his big brother, and for the first time had to face up to what it might be like if he never caught up to him.

Tom Pate sat alone in the bleachers watching the Greenmont Cemetery and Mortuary truck creep around the race track. A man stood in the back with a shovel, throwing the red clay into the potholes cut out by Saturday's race. Tom hadn't driven in the last race. He hadn't gotten a ride yet this season, and four races had already been run. When the truck left empty, Tom walked across the track. The car smells were gone, leaving only the scent of fresh clay, smelling a little too much like a farm to suit him.

On the far side was one of the jalopies that crashed on Saturday, its frame too twisted for the wheels to roll. He saw that the carcass had already been picked: the engine, the transmission, and the only good wheel gone. Tom looked inside. The water temperature gauge hung like an eye from its socket. He crawled through the window and removed the gauge.

He slid the gauge inside his jacket and walked back across the track before the next load of clay came in. He went out the gate, stopped, then flung the gauge at the side of a trash can before heading back towards the bus stop.

Cy Thomas, the other teenage mechanic at Maurice's Pure Oil where Zack worked, sat with his long legs dangling off the edge of the porch of his family's row house on McGee Alley. His straw-colored hair had a ragged cut, his own handiwork. He would snip it off in chunks when it started to fall into his eyes. Cy's movements were angular, reminding Zack of the scarecrow he had made for their cornfield out of nailed-together two-by-fours dressed in throwaway clothes. Yet he took the long leap from the porch to the front yard, an act that Zack would have had to muster up the courage to attempt, as absently as an ordinary man would take a step.

When Zack walked into the narrow yard, a rooster began to kick like a miniature bull preparing to charge. "That's Charlie," Cy introduced the rooster. "Come on out back where the car is." Zack followed him through the strange house that was connected to the other houses on both sides.

A loud female voice blasted from the kitchen, "Get that goddamn rooster out of here!" Charlie jumped out through a hole in the screen. "Rooster crowing in the doorway, man in the coffin before dusk," she warned.

"Charlie didn't make a peep, Ma."

Zack saw flour scattered across Cy's mother's bosom, which hung over her belly like a snow-covered awning. Her dress, buttoned up wrong, gave her a lopsided appearance. Noises bubbled from her, mumbo jumbo like from Soho the palmist, and she wore knots tied in her skirt to ward off demons.

Cy's father, Horace, lay on the couch in boxer shorts and an undershirt, balancing a bottle on his chest with fingers so stubby they looked like little fists. His hair, the color of mildewed straw, was cut to match his son's. Cy had introduced Zack to his rooster, but not to his parents.

"Hey, Pop," Cy called. "I'm pulling the transmission out of the Chevy and when I get it running, I'm driving it. You ain't never going to get it running."

"I'll be out," Horace replied. "Might just get in my milk truck."

"Pop, you're going to smother to death in there. I thought you bought it to make Charlie a house."

"Too good for a chicken. I'd still have my hands if I'd passed out in there. She left me out in the snow."

Through the afternoon, Cy and Zack struggled with the '49 Chevy, a two-door Deluxe model that had been mechanically mistreated as well as dented on numerous occasions. Horace and Charlie both cocked their heads to watch, the former an almost nonstop talker except for lapses when he would fall asleep.

"The ruin of this country," Horace began to hold forth, "is industrialization. The machine age. When a man can't look at an automobile and tell you, 'I made that automobile with these two hands.'" Horace held up his mutilated hands from his prone position. "You got no way in this world of knowing what dumb Polack put that sorry transmission together."

"No," Cy winked at Zack, "but I know the drunk jackass who tore it up."

"You know, if I'd known I was gonna live so long, I'd taken better care of my teeth." Horace jabbed at his teeth with a white sliver, then held the sliver out on his tongue like a woman serving a platter of cookies. "See that. Made out of a coon's dick bone. Fabius Herd uses one just like it."

"You knew him?" Zack exclaimed, recalling Tom's stories of his exploits. "You knew Fabius Herd, the stock car driver?"

Horace nodded. "I been around. I wasn't born yesterday, you know."

"Tell him about Fabius' monkey, Pop," Cy urged.

Horace scratched his stomach until Charlie jumped on it. "Fabius Herd," he began, "who used to race for Ford, had this little monkey who rode with him in his race car. One day at Rockingham old Tonto Monkey stuck his head through this little trap door in the floor that Fabius would lift up to check his tires. Monkey skint his head and Fabius had to make a pit stop to let him out. Cost him a position. Oughta wrung his neck.

"That Fabius was a strange bird," Horace went on with a

chuckle. "Actually he *had* himself a strange bird. Had this crow used to sit on his shoulder. Loved that crow to death."

"What'd the monkey think of the crow, Pop?"

"Poor little ol' monkey. Like one day Fabius didn't care a thing in the world about him anymore. Then the same thing happened to the crow. Fabius told me one time, 'I'd die for this old crow.' Six months later, he went out in the backyard and turned it loose and shooed it away when it come back."

"What about the monkey?"

"Died of something. That damn Fabius," Horace went on, "hell of a good race driver till he went to drink. Saw him racing so drunk one time he had to stay down on the inside of the track, where it was level, to keep his stomach. Had this pretty little '39 Ford road car, dark brown with a painted wood dash. He loved it so much he kept a rattlesnake in the trunk to keep it from getting stole. Then he got drunk and busted it up and didn't care about it no more. I was helping him pull it out of a ditch and opened the trunk to get the jack and out come that goddamn snake." Horace began to cough, and Charlie fell off his chest. Then Horace wiped his mouth on the bottom of his undershirt and the rooster jumped back up. "That's the kind of guy who races cars," he said clearly.

"Guys who keep monkeys, crows, and snakes?" Cy asked.

"Boy, have I got to hit you over the head to make you get the point of something?"

"Guess so. But you can't reach me without getting off your ass so just hit my buddy, Zack, there instead. Slide that jack a little more, Zack."

"The point is I'm telling you what them race drivers is like."

"What's that?"

"They're assholes."

"All of them?"

"Every damn one of them," he sputtered. "Gotta be to be any good. Act like they love something to death at first, love it twice as much as their next breath. Get tired of it just as hard and fast as they love it. This town is full of race car drivers."

"Zack's brother is a race car driver."

"Yeah? So he's an asshole, huh?"

"Don't know. Haven't seen him in four years," Zack admitted.

"You haven't seen your brother in four years? He's an asshole. What'd I tell you. You'll see him. He'll want to borrow money. That's always their problem. Need money. Everybody else's always got a better car, which is why they don't win. Spend every dime their friends and kin can lay their hands on, then they're gone."

"Where's Fabius?"

"County Home, I guess. Was last time I asked. He can't drive no good anymore anyway. Too old. But he was good in his day."

Horace lay back, pulling his undershirt out from under the rooster and using it to cover his eyes. The rooster settled back in place on his hairy stomach.

"One more tug, Zack."

Zack pulled on the jack and the transmission dropped.

"Okay. Now let's see how many paychecks this is gonna take."

"Pour some Co-cola on those bolts," Horace mumbled through his undershirt.

"What for?"

"Rust never sleeps," he said, and immediately began to snore.

One Friday night in June, after Zack and Cy cashed their paychecks and finished paying off their transmission parts for the Chevy, they went to pick up their dates. The Chevy had become one of those things in life that, after you've had it for a while, you can't imagine life without. For Zack it was like when his father had built two new rooms on the back of their house; afterwards it was hard to believe all six of them had lived in that little space that was the house before. For Cy, the Chevy was a practice race car on the back roads of Greenmont; he burned each set of its used tires down to the cord as fast as he could retrieve them from the trash pile behind Maurice's Pure Oil. And for both of them, it was a chance to go out with girls.

They were picking up Sue Ann and Hazel, two women they'd met at Auntie's Grill. Hazel, the plump one, worked at the cosmetics counter in Kress and had taken a liking to Zack because he looked intelligent with those glasses. When Zack met her, every time he got close enough to her to feel her warm skin, every flaw on her body, from the deep pores in her face to her saddlebag legs, evaporated. His brain airbrushed her body till it resembled the photos he'd bought from Sherwin Greenburg in eighth grade.

"I don't know about them women, Zack," Cy said on their way to pick them up. "We ain't even seen them in the light of day yet." He blew the horn in front of Sue Ann's house instead of going to the door.

Hazel had looked a lot better in the dark at the bar than she did now. She had covered the rough places on her face with pancake makeup; her skin was like a fender smoothed out with bondo, ready for sanding. Sue Ann, on the other hand, looked like she had experimented on her own hair with every new style and tint she learned at the Greenmont Beauty College until it looked like singed corn tassels. When she got into the car, she crossed her arms and looked straight ahead. "My daddy says he's heard you drive too fast. He almost didn't let me go out with you. You're reckless."

"Not me. Musta got me mixed up with somebody else," Cy replied.

"Well, I don't know what you think is so exciting about somebody who thinks they're a race car driver."

Without another word to her, Cy dropped the Chevy down a gear and gassed it; the tires screamed down Sue Ann's street. He headed up the hill behind Greenmont to Rolling Pen Road, turning the radio up and waiting for a song to begin before he floored the pedal. Both girls squealed and screamed for him to stop as the car began to whip through the switchbacks, the wheel sliding easy through Cy's hands.

Hazel jabbed her high heel into the top of Zack's foot, yanking his loafer off when Cy dropped the inside right wheel and sent a flurry of rocks into a Sweet Peach Snuff sign on a tobacco barn, sounding like a snare drum roll.

"Hang on, good buddy. Got a record run going this time!"

At the top of the hill Cy hit the hand brake for a bootleg turn. Sue Ann, grabbing for the dash, dumped off the seat onto the floor. Cy let the engine idle, waiting for Elvis to finish "Devil in Disguise." "All right! I beat it a bunch, Zack. He had to sing 'devil in his eyes' two more times before he was through."

"What?" Zack was confused.

"Elvis! 'You're the devil in his eyes.'"

"'Devil in *disguise*,' Cy. Not his eyes."

"Dis guys, dos guys, don't matter. I beat him."

"You're racing songs?" Zack shook his head. "How do you know they're all the same length?" Sue Ann climbed back onto the seat and straightened her skirt.

"Hey, good buddy. Ain't you ever seen a stack of records? They're all the same size. Hang on! I'm going to blow off old Martha and the Vandellas on the way down. *Heat wave!*" Sue Ann was thrown forward again onto the floor.

After another run up and down Rolling Pen, up to Peter, Paul and Mary singing "Blowing in the Wind" and down to

Del Shannon's "From Me to You," Hazel sat stiff as a dummy, one set of fingernails digging into the seat, the other set into Zack's arm. Sue Ann rocked to her sobs as she cried, "I-wanna-go-home, I-wanna-go-home . . ."

Cy zigzagged through the dirt roads to the back streets, finally pulling up in front of her house, sliding to a stop against the curb. The Chevy stopped so fast, Zack hit the back of the seat. As soon as the car was still, both girls jumped out and ran like cats dumped out of a sack. Cy dropped the Chevy in low and drove away as slowly as the middle car in a funeral procession. "As my old man would say," Cy drawled, "'Whiskey eyes, lies.'"

"How'd you get so choosy?" Zack complained, crawling over into the front seat. "Man, I'm hornier than a four-peckered goat."

"Hey, man, we've got a car. A car." Cy patted the seat. "A Chevy. Remember that. We don't have to take the first two that come along. Hey! We can still get inside in time for practice!" Cy turned into the lot at Greenmont Raceway.

"How much are programs?" Zack asked Cy.

Cy put his arm around the girl selling them, and smiled. She handed him a program, smiling back, as if that was the proper way to buy one. That program was the key to what Zack was looking for. On the third page he found it: a photo pasted into a collage, a weak shot, but clear enough for him to be sure. The driver dropped his arm out the window and looked straight at the camera. Number 7 was on the door. He wore a helmet with a leather chin strap that fit his head like a white bowl.

The track opened for hot lapping. Zack's eyes searched the moving cars. There was no number 7 on the track.

"Cy, this guy, do you know him?"

Cy squinted at the photo and shook his head.

"Can you read what it says on the door?" Zack insisted. "Does it say Pole Cat?"

Cy shrugged. "Hell, I don't know. There used to be a Pole Cat Somebody."

Zack brightened. "How good was he?"

"Pretty good. Fast while he lasted. He only come once or twice last year that I was here, maybe four times at the most."

"What else?" Zack pressed.

"I never seen him win one. But I don't believe he had much of a car. Hard to remember. Why?"

"It might be my brother is why. Tom."

Zack pounded his fist on his knee, irritated with Cy for not knowing more. He watched the race anxiously, searching the pit area, cleaning his glasses and searching again. When the race was over, the two boys crossed the track into the infield, shoving into the crowd that funneled through one small opening in the fence before heading across the now-dry track, its surface blackened and pounded as hard as asphalt.

A group of men stood in a circle. Others tried to squeeze through to see what they were laughing at. Zack felt a magnet pulling him towards that group. He climbed up on the roof of the concession stand; Cy followed him. When Zack looked down, he spotted the top of the man's head in the center of the group. Everyone was watching this man. His hair was blue black and thick.

"Do it, Pate, go ahead," a big red-headed man said.

Tom turned towards the man and laughed.

"Hey, give me a minute. This takes some concentration."

When Zack heard his voice, it was as if he had finally remembered the name of a song that had been driving him crazy. He started to call Tom's name, but something kept him quiet, like when he was a little kid and Tom would get mad if he interrupted him.

In Tom's left hand was a mousetrap. The spring was set and he was slowly sliding his index finger towards the release. It was a reflex game Tom and Zack used to play. Zack was always chicken because he knew what would happen to his finger. He would have taken pride in waiting for his smashed finger to heal up, but he just couldn't let it happen. At home Tom used a trap so old and rusty that sometimes even the mouse beat it, stealing the cheese to boot. This trap was brand-new shiny metal.

The race track was so quiet he could hear Tom breathing. Zack's index finger ached as though the trap had already snapped shut. The wait was almost unbearable. Suddenly Tom's shoulder jerked. As the trap shut, Tom's finger lifted to point at the sky, no trap attached. A cheer went up, and a few men clapped. A young man started handing out money, paying off the bets. The red-headed man didn't get any money.

Just as Zack was getting ready to hop down, the red-headed man reached into his tool box, pulling out another trap, three times as big as the mousetrap.

"Okay, Pate. You've won the heat. Let's see how you do in the main event."

"Aw, come on, Daddy, that's a rattrap," said the young man who held the bets. "That mother will break your finger."

"Just take the bets, Allie," Red said.

"Burcham likes to separate the men from the boys," one man commented.

Red Burcham grinned at Tom, saying, "Or the mice from the rats."

Tom studied the trap while the bets were placed. His eyes hadn't moved from it since Red had produced it. He reached into a tool box for a screwdriver. When he set the trap and touched the release with the screwdriver, the trap sprang shut so violently, it flipped out of his hand.

Red Burcham picked it up, the screwdriver still in its jaws, and laughed. "Look at that. Bent my best screwdriver."

"Take it back to Sears," one of them said.

They all looked back at Tom, waiting for an answer.

"Whatcha say, Pate? Met your match?"

Tom didn't answer. He took the trap back, then walked back over to the tool box. He released the spring and dropped the screwdriver back into the drawer. He shut the tool box lid and placed the trap at about waist level, pulling back the lever to set the spring. The men began to gather closer around him again.

"That guy is nuts," Cy whispered to Zack. He had forgotten Cy was on the roof with him. "But I think he's got the guts to try it."

Zack felt a gust of wind hit the side of his face, just like the day ten years before when the corncrib door had blown shut. A bad feeling ran through him. The men placed bets, but Zack already knew what the outcome would be. All of his excitement at finding Tom was replaced with a terrible sadness. He hated that red-headed man, and his rattrap.

Tom's shoulders moved and almost instantly, Zack heard him cry in pain. Tom dropped to his knees, moaning. His hand lay on the ground, two fingers caught in the giant trap. The red-headed man's son dropped the money and stooped beside Tom. He moaned once again, as Allie Burcham released the trap.

"It just got the tips of his fingers, Daddy," Allie said, holding up Tom's hand. "That ought to count for something."

"Give you a quarter change on that ten you just lost, boy."

Tom yanked his hand away, jumped up from the ground, and butted his way through the group, walking on the money and scattering the men who were collecting it from the ground. Two of them slapped him on the back and one said, "Bet that hurt like a sonavabitch."

"The guy's got some guts. I'll give him that."

"Shit for brains."

Zack jumped from the stand; it was too long a drop and he crumpled to the ground in the midst of the men. He jumped back up and ran to an open cooler where he fumbled for a handful of ice. Then he ran after Tom yelling, "Tom, wait!" Tom stopped and turned around. Zack's hands were cupped out in front of him. "I got you some ice," he said.

Tom winced as he stuck his fingers between the cubes. Zack's hands were aching so from the cold, he could barely keep them cupped.

"Thanks, buddy . . . sonavabitch." When Zack looked up at Tom's face, his brother shook his head and smiled. "How the hell did you find me? Hey, you didn't get much taller." Tom paused. "But those new glasses make you look smart instead of sissy," he added.

When they got to the parking area and Tom saw the Chevy, he said, "You already got a car."

"It's not mine, Tom. Belongs to Cy here. I helped him get it running is all."

"You been doing cars?"

"A little. Not as much as I'd like. How about you?"

"About the same for me." Then he was silent again.

When they reached the car Cy asked him, "Where you headed?"

"Home, I guess. I mean, nowhere really."

"Let's go get a beer or something," Cy suggested. "Celebrate Zack finding his long lost brother."

Cy jumped behind the wheel and started the car. Before they left, Tom's friend, Allie Burcham, ran up and asked if he could go along. Allie resembled the red-headed man only he appeared undeveloped, his skin and hair lacking color like a piglet that had been born too soon. As they left the track, Cy peeled a wheel on the pavement, the squeal floating over the racers in the parking lot. If they'd been in Summit, some-one would have said, "Get one." Or "Get on it." Or "Do it." "So you laid Rubber, man. What's her sister's name?" No one inside the car said anything. Zack felt embarrassed, like Cy'd lit a cigar with a dollar bill in front of a bunch of millionaires.

He kept telling himself that this was his brother sitting be-side him, the brother he had been waiting to see for four years. He was thankful for Cy, who was the reason Tom came with them. Here he was, really riding to get a beer with Tom, like it was anybody on any day of the year. Zack thought about punching Tom's leg to see if he was real.

"Your hand hurt pretty bad, Tom?" he asked.

"Hurts like a son of a bitch. I could have beaten that rat-trap. I just didn't get my concentration going good before I tried it. Should have held it in my other hand instead of put-ting it on that tool box. I'll get it next time."

"That's a hell of a act to practice," Allie Burcham laughed. "Like practicing sticking your head in a lion's mouth. Oughta ask my old man for his trap. He'd probably love to watch you practice. He's had it for two weeks." He turned to the boys. "Couldn't wait till he saw Pate. Said he'd let him drive one of our race cars if he beat it."

"I guess he's thinking of another way to rub my face in it tomorrow. He's never going to let me drive his damn car. Why don't you just quit screwing around with that car of yours and let me drive it, Burcham? You can't drive a nail in a snowbank."

"I'm getting better. I went half a second faster tonight."

"Yeah, in qualifying. Then you race like you got an anchor tied on your ass."

Cy pulled up in front of the Speedway Bar and Grill. When they got out of the car, Allie held his white palms up and teased, "Slap my hands, Pate." Zack recognized the hand-slap game that he and Tom used to play.

"Kiss my ass." Tom held his hurt hand against his side as if it were paralyzed. "I don't plan to be feeling any pain pretty soon."

All of Zack's nights of eating supper, then going right home to his room, and saving his money came to a halt as he put down dollar after dollar for beer after beer. The more Zack drank, the more he wanted to talk. Tom was the opposite. He was so quiet, Zack started worrying that maybe he wasn't his brother after all. Up until that moment, Zack had spent four years thinking about being with him; now he was here and he could see Tom like a person in a glass box, but he couldn't get to him.

"Remember when we had storytelling contests, Tom?" Allie and Cy weren't listening; they were watching a blond who was dancing by herself. Zack couldn't wait for an answer from Tom. "That was the only contest I ever beat you at." Tom looked up, his back straightening a little, his chin lifting from his bottle. "Don't you remember the one I beat you with? I told you I could tell a story that would make you cry and you dared me to try. It was about an old dog. His master had left him behind because he thought he was too old to make the trip west, but the dog followed anyway, dragging his bum leg. The dog limped for days across the blistering desert. He finally made it to the house where the man lived."

Tom yawned and leaned back in his chair, but Zack continued, "The man's house had a new doghouse in front. While the old dog was heading up to check out the doghouse he thought was for him, a puppy ran out of the people house and into the doghouse." Tom took a swig of his beer, but still didn't speak. "A garbage truck sped around the corner," Zack went on, "and drove over the old dog and smashed him. And the garbage man threw him in the truck so the man never even knew the dog had followed him for two thousand miles. That was when I saw the tear. It rolled out the corner of your eye and you tried to wipe it away before I saw it, but I saw it. You knew I'd won."

"I don't remember that story," Tom said flatly. His eyes were glassy in the bar light. He had cried before, Zack was sure of it. Maybe he had changed. He tried to look at Tom through his brown beer bottle.

"Tom, do you remember the idea you had about a bottle that would turn back to sand if you busted it?" he blurted out.

Tom turned his beer bottle in his hand, staring at it like it was supposed to tell him the answer.

"We were down at the trash pile," Zack insisted, "and had busted a bunch of bottles shooting at them. You were afraid Daddy was going to see the glass and we'd have to lie and say somebody else did it."

Tom shook his head slowly, nothing appeared to snag on his brain. He absently tried to tap his cigarette pack with his hurt hand. He groaned and shook his hand, then stared at the cigarette stuck inside.

"The experiment," Zack urged. "Jigger Carmichael was always trying to turn some junk metal into gold and you told him what a dumbass he was because iron had never been gold. You were going to turn glass back to sand. You were going to sell the idea as a way to keep people from getting cut with broken glass." He tossed words until finally one caught. "Sand. Broken glass. The chemistry set."

"Chemistry set," Tom responded slowly, as if he were speaking his first words from a coma. "I wanted the deluxe set for Christmas."

"Right!" Zack said, too loud.

"Mama said it was too dangerous," Tom went on. "She was afraid I'd blow us all to pieces. She gave me an Erector Set instead. Typical Mama." Tom leaned back in his chair. "Wait until somebody lets me drive their car again. It'll drive her crazy," he said with a grin. Then he looked at Zack suspiciously. "What made you think of that bottle stuff?"

"I read where this guy came up with a bottle like that. To prevent litter. You smash it and it turns back to sand. Or maybe it was water."

"Damn," the old Tom filtered through. "He'll be a millionaire." Then he was quiet again.

"Speaking of smashing stuff, you aren't going to believe what we found at the trash pile, Tom. We found Daddy's lost wallet. Remember?"

"Yeah," Tom said. "He told me I stole it."

"It was in the commode. It must have come out of his overalls when he was taking a crap, and he flushed it."

Tom frowned. "How'd it get in the trash pile?"

"That's where he threw the commode because it kept plugging up and then I busted it open shooting."

Tom stared at his beer bottle, tipping his head from side to side.

"'You busted up a perfectly good commode, boy,'" Zack grunted in imitation of Hershel.

Tom began to laugh. Soon both of them were laughing so loudly that a man said, "Hey, buddy, that one's too good not to share." Tom wiped tears out of his eyes with the back of his good hand and laughed some more.

"Your family sounds as fucked as mine," Cy said to Zack.

Zack went to the bar to get another beer; he got one for Tom and paid for it. Tom didn't give him any money. Each time Zack got up to go to the men's room or for another beer, his body felt heavier and his head lighter. He was starting to veer off course and bang into things. He could hear his words and they were slurred. He couldn't remember what anyone said long enough to answer them. He reached into his pocket for a pencil and piece of paper when Tom told him where he lived. He didn't have a pencil or piece of paper. He was as drunk as he'd been the night that Hershel smashed his guitar. He was drunk enough to try to tell Tom the news he had been carrying for weeks. "Hey, Tom. Remember that Holly Lee?"

Tom frowned as though a hammer had tapped him between the eyes.

"Yeah, my girlfriend. What about her?"

Tom's words hit Zack hard, sobering him momentarily. "Uh, she married Buck Herndon," he answered, then quickly changed the subject. "Me and Cy here want to be your racing crew, Tom. We talked about it a lot. We'll work for nothing."

"Well, that sure as hell's a good thing, because I haven't got a dime," he said bitterly.

"Or a car," Allie added, his smile fading under Tom's stare. They sat in silence for a few minutes. Cy got up and went to the men's room.

When Cy got back, Allie said, "You better go tell that big guy over by the bar you're sorry or he's gonna kill you. That blond dancing by herself is his wife and he said he don't like the way you was looking at her."

Cy stumbled over to the bar and stood in front of the man, who was double his weight. They could hear the man's laugh boom across the room. "Allie, did you tell this asshole that whore was my wife?" he called.

Cy came back with a big grin on his face. "I owe you a big one, shithead."

Allie laughed so hard his eyes started to tear, then he sneezed. When he unfolded a perfectly ironed handkerchief, all three of them stared at it before he caught their glance and stuffed it quickly back into his pocket.

The lights started going off. Cy had been trying to outstare a cross-eyed drunk who was slumped in the corner. "Nine days of bad luck, if I don't," he told them. "See, I did it. He give up."

"He didn't give up," Allie replied, looking at the drunk, whose eyes were closed. "The fucker passed out."

"Bar's closing," Tom said, and stood up, steadying himself on the chair back before heading for the door. Allie followed like a pet dog.

Outside, Zack leaned against the car, trying to decide if he needed to pee again before he got in. He heard the engine start, so he crawled in. Cy gunned the motor and slid through the lot, kicking up gravel that bounced off the fence and the cars that were left.

"I think you just totaled the bartender's car," Allie sputtered. Cy laughed as the wheels whined onto the highway. Zack leaned back and looked at the roof. It dawned on him that he might get sick. The next thing he knew, the car was stopping on a bridge. Everyone got out and stood in a row and peed over the side.

"I'm writing my name," Allie said.

"Not me," Cy said. "I'm just pissing."

"Let's see you dot the *i* in Allie," Tom countered.

"I'm just going by Al tonight. That's my real name, Al."

"Your real name is Alfonzo."

"Is not. It's Al."

"It's Albert or Alton or something like that. Take a whole six pack to write it if it's Alexander," Tom argued. "Nobody's real name is Al."

"Well, you can tell my mama that because she named me Al and didn't even know it wasn't my real name." Allie looked over the edge, wobbling as his gaze tried to follow his stream to the water below. "Boy, it's sure a long way down there."

"Nah," Tom answered. "Not so far. Fifteen or twenty feet at the most."

"Have you ever dived that far?" Allie asked.

"Sure. Lots of times. The quarry is twenty-five feet up and a hundred feet deep."

"How deep is the river?"

"Don't know. Why don't you jump in and find out?" Tom laughed.

"Dare me."

"I dare you," Zack said.

"Pay me."

"Bullshit," Tom replied.

There was a moment when no one talked. Zack stared down at the water and could see shiny spots where the moon looked back in broken pieces.

"Ten bucks says you won't do it," Cy said. He didn't have ten dollars to his name.

Suddenly they heard someone cry out, an exaggerated yell as if someone were pretending to fall. A dark object blocked the light from the moon, then scattered the pieces of light. A splash rose over the sound of the running water. Then everything went back like it was. Except for one thing: there were only three left on the bridge.

"Holy shit." Cy turned to Zack. Zack felt a rush of sobriety before his drunkenness came back. He gripped the cold metal post in the center of the bridge with both hands.

"He jumped," Zack said.

"The dumb fuck jumped," Tom echoed in disbelief.

They all turned and started moving. Cy and Zack tried to follow Tom down the riverbank, slipping on the rocks and banging on their backsides down to the edge of the water. Tom headed out into the water.

"He's walking on water," Cy said.

Zack slogged out into the knee-deep water behind Tom. Allie had dived headfirst into water two feet deep.

Tom found Allie. He tried to drag him out by the arm. Zack lifted his other arm and they tugged him towards the shore. Dragging Allie's limp body was as hard as pulling out a stump.

When they got to the bank and let go of his arms, he fell face down into the mud, his feet still in the water.

Tom whispered to Zack, "I think he's dead."

Zack heard someone coming down the bank. They were silent until they saw it was Cy.

Cy looked down at Allie. "I went to see if he got back in the car. He wasn't there," he said dumbly.

"I think he's dead," Tom repeated.

"Oh, shit," Cy said. "He's dead. We better bury him fast." Cy began scooping up leaves and sticks and throwing them on Allie's back. Then he lost his balance and fell down. "I better go find a shovel," he sputtered.

"Get quiet. I hear a car," Tom whispered.

Headlights flickered through the bridge railing, hesitating for a moment near their parked car, then moving forward slowly.

"You think they saw us?" Cy asked.

"Yeah, they saw us," Tom answered. "We've got to get him out of here fast."

They began to tug on Allie, dragging him back up the bank towards the car. When Zack pulled Allie's arm, he felt his shirt rip under his arm. Dragging Allie up the bank was like carrying a sack full of rocks that rolled and shifted in all the wrong directions.

Zack felt a sudden burst of strength. Inside his head this seemed like something he would wake up from, but his body knew it was real. Allie's weight was real, the slippery bank, his water-soaked shoes. Finally they shoved him into the car with Cy tugging from inside and Tom and Zack on the outside pushing, trying to get the doors closed before another car came by. Cy started the car. Zack felt the car start moving away from the bridge. His feet were on top of Allie, who was on the floor in the backseat. Tom was in front.

"Where are we going to dump him?" Cy asked. "We could leave him in a gas station."

"Dump him at his house," Tom answered.

That was the last thing that Zack remembered until he woke up when the sun came in the windows of the car. He looked over the front seat where Cy was stretched out asleep. Tom was gone. Then he looked under his feet in the backseat. Just sticks and mud and leaves. Allie was gone too.

Zack threw the car door open and started screaming Tom's name. He woke Cy up. Cy crawled out and grabbed his arm, shoving him back inside. A man on the sidewalk was staring. They were in a vacant lot in a place Zack had never seen before.

"Tom is gone again and I don't have any idea where he went." Hot tears hit Zack's face like spattering grease.

"Shut up and go back to sleep. Tom went home."

"Home?" Zack's voice was thin.

"Wherever he lives, that's where he went. You couldn't find the key to where you live, remember?" Cy dropped back inside the car, grabbing his head as the sun hit his face. "Shit, I don't see how my old man can stand feeling like this every day."

Hours later Zack and Cy went by Red Burcham's shop, where Tom worked. The ghost of Allie Burcham was using the drill press, his head tipped so he could see through a swollen-shut eye, his arms scraped red from the wrists to the elbows.

Tom had his back to them, pounding on something in a vise.

Zack Pate's early years on the Goose Bottom farm had been like a black and white picture show with his brother stuck in there in Technicolor. After he found Tom in Greenmont, the Technicolor came back into his life and spread into every corner.

Greenmont was everything Zack had dreamed it would be, a little kingdom of dirt track racing with seemingly every auto repair, paint and body shop, and parts supplier with a race car waiting in the wings on weekdays. With their bread and butter businesses going on out front all week, on Fridays and Saturdays the racers gathered for their weekly showdown at Greenmont Raceway. Tom didn't seem to share Zack's enthusiasm. It was what Tom had left home for, to be a dirt track racer, but he was still on the outside looking in.

"We'll buy our own car," Zack proposed. "Me and Cy can help. We'll put all we can save together until we get enough."

Cy knew every junkyard in Greenmont, so they began to search for the car Tom wanted. Each time they would find a good '32 or '33 Ford that wasn't rusted out, Tom would ask the price. "A hundred and fifty dollars," the junk man would say, and Zack would write the car and price down in a notebook. Tom would walk on, as if something magic were going to make the next one he found cheaper. Or free. Then one afternoon Cy and Zack got off work and hurried to find Tom to show him a '33 for a hundred and a quarter, but Tom shook his head and went back into his apartment.

"Forget it, you two. You think all we have to do is buy a car? Where are we going to work on it? Who's going to pay the entry fee? What are we going to buy parts with?"

For the first time, Zack realized his brother's confidence had slid away. "The truth is that I wasted a hell of a lot of my time before you got here," he confessed to Zack. "All I got was four years older. It's like a girl wants to be a movie actress, only she got born ugly as sin. Or a cripple wants to be a tightrope walker. I felt about that hopeless at times."

Tom's mind had been obsessed with a nonexistent race car, the one he was going to prepare, as soon as he figured out how to get it. "I used to be just like you guys, thinking if I can just get in a car, then I'll show them. None of those guys banging around out at Greenmont are as good as I'm going to be, I told myself. Then one day I thought about it different. I don't know why, but one day I saw you don't just get in a car like some kind of fairy tale and already know everything there is to know and impress the hell out of everybody. You have to drive for a long time to get good and you have to have a good car and a good team. And even then everything can go wrong and leave you looking like an ass. So don't think I'm so stupid I don't know all of this, Zack. I just can't stand to let myself sit around thinking about it."

Zack had learned that Tom's friend, Allie Burcham, was his constant reminder of how the other half lived. Allie raced every weekend in both the Jalopy and the Modified Sportsman races, yet he never seemed to get any better. Tom had met Allie at Greenmont Raceway. His father, Red, owned a parts supply and car repair business and several cars, the best one a '34 Ford. Allie's brother Giles was his mechanic. After Tom took a job working as a mechanic in Burcham's shop, going with them to races every Friday and Saturday night, Red Burcham teased Tom with his Sportsman car, dangling it in front of him like a carrot, then let his son—who had no natural ability and next to no desire to race—drive it.

"If I had Allie's old man, I could race until I got sick of it,"

Tom said. "So he ends up with a son who can't drive out of a wet paper sack."

Cy thought about this, then offered another idea. "I know this guy named Ned. He's got a '40 Ford flathead in his shop—Ned's All-American Automotive. His old lady is getting on him all the time to quit driving."

"And I bet he's got a son who can't drive," Tom replied.

"Naw, all's he's got is a beautiful daughter. He don't have no Whitworth tools, so I fix her MG over at the Pure Oil."

On the way home from work Tom found himself stopping by Ned's shop. The race car sat in the corner, still splattered with mud from the last race. When Ned Morris walked up, Tom asked him for a job. He started work the next morning.

Ned fixed street cars during the day and at night had his shop mechanics work on his race car. His graying hair was always neatly wet-combed into place, and he wore a crisp blue uniform that he never seemed to get dirty, with his name in an oval on his chest. He was part of the Greenmont racing scene, another of the local drivers whose work and recreation merged at the raceway every weekend he could afford to enter. He was a middle-of-the-pack racer. Ned knew Tom was waiting like a buzzard for him to call it quits.

One night when Tom was sitting on the creeper beside the race car eating his hamburger supper, Ned sat down next to him to talk. "Listen to me, Pate," he said with a smile, "don't think I haven't got your kind figured out. Guys like you think some fairy godmother ought to come along and put everything together for you. See, you'll get up to one level in this racing business and you'll look up at the rung above you. You can't enjoy where you're at, because you're close enough to see somewhere else you want to be."

"How do you know where I want to be?" Tom asked.

Ned laughed softly. "Trust me, I know. And even if you

were to win the feature at Greenmont, you'd think, 'I'd have rather won at Hickory.' If you win at Hickory, you'll be jealous of the guy who wins at Daytona. You win at Daytona, some guy younger than you beats you the next year, then you're miserable because you can't win it twice. You'll never be satisfied. It's part of the deal. You get satisfied, you're finished."

Then he added with a grin, "Or one day you get old. Just like me. You get one or the other. Satisfied, or old, or both. Or dead. That can be in the cards too. You remember who told you this, Pate."

Tom smiled, tossed his empty wrapper, and shoved himself back under the car, but he quit smiling when Ned couldn't see his face. Ned was right. If he'd thought his racing career would begin and end with a car like Ned's, he wouldn't have bothered doing it at all. When he left Summit for Greenmont, he was looking for a better track and better teams. Then, working at Ned's shop, getting the jalopy ready for the dirt track outside of town, he was thinking maybe after Ned let him drive the jalopy, next he could talk him into getting a Modified Sportsman. Then, after they won in that, they'd go to Hickory. Then if he got there, maybe he could see that the asphalt superspeedways at Darlington and Daytona were next in the late models. Ned was no dumbass.

Cy and Zack began to hang around Ned's shop at night, helping with the race car. "Isn't it amazing how much help an old man like me is getting with his race car?" Ned teased. But he had enough street car work coming into the shop, so Ned hired Zack and Cy away from Maurice's Pure Oil to work during the week for pay and let them go to the races on weekends. But he hadn't said Tom could drive.

Cy used tools as though he were born with them attached to his hands, picking up the right size wrench the first time, coupling sockets and drives and speed handles by just looking at the nuts he wanted to turn. Zack would be struggling and

Cy would thread a long arm to him with the right tool, saying, "Here, try this," making it seem simple.

Zack admired Cy's mechanical finesse because he spent a good deal of his own time taking things apart he'd put together wrong. His first day on the job at Ned's, Zack had said jokingly, "Watch me slip and drill a hole in this tire," as he braced a piece of metal against the trailer tire. Shortly after his announcement, the tire hissed flat.

After Zack broke a plug off in one of his engines, Arnold Morgan, Ned's engine builder, lifted Zack away from the engine by grasping the back of his T-shirt. "Where did you find this fuck-up?" Arnold asked.

"He's my brother."

"Does that mean we're stuck with him?"

Arnold regarded Zack with a look not unlike a snapping turtle about to emerge from his shell; thereafter, he took advantage of Zack's inexperience. Before Zack learned to weld, Arnold made him hold pieces while he tacked. Arnold, who used coat hangers instead of welding rod to save money, would fill the air with sparks. Zack would smell singed hair, knowing it was his own. One day Zack stood inside a chassis, holding an exhaust pipe for Arnold to weld to the back of the gas tank. When the tank, a used jerry can from the surplus store, caught on fire, Arnold threw a jacket—Zack's jacket—over the flames, and ran.

Zack admitted to Tom later, "No, it didn't seem like a good idea to weld something to a gas tank."

"So why did you do it?"

"I don't know. I mean, he's twice as big as me. I'm low man on the totem pole around here. I'd be looking for another job . . ."

"Looking for a job! Next time you better try complaining, or I might be picking what's left of my little brother off the ceiling."

"Hey, Tom. Remember the Speed Seat?" Zack asked brightly. The Speed Seat, a car powered by a gasoline washing machine motor, had been Tom's first motorized vehicle.

Tom looked puzzled.

"The fire?" Zack insisted. "Remember when I did a pit stop for you and spilled the gas on the motor and we set the lower field on fire?"

Tom went back to work. "Yeah, I remember," he muttered.

On Sunday afternoons when they worked on the race car in Ned's shop, the radio was always on, tuned to the races. Muted engine sounds brought Cy's finger to the volume dial of the radio; then he danced across the shop with an imaginary steering wheel in his hands. They listened to the engines screaming around the funneled pavement of the superspeed-ways, the big-time racing where tires ground down and blistered, sometimes exploding beneath their heroes—Lee Petty, Fireball Roberts, Junior Johnson, Little Joe Weatherly, and the new sensation, Freddie Lorenzen—slamming their cars into the walls at Charlotte, Darlington, Daytona. Even though Charlotte Motor Speedway was just down the road, it seemed like a trip to the moon.

The announcers were breathless, their voices bubbling over with excitement, milking every incident while the listeners at Ned's All-American Automotive waited in their blind world for their commentary. "Tell us who crashed, you big-mouthed son of a bitch," Arnold shouted, and slammed the radio with his fist, his belly banging the workbench. "We can't see the goddamn track, you loudmouthed, bullshitting . . ."

"It's Buck. Buck is in the wall," the radio sputtered under Arnold's heavy hand. "Took the right side clean off . . ."

Zack noticed that Arnold's eyes were small and closely spaced, a trait that indicated stupidity in farm animals. The self-proclaimed expert on everything, Arnold had seen races at Darlington and Rockingham and gave his version of superspeedway versus dirt track racing to Tom: "You drive on pavement onct, Pate, and you'll see it ain't got a thing to do with running on these rinky-dink dirt tracks. Throw the son of a bitch sideways and you got a date with the fence.

"A tire lets go on one of them big tracks, and it's bam-bam. Bam the tire, bam the wall. Turn right to the cemetery, motherfucker. You run up on a guy like they do at this hick-town track here, bust his tire, and he'll kill you for it. I seen Lee Petty and Junior fighting in the infield. Lee slides up on Junior, cuts his tire. So Junior goes in to get a tire and picks him up a bottle at the same time. Then they got into it. You don't fuck with Junior.

"Don't fuck with the Pettys, neither," he went on, pointing at Zack, who backed away. "Tiny Lund was driving on the same team with Lee, and Lee got pissed at his driving. Didn't like the way Tiny would go for it. Figured Tiny ought to puss along like he did, waiting for everybody to break, but Tiny went for it and he put this little bitty crease in Lee's car when he passed him because Lee wouldn't move the fuck over. So Lee come up and started one with him at the payoff window. And I kid you not, ask Ned, next thing Tiny knew he had Richard and Maurice jumping all over his ass and old lady Petty kicking him in the nuts and busting him over the head with her pocketbook.

"That Lee is a prick," Arnold added, "Wouldn't say shit if he had a mouth full. Goody-goody. If he hadn't been pussing around at Daytona in 'sixty-one, Beauchamp wouldn't have shoved his ass in the fence. Richard thinks he's so hot. He wouldn't get in the front gate if it wasn't for his old man. Now, Tiny, there's a real driver. Marvin Panch would be a well-done hamburger if Tiny hadn't pulled him outa that Italian piece of shit he tried to drive in the sporty car bullshit at Daytona . . ."

Arnold talked a lot, so much that Tom wondered if it all were true. He seemed sure of himself. He was known to be a hothead. Ned told Tom that once when he got punted into the wall, Arnold took a brick, went to the edge of the track and threw it through a driver's windshield, getting him banned for two races. Now, when Arnold got mad during a race, Ned made him go sit in the truck until he cooled off.

Tom and Arnold argued constantly, mostly about who was the world's greatest stock car driver, Fireball Roberts or Freddie Lorenzen. Tom could flare up, then quit arguing and go back to work and forget about it, with that same flash-fire temper he had as a child; but Arnold would hit things too hard and cuss under his breath for hours afterwards.

"Fireball can blow Lorenzen in the weeds any day of the year," Arnold blasted at Tom. "They give Lorenzen the best stuff."

"Maybe he could have ten years ago," Tom came back, "but not anymore."

"You don't know shit, Pate. The year Darlington opened, Fireball started in sixty-third place and finished second."

"That's what I mean, Arnold. That was a long time ago."

"He won the damn thing in 'fifty-eight. I oughta know. I was there. I got his autograph. It's right here in my wallet. Where were you, asshole? Watching the sun come up behind a plow? Fireball was winning races when Lorenzen was still driving nails."

"Let's put your money where your mouth is, Arnold. I bet you Lorenzen will win twice as many races as Fireball this summer."

"You got yourself a bet, Pate."

"Lisa's got money," Tom told Zack, sitting outside at the hotdog place down the street from the shop. Lisa was his new girlfriend. "All those girls at Rosemount College got money to burn. Lisa doesn't have to work for it. Her old man just gives it to her. I go to the store with her, she doesn't look on the shelf until she finds the cheapest, biggest one for the money, she just picks out the best one. Or the one she likes. And then they tell her how much at the cash register and she pays it like she's dealing out cards."

"Must be nice."

"Yeah. Lisa wants to go somewhere, say, to Hickory for the weekend, she just unsnaps this little checkbook in a case with her lipstick stuck in beside it and writes down a hundred dollars and goes to the school cashier and gets the money, just like that. Doesn't even write down the amount. 'I find out at the end of the month,' Lisa says, 'how much I spent.' I asked her what did her old man say about the money she spends and she looks at me like I asked something she never gave a thought to. 'Nothing. Now, if I go buy a new car,' she tells me, 'he'd have something to say about that. It hurt his feelings when I didn't ask his advice about the Healey. Said he never would have gotten it.' I told her her old man was smarter than I thought and she rabbit-punched me, but I tell you, Zack, that Healey was a fancy piece of junk. Lisa just liked the way it looked.

"I took her looking for race cars with me and she said, 'They're so cheap. A hundred and fifty dollars. It's just an old junk car with torn up insides that nobody would drive. My new car cost three thousand dollars. Why don't you just buy you a race car?' Just like that, just buy it. Makes me want to smack her sometimes."

"So what does Princess Lisa see in you?" Zack asked with a grin.

"I don't know. Bored, I guess. Maybe she just hangs around with me because she gets to be around exciting things, but doesn't have to take any chances herself. She's not impressed with those sporty car jerks, like our old buddy Harris Carmichael back in Summit, who go around talking about taking a turn at nine-tenths, like they know what fast is. She's met him. He's in the sports car club that a bunch of her friends are in. She said he was going to drive in this race they have at Danville and his old man wouldn't let him. Shows you how much he really wants to drive race cars and the jerk has a whole garage full of them." Tom remembered how he and Holly Lee had stolen a look at Harris's garage when they'd climbed the fence to his estate and skinnydipped in his pool.

"Remember when you thumbed a ride with Harris in his Jag and he was going the wrong way but you rode anyway?"

"Yeah," Tom grunted.

"Daddy beat you when you got home. It was one A.M."

"I don't remember that."

Zack met Lisa one afternoon when she came by the shop. She was tall, almost as tall as Tom, with legs that seemed longer than Zack's whole body. Her legs were there in clear view, perfectly formed, tan and smooth as polished wood, except for a soft blond down on her thighs where she didn't shave. She was wearing a white tennis outfit that glowed like her perfectly spaced teeth. She had thick, curly brown hair that she pulled back with a clip, but little curls came out and reached around her face. Skin peeled off the end of her nose, the only part of her that hadn't soaked up just the right amount of sun. She had come to pick up Tom in her new red Corvette Stingray. Her daddy had taken the Healey away from her after it quit on her one night at midnight with a jammed fuel pump. She rested against the fender of the Corvette, picking the skin away from the callouses on her palms. She wore white terrycloth bands around her wrists.

"What are those for?" Zack asked when she didn't speak.

She looked at him dumbly a moment as if she had forgotten what they were for. Finally she answered, "Sweat bands." Then she rolled over her hands and looked at the bands.

"Only I don't sweat enough to wear them. I guess they're really just to look good. Tennis players are supposed to wear them." Then she flashed him a smile with those perfect teeth, as if he had caught her at something.

She crossed her arms and threw back her head, staring at him with eyes so blue they looked polished. Lisa was a strong kind of pretty. She was almost too big to be a girl. Her stare made him look at his feet.

"So you're Tom's kid brother," she said.

"Did he tell you he had a kid brother?"

"He said he had a whole family somewhere, I don't remember where."

"Summit."

"Summit. Never heard of it."

"You didn't miss much," he answered.

"Got a track?"

"There's a track. Only not worth staying there for. Guess Tom could account for that."

"I never saw a race in my life till I met Tom. The first race car I ever saw was on a trailer going by school when I was looking out the window in history class."

"Do you like it?" Zack asked, even though Tom had told him she was crazy about racing.

"It's a real good party, yeah, I like it. The cars aren't pretty like the ones at the sports car races, and I don't like the way they sound as much. Crashes kind of give me the willies, you know what I mean? I mean they're kind of neat to see and all that, but I never saw Tom get into a big one. I don't think I'd like that very much."

"I saw him get into a really big one," Zack offered.

"You did? Where?" She seemed excited.

"Summit. A long time ago. Four years."

"Did it scare you?"

"A lot. I couldn't stand it until I saw him. Then I knew he was okay. There was gas all over the place and I thought he was stuck in one of the cars."

"Did you think about what could have happened?" Her eyes were wide. "That it could have torn his arms and legs off, or burned him up?" She shivered at her own words, and real goose bumps came on her arms. She wrapped her arms around her chest.

Zack responded, reciting his brother's philosophy: "If you can get hurt really bad doing something, that makes it harder to do."

Lisa absently reached behind the seat of her car and pulled out her tennis racket and a ball. She bounced the ball on the strings in such a detached way that Zack started back into the shop.

"Come on over to the courts today," she called. When he turned she added, "if you like," but she didn't smile.

That afternoon Zack and Cy watched from the bleachers at Rosemount College as Tom attempted to play tennis with Lisa. While they were waiting for a court, Cy had entertained her with the story of a murder: "They caught the guy because he left his picture behind, up here"—he pointed to his left eye. "Froze in his eye."

"No kidding," Cy added, when she frowned at him in disbelief. "It happens if you shoot somebody straight on. There's a picture of you froze right there in the dead guy's eyeball."

Lisa smiled to end the story and summoned Tom to enter the court. Everyone else on the courts was wearing white; Tom wore cut off jeans and black basketball shoes.

Lisa said, "The other side of the net, Tom. You're my opponent." Cy and Zack laughed. Tom began to swing at the balls she fired at him. The first five went past without touching his racket. His wolf tattoo moved over his muscle like a dirty spot as his arm swung beside his body.

"Hey, Pate. Got a hole in your racket?" Cy heckled, ignoring the other players. One player was an older man Lisa had pointed out as her history teacher. He threw the ball up once to serve, but Cy whistled at Tom and he caught it without swinging, and sighed. Lisa hit another fast ball past Tom that hissed when it hit the gray court, then jingled into the fence. By the time Tom swung the racket, the ball was rolling behind him.

"Hey, Pate," Cy kept on. "Maybe you should put on a wig and run the Powder Puff next Saturday."

Tom walked to the fence and ran his fingers through the wire like an ape in a cage. "OK, hot shot. You want to get in here and beat her? She plays this candyass game all day long."

"Her? Not a chance. It's your ass I want to whip."

Before Tom could reply, Cy was inside the court, walking over to Lisa. She seemed reluctant at first to let him use her racket, but finally handed it to him, then came out and sat beside Zack. Cy looked even more ragtag than Tom, with the knees torn from his jeans and a dirty T-shirt. He had on his work brogans. Cy was so thin he would have disappeared had he stood behind Tom, but neither of them appeared to have an advantage.

The ball bounced back and forth, into the net more than over it. They argued loudly over the score and whether balls had hit the line or bounced twice. Soon both of them were angry. Lisa remained silent until Tom ran up the court to attempt a shot that had hit the net and rolled over. He missed the ball, but hit the net with the racket.

When Tom banged the racket on the net post, Lisa whispered, "Shit," under her breath.

"It counts," Cy yelled. "It went over."

Tom hit a ball towards Cy, scoring his first shot of the day as it caught Cy in the stomach. While Tom laughed loudly, the history teacher on the next court began collecting his balls and zipping his racket into a case.

"See you Monday, Dr. Stallings," Lisa called. The teacher waved briefly at her, shaking his head. After the teacher and his partner left, Tom and Cy got worse, screaming insults and hitting the balls at each other instead of at the court. The once-smooth court began to look like a plowed field.

Finally Lisa turned to Zack. "I'm bored," she said. "Let's go get something to drink."

"Bored! With the championship of the world in the last round and you're bored." She flashed Zack that white-toothed smile as they climbed down the bleachers. With the noises of Cy and Tom fading into the distance, they walked over to the snack window. When Zack reached for his wallet, she shook her head. A woman handed Lisa two lemonades and she signed a ticket.

"It is so boring here in the summer, I almost go crazy," she said.

"Are you in summer school?"

"No. I'm going to Europe next month. I can't wait."

She sounded as bored when she said that as when she'd said she was bored.

"Have you been before?" he asked.

"Three times. Four, actually, if you count when we went skiing last Christmas, but we didn't see anything but Switzerland. I just skied the whole time because you can imagine how much fun it is with my father around."

Zack had a quick comic flash of his father, standing on skis made of barrel staves strapped to his feet—an old photo in the family album, with his father a young man, no older than Zack was now. It was one of the few pictures he'd ever seen of his father having fun. The fun didn't last because that was the same snowstorm when Hershel had ridden a sled under a car that had stalled on Highway 43, opening his head above his now-bushy eyebrows. His skin was stained where it had been stitched, because his mother had stuffed the wound with cobwebs to stop the bleeding.

"My father made us come in every night by midnight," Lisa went on, "because that was when he wanted to go to bed. He never cares what anyone else wants to do."

"My daddy probably never stayed up until midnight in his life. Even the night Annie was born, he was snoring on the couch and didn't know until morning he had another daughter. At least that was what Mama said."

Lisa's pout went away. She laughed at something inside her head and gave Zack a guilty smile. "I'm sorry. I didn't mean to be rude. I was just thinking of something funny. My little brother started having one of his tantrums one day when Tom was over. After Tom left, he told me why he was so mad. Mother said he couldn't have a blue wolf on his arm just like Tom's." Lisa pitched a stone sideways and hit the trash can. Then she struck another one in the same place, proving she hit what she meant to hit. "Brat," she mumbled. She was silent. Then she asked, "What's your daddy like?"

Zack didn't know what to say. "What has Tom told you about him?"

"Zero. Nothing. Is he handsome like Tom?"

Zack laughed. "No, he's homely like me."

Lisa flashed him that smile again.

"When did Tom get that tattoo?"

"Right after high school. It was supposed to look like a wildcat, like the one on the Jaguar steering wheel."

"Sometimes I wish he didn't have it. I mean, sometimes I think it's neat because I know it really gets to my father. I mean, he can't stand it, if you want to know the truth. Tom could have a mind like Einstein and a million dollars in his pocket, but Daddy wouldn't see anything but that tattoo. One night when I was really mad with Daddy, I said right in front of Mother that I might get me a tattoo too, a little rosebud right here on my leg." Lisa made a tiny impression in her tanned thigh with her fingertip. She saw Zack frown.

Her eyes changed. Lisa went from strong to weak, like a little girl who was afraid of something. Then she lifted her chin in a way that reminded Zack of Annie when she was getting ready to be brave.

"If Tom said he thought it would be neat for me to get a rosebud tattooed on my leg, I would go do it without giving it a thought." Then she looked at him again with that clear stare that said she wanted information. "Girls always feel that way about him, don't they?"

Zack shrugged and stared at the ground. Lisa fished ice cubes out with her fingers and crunched them noisily. His mother would have corrected him for that. Rich girls could do anything they wanted to; when they didn't have good manners, it wasn't because they didn't know any better, it was because they didn't give a damn.

"Do you mind if I ask you something?" she said finally. "You have to promise not to tell Tom that I asked."

"Okay," he replied, his voice weaker than he had intended.

"Has he got something going with that Roxanne girl where he works?"

"Roxanne Morris? She's the boss's daughter. Allie Burcham says she's his girlfriend."

"Good. She isn't his type, but you never know," she concluded, but not with the confidence she showed about other things. Then her personality popped back. "Look at that jerk banging my racket on the ground. He doesn't have any right to get mad. He doesn't even know how to play the game." She laughed. "Your brother thinks he is supposed to be great at everything. He can't believe he picked up a tennis racket and it didn't start working like it was supposed to. It took me a whole summer of private lessons every day to learn how to hit a backhand right." Lisa got up, so Zack got to his feet and followed her back towards the courts. "By the end of the summer, though," she went on, "he will be able to beat me." A quick, sad look that she couldn't control rolled across her eyes before the Lisa she intended to be flashed back. "But until then, I am going to enjoy it. I am going to enjoy every point Tom Pate loses."

Tom and Cy were coming out the gate.

"Game over, boys?" she asked. "Or did you lose your balls?"

"Pate lost both of his," Cy said and punched Tom. Tom didn't smile back. Cy took off running to retrieve the balls, which were all outside the court fence.

"This is a real pussy game, you know?" Tom said to Lisa as Cy dropped the balls in her can. "Who was that sissy-looking doctor you spoke to next to us?"

"That was my European History professor. He's a very good teacher and not a bad tennis player, either."

"I like a game where you don't have to pat the ball around, you know?" Tom insisted. "This is like playing some little kid's game."

"Oh, and those aren't grown men hitting baseballs that I saw in the World Series? And Tony Trabert isn't a grown man?"

"Who's he? I've seen his name somewhere."

"Yeah. On the racket you just broke."

Tom read the name on the racket throat. Cy's racket had a broken string and the one Tom had used had a crack through Tony Trabert's name.

"Want to go over to the snack shop?" she suggested.

Lisa was looking just at Tom so Zack took it as a hint to leave, but he couldn't get Cy's attention away from her. Before he could say anything, Tom answered, "No. I have to get back to the shop. Take me back," he said. "I want to see if there's a car there yet."

"Hey, it's Christmas Eve," Cy teased. "Santa just might have brought Tom a car."

"I'm getting my own car. I don't have to wait for Santa to bring it to me," Tom snapped, then looked at Lisa. Zack couldn't be sure, but he thought he saw a knowing smile that said she intended to buy Tom a car.

One Sunday evening, Zack and Cy went to Tom's apartment to watch TV. Lisa had given him an old black-and-white one as well as having filled his house with furniture from her parents' attic. She'd had a telephone put in.

Zack decided to present Tom with his inheritance. He put it in a paper sack and set it on the kitchen table beside the greasy bag he'd brought full of fries and hamburgers.

"What's that?"

"I'm Michael Anthony, the Millionaire's secretary. It's your inheritance from Aunt B.B."

Tom grinned and reached into the sack, lifting out the hand-made globe in both hands. The colors were still rich. Zack had cleaned the dirt off the snow on the Alps.

"B.B.'s globe," he said mildly, but he seemed pleasantly surprised.

"Yeah, she always thought the world of you," Zack replied, the remark he'd practiced in his mind before he got there.

Tom rolled it in his hands. "She always took this globe away from me and now she gives it to me. She didn't really think the world of me, you know."

"You got anything to drink?" Cy asked. "Hey, what's that?" He pointed at the globe with one hand and reached into the bag for his food with the other.

"What's what?" Tom countered.

"That blue and green ball. What's it for?"

Tom looked at Zack and back to Cy.

"Do you want to explain it to your friend?" he smiled, handing him the globe and reaching into the refrigerator. Zack held it closer to Cy for a better look. Cy took it from him.

"What are all these bumps on it for? Come on, tell me what it is. Some kind of ball for a game?"

"It's a globe, Cy," Zack blurted out. "It's the world, a small version of the world."

"The world?" Cy said, his voice a little weak.

"The world is round, you know. You did know the earth was round, didn't you?"

"Yeah, I learned that in school, I think."

"Well, a globe is a model of the world. The oceans." He pointed. "And the mountains. And here's the United States with us about here." He found North Carolina.

Cy took it, rolling it around to see where Zack had pointed. "You mean we're on the outside?" he asked.

Tom glanced over his shoulder at him before he walked into the living room with three beers against his chest. "Bring the food in here. You can give your friend his geography lesson while I watch 'Ed Sullivan.'"

"What keeps the water from running off?" Cy asked.

"It doesn't run off because the earth is spinning," Tom answered from in front of the TV. On the screen five men stood on each other's shoulders juggling bowling pins. "Like at the state fair, the Dome of Death with the motorcycles," he added.

"I never seen that." Cy came to the door.

"Well, go this year. I'll buy you a ticket. Now get quiet. I want to watch this."

Cy looked at the globe awhile more before he set it on the kitchen table, shaking his head, and joined Tom on the couch.

When "Ed Sullivan" was over, Tom told Zack and Cy about a dream he'd had. "I was on this race track, only it didn't really seem like a race track. It was green with white stripes on it. It was driving me nuts. I kept running off the track. The turns were too sharp. It had corners that weren't curves. It was too square or something." Tom lifted his hands and made a right angle. "I couldn't even figure out what kind of car I was in," he went on. "Something kept telling me that Lisa was in one of the cars. Then I saw Lorenzen right in front of me, and said to myself, 'I'll follow Lorenzen. If anybody out here knows what he's doing, he does.' So I followed him and didn't go fifty yards before he went smashing right through the fence. I went through right behind him and when all the boards started flying at me, I put my hands in front of my face. Then I got all tangled up in stuff and couldn't get loose and woke up with the sheets so wound up on me that I fell out of bed like a mummy."

Tom stopped talking and looked at Zack. "Well?"

"Well, what?" Zack said.

"Well, what does it mean? You're the one who's always telling me what things mean."

Cy answered, though Tom wasn't asking him. "I think it means you've got no business racing cars, Pate, if the first thing you do is let go of the steering wheel when a little trouble comes up." Cy started laughing, but Tom didn't join him.

Finally a light bulb popped on in Zack's head like a comic book character: "Tom, that green race track was a tennis court. That's why Lisa was there. Because she beat you at tennis and because she's thinking of buying you a race car."

Cy mocked him with his own words: "'I don't see what's the big deal. That tennis is just a pussy game.'"

"She doesn't think she's buying me a race car, does she?" Tom asked Zack.

"You're asking me?"

Tom looked at his brother squarely in the eyes and said, "She's not buying me a race car." Then he opened the door for them to leave.

Tom waited until he heard the engine start on Ned's pickup and saw their boss headed home for supper before he turned to Arnold, Zack, and Cy.

"Next weekend!" he shouted. His words wouldn't come in sentences. "Me. The driver!"

They all understood him perfectly. Ned had finally stepped aside and had told Tom he could drive the flathead at a race at Tar Valley Fairgrounds, a quarter-mile dirt track in Simmons, about thirty miles north of Greenmont. "I'll let you give it a try," Ned had said. "Me and Roxanne gotta take Mama to the cemetery in Franklin next weekend."

After that, the time spent getting the car ready doubled. Tom wanted all the jobs done they had put off when Ned drove. They worked so late, they hardly needed to go home before work the next morning.

"Our new boss is a mean son of a bitch," Arnold pretended to complain. "All this work and he probably can't drive his finger up his butt any faster than Allie Burcham."

"If I don't blow Allie in the weeds my first time out," Tom countered, "I'll retire at twenty-two."

"Hey, Tom," Zack blurted. "Remember when we ran your Speed Seat in Bunker's Field? You told me you'd go by so fast, if I blinked my eyes, I'd miss you."

"Yeah, and you blinked them, didn't you?"

"Did not."

On the drive to Tar Valley Raceway, Tom was silent, his nerves taking over. When Lisa phoned before he left, he lost his temper and hung up on her. "Can you believe she thought I was going to play tennis this weekend?" he told Zack. Cy and Arnold rode in the back of the pickup. Zack could see

Arnold talking, but couldn't hear him; Cy's eyes were closed, the extra-long hours they'd put in taking their toll.

"We got a chance to do something this weekend," Cy had told Zack when he drove him in the Chevy to pick up some clean clothes. "Old man Ned is a nice enough guy, but he's not going to win any races."

"How do you know my brother will be any good?" Zack asked him.

"He'll eat 'em alive," he smiled. Zack had no idea why Cy was as biased about Tom as he was.

When they got to the track Arnold began dragging his tool box from the pickup. Arnold's pants rode under his belly and were so low on his rear that his crack was exposed when he bent over. "Hey, Arnold," Cy teased. "That girl over there thought you were mooning her." Arnold tugged his pants up then leaped forward when the ice cube Cy had dropped in the back of his pants rolled under his balls. "Arnold's actually a nice guy," Cy remarked, jumping out of reach. "He's just been in a bad mood for the last five years."

To Zack's dismay, Arnold took over as crew chief.

"I was going to organize Tom's team," Zack complained.

"Screw off," Arnold replied. "You couldn't organize a fuck in a whorehouse."

Arnold told Zack to clean the windshield if the car came in the pits for any reason during the race. Most of the other teams had replaced the glass with wire mesh, enabling the driver himself to knock the mud off, but Ned had kept the windshield to keep the dirt off his glasses. The rest of the time, Arnold said, Zack would just hand the tools to them. "I don't want to take a chance on you leaving nothing loose," he said.

Tom qualified fourth, higher than Ned had ever run and five rows ahead of Allie Burcham. When the green flag waved, Tom moved from his fourth starting position into third, holding it for four laps. By the tenth lap he was in second, leaning on first place in every turn.

"He's gonna get him!" Arnold shouted. "Nail the sonava-bitch. Shove him in the wall. Get out of the goddamn way, Burcham. He's lapping your ass." Arnold's overheated face was red with white splotches in his acne scars, like bleach spots on a shop rag.

As Tom drove to the inside, shooting past the pits in first place, they hardly had time to cheer before trouble hit. When they heard Tom's tire pop, Arnold grabbed the spare wheel and climbed over the wall. Cy handed the jack over and set a bucket of water by the wall before picking up the fresh wheel. Zack crawled around on the ground, looking for the clean rags.

Tom came in, sliding to a sideways stop, the blown tire shredded and wrapped around the axle. While Arnold shoved the jack under, Cy pulled the torn tire away. After Arnold jacked up the car and loosened the lugs, Cy pushed him aside to pull the hot wheel off with his gloved hands. Then Arnold stuck the new wheel on, picking up and dropping the nuts like hot peanuts. Cy scooped them up, dropping them into the water he'd brought to pour over the radiator, where they sizzled like hush puppies in hot grease. He fished them out for Arnold, who spun them on and tightened them with a lug wrench, grunting like a weight lifter over each lug. Neither of them had time to pay attention to Zack.

After the car had limped to a stop, Zack had crawled across the hood to start scrubbing the mud off the glass. Tom revved up the engine, holding the car back like a horse in the gate while the crew worked. When the new wheel was on, Arnold dragged the jack back out and Cy dumped the water over the radiator to cool the overheating car. Arnold jumped to the side to signal Tom out before he noticed Zack was still on the hood, scrubbing the window. He'd taken a clean rag out of his back pocket and was wiping spots as if he were still working at the filling station, looking through the windshield up a girl's skirt.

"Zack, get the fuck off of there!" Arnold yelled. Zack looked at Arnold as the race car hit the ground, the wheels spun, and Tom took off. Instead of dropping off or falling and getting skint up, Zack left the pits hanging on. The last thing Arnold and Cy saw was the bottoms of his shoes dangling over the fender.

"Jesus H. Christ," Arnold shouted, "that dumbshit's still on the race car!"

Zack held on to the hood latch, the engine heat burning his bare stomach through the metal. The car limped over the ruts with cars passing on both sides, one nudging into Tom's car and shoving it sideways, barely missing Zack's foot. Zack could see his brother's contorted face through the clean windshield, but couldn't hear his words over the screaming engine. Cars passed them on both sides, but the competition was a blur to Zack, because the rough track bounced his glasses on his nose.

Tom swerved back into the pits and jammed the brakes, dumping Zack onto the ground in front of the car. Zack crawled out of the way, grabbing for his glasses that hung off one ear as Tom went back out. Arnold gathered up the back of Zack's shirt in his fist and tugged him over the pit wall, keeping his eyes on the track. Then he shook Zack like a bulldog with a rag in his mouth.

"Burcham got back in front of him. I can't believe it!" Arnold shouted. He pushed Zack to the ground at his feet. Zack crawled to the water bucket and soaked his burned and scraped forearms.

Tom struggled to repass Allie, but his car had lost its edge. Cars were passing him on both sides. "How many laps?" Arnold asked Cy.

Just as Cy shrugged, the white flag came out.

"One," he held up a finger to Arnold.

"I can fucking see, you dumbshit," he grunted. Arnold began to count cars: "Eight, or maybe nine." Zack backed up, standing behind Tom's tool box like a kid behind his mother's skirts. His arms and knees stung, but he wasn't badly hurt. No one asked if he was.

The car crossed the finish line, the fresh wheel glowing white on the mud-spattered Ford. Allie had taken the checkered flag two positions ahead of Tom. Tom drove into the pits.

"Goddammit, Zack," Tom started yelling as he climbed out the window, "you think I've got time to just sit and wait for you? Because you're not done yet, I'm supposed to sit there, twiddling my thumbs?" He pounded on the roof, then began picking up tools and throwing them. "This was a goddamn *race,* you know. As soon as I feel my wheels hit the ground, I'm off. You think I'm supposed to worry about you?"

Arnold butted in, never one to miss a fight. "The car leaves the pits and I see that dumb little son of a bitch is still on the hood. Well, he is going to fall off, I tell myself, before the end of the pits. Or jump off, if he has any brains at all, and then the car hits the fucking track and he's still hanging on for dear life like he thinks that's what you're supposed to do. Race car's not a circus ride, you know? You're too stupid to live, you know?"

"I'm real sorry, Tom," Zack said weakly, not looking at Arnold. "I didn't mean to mess you up."

"We was winning when the tire blew, you know that?" Arnold insisted, reaching around the tool box to yank at Zack's sleeve. Tom turned his back and leaned on the car, unstrapping his helmet. He didn't say any more.

"Yeah. That's why I was trying to do such a good job on

the glass, so Tom could catch back up," he explained to Arnold.

"You mean me and Cy changed a flat in the time it took your ass to wash half a windshield?"

"I guess so."

"You guess so. Well, just shut up. Everything you say makes me want to kill you more. Did you know that seven guys passed him when he come back in the pits to let you get off? Even that goddamn slug Allie Burcham got ahead of him." At that moment Zack missed Ned, who would have shoved Arnold into the pickup.

Cy butted in on Arnold's tirade, "Yeah, but Zack didn't make the motor go flat."

Arnold, who outweighed Cy two to one, had built the motor.

"I guess you didn't hear what I just said," Arnold threatened. "I meant for you to shut up too."

"I mean, he wouldn't have won anyway," Cy blurted to Arnold.

"You got bad ears, asshole?"

"My ears are just fine. Your engine took a shit," Cy insisted. "You heard it go flat, same as me."

The engine had gone off two laps from the end when Tom was still down a lap, desperately trying to unlap himself, and the same seven cars had passed him again. Zack felt his heart beat faster as he stood waiting for Arnold to grab Cy and shake him too. When he and Tom would be in bed as children, and their daddy would open the door and say, "I don't want to hear another peep out of either one of you," Tom would say, "peep," just before the door closed. All he could think of to say right then to Arnold was "peep."

Then to everyone's surprise, Tom broke the silence. "Go buy us some Cokes, Arnold," he said. Arnold danced in place like a fighter waiting for his trainer to tell him to throw a punch. When Tom handed him a dollar, he dropped his arms by his side and backed away.

"Cokes, Arnold, Cokes," Tom insisted. "Four of them." Then he said to Cy, "You and Zack get the stuff loaded. I gotta unwind a little." His voice had totally changed, the anger gone, replaced with disappointment. Tom didn't have to stuff Arnold in the truck; the calm around Tom forced Arnold to back off in confusion. When Arnold got back from the concession stand, Tom took two drinks and handed one each to Cy and Zack while Arnold looked at him in total puzzlement.

"The race's over, Arnold. You gotta learn when a race is over."

While Arnold drove down the highway, Tom rode shotgun, talking about the next weekend, the things he wanted to do. Cy and Zack rode in the back of the pickup.

"Somebody other than us has got to tell Ned how good I was doing," he said.

"Old man Burcham will tell him," Arnold replied. "He was so jealous he couldn't see straight. Did you see him after qualifying, sniffing around the car, figuring we used nitro to go so fast? Red knows you don't have half the car he give his dipshit son. Don't worry about it. By the time Ned gets to work Monday, he'll know. The old man is getting tired anyway. Ned thinks he needs an excuse to save face. No sense in our working our butts off on that car with him driving it like a little old lady with a load of eggs in the trunk." Arnold kept talking as he muscled the steering wheel that crowded his belly. "We'll get you together a better bunch of guys. We can get Ralph Bailey to come along and we can use Richard to do some of the shit work. We can leave those two in the back of the truck at home." He rolled his pig eyes towards the cab window, where the back of Cy's head rested against the glass.

"Cy's a good mechanic," Tom said. "He can weld, too. He's a lot better than Ralph Bailey."

"Yeah, but he's two bricks short of a load," Arnold said. "And your brother is useless."

Tom's cheeks burned red, splotching his skin with an emotion that resembled embarrassment or anger, but Arnold never noticed. He pulled into the parking area beside Agnes' Place, stopping the truck and trailer beside two rigs that had finished loading up before they did.

The café used to be J.B.'s Place, which was what some of the older drivers still called it. When J.B. was killed—he'd been thrown from his '34 Ford at Cowpens and crushed when it rolled back over—his wife, Agnes, put her name where his was on the outside sign. She didn't repaint the crossed checkered flags above the name; they were so faded only the old racers still saw them.

Tom spoke to some men they had seen at Tar Valley. Zack slid into a seat in a booth, but Cy tensed up like a cat that had been dropped into a new yard. Tom shoved him towards Zack's side of the booth. "Sit with him so I got more room," he said.

Cy dropped into the seat. Arnold went over to sit with the Burchams at the next table.

"Pretty junk day for the hometown boys," Tom said to Allie Burcham.

"Don't get much junker," Allie replied. Allie's arms were spotted with scabs from his dive into the creek. "But you had a good one going, Pate. Ned should have been there to see it."

"You make sure he hears about it, Allie, you hear?" Arnold put in. Tom had a faint smile on his face. "Only leave out the part about Dumbshit riding on the hood," Arnold added.

Zack stared at the paper place mat, the kind of mat that was meant to keep little kids busy till their food arrived. "Find twelve squirrels," he read. He counted out loud. "I can't find but ten."

Tom reached over and shoved him like he had Cy. "I know where the other two are," he said.

Agnes's daughter, Agnes Junior, threw green plastic menus in front of them and set down three glasses of water with no ice. Tom held up his glass to her. "Ice," he said. She snatched it back with mock anger.

"Nice tits," Allie Burcham said after she was gone.

"God gave her nice t-tits, so you wouldn't look at her face," his brother Giles stuttered. "Looks like she's doing a stress test on that p-p-p-pink nylon uniform." The "nylon" came out so loud the deer hunters and pig farmers at the other tables turned around. Zack got ready to punch Cy, afraid he was going to comment on Giles's speech problem, but Cy was speechless himself.

After Agnes Junior returned with the ice water, Tom opened his menu. "Son of a bitch, Junior." He pointed to a blackened area. "Only decent thing you had was the catfish and you marked it out. You trying to make us stop coming here?"

"Right," Agnes Junior said with a laugh. "Why don't you just take your business to one of the twenty other places on this godforsaken road?"

"Come on, Junior. Where's the catfish? Your old man getting too lazy to catch them?"

"Guy died on the catfish is why it ain't on there."

"Shit." Tom dropped his menu.

"I'm not kidding you. That table over there by the window? That's where the guy was sitting."

Tom looked at the table where Arnold sat, just as Arnold

picked up his place mat and glass and moved to a booth. The Burcham family followed him, as if their seats had suddenly got hot.

"This guy says to Mama," Junior went on, " 'This catfish got bones?' and Mama said, 'Naw, mister, it's a fillet.' You know how Mama is. She didn't know the stupid, goddamn Yankee believed her. When it was done—it took four men to haul him out—she said to me, 'Junior, any moron think you can fillet a skinny little Cowpatch Crick catfish ain't smart enough to live.' "

By now everyone had stopped eating and was listening to Junior rattle on. "He had on these big, thick glasses made his eyes look like they were floating in buttermilk. Ugly sonava-bitch. Stuffed his mouth full, musta swallowed it without chewing because the first bite, he went into this coughing. It was such a peculiar-sounding coughing and to tell the truth, I thought he was putting on. I come to the kitchen door when I heard this thud and some glass breaking and he was rolling around on the floor. He started into kicking and heaving and turning over chairs and he was so damn big and fat, nobody could get him up. So about ten people started beating him on the back like they was burping this great big old baby and he made this noise—I can't repeat it to you, but it was awful-sounding, sort of like a burp and a sneeze. Like if a hog could burp and sneeze at the same time, and that was it. Dead as a doornail."

When Junior finished, she looked around and was shocked. Every man in the restaurant was laughing except Tom, who just leaned back and looked at her with a big grin on his face.

"You think it's funny somebody died? Man walks in here on his own two feet and the undertaker has to haul him out? It's my restaurant. It ain't funny to me. He had a weak heart or something. He was fat as a pig." The men were all still laughing. "I know what I think. All of you can get the hell down the road. People dying ain't funny. You might yell and cheer at your rotten race tracks and think people dying in them cars is funny, but I don't. Anybody who races cars is crazy in the head is what I think." Junior started crying. "Dying ain't one bit funny. It don't even have to be somebody you care about. Just a fat old ugly man I don't even know." She went back through the swinging door into the kitchen. Soon an older woman came out. She looked just like Junior except her hair was sealed down with a net and her breasts hung lower, down past her waist.

"You boys giving Junior a hard time."

"Damn, Agnes, she's getting too sensitive," Arnold said. "Must be that time of the month."

"Junior took it pretty hard, that fat guy choking," her mother answered. "She ain't never seen a dead man before. I had her daddy's box shut up after his wreck. His face was so mashed, I couldn'ave told it was him. What you having?" she said to Tom.

"Catfish."

Agnes smiled and picked up his menu, swinging it at him. "I got a nice little fillet I fixed just for you. How 'bout the boys?"

"What you have, Cy?" Tom asked.

Cy was silent.

"You haven't even looked at the menu," Tom said. "Make up your mind."

"Nothing. I don't want nothing."

"Aw, don't let all this kidding get to you. You got a weak stomach?"

"Naw."

"Well, order something. I'm buying, if that's what's worrying you."

"Steak."

"How you want it cooked?" Agnes asked.

"Fried, I guess," Cy replied.

"Wait a minute, wait a minute," Tom put in. "I'm not buying you a damn steak. We didn't *win* the race, you know."

Cy's eyes began to roll around. He still didn't open the menu.

Tom stared at him until Zack said, "I want the Double Burger Special, lettuce and tomato, hold the mayo, with fries and a Dr. Pepper."

"Me, too," Cy said quickly.

Tom lifted his eyebrows and stared at Cy briefly, then he nodded. Agnes collected the menus and walked into the kitchen. Cy didn't talk during dinner, but when he was through with his food, he took his empty plate and glass, stacked up his dishes, and carried them over to the opening where the food was handed through.

"You've never been to a restaurant?" Zack asked the next day. "You must have looked in windows before or through doors and seen people sitting around a bunch of tables that weren't home."

"I reckon I never put any thought into it," Cy said quietly.

"You've been down to Edna's to get hamburgers for lunch."

"Edna's ain't got tables and chairs."

"Yeah, but it's got a menu."

"If we go there again, you pick for me, okay? Like you done, okay? That suits me fine."

The look in Cy's eyes begged Zack not to question him further, to set him free like a garter snake trying to wiggle away from his fingers.

After work that day, Ned Morris gave them forms to fill out, telling them to put down their full names and Social Security numbers. When Zack finished his, he noticed Cy had his back to him, hunched over the lunch table. Cy looked back and forth from his Social Security card to the form, drawing just a little more of one of the numbers each time. He held the pencil like a chisel. When he got to a three, he made it backwards, then tried to rub it out with a wet fingertip even though his pencil had an eraser. Then he marked over the smudged numeral.

Zack looked over his shoulder. "Cy, you're supposed to put your name there," he pointed out, "not your number."

Cy threw down the pencil, wadding the paper up in one motion. He shook his head, got up, and walked towards the door. "Cy, hang on. Don't leave. I'll fill it out for you. Give me your number. Or just give me your card and I'll copy it."

Cy came back and handed him the card, but never looked him in the eye before going back into the shop. Zack got another form out of Ned's file cabinet to fill in for Cyrus Horace Thomas II.

Back in the shop area, Cy beat so loud on the fender he was straightening that Arnold hollered at him to pipe down. Cy's out-of-control arms slowed like a battery toy running down. He went to his tool box and began to pick up the loose sockets, jabbing them back onto their rack, each fractional size registering in place on the right stob on the first try.

12

Cy had met Roxanne Morris months before Zack, while he still worked at the Pure Oil station. Zack hadn't seen her yet, and for reasons he didn't comprehend, Tom hadn't mentioned her.

"The first time I seen her," Cy had related to Zack, "she was standing out in the rain in this yeller raincoat after her puddle jumper didn't clear a deep one off of Main Street. I'm not kidding you, the water was clean up to her . . . up to her door," he laughed.

The first time Zack saw Roxanne Morris, he was lying on his back on a creeper under a '61 Ford convertible in her father's shop. After Roxanne walked into the office, Zack stuck his head out from under the car. "That's her?"

Cy nodded with a smile.

"That's her?" he repeated in disbelief. "Jesus, I see why you were hiding her from me."

"She'll make you get religion," Cy laughed. "I hear on the grapevine that she's going to be the shop secretary as soon as she finishes night school."

Zack waited for Roxanne to come back out to see if the second sighting was as favorable as the first. To his mind, she looked darn near perfect.

Roxanne picked her way across the tool-and-rag-strewn floor.

"Come on, Roxanne," Allie called, "you act like you're afraid of stepping in dog shit."

Her feet were only a few feet from Zack's face. She had on white patent leather high-heeled boots with red stars at the ankles, the stars peeking from under the cuffs of her white pants. Zack pushed himself over to the edge of the car where he could see her backside, the kind of bottom that most girls thought was too big and guys thought was just right. Her long blond hair, tied back with a black ribbon, was almost as white as her pants. He couldn't tell if it was bleached, but it seemed too blond to be real. Her blouse was checked like a race flag.

"Hi, Roxanne," Cy said bravely. "Guess you're the only way old Allie is ever going to get to see a checkered flag."

"Very funny, *Cyrus.*" Allie's voice got higher when he was beginning to get upset.

"I thought it was, *Alvin.* You didn't just go in a store and buy that shirt without thinking of that, did you, Roxanne?" Cy asked her.

"My name isn't Alvin. It's Al, just plain Al."

"Without thinking what?" she asked. Her voice was almost a whisper, like she was somewhere that she wasn't allowed to talk.

"She don't think, Cyrus, see? That's not her job," Allie answered for her.

"Knock that off, Allie," Ned snapped.

Allie backed away from Roxanne. There was no doubt in the tone of Ned's voice; kidding his daughter and cussing in front of her was okay, but don't call her stupid. When she frowned at Allie, Zack saw her face for the first time. Her bottom lip was sticking out. She wore a lot of makeup she didn't need, but he could still tell that, except for maybe her eyes being a little too far apart, she was as pretty as the girls in ads in magazines. He wanted to crawl out and slug Allie for talking that way about her. He slipped from under the car and stood up to get a better look.

Roxanne walked over where Cy was taking a carburetor apart. While Cy talked softly to her, the banging in the shop went away except for Tom's. Tom hadn't looked up since Roxanne came in, and he continued to pound on a bent suspension arm in a vise a few feet away. She stared at him and his noise.

"I think you look real pretty in that blouse, Roxanne," Cy commented, distracting her. Then he said something no one could hear. She giggled and began picking up the tools on his bench, fingering them as if they were nail files and fingernail polish.

"Careful, Roxanne," Cy cautioned. "That stuff is greasy." He gently took a box wrench away from her, inspecting her palm and finding a black smudge. He held her hand in his while he rubbed the spot with a cloth. She glowed, standing beside that workbench on the dark side of the shop as if she were lighted from within like a fairy princess in a cartoon.

Still Tom banged. Zack cupped his hand around his right ear. No matter how hard he tried, he couldn't hear what Cy and Roxanne were talking about. Finally Allie could stand it no longer.

"Come on, Roxanne. I want to show you something outside."

Cy watched Allie tug her away like a poodle on a leash. A slow smile spread across his face. He held his chin up, breathing deeply as if to suck part of her up his nose to keep. Zack waited for a Coke to move over in the drink machine. When she walked by, he picked up the cold bottle and stuck it to his lips, forgetting to pry off the lid. He got a whiff of her perfume, the same sweet scent that he'd smelled in the office after she did the books on weekends while they were at the races. He looked around, hoping Cy hadn't noticed the lid was still on his drink, but he had. Zack's ears blazed red.

After Ned went back into the office, Cy sang a little song. "Allie paraded sweet Roxanne through, to make the boys' weinies get hard and their balls get blue."

"Okay, what were you and Roxanne talking about?" Zack asked when they took their break.

"I was telling her about the guy and the popcorn box."

"Baloney, you were," Zack replied, only half-believing Cy hadn't told her the story he had told them that morning. Cy said a guy he knew sat next to a girl in the movies and offered her popcorn. "He poked his dong up through the bottom of the box and when she reached in and grabbed it, he said, 'Excuse me, Madam, but I just offered you my popcorn.'"

"That's bullshit," Arnold had scoffed. "I heard that old story a hundred times."

"Come on. What were you saying?" Zack asked again. "Really."

"Nothing much. Just asked her if she was going to be Miss Greenmont Raceway at the big race next month."

"What'd she say?"

"Maybe."

"You planning on cutting out old Allie?" Zack said.

"Maybe," Cy repeated with a grin. "I told her I just might get to drive her old man's car that weekend."

"Yeah, and I'll get to ride the first rocket ship to the moon," Zack answered.

They heard a familiar voice behind them. "Looks like it's going to get pretty damn crowded in that race car," Tom said as he popped his Coke cap off on the edge of the bench.

Cy knew that he had stepped out of bounds.

"Okay, okay," he said quickly. "I'll wait until Ned buys a new car for you before I ask if I can drive his old jalopy, Pate. Your leftovers will suit me just fine." Cy laughed uncomfortably. "Maybe Allie will give me Roxanne. Roxanne and the jalopy and I'll be in Fat City."

"Yeah, and while you're at it," Zack put in, "see if Roxanne has a sister." He leaned against the workbench and sighed, unable to hide his feelings.

"I heard she had one with buck teeth that makes all her own clothes and, for a fat girl, doesn't fart much," Cy answered.

"Doesn't sweat much, Cy," Arnold corrected.

"Oh."

When Tom didn't respond with a laugh, Cy and Zack stood in place like two corncrib mice facing the barn cat until he turned around. Tom drew down the last half of his Coke with one swallow, dropping the bottle in the rack with a thud before he walked to Arnold's bench and started back to work.

Zack turned to Cy and whispered, "Fat City, my ass. Up Shit Creek is more like it."

Cy chuckled. Out of Tom's earshot he asked, "Hey, if Ned said, 'Zack, old boy, you can have one or the other: my daughter or my car,' which one would you take?"

"Oh, man, I'd take the car. How about you?"

"Me, too."

That was the first time Zack had lied to Cy since he'd pretended his own father was a drunk, too.

Tom was grilling Arnold about the race.

"So why did it go flat at Tar Valley, Arnold?"

Arnold held out both hands like a beggar, except that each palm cupped a part. "This or this," he answered. "Bum condenser or this crack in the distributor cap caused it. Might not be the condenser at all, but I'm throwing it out to make sure." He dropped the small part into the trash where it rattled between the empty oil cans.

Tom took the distributor cap and examined it. "This is probably it," he said when he located the crack. "Makes sense. You probably threw out a perfectly good condenser."

"Want me to fish it out?"

"No. No need to take a chance." He tossed the distributor cap into the same garbage can. As he walked back to his bench, Ned called him into his office.

In about fifteen minutes he came out, moving slowly, as though his brain wasn't guiding his feet.

"What's the matter, Tom?" Zack asked. "Something bad?"

"No, no, something good," Tom replied incredulously. "Something real good. Ned says we got gas money and entry money for Tidewater."

"No shit!" Arnold exclaimed. "Then we're going."

"And he'll let me drive from now on. Long as there's money. We gotta write some guy's name on the car, Maurice Somebody with a gas station."

"Maurice Penninger," Cy put in. "Our old boss at the Pure Oil, I betcha, Zack. Him and Ned are buddies."

"I didn't think we had a ice cube's chance in hell of going that far," Arnold said. "What about some tires?"

"I didn't ask him. Took me by surprise."

Tom stared straight ahead, afraid that his news was going to evaporate like a waterhole in the desert.

"Our tires are really junk now since Tar Valley," Arnold said. "We shoulda just stopped down there after we knew we weren't going to do any good and saved them for this weekend."

Tom's face snapped around to Arnold. "Why would we have done that when I just found out five minutes ago we were going to Tidewater tomorrow?"

"Allie said we could have his old ones," Cy offered. "He didn't run hard enough to hurt them. Me and Zack'll go get them." He trotted towards the door, tugging Zack along with him.

That evening they loaded the pickup to be ready to go first thing in the morning. Tom asked Zack, "You guys aren't planning on riding in the back of the truck, are you?"

"Hadn't thought about it, to tell the truth," Zack answered. "We could take turns riding up front."

Tom shook his head. "Won't be room with Arnold up there. That's a long drive to go crowded in a cab."

"Hey, Zack. We got a car, remember?" Cy said. "We get some gas money, we can drive."

"Consider it yours," Tom said.

"Look what he'll do to get rid of us," Cy joked.

"Tom, look here at the map. We go right by Summit."

Tom glanced over Zack's shoulder. "Yeah, right on by it."

"What if we see Daddy up there tooling around on his tractor?"

"They don't let tractors on Seventy. He probably doesn't even know it's there."

"We better get disguises, Tom," Zack said, only half kidding.

"You act like somebody who's escaped out of jail," Tom said. "You don't ever have to go back there. You don't owe them anything."

"Well, I would kind of like to see Annie."

Tom stared at him, not breaking his glance until Zack looked down. "In a couple of years," Tom said, "Annie won't even remember she ever had two brothers."

They left for Tidewater, Virginia, the next morning before dawn; the race would start at four o'clock that afternoon. Before Cy and Zack reached the Greenmont city limits in the Chevy, they had to swing back to get Cy's forgotten swimsuit. Cy ran out of the house with the suit, then stopped dead still in front of his house. He closed his eyes, walked nine steps backwards, tripping twice over Charlie the rooster before spitting over his shoulder. Zack turned away from this ritual. He was reminded at least once a day that Cy was the son of a woman who spoke mumbo jumbo and tied knots in her apron. If a black cat had crossed their path that day, they'd have stayed home.

Zack turned on the radio and began to sing with the faint tune under the static overlay: "You don't own me, I'm not just one of your little toys . . ."

"Hey, good buddy," Cy said, "as my old man would say, you can't carry a tune in a bucket."

Zack stopped singing and, when the static overruled the song, he shut the radio off. They soon caught back up to Tom and Arnold. Cy passed the truck and trailer with a loud blast of the horn. "We'll have time to swim in the ocean before they get there," Cy said. Greenmont was only five and a half hours from the ocean, but Cy had never been there.

When they reached the open road, a Trailways bus lumbered past on their left, filling the air with diesel fumes. "That's how I got here," Zack told Cy. "On that bus."

"No kidding. I never rode a bus, except around town."

"That bus stops at every eye's blink between here and Durham. You gotta wait for all these people to get on and off, wait while the bus driver tries to make time with the waitresses in the cafés at the stations. Wait, wait, wait. Poor people know how to wait. They know how to go to sleep without closing their eyes."

"Hey, good buddy, we ain't poor folks. We rich. We high rollers, going to the beach in our very own car. Week's pay in our pockets. We can pull over and take a leak in the woods when we have to go. We stop for a drink in a filling station when we get thirsty. If that ain't rich, I don't know what is. Hey, did you see that 'forty-six?" He pointed to a junk car sitting in a field.

"Are you sure? Looked like it could have been a 'forty. I think it might still have a motor." A car with a motor was always worth checking out.

Cy slid the Chevy into a side road, grabbing the emergency brake as the wheels hit the white dust turnout, spinning the car back in the direction they had come from, and coating it over with a powder as fine as flour. When they got closer to the junk car, they found they were both wrong. Instead of being an eight-cylinder Ford, it was a six-cylinder Plymouth, a dark blue '46, sitting in the sandy field like a giant blood blister.

"Damn, it's a shame to let it rust in the ground," Cy said. "I'd give him twenty-five bucks for it, as is."

"How would you get it home?"

Cy scratched his head and swung the Chevy back onto the highway, but as soon as he was back up to speed, he hit the brakes again.

"Did you see that rock?"

"What rock?"

"There by the road. I swear it had a hard-on."

This time Cy did a bootleg turn on the pavement, squealing in a circle. "For Christ's sake, Cy, warn me next time. You're like the frog in the well, hop up three feet, slide back two. We're never going to get to the ocean. You made us a set of square tires for sure now, too."

Cy ignored him with a chuckle and drove back to the rock that had a hard-on. It was a snapping turtle. Zack jumped out and grabbed a stick, holding it in front of the turtle, who grabbed the bait like a bass, chomping into the wood.

"Golly," Cy exclaimed. "We could use that son of a gun for a vise."

"Yeah, except he won't let go till it thunders."

Zack pulled the turtle to the other side of the road, its neck stretched so thin it appeared it could break. After he dropped the stick, the turtle kept walking, dragging it like property.

"I pulled him over here to keep him from getting squashed," he explained to Cy. "See, a turtle won't change his direction, once he's started heading for the water."

"Hey, this is better than the nature walk at school."

"When were you in school long enough for a nature walk?"

"I took a bunch of them. Out the back door, down the riverbank, through the woods . . ."

150

They got back in the car just as the truck and trailer was coming into sight. Cy pulled out in front and got up speed.

"We had those big turtles on our pond at home," Zack related. "I saw one of them once swim up under this little duck and swallow it whole. . . . Summit, three miles!"

"Huh?"

"That green sign with the white writing: SUMMIT. I never saw it on a sign like that before. I wonder of Tom sees it."

Zack looked back at Tom. The headlights flashed on the pickup and Tom's arm waved out the window. Go faster, Tom was motioning. Did he want to get there or go past it faster? When Cy slowed, Zack could see that Tom was wearing the glasses with bushy eyebrows and moustache and big nose that Zack had given him that morning for a disguise. Zack took his from the glove box and removed his own glasses. The next green sign he saw was blurred through the novelty shop glasses.

"Cy, did that say Summit?"

"Shoot, I don't know."

"That's it! There are the towers from Solomon's Hosiery."

Cy hit the brakes.

"No, don't stop. Keep on driving," Zack urged.

Cy turned suddenly down the ramp into Summit.

"Are you nuts? What are you doing?"

"This is where you lived, huh? I've never seen a town anybody else lived in before."

Zack spun around in the seat, frantic. To his amazement, Tom followed them, towing the car that had POLE CAT lettered over the driver's window. As they turned onto the old highway, Zack made out a sign on the side of a barn, SEE ROCK CITY. He couldn't see Tom's face. He stuck his regular glasses under the others. A Burma Shave sequence appeared: SAID FARMER BROWN / WHO'S BALD ON TOP / WISH I COULD / ROTATE THE CROP / BURMA SHAVE. They were on Highway 43, heading east, right past their house. No one would recognize Tom. Zack looked even sillier than his brother—light brown hair, a black mustache, and two pairs of glasses—so he slid down in the seat.

"Hey, man, did you leave here with your face on a wanted poster or something?" Cy asked. "Like the guys on TV with a bounty on their heads?"

"My old man has probably put a bounty on my ass."

"Would he pay me if I dumped your ass in his front yard?"

"Just keep driving, okay? No kidding. This goes right by my house."

The familiar scenery went by. There were a few changes: a dead tree here, a new paint job on the Plymouth that belonged to old man Gunter at the sawmill. They were getting closer. For Zack, waiting for his house to pop into view was like waiting for Tom to pop from under the water—inevitable, unless he had sunk to the bottom forever. There it was.

The tobacco field beside the house was clean of weeds, the plants he had set out as slips now full grown, but his mother's zinnias reached out above a tangle of wild grass, their brightly colored heads fighting for air. It wasn't like her to let the grass take her flowers. Chills swept across Zack's arms; what if she were no longer there, gone like old B.B.?

Tom noticed the Burma Shave signs had changed since he'd left. Four years ago it had read: THE WHALE / PUT JONAH / DOWN THE HATCH / BUT COUGHED HIM UP / BECAUSE HE SCRATCHED / BURMA SHAVE. The Burma Shave signs were new now, but everything else was older.

Their house on Highway 43 looked tired and old, like a woman who had aged suddenly with lines in her face and streaks where her hair has lost its color. Women were chopping grass away from the corn, swinging hoes mechanically, one woman per row, four women altogether. On the front lawn a tricycle lay on its side; it had been Tom's first, then had passed down through the offspring to Annie. She had painted it pink, the color it was now. But Annie was too old for a tricycle.

After the house was past, the four women and the pink tricycle stuck in Tom's mind like color spots when the lights go off.

"Blow the horn," Tom told Arnold. "Right up there is where we get back on Seventy."

Arnold blew the horn and Cy swerved the Chevy up the ramp, back onto the highway to Tidewater.

Cy and Zack had reached an area where the ground was so white on either side of the road that the glare hurt their eyes. Zack began to sneeze. They stopped and bought some sunglasses in a gas station. Then they went out back and put on their swim trunks, pulling their jeans back on over them.

"Turn left over there," Zack said, pointing to a sign to Hooker's Beach, "then back to the right."

Cy slowed almost to a stop. "Which way is that? I mean, *point* which way. Don't give me this left-right business."

When Zack stuck his hand under Cy's nose and pointed, he followed his directions like a mule. They drove down a street that dead-ended in the sand. The trip had ended almost too abruptly for Cy. He sat there a minute, speechless, staring at the water. The sun was full between white clouds and the waves slapped hard, spraying higher than the crests. No humidity hung in the air here as it had inland; the air was so clear it was as if their eyesight had improved. Zack tried to feel like Cy, pretending he had never seen it before.

As they walked across the beach their shoes soon filled up, so they went barefoot in the hot sand. For the first time in his life, Zack felt his feet had gotten too used to shoes. He ran down closer to the water, to where the tide had cooled the sand, to soak his burning feet. Cy trotted behind him like a little kid, picking up shells and throwing them at the water. Soon he started whooping like a crazy man.

"Sonavabitch. I've never seen anything like this in my life. I've died and gone to heaven. I coulda died in Greenmont and never seen nothing like this."

Zack dove through an incoming wave. As he surfaced in the still water behind the wave, feeling the suction of the undertow pulling him out, he heard the thud of the wave. As it leveled, he saw Cy's white legs shoot up out of the spray like a crane caught unaware. Zack went through the next wave and the next until his feet felt the swirling sand of the bar where he could see the bottom quivering through the water. On his last trip to the ocean he had spent the first three days getting knocked down, his head stinging with salt, until he finally humbled himself and went in with one of the trip chaperones, a deacon at Cedar Grove Baptist, who shouted in the same baritone he used in the choir box, telling Zack each time he must hurl himself into the water wall.

Cy, his wet hair reaching down his face like a yellow hand gripping his head, still struggled to get beyond the breakers. He challenged the waves upright and lost. Zack floated on his back beyond the breakers, buoyant in the salt water. As he drifted over a giant wave, he glanced towards Cy, thinking that this one was going to wipe him out, but Cy sat on the sand with his limbs lax like a discarded puppet, his trunks split down the side. Zack caught the top of the next wave and rode in. When he got closer, he could see Cy's sides heaving from exhaustion. Zack hurried through the breakers, then trudged along with the foam around his calves to sit beside him on the wet sand.

"You've got to get past the breakers, Cy, to have any fun."

"I gotta get past those damn big waves that keep knocking me down." He snorted like the victim of a bully as water drained from his nose over his upper lip.

The tide moved around their feet, sucking holes beneath them as it retreated. Cy jumped up and stomped back towards the water.

"You want me to show you how?" Zack offered.

Cy stopped. "After you, good buddy," he answered, his anger burned off like rain on hot pavement.

On his next attempt, Cy made it through a wave, diving into the wall of water beside Zack, and swam awkwardly in the calm water beyond like an animal with an instinct for staying alive, but one not designed for the water.

When they returned to the car, Cy pulled his jeans back over his split trunks and pounded the steering wheel twice with the palm of his hand, happy to be back in his natural habitat.

"Goodbye, Ocean," he grinned as he spun the wheels in the sand and pulled away from the beach. The tires sang as he went quickly into a turn, controlling the slide through loose sand that had blown onto the pavement. "Roxanne won't look twice at Allie Burcham or even that hotshot Tom Pate again, after she sees me in a race car," he stated out of the blue.

"You better slow down or a cop's gonna have your license. You don't know the places they hide out down here."

"What license?" he laughed. Then he drove so fast on the way towards Norfolk that Zack looked for a cop behind every billboard.

13

The cars were lining up on the track. Tom helped push his '32 to his second row starting place beside the canary yellow '40 Ford of the local star, Crawdaddy Crawford. The sun beat down on Tom's back until he threw his arms backwards, pulling his sweat-soaked T-shirt off his skin. He tossed his Big Mac work gloves inside the car before he lifted his legs up and through the window. The seat felt better; Cy had stuffed rags and foam inside it to keep his hips from sliding around and bruising. Zack handed him his Air Force helmet through the window. When he pulled it on, the voices around him were muffled.

"Hey, Allie," he heard Cy yell. "I just heard Jim Reeves singing your theme song."

"What's that?"

"'Hello Wall.'"

Allie shot Cy the finger, then stuck his face in Tom's window. "I got me some of that acetone stuff, too," he whispered.

"What?"

"Acetone," he said louder, his hands cupped around his lips. "So my engine will have as much power as yours. I got it at the paint store."

Tom shook his head and looked away. He didn't want to hear any more talk. Red Burcham was rumored to have added nitro to Allie's fuel. But no one in Greenmont cared if Allie cheated; he wasn't a threat anyway. Now someone on Tom's team had told Allie to get acetone and he'd been dumb enough to believe them. Must have been Arnold. Or maybe Cy.

It was Tom's first afternoon race in Ned's car; the sunlight glared off the white hood. The locals, accustomed to daylight races, knew to paint theirs flat black. The ocean wind that blew inland at Tidewater didn't cool the air but dried the track instead, the steam rising off the packed sand. While the water trucks circulated, preparing for their event, Tom waited inside the car where the dark felt like he'd crawled under a tree. His momentary relief left when the engines began to start up around him, the heat curling off them in visible waves.

"Fire her up," Arnold called.

Tom turned the key and tapped the throttle twice as Arnold had instructed him. The starter turned over but the engine didn't catch.

"Ah, shit," Arnold muttered. "Flooded the goddamn thing. Open it wide and we'll push it." When the car was rolling quickly, Tom popped the clutch. It didn't start. Cy lifted the hood and looked inside.

"Zack," Cy instructed, "go get a condenser, that old coil we took off yesterday, and two sets of points. You know where they are."

Zack ran towards their pit area, his short legs reaching out like a man in a race from a bear. Cy patted his back pocket, checking on his tool supply. Arnold's face was red as he puffed and fretted over his motor, patting everything under the hood.

"It ain't getting no spark, Arnold," Cy noted.

"I'm not fucking blind," Arnold shot back. "It's not the distributor cap again, if that's what you're thinking. Both of them are brand new."

An official walked to Tom's window. "Want a jump start?"

Tom shook his head.

"Not the battery," he replied. "Starter's fine."

"Then roll her out of the way. We got to get this race going."

Tom cranked the wheel to the left and, as two mechanics from the car beside him gave him a push, the car began to roll down to the apron. Cy danced along beside the rolling car, then reached over and yanked out the coil wire. He put his finger in the hole. Arnold looked at him incredulously.

"Turn her over, Tom," Cy called, bracing for the shock.

Tom turned the starter. The battery was getting weaker and the engine didn't fire.

"No spark at all," Cy answered, pulling his finger out. Cy popped off one of the distributor caps. Zack had arrived with the parts. "Nothing looks wrong here. Gimme one set of points, Zack. Change the other set, Arnold."

Cy removed the points and put the new ones in place. "Condenser," he said, so Zack handed him the part like a nurse. The cars began to move away behind them, heading onto the pace lap for the start. Cy clipped the distributor cap back on, attached the condenser, and reached for the coil. The field went rumbling past behind them. The starter wasn't pleased with the lineup so he gave them one more lap.

Cy put his finger back into the plug to the coil. "Crank her again, T—motherfucker!" he cried and jumped back. "She's getting some spark *now*," he panted.

Arnold jabbed the wire in the coil and shoved Cy backwards.

"Fire her up," Arnold called.

Tom cranked the starter and the motor fired, wrapping the car in smoke as Arnold held the fuel valve open. Then he slammed the hood and yanked Zack back by the shirttail as Tom spun away, sliding into the first turn as he rushed to catch up to the back of the field. The three of them ran to the pit area. They passed two teams, who applauded.

"All right!" Cy called, sticking a thumb up beside his index finger that still tingled. By the time they climbed over the pit wall, the field was coming through the third turn.

Tom caught the field and moved down onto the apron, bouncing along the rough track as he headed for his qualifying slot. He passed Allie Burcham in the tenth row, who was so startled he slid up the track, bumping into the car starting beside him.

When the flag dropped, the momentum Tom had gained when he was forced to catch up to the field propelled him past two cars before the first turn. By the end of the first lap, he was in second, with only the bright yellow rear end of Crawdaddy's Ford ahead of him. Tom chased the yellow car, backing off later each lap as he entered the turn. When he put his foot on the throttle, he felt the engine rush to its peak, but it would go no faster. He tried driving lower on the track as he entered the turn, then jumping onto the throttle quicker. Still the gap didn't close. He slid sideways through the turns, setting the car up sooner so he could jump on the throttle sooner, but still the yellow car stayed ahead, too far away to tap if he wanted to try nudging him out of the way. His car got a little unsettled once and he lost some ground.

Lap after lap he struggled, but could get no closer. He felt a jolt to his side when he was going through traffic. He had let off sooner because a lapped car was already in the turn. Until he felt the jolt, he didn't know how close the third place car had gotten. He drove harder, cutting across the road, blocking the car behind him.

When he passed the start-finish line, a man leaned down from the starter box with a white flag. Only one more lap. It would be over with so fast. Still the yellow car was ahead, as if there were an invisible block of glass between them that kept him from getting any closer. On the last turn he saw Crawdaddy go across the finish line, the checkered flapping above him; in that moment, forgetting for an instant his race wasn't over yet, he felt the jolt again. He put his foot down harder, but the pedal was on the floor. Now the jolt came from behind. The two cars crossed the line together.

Tom let off, angry at himself for letting the other driver get so close, but the car beside him didn't back off, it went straight into the first turn as if they were still racing.

"It's over, you bastard," Tom said out loud. "And I beat your ass." But he wasn't sure.

The other driver threw his car sideways too late and bounced into the berm, unsettling it and tossing it up into the dirt that had piled up against the wall. Tom dropped down onto the apron as the other car struck the wall and shot backwards down the track. He cleared the out-of-control car, but when he turned into the pits, saw the field behind him begin to pile up in the turn. He couldn't believe it; the biggest accident of the day was happening after the race was over. He drove over to the trailer where his crew waited for him.

"You beat the son of a bitch," Arnold shouted. "And I'll break anybody's neck who said you didn't."

Tom lifted his body out of the window and shook hands with Cy, then Zack.

"You beat him by a foot across the line," Zack added.

"Are you sure?"

"I'm sure."

"I shoulda blocked him off that last turn. Dammit. Had my mind too much on trying to win. My own fault. Shouldn't have let him get that close."

Tom looked up to the top of the bleachers, where the scoreboard numbers showed the top three: his number, 7, was in second place.

"Second place. Look, they have it up there!"

When they saw it on the scoreboard, it became real.

"That should be some money for a change, huh? We better get to the payoff window before they change their minds."

"Hey, Pate."

It was Allie Burcham.

"How'd you like the way I got out of line and made them have to do two pace laps?"

Tom looked at Allie. "You did what?"

"I got out of position so they wouldn't give the green flag so you could have more time to get your car running."

"Thanks, Allie," Tom said. "I needed all the help I could get. What did your old man say?"

"He says the dumb little shit cost himself a position at the finish," Red Burcham answered from behind Tom. "You're lucky I wasn't driving that car. And you can tell that skinny little asshole you got working for you to drink that damn acetone. It'll be a cold day in hell when I let you drive my Sportsman."

"Yeah, Red, I know. I expect hell to freeze over first."

Tom looked at Cy, who was standing in front of his toolbox, pretending not to hear Red, while he juggled three of his wrenches.

Tom collected his winnings at the payoff window while the others loaded the tools and hooked up the car. The feature race got under way before they could get out of the infield, so they had to stay till the finish. Allie drove his Sportsman car in this one. He started at the back of the field, and that was where he finished.

"Nice run, Pole Cat," a man called in passing.

Tom nodded.

"I bet they're pissed having some guy they never heard of show up down here and run off with their prize money," Arnold commented.

"Yeah. If I run here again, I'll beat that Crawdaddy, too. He just knows the track better is all. If he comes up to Green-mont, I'll blow him in the weeds."

"He's got some dough, too," Arnold added. "Do a lot better job if we didn't have to make do with a bunch of used-up parts."

"Glad we had old Ready Kilowatt troubleshooting for us," Tom replied, nodding at Cy.

Cy held up his stung finger with a smile. "Didn't hurt half as bad as the time I pissed on that electric fence. Got out to take a leak in the dark on Rolling Pen Road, about three sheets to the wind. Woke up flat on my ass in the middle of the highway with these headlights coming at me . . ."

"Yeah, I bet," Arnold grumbled.

"I did, I swear to you. Had a hard-on for three days."

Later, when they were sitting outside a hamburger place on the highway, Tom made them move to another table because there was a middle-aged woman with a grating voice talking a steady stream to her husband.

"I wonder how many years that poor son of a bitch has listened to that mouth," he said.

A car drove up and an attractive woman got out. All of their eyes followed her until she walked around to the other side of her car and took out what looked like a tray wrapped in a blanket. When they heard the gurgling sound of a baby, all of their eyes turned away as quickly as they had found her.

"Hey, Tom," Zack said, between hamburger bites, "remember when you made all that money jumping the cotton bales? He jumped fifteen bales going down this ramp on his J. C. Higgins."

Tom laughed. "Yeah, I made a bundle. Zack took up a quarter admission from a dozen guys, then I bent the front fork and the wheel rim when I landed, which cost about three times as much to replace."

"We made money today," Zack said.

"Just wait until Ned starts adding it all up. He'll make us come out losing money," Tom answered.

While they were eating, Allie Burcham drove past with his father and brother, BURCHAM BROTHERS AUTO PARTS AND REPAIRS lettered on the side of their double-decker trailer to match their red pickup.

"Hey did you see what I got Allie to buy for me at the paint store?" Cy asked, holding up a can of yellow spray paint.

"So you did send him after the acetone. What you planning to do with the yellow paint? Paint my car like Crawdaddy's?"

"Naw. Got it for Allie's guard dog. You know that dough-boy-pinch-whatever-you-call-it he keeps bragging about? I'm going by tonight and put a yellow stripe down his back."

"Gonna get your dumb fuck arm eat off," Arnold said. "Those Dobermans are real bad asses. Hey, Tom, what you think of Allie's new pickup? His old man acts like he's made out of money. Comes from gypping the hell out of everybody in his store. I wouldn't buy shit there if there was anywhere else to get it. Acts like he's doing Ned such a big favor giving him a ten percent discount and he still gets double what he oughta. Guess that's what Roxanne sees in him. Money. Sure as hell can't drive a race car."

"Roxanne's just looking for husband material," Tom commented.

"How do you know Roxanne wants to get married?" Zack put in.

"They all do. All the little Roxannes do. As soon as they can and to a guy with as much money as they can find. Then they bitch at him the rest of his life because they're so damn bored they can't stand it."

"And why are they bored?"

"Because they didn't marry a race car driver," Tom laughed.

"I got girls figured out," Arnold explained. "Act like they love you so much and the reason you're supposed to believe it is they're scared to death when you're racing. They're not worried about your ass. They're just worried you'll get banged up and leave them with nobody to pay the bills."

"Naw, I think they just *think* they don't want you racing," Tom said. "All that worrying about you and they'd find something else to harp on if you went out fishing or something. They love it you're a race driver. Just won't admit it. They get all that attention when you win and never have to worry about hurting one little finger."

"You should have seen this movie me and Cy saw the other night," Zack said.

"Yeah, they didn't talk English, but it had a lot of neat cars. A Duce Evita Caddy."

"That was an Eldorado, Cy. The movie was *La Dolce Vita.*"

"Then what's the point in calling it that? I know there was a Triumph and a 'Vette older than Lisa's that Tarzan drove . . ."

"Anyway," Zack interrupted Cy, "this rich woman says to this guy who's got the hots for her: 'My trouble is too much money, yours is too little.' That's like you and Lisa, huh?"

"Let's hit the road," Tom said, standing up. "We've got a long row to hoe."

Arnold drove alone in the pickup while Tom stretched out in the back seat of the Chevy. By the time they passed the turnoff for Summit, the sky was black.

"We just passed Summit," Zack said. Tom grunted but didn't sit up.

The green sign with white writing reflected back at Zack, putting Summit into a neat square like every other town that was beside Route 70. Moonlight flashed between the straight pines, planted in rows. That morning there had been four women, not three, in the corn rows at the Pate place. And a tricycle.

"Tom, how many women did you count at home this morning?"

"Four."

"Yeah, me too. She wasn't colored. Wonder who she was?"

"Don't know."

"Annie's too big for the trike that was in the yard."

Tom didn't answer.

Every Friday night Tom battled it out at Greenmont Raceway in Ned's '40 Ford, going for the jalopy win three times, a win that at the time paid fifteen dollars. Then he watched the Saturday feature race, the better, faster Sportsman cars that put on the show everyone came to see. The space between him and the winner of the feature race seemed as impossible to cross as the distance between the nose of his jalopy and the rear of Crawdaddy Crawford's yellow Ford. No one offered him a ride in a better car. There was one answer that Tom would always refuse to accept—that Crawdaddy Crawford was a better driver and might always be better. That couldn't be it; there was only lack of money and lack of experience separating the rungs on his ladder. Then one day in that summer of '63, the next rung got within grabbing distance.

"Look at that, Zack," Cy exclaimed. "Can you believe we've finally got us a real race car?"

The crew watched the '33 Ford come into the lot as if it had rolled down off a cloud. Ned had given up the jalopy, plus two hundred dollars. The car would run the feature race on Saturday night: eighty-over standard bore in the Modified Sportsman class, racing for fifty dollars to win.

To get the car prepared, Tom made a deal with Ned to have money come out of his paycheck a little at a time until his winnings were enough to pay for racing it. He would come to work an hour earlier every day so he could put in his eight hours then start on the race car before the shop closed.

"Aren't you excited?" Zack asked Tom, who seemed subdued.

"I knew it was coming," he answered simply.

Cy couldn't quit talking while they pushed the jalopy out and the new car back into their work area. "It's like the golden punkin, you know, like in that Mickey Mouse movie?" he said.

"You mean the pumpkin that turned into the gold carriage, Cy?" Zack asked.

"Yeah, that one. The golden punkin," he insisted. "We're going to make this into a golden punkin and nobody is going to be able to touch it."

He walked around the car, stroking its pale green sides like he was feeling to see if it were ripe. Zack could feel Tom's blood rising as though it were his own. When Cy climbed into the driver's seat, Tom asked, "How come you're so excited about it?"

Cy looked out at him through the open window. Then he tugged on the door handle, which didn't work from the inside, and finally pulled his bony frame back out through the window. He glanced nervously back at the car, wondering if his golden punkin had turned back to twenty-nine cents' worth of pie filling.

"Because we got us a— a real race car," he stammered, his voice thin and childlike. "Because now we get to race in the *feature*."

Like a cat who would turn on his own littermate if there was only one sardine to go around, Tom eyed him coldly. "I just don't see where you're coming from, kid," he said.

Cy stopped talking. He was confused. The conversation had gone over his head. He looked at Zack in desperation, hoping he would answer for him, but he didn't. Finally he said, "You know me, Pate. I get excited about things. But I don't never get nothing. My old man tells me, if my ship come in, I'd be at the train station."

Tom still stared at him.

"The car's a piece of shit, Cy. Why can't you see that?"

166

"Naw. Don't say that."

"Yes, it is. But it's the best we can get right now. You start believing it is more than a piece of shit, then you'll never know any better. If I thought this was the best car I'd ever drive, I'd hang it up, right now."

"We can run with the good guys now," Cy said weakly.

"Just the good guys around here. These guys around here are nothing. If you look at the big picture, Greenmont Raceway is nothing."

Arnold had started to look through the inside of the car. Now he interrupted, "Hey, Pate. Look here."

Arnold held out a photo of a small Negro boy that he had found in the glove compartment. Tom handed it back to Arnold, who jumped back from it.

"I don't want it," he said. Then he looked over his shoulder to see where Richard, the Negro who worked there, was before he whispered loudly, "You got yourself a nigger car, Pate."

Tom wadded the photo and threw it back in before he went outside where Ned was paying for the car, counting out the cash. After Tom left the shop, the crew began checking out the green Ford.

"This thing smells like a cow stall," Zack said, as he caught a whiff of its rotten leather interior.

Arnold had the hood up, jabbing the engine mounts with a screwdriver.

"What's eating your brother?" Cy asked Zack.

Zack thought a moment. "He just doesn't understand why anyone wants to be anything but the driver," he offered.

"Yeah," Cy answered. "I know what he means. Me neither."

On Sunday evening, following an afternoon swimming at White Lake, Cy and Zack dropped off their dates and drove by the garage to see if Tom was working. Zack unloaded the scraps of metal he had picked up from under the shear at Burcham's shop to use in practicing his welding. Cy's daddy, Horace, had shown him the technique, the old man's stubby hands shaking with the torch, but steadying as the heat, rod, and metal began to connect.

"See, Pop. I told you you could still do it," Cy had said.

After he finished three rows, Horace shut off the torch and pulled off the glasses, handing them to Zack. "Yeah, and you tell your mother I can still do it and I'll break your neck. Next thing you know, she'll expect me to get a job."

Zack continued to practice, trying to produce a weld that Horace wouldn't dismiss as "bird shit." Actually, it was the first activity around a car that didn't make Zack feel inept; his patience and steady hands were finally scoring on the plus side.

The lights were on in the shop and in the office when Cy and Zack arrived. A sweet smell floated out as soon as they opened the door. Both of them leaned into the office at the same time and saw Roxanne, the ledger open in front of her. She looked like a little girl reading an oversized book. She was rapping the desk with her pencil like a drumstick. If her father had been there, he would have walked over and taken it out of her hand, like he always did.

Back in the shop, pieces flew out the open windows of the new race car that sat wheelless on jack stands: handles, chunks of upholstery, and the hand brake lay scattered on the floor. As Cy and Zack walked up, the door to the glove compartment flipped out the passenger side.

Cy stuck his head in the window. "Hey, Pate, you wrecking the inside first this time?"

Tom lifted himself out of the window with one hand as if the door were already welded shut. He tossed a rusty makeshift heater into the pile of discarded innards. Leaning back against the car, he wiped the rust off his hands down the tail of his T-shirt and took a cigarette from a pack on top the car.

"There was a lot of extra weight in there."

"Hey, you should have seen your little brother making time today, Tom. Him and Nadine were in the woods so long, I almost sent the Boy Scouts out looking for them."

"Nadine, huh?"

"Yeah, you saw her," Zack said. "You said she was chunky. I thought you and Lisa went somewhere today. It looks like you spent all day working here."

"Yeah, pretty much." He looked around the shop as if he had forgotten where he was. "There's a lot to get done before I can race it. Ned keeps this place so filled up with street junk. That's where the money is. I can't blame him. I just don't have to like it."

Like a bee to a flower, Cy wandered over to the door of the office.

"Cy might not know how to read and write and that the earth is round," Tom said, nodding at the office, "but he sure knows how to chase women."

"He knows a lot about cars. I wish I knew half as much."

"You oughta learn something. Like how to weld."

"I am learning to weld," he defended. "I'll show you when I get some good. Cy's daddy is teaching me."

"If you learn that then everybody will want you. There's really only two kinds of guys you need to work on race cars: those who can make pieces and those who bolt them together. The ones who can make them get about three times more money."

"Cy's daddy taught him when he was a little kid. His old man doesn't have any ends on his fingers, so he reached around Cy and used Cy's hands to hold the torch and rod. Pretty neat way to learn, huh?"

Tom didn't hear him. He lit the welding torch, shooting out

a long blue flame as he pulled down his goggles. He lay on his side across the seat, his legs dangling out the door, while he tacked a hook in place on the dash. When he shut the torch down, the hook broke loose and tinkled into the floorboard. "Dammit. I'm telling you, you ought to learn to weld. I ought to learn." Tom lifted the goggles and rubbed his eyes. "Guess I should have used a clamp." His shoulders fell forward from fatigue. He pressed the side of his face against the door frame.

"I'll do it for you," Zack said eagerly. He took the torch from Tom's hand and climbed inside.

"Hey!" It was Cy. "I talked Roxanne into taking a break. Want to go somewhere and get something to drink? The machine's empty."

"Nothing's open on Sunday night," Tom answered, just as Roxanne walked out. Her hair and clothes glowed like a lighted Christmas angel against the dark clutter of the shop.

"You mean I got us the best-looking date in town and there's nowhere to go?"

"We could get a Coke at Auntie's over near where I live," Zack suggested from inside the car. "She stays open till eleven-thirty on Sunday."

Cy waited a moment, but Tom didn't answer. "I'll help you with that hook tomorrow," Cy offered. "I seen how Giles Burcham did his."

"What is it for?" Zack asked from behind the sputtering torch.

"Hooks it in second," Tom replied.

"They pop out real bad," Cy said. "Seen Allie go from first to last 'fore he knew what hit him. 'Course that happens to Burcham about half the time anyway. 'Scuse me, Roxanne, but he's not exactly Curtis Turner. You knew that. Whatcha think, Pate? Knock off till tomorrow?"

Tom wheezed and headed over to the sink. "Yeah. Let me get washed up. Hard to know when to stop." Roxanne's eyes followed Tom's back. As soon as he finished and returned from the sink, she began to smile as though someone had said the camera was on her.

"Where's Lisa?" Zack asked pointedly, putting the torch and goggles away. "Your hook is welded on," he added.

"You did it?" Tom asked, looking inside. "Damned if you didn't. Lisa's over at her parents. Arnold left early because he gets bent out of shape every time she comes back in the shop. Lisa hung around after Arnold left until she got so bored she couldn't stand it. She really likes the races. She just can't put up with getting ready for them. Kind of spoiled, I guess."

"Did you hear what Arnold told her Friday?" Cy asked.

"Shut up, Cy," Zack warned.

Cy continued undaunted, "He said he'd let her drive his race car if she could piss through a knothole at twenty paces." Cy laughed as Zack began to shake his arm. "I told him, yeah, Arnold, old buddy. We know you can hit a toilet seat at three feet—"

"Cy, for crissake," Zack interrupted, "there's a lady present. Watch your mouth now."

Roxanne walked behind them in a cloud, as if she lived in a world with no sound. Cy opened the door of the Chevy for Roxanne to sit up front. He leaned back and closed his eyes. Tom locked up the shop and got into the backseat with Zack.

"What are Lisa's folks like?" Zack asked.

"They're okay," he answered without opening his eyes. "Her old man is a little stiff, but her mother seems pretty nice. I argue a lot with her old man about golf and racing. He gives me this business about how thrilling it is to chase a little white ball through the grass, how I don't understand the tension of the sport. Finesse, he calls it. He pretty much thinks stock car racing is for a bunch of low-class boneheads."

"Hey, watch it," Cy put in. "I resemble that remark."

"Then he gets into this technology thing and European cars and how he can't see the skill in driving a four-thousand-pound lump of steel in a circle when a Ferrari right out of the showroom is faster."

"What did you say to that?" Cy asked.

"I told him I'm driving a real car, one that every man in America can drive, not just some millionaire. I said you try filling up the stands at Charlotte with millionaires and they'll get pretty lonesome up there."

"Hey, that's no foreign car Lisa's driving now," Cy put in. "That's a Chevy."

"Right. And you know who talked her into that. She wanted me to go on this rally thing with her in the 'Vette, so, I thought, okay, might be fun. I can haul ass in that car and blow her hotsy totsy friends in the weeds. So I find out you aren't allowed to do that. You drive to these checkpoints and if you get there too fast, you lose. I mean those people with money get a fast car and don't have enough sense to know what to do with it."

"What do you think of this racing business?" Zack asked Roxanne, leaning over the back of her seat. "Pretty boring, huh?" Her perfume made him want to get closer; Nadine smelled like she soaked in hers. Roxanne didn't answer for so long he thought he should tap her for her attention.

Finally she spoke. "I don't know why Daddy does it, really. All he does is spend money. He makes money fixing cars then loses it all racing them. That's what drove Mom crazy. Sometimes I think I should tell him when he spends too much, but I don't think he wants to know."

"Hey, do us a favor," Tom put in. "Don't tell him, okay?"

"I won't," she answered, almost in a whisper.

When they walked into Auntie's, all the men at the counter turned around, their eyes staying on Roxanne as she headed to a booth. She was the only woman in there besides Auntie behind the counter who had tattoos on both forearms like a man. Cy jumped in beside her in the booth, grinning at Zack and Tom as they sat on the other side.

"No beer on Sunday," Auntie called from behind the bar. "Kitchen's closed."

"How about four Cokes, then?" Zack asked.

"We start winning a few features and get the car looking good," Tom said to Roxanne, "your old man won't have to spend his own money and beg his friends to help. Some big company will pay him to have their name on the car."

"Yeah, like Greenmont Bail Bonds or Greenmont Sand and Gravel," Zack put in.

"Why'd you think of them?" Tom asked.

"I saw their names on the fence at the track."

"Probably because they paid for the wood. I don't mean some five-and-dime local outfit. I mean some big money like Lucky Strike or Sweet Peach."

"You better tell them your name is Buck Fireball Junior Pate," Cy said.

"Maybe it will be," he said, a little irritated. When Auntie set down four Cokes in the bottles, Tom told her, "I want a glass of ice."

"I ain't got no ice. Feel that bottle. It's cold enough. You lucky to get that at this hour," she replied.

Tom leaned back in his seat, his face falling into a shadow. He quit talking. After Auntie walked away, Roxanne broke her silence. "Anybody's got ice. She could have gone to her refrigerator and taken it out of the trays. She was just too lazy to do it."

"Hey, Roxanne," Cy asked. "Aren't you just a little bit glad your old man is in the racing business? Don't you think it is a little more fun than, say, if he was selling groceries or fixing shoes?"

Roxanne's chin tipped up. "No. I mean it might be more

exciting, but I don't think he has to do something exciting. I'm just glad he's not driving them anymore. I worried to death about him."

"Yeah, but if he sold cabbages you wouldn't get to be Miss Greenmont Raceway. You'd have to be Miss Produce for Less. Or Miss McMillan Street Shoe Repair. That don't sound too hot to me."

"Who told you that?" she asked, a little miffed.

"About Miss Greenmont Raceway?" Cy began to chuckle. "Allie Burcham."

"He has a big mouth. I don't care whether I'm Miss Greenmont Raceway or not. And I'm not going steady with Allie Burcham, if he told you that too."

"Aw, come on," Cy insisted. "You're not going to turn it down if they offer it, are you?"

"I might. I just might."

"Boy, look at your eyelashes, Roxanne," Cy exclaimed.

She began to rummage through her purse. "What's wrong with them?" she asked, squinting into her mirror.

"Nothing. They're about an inch long and they curl up, is all I mean," Cy answered.

She looked down, dropping the mirror back into her purse.

"Remember when you cut your eyelashes off, Tom?" Zack asked.

Tom wheezed as Zack continued. "This ugly lady our mother knows said Tom's eyelashes were so long he was the spitting image of Tyrone Power, so he went in the bathroom and cut them off."

"You cut your eyelashes off?" Roxanne exclaimed.

"Shut up, Zack," Tom grunted.

Auntie walked back to their table. She threw out four small bags of potato chips like she was dealing cards. Then she sat down a glass of ice with a clunk. Tom reached for it as if he'd expected her to do that all along, and began to pour his untouched Coke into the glass. When the cubes made a cracking sound, Roxanne winced as though she'd heard something shatter. She struggled to tear her chips open, her pink nails jabbing helplessly against the bag. Cy took them from her and, as usual, overdid it, ripping the bag open, spilling the chips on the tabletop. He tried again with his own, opening it neatly, so he gave it to her, sweeping the broken chips into a pile in front of himself.

"Hey, Pate," Cy said. "You win the Labor Day Classic and you get to kiss the queen here."

Roxanne lifted her hands to cover her flushed cheeks, but when she glanced across the table towards Tom, she saw that he was slumped in the corner of the booth, asleep.

The next morning, when she brought Tom a package of parts to his workbench, he nodded as she set it down.

"How come you don't like Roxanne?" Zack asked after she left.

A strip of metal spiraled up from the hole Tom was drilling. "I've got nothing against her," he answered, moving the drill to another spot.

"How come you don't pay any attention to her at all?"

Tom started smiling. "Sounds like somebody's got a crush on her."

"Yeah, I like her. And so does Cy. I mean, she's too pretty to ever pay any attention to me." Zack shuffled his feet. "I mean, I had a pretty girl once."

"You did it with her?"

"Yeah, back in Summit."

"Yeah, who?"

"Uh, she was a singer at the Stallion Club."

"Yeah, a singer?" Tom smiled. "I'm proud of you."

Zack looked at his feet. "About Roxanne. I mean, it just seems weird the way you treat her is all I'm saying. It may just be some kind of hard-to-get you're playing. I mean, anybody can see she's real pretty." Tom didn't respond, so he added, "Anybody can see she's more interested in you than the rest of us."

Finally Tom stopped working, appearing a little irritated with Zack's persistence, but stopping to think about what he'd said.

"Okay, okay, I'll tell you why. I don't mean any harm to Roxanne or any of the other little Roxannes in the world . . ." Zack felt a sting, because he was convinced there was no one like her on earth. "They don't want a boyfriend. They want a husband. What if I want to buy some tires for my car and she says, 'I need a new stove.' And I want to work late on my car and she says I have to come home because she's got people coming to supper. I just don't need that, Zack. And you remember I told you this. Roxannes want houses and babies and, soon as they get a man, they start bitching about how they want him spending his weekends at home and how he doesn't give them enough attention and how they want him done over to suit them. And, most of all, how they want him out of race cars."

He started drilling again. Before Zack walked away, Tom looked up and said with a smile, "Hey, Zack, remember *The Crash Helmet.*"

Zack didn't answer. He did remember the beautiful woman who was drawn to the race driver, yet begged him to give up racing as soon as they were married.

"I don't care how good-looking she is," Tom added. "She's just not worth it. Twenty years and a couple of tattoos and she'll look just like Auntie. She'll fall all over you to get you a glass of ice cubes now, and in twenty years she won't lift her butt out of a chair. Women always want to be number one. They just don't understand that the beauty contest for a race car driver is already over before they enter it."

14

Zack and Cy drove the Chevy, loaded with groceries, camping gear and Horace in the back, into the parking lot at Ned's where Arnold and Tom waited. They were heading to the Charlotte Motor Speedway to watch the World 600. Tom and Arnold were prepared for the showdown between their respective heroes: Freddie Lorenzen and Fireball Roberts.

"Who's that?" Arnold asked Cy, looking into the backseat.

"Oh, that's Pop. Horace is his name. Pop, this here's Tom and Arnold." Instead of speaking, Horace wiped his nose on his sleeve. Zack got into the back beside the old man. Horace, who had more skin than he had insides to fill it up, slumped forward like a sawdust-filled teddy bear that had lost half its stuffing. When he smoked, he squinted at his cigarette as though he was mad at it for making his eyes water. The boys rolled down all the windows, because Horace didn't smell fresh as a daisy, either.

After they got under way, they began playing riding games to pass the time. Cy dreamed up a story for a wrecked car they saw with a number painted on its side, rusting in the bushes off Highway 29: "It happened coming off the third turn in the 400," he began. "Tiny Lund tried to put a wheel under me, so I leaned on him just a little and shit, he lost it. Took out five cars. He come up after the race—which I won, by the way—had half a pop bottle in his hand, and I said, 'Tiny, did you bust your Coke? Want me to loan you a nickel for another one? I can spare it since I won.' So Tiny says, 'I'm gonna bust your ass, Boney Baloney,' so I told him if he had any problems, that my good buddy Arnold over there took care of my light work."

"That's probably exactly what you would do, you asshole," Arnold replied. "Get my ass broken instead of your own."

"Hey, look at that one," Cy exclaimed.

They caught up to a mud-covered car on a trailer.

"That's just some piece of shit they raced down in Cowpens last night," Arnold said as they passed the truck and trailer. "They don't run shit like that at Charlotte." The driver glared at them as if he had heard what Arnold had said.

"It doesn't look any worse than what we run in Greenmont," Tom put in.

"Yeah, you're right," Arnold had to agree. "You just get used to them is all. Guy puts a new coat of paint on something and everybody notices it. After you see this race, I kid you not, you won't even want to go to work on Monday. That 'thirty-three you think is going to be so hot will look like it ought to go in the garbage pile."

"Lorenzen drove junkers, right up until he got his break," Tom replied. "He didn't even have enough money to buy a hot dog the first time he came to Darlington, and the next year he won."

"Yeah, he didn't work his way up like Fireball," Arnold argued. "He'll be one of them fly-by-nighters, you just wait and see. He ain't paid his dues. He's a goddamn Yankee come down here after our prize money and our women. Thinks he's hot shit getting something going with Linda Vaughn. You ever heard him talk? Makes you want to smack him just hearing that fast-talking Yankee mouth."

Horace finally came to life. "Junior Johnson can put all their asses in the grasses. Mind my words, Junior'll blow up or win today, one or t'other."

Everyone got quiet. They'd thought he was asleep.

"Ford figures they got their motor problem fixed," Horace added, then belched loudly.

"How come you know so much?" Arnold asked.

"They're cross-bolting the main bearings to keep the blocks from cracking," Horace said and belched again.

Arnold was truly amazed. Cy looked at him, grinning.

"Fireball'll be the first to tell you," Horace went on, "money talks, bullshit walks. He's as big a whore as the rest of them. Ford shows him big money and he kisses GM good-bye. All them fools went out and bought a Pontiac 'cause Fireball drives a Pontiac. Look how long Fireball keeps driving that Pontiac when Ford greases his palm a little slicker. You win a race with a turd in your pocket, next race every driver there has a turd in his pocket."

While they were waiting for the next words of wisdom to come from Horace, they heard a snarling sound. Horace was snoring, one side of him so bored with the other side that it fell asleep.

"Tune in tomorrow," Cy laughed. "That's how he goes 'bout half the time, nods in and out. He don't sleep like a normal person all at once at night. Unless he passes out. He don't think you oughta waste a big hunk of every day asleep."

"Our old man was just the opposite, wasn't he, Zack? Never let the chickens get to sleep before he did." That was the first time Tom had mentioned their daddy since Zack found him. "I suppose he's still that way," Zack said lamely.

"Your old man still alive?" Arnold asked.

"Yeah, far as we know," Zack answered. His answer made him feel uneasy. He had a quick image in his mind of his tractor rolling down the hill behind the barn, a burning ball that hit the pond and sizzled like a hot coal.

"It's Saturday so he'll be tooling around on his tractor today. Tomorrow Mama'll be chewing him out for chasing the hogs back in the pen in his Sunday pants and getting mud on the cuffs, right, Zack?"

"Naw, Tom. He'll be sitting in the living room by the radio listening to the World 600 like he always did," Zack joked.

"Right, sure," Tom replied bitterly. "Why don't you pass that goddamn truck, Cy," he snapped, "or you just like riding his ass?"

"I'm drafting, man. Saving gas."

"Drafting," Horace sputtered to life again. "Tiny Lund won the Daytona 500 'cause he was smart enough to figure out drafting."

"Yeah, Pate," Arnold picked up on Horace's remark, "Jarrett and your buddy Lorenzen had to go in for gas, but Tiny was letting them suck him around with his pedal halfway to the floor."

"He damn near blew it and you know it," Tom put in. "Lorenzen was catching him. Tiny just got lucky when his engine caught on the fumes. He was out of gas."

"But who crossed the finish line first? Tiny did, that's who." Arnold put in, "I don't care if he rolled across two miles an hour backwards, if he got there first, he won it. Right, Horace?"

Horace grunted.

"Just lucky," Tom said.

"Smart," Arnold put in.

"Lucky," Tom repeated. "Could have screwed up big time trying to make it."

"So what would you have done, hot shot? Come in for gas and let Jarrett and Lorenzen beat you for sure?"

Tom was quiet a moment. "I'm not sure what I'd have done. Maybe took the chance, maybe not."

Horace reached over the front seat and pushed Tom's shoulder. "You think drivers on the big teams make them decisions? You do as you're told, big boy. Wood Brothers figured all that out for Tiny."

"He's right," Arnold put in. "You watch them guys work. Bust your ass on the race track and they get you three times as much in the pits. In the big time, a good crew wins as many races as the driver."

"Yeah, maybe that's the reason I'm not winning any races," Tom said.

"You ever been to a race here, Horace?" Zack asked.

"'Forty-nine. The year they opened. First new car race. Busted up a bunch of nice cars. Tried to borrow me a car to race. Lee Petty borrowed a guy's car, didn't tell him what he was up to, and turned it over. Nobody knew what the hell was going on. I didn't care much. I was drunk, I reckon."

Horace chuckled and soon was snoring again.

"What does your old man do?" Arnold asked. "He knows his shit."

"Eat, sleep, drink, and talk," Cy laughed. "Ma says he's useless as lace toilet paper."

"What's he live on?"

"He lives with me. Him and Ma don't get enough to get by. He was in the war and messed up his knee. Got drunk and fell out of an airplane he was making. He gets out of bed and takes a bath the day his government check comes."

"Guess he hasn't gotten a check lately," Arnold remarked and stuck his nose out the window, but Cy didn't seem to catch on. "How come you let him come to the race with us?" Arnold asked.

Cy was a little slow with his answer. "Because he wanted to come real bad, I guess. He don't get to go many places. He loves racing," he said apologetically. "He was near 'bout a race driver himself. Had a car all ready to run down at Daytona Beach in 'thirty-six. His partner run off with a girl and took their racing money." He looked over his shoulder at the slumped teddy bear body sleeping like a toy beside a kid's bed. "He won't cause no trouble."

"I got in this big argument about Lorenzen with Lisa's old

man, Harry's his name," Tom told them. "Harry thinks because he's rich, he knows everything about everything. He's telling me how Freddie Lorenzen, who I told him was the best thing going, would never be able to cut it in sports cars. Sophisticated cars, he calls them. Then old Harry stepped on his dick: 'Freddie Lorenzen couldn't make the field at Le Mans,' he tells me, sucking on this stupid pipe."

"Lorenzen and Fireball would blow those Le Mans pussies in the weeds," Arnold said.

"Here's what I told him," Tom went on. "'Ford begged Lorenzen to go to Le Mans, Harry'—he hates it when I call him by his first name—'and Lorenzen turned them down.' And old Harry says, 'I find that hard to believe.' 'Why's that?' I say. 'Le Mans pays five thousand to win after you drive for twenty-four hours and you have to share it with your co-driver. Lorenzen's not going to race for peanuts.' You should have seen old Harry's face. So he shoveled in a little deeper: 'There is more to racing than mere money. There are sportsmen,' he tells me, and I say, 'And I thought you were a businessman, Harry. Me, I'm a businessman. Cars are my living. If I wanted to be a sportsman, I'd get me a shotgun and a fishing pole. And your sporty cars are just playthings.'"

"Did you tell him you made thirty-two dollars at Tidewater?" Cy laughed. "Boy, twenty-four hours is a long time to drive."

"They have co-drivers, Cy. They change drivers when they make pit stops."

"So he can run take a pee and get a hot dog, huh? That makes sense. We'd have to get a couple of days off work just to watch that Le Mans. What's it near?"

"England, you dumbshit," Arnold snorted.

"France," Tom said.

The traffic began to slow so they knew they were getting close to the track. They needed to get into the infield, where they were going to spend the night. A spectator in a pickup had tried to go through the tunnel and got stuck because of a stand he had built into his truck bed. They had to wait while the man knocked the stand apart and freed his truck. After they finally got inside, they parked and looked out across the speedway. It was all Tom could do to keep his balance when he saw how big it was, that black banking too steep for a man to climb. He had to admit Arnold was right; a superspeedway was awesome.

"That goddamn Allie is up there," Arnold pointed. "Cost them nine bucks apiece for seats and they're staying in a hotel to boot."

"Yeah," Tom answered, "he thinks he's hot stuff with that new rig and look at what these guys got. The worst guy here has a better setup than he does."

"Guess how much they can win, Tom?" Zack asked. "I saw it in the paper. Twenty-seven thousand, eight hundred and thirty dollars."

Tom leaned back against a post when he said that.

They unloaded the trunk, and struggled to put up the army surplus tent. Horace crawled back into the car to sleep.

A man played a piano in the back of a pickup as long as a beer was kept beside him on the bale of straw he used for a seat. People danced barefoot, and scolded like old maid schoolteachers anybody who let his bottle break. When the first fights broke out, everyone moved over to watch, but they soon got to be old hat.

After dark Tom and Zack looked out from under the tent flap and saw a woman dancing nude in the moonlight, her white breasts slapping against her naked chest. Her feet were brown, moving up and down around the broken brown glass. Horace saw the dancing woman and said loudly: "Boobs like two baseballs in a pair of socks." Cy giggled at Horace before they settled to sleep in the car.

Towards morning when the sky was starting to turn gray, the piano finally fell silent. The piano player slept underneath the keyboard, surrounded by beer bottles, with his back arched over the pedals.

A couple in a black '58 Ford pulled up beside their Chevy, the number 28—Lorenzen's number—on both doors in shoe polish. The woman wore a black shirt with FEARLESS FREDDIE lettered on it with the same shoe polish, the LESS blurring with the sweat in her cleavage. Her mate had a picture of Lorenzen's Ford taped to the brim of his cap, spread out in front of the embroidered names HOLMAN AND MOODY.

The man and woman got out of their car and he climbed to the roof. The Ford groaned under their weight as the man tugged the woman up beside him. Together they stretched their necks to see Freddie in the garage area. While Tom and Zack folded up the tent, skydivers began to drop into the track, trailing colored smoke and aiming for a white X on the apron. Each time an engine started in the garages, Tom turned his head like a dog hearing a whistle. Zack imagined his brother could climb over the fence and push a regular driver aside.

"I think I see Junior. Is that Junior?" Tom asked. "Over there by the white Chevy with his arm resting on the roof?"

"That's him," Arnold replied. "The one who looks like he swallowed a watermelon." Junior Johnson's stomach was round and high, a solid-looking structure unlike the apron of fat that rolled over Arnold's belt when he sat down, hiking his T-shirt up in the back.

Before the race started they had for sure picked out Lorenzen, Fireball, and Ned Jarrett in the crowd in the pit area. Arnold said he saw Tiny Lund, the Wood brothers—Glen and Leonard—and Marvin Panch. "And over yonder by that Mercury is Joe Weatherly."

"Naw, ain't him," Horace stated flatly. "Ain't Weatherly."

Arnold looked down at the little man beside him who wobbled beside the fence and squinted across the neck of his liquor bottle like it was a gun sight. "What makes you so sure it ain't? I bet you can't see past your belly button."

"Little Joe's a deal shorter and wears two-toned shoes."

"That's for sure Linda Vaughn," Cy broke in. All of them sighted the unmistakable tall blond with the giant chest. "She looks like Daisy Mae, don't she, Pop?" Cy exclaimed. "And I thought that funny-paper guy you read me just dreamed her up."

"Al Capp," Horace grunted and looked at the ground.

"He reads you the funnies?" Zack asked.

"Every Sunday. And the pinkies on Saturday."

The woman in the Lorenzen shirt squealed, claiming to have sighted her hero. She fell back onto the roof as the man laughed, spit, and said, "You don't know Freddie from Fireball's house cat, woman." He whistled, then spit a long brown thread of tobacco that hung in the air a moment like a stick.

She struggled back to her feet, flailing at him.

"I know Freddie. I know Freddie from a mile off. He has the sweetest little ass." He pushed her and she dropped onto the roof again, the metal snapping under her weight. The roof didn't pop back out as she struggled to her feet. "I think he might be Jesus," she sputtered. "Jesus was a carpenter, too, you know?"

"He's a goddamn race car driver, woman," the man replied.

"Those two are disgusting," Arnold said. "Oughta be ashamed to be Southerners showing theirselves like that."

The showdown of the race was touted to be between Ford and Chrysler, but Junior had put his Chevy on the pole at 141 miles an hour. When the field came around for the green flag, Tom watched Lorenzen, and Arnold watched Fireball. After the skydivers had gathered up their chutes, Horace crawled out of the car where he slept and said, "My money's on Junior."

Junior didn't disappoint Horace, jumping into the lead when the flag waved, with Lorenzen taking up the chase in second. When Fireball fell back, Arnold began to grumble about his engine being flat. "Poor old Fireball just ain't got Arnold doing his motors," Cy teased.

Halfway through the race, Arnold decided to park the car over near the tunnel so they could beat the traffic out. "People start wrecking left and right leaving these big races," Arnold related. "They all start thinking they're racers. Some rich jerk in a pink Caddy passed a whole line of cars leaving Rockingham right over a damn hill. Took his head off under a semi."

"Fireball is breaking old Arnold's heart," Cy said as he left. "He can't even stand to look anymore."

"I heard you," Arnold shouted back. "Fireball's gonna get him next year. His team let him down today."

Lorenzen chased Junior the whole race, but Junior seemed unstoppable.

Tom told Zack, "I know what he feels like. Seeing the back of that car the whole damn race and not being able to catch it."

The race continued to run at a furious pace. It wasn't until the first of only two cautions that the loudspeaker could be heard, the same voices they listened to every weekend in the shop.

"Listen to that jerk talking on the speaker," Arnold complained. "He's the same SOB on the radio who don't never tell you what's going on."

In the closing laps, Lorenzen's two fans jumped up and down like two hogs on a trampoline, waving at his Ford each time it passed. The roof of their car collapsed, resting on the top of the seat inside. Freddie stayed close, but he couldn't catch Junior.

Then, three laps from the end, the woman shrieked, hanging over the windshield of her wrecked car like she was climbing out of a hole.

"Junior blew a tire. Junior blew a goddamn tire," she hollered. Everyone had seen it at the same time, but she kept repeating it like a stuck record. As Junior dove into the pits, his left rear tire shredded, Freddie blasted past. Junior's crew changed the wheel and sent him back out—on the same lap, but hopelessly behind.

"Two laps, two laps, two laps," the woman kept shouting until, "Last lap, last lap. Oh no-o-o. Oh no, oh no, Freddie, oh no."

Again they all saw it, but she kept shouting. Freddie had slowed. His engine was sputtering, barely moving, and Junior was charging around like a lion after a wounded rabbit. Lorenzen was out of gas. The woman jumped off her car and ran against the fence, shaking it in her hands. "I'll push you, Freddie," she screamed.

The '49 Chevy purred to life, taking a short hop forward into the fence when Horace got second instead of reverse, then a longer hop backwards as he found the right gear. He sent an oily blue Dynaflow rocking in place as he knocked the front bumper. Right then nobody was noticing any metal-to-metal except on the race track.

Horace grabbed the clothes left on the seat and stuffed them behind his back so he could reach the pedals better. That damn Cy was a stringbean. It had been a long time since Horace had been at the wheel and felt the crunch of gravel beneath his tires. Give three hundred for this old Chevy, but it was a good one, one owner, kept inside at night. That damn Cy was a sight taller than he was, wonder how come? Pop.

There went a beer bottle, saying his name. He swerved and got another one. Pop goes the weasel. No problem; never seen a tire punctured by glass in his life. He hadn't lost the old touch. Could wipe the snot off that kid's nose over by the gate if he was of a mind to.

The best time to get out. Beat the crowd. Not a person in that place was looking at him, their eyes glued to the race track. Junior was stomping them, what'd I say? He turned on the radio and there was the race. He pulled onto 29, waved at the motorcycle cops sitting over by the fence chewing the fat. Have to get off their asses and get to work soon enough. Cops go around with their heads up their asses, sitting out here, missing the race. Hey, this was the life; no crowds to fight, hearing every last thing that was going on on the track, humming down the road in his Chevy at the same time. It had been too damn long. Now up through the gears just as smooth as silk, one, two, three. Cy fixed her all right. Son of a bitch stuck in neutral on him more than a time or two. Kid's one hell of a mechanic.

Goddammit. Goddammit to hell. Junior lost a tire. Son of a bitch. Don't that beat all? Could hear that crowd moaning clean out on the open highway. Damn that Junior. He'll win or bust, what'd I say?

Whoops. This little baby will slip right on up on you. Sixty-five miles an hour and more where that's coming from. That kid of mine has got a hell of a knack with cars. Never saw the day it ran like this when it come out of Detroit, no sirree. Got the personal touch; not some dumb Polack turning nuts. Needs him some new tires. I ought to buy the boy a set of new tires for getting it to run so good. I'm going to remember that my next check.

Come on, Junior. Pedal to the metal. Go. Go. Go. It ain't over yet. You can catch that Yankee SOB. Put his Chicago ass in the wall.

Now what's all that? What's all that blue light flashing?

Now, hold your horses till I get her slowed up. Running me off. Quit it, son of a bitch. I'm trying to get her stopped. This is one fast car, cops, so hold your goddamn horses, oh my God. I'm off now. Slicker than two eels fucking in a bucket of snot. Can't get her stopped. Gimme a hand, Junior. Got no fingers to hang on that frigging wheel. Bitch of a woman left me out in the snow. Goddamn, Junior, I'm a flying motherfucker.

Junior pressed the throttle to the floorboard, but Freddie coasted across the line to take the checkered before he could catch him. The woman sobbed and clutched her husband, who pulled her off the fence. Her face was blood red.

"Somebody ought to take that disgusting bitch out back and shoot her," Arnold snorted.

Tom grabbed Zack then Cy by the shoulders and shook them. "I'm telling you," he said, "this is the last time I'm coming here on this side of the fence!"

Cy laughed. "Hey, Pop. You were right. It was win or bust for Junior. He busted." Cy turned around. "Pop? Where are you?"

"Where the hell is he?" Arnold asked, irritated, sunburned, still mad about Fireball's engine.

If Horace had been trying to get back to them, he would have been like a salmon swimming upstream as the crowd rushed for the exit, but his bent old body would have been no match for this mob.

They looked everywhere for him, in all of the restrooms, behind the concession stand, crossing the same areas over and over, running into each other. The crowd started to thin out.

"Maybe he's waiting at the car," Cy offered.

"Well, if he isn't, we're leaving him," Arnold grumbled. "We've got a hell of a drive and gotta get up early tomorrow. You've got the keys, right?"

"Who's got the keys?" Tom asked.

"I gave them back to Cy," Arnold answered.

"Naw, Pop's got them," Cy replied.

"Jesus H. Christ," Arnold mumbled. Tom just shook his head.

"That's where he is," Cy said brightly. "I forgot. I gave him the keys so he could go take a nap."

Soon they were staring at the empty spot where the car had been. "Maybe things look different now that most of the cars are gone," Cy offered lamely.

"I know where I left the goddamn car!" Arnold shouted. "I left it right here," he pointed at his feet. Arnold's face became a deep red and his nose puckered like a strawberry. Before Tom or Zack could stop him, he grabbed Cy and, with one blow to the face, Cy was on his back, his nose and mouth spouting blood.

"I heard that Lorenzen had to sleep in his car before he made the big time," Cy commented later into a chorus of grunts, "but I bet he never got to ride home in a pig truck."

It was dawn before the Piedmont Porkers truck that picked up the four of them pulled into Greenmont. From there, they took city buses home in their different directions. Their clothes were so saturated with the smell of the cargo they'd shared their ride with that the passengers near them moved to other seats.

Cy walked from Main down McGee Alley towards his house, hoping the Chevy would come into view parked in front. It wasn't there.

"You can just turn right around and go back and get him!" his mother shouted from the porch, still in her bathrobe.

"He left us, Ma."

"Maybe it'll be a blessing to all of us when he leaves us. Right now his behind is in the Cabarrus County jail."

"Where's my car?" Cy asked.

"Your car is in the pond where your father parked it."

Cy dropped to the steps and wrapped an arm around Charlie's sunsoaked feathers. "Damn, Charlie," he said as the rooster pecked the dried blood on his hand from his bloody nose. "I sure hate to admit that Arnold was right. He said you go to a race and on the way home, every Tom, Dick, and Horace starts thinking he's a race car driver."

Tom won his bet with Arnold that Lorenzen would win twice as many races as Fireball when Lorenzen won six Grand Nationals that year. Freddie's picture sat in the lid of Tom's tool box in front of the nude woman on the Ajax tool calendar. Lorenzen's goggles hung around his neck, his dirty face like a raccoon in reverse, his arm around racing's golden girl, the long-legged, huge-chested Linda Vaughn, who rode around the big tracks astride a giant red Firebird, her body swelling in her red suit like a ripe tomato.

Tom's picture of Lorenzen wasn't like Rachel with her movie magazines. That picture of Lorenzen was real, the races he won, the cars he drove, the money he made. And all of the guys in Ned's All-American Automotive believed they were a part of that same picture.

It was a long time before Tom remembered what Ned had told him about becoming a race car driver: "You'll never be satisfied. It's part of the deal. You get satisfied, you're finished. Or one day you get old. Satisfied or old or both. Or dead."

By the time Tom remembered what Ned had said, Fireball Roberts was dead and it was too late to recognize that teaching and learning don't necessarily happen at the same time.

15

Aurora ran down the path because she heard a strange noise, a moaning. She imagined the girl with a heart-shaped face and violet eyes in the picture show she'd gone to with Annie, trapped under a fallen tree, trying to reach a drop of water that hung from a leaf. But instead she saw the tenant woman, Aunt Tillie, rocking in her porch chair, her arms clamped around her bosom big as a bed pillow.

While Aurora peeked from behind the smokehouse, the woman rocked in silence. Suddenly the noise swelled from her again, scattering the chickens around the porch. They soon resumed pecking and scratching, but Aurora couldn't forget the sound. Up close she could tell that the moaning didn't come from pain here on earth; Aunt Tillie had left her chair and was hurting somewhere far away.

The third time she moaned, Aurora ran to tell Gladys Pate. Aurora's own mother had taught her that things came and went in patterns of three; the third night that Tom didn't come home and she felt the baby move inside her three times, she knew he was gone for good. She and her baby had come to Summit three years and three months after Tom left.

After Aurora described what she had heard, Gladys moved automatically, as if a key in her back had been wound up tight. She went into the pantry, took an old pan and poured in part of the stew she was cooking, covering it with a lid. Then she opened the refrigerator, removed a plate of cold biscuits and dumped them into a paper sack. She placed a slab of butter on wax paper and rolled it up.

"Come with me," Gladys said. "We're going down there." She handed the sack of biscuits and the butter to Aurora.

"Aurora, her baby has died." To Aurora, Aunt Tillie looked like an old woman, too old to have had a baby just four years ago.

They walked down the path, Gladys Pate ahead, with the stew sloshing in the pot. Aunt Tillie still sat on the porch. A howl stopped in her throat as though someone had turned off a button. She stood up to greet the women, opening the door to the house. Gladys took the stew to the kitchen, setting it on the stove. Tillie lifted the pot lid and said, "You real kind to me, Mrs. Pate, I declare. There's lots of big chunks of meat in that stew."

"I was fixing it for dinner, Tillie. We had plenty."

Then they were silent, Tillie looking at Gladys as if Aurora wasn't there. "I b'lieved God done sent him to me," Tillie said, "to take care of me in my old age." As she talked, her voice reached a higher pitch until she sounded like a little girl. "I declare I b'lieved I done gone through the change and along he come."

"God giveth and God taketh away," Gladys replied then reached over and took Tillie's hand like a preacher. Tillie bowed her head and began sniffing.

"Amen. Amen. You's a good woman, Mrs. Pate. A good, good woman."

They walked into the living room, Gladys still holding Tillie's hand. Aurora didn't see where a baby would ride, under that fluff of a body. Her own boy Tommy rode under her black-and-white uniform even after the truckers began to laugh at her shape, her white apron standing straight out like a tray she carried in front of herself.

Aurora had seen the little colored boy, running through the fields behind the older children, riding the mule when it pulled the wagon. He would chase Tommy, grabbing at his heels like a little dog, but Tommy ran and hid under the bushes. Aurora saw the little colored boy shove the drinking water off the wagon and laugh. An older girl said, "Tigger, you spoilt rotten," but no one spanked him.

Gladys and Aunt Tillie walked over near the window. A cradle was up on the table. Aurora rubbed the chills from her arms; she had walked right by Tigger's dead body. Aurora didn't understand grown women at all right then.

"So, so little," Gladys whispered. "Such a shame. He was sick?"

"Yessum. 'Fore he took sick, he'd outgrowed that rocking box. He got droopy. It being the summertime, I reckoned it was just the heat, you know, and set him in the shade. But when I felt 'neath his clothes, he was hot as a firecracker. 'Fore we knowed it his little bowels was water, just pure water. Every scrap we got in him, he turnt to water till he won't big as a minute."

"Did the doctor come, Tillie?"

"Yessum. Colitis. He said was colitis and give me some pink stuff in a jar, but it didn't do a whit of good. He went to sleep yest'dy and never waked up." She began to sob and started to rock the cradle. The little boy shifted, stiff as a log. "Mallard be doing him a box, soon's he gets in tonight." Gladys didn't say anything else so Aunt Tillie went on, "I fanned him till my arm was sore. Wiped off his sweat. He burnt up with fever. But he was sleeping peaceful. 'Cept his little face don't look peaceful to me, do it to you, Mrs. Pate? He spit up that pink stuff." She reached in and wiped his face with the corner of her apron.

"He's peaceful, Tillie. Don't blame yourself. You did all you could. It isn't for us to question the Lord's will." Gladys paused and looked out the window towards the path. "My very own mama lost three babies to colitis."

Tillie's eyes grew wide as a child's. "Do tell? Do tell, I declare. I declare I didn't know that white babies took it too." Then Tillie shook her head. "'Scuse me, Mrs. Pate. I don't know what I'm saying. I be all right 'fore long. Just a shock, that's all. He was so full of life to go so fast."

Gladys let go of Tillie's hand and patted her on the back. "Now, don't you hesitate to give us a call if you need anything. Hershel can build you the box if Mallard doesn't have time. And I have some nice soft cloth to put inside. My cape jessamine has oodles of blooms this year. We'll make Tigger a pretty bouquet."

Tillie nodded and bowed her head. Before they left, Aurora stole a look at the dead child that lay in the cradle, no more real-looking than a wooden doll with half shut eyes. There was a smell she didn't recognize, but she wasn't sure what death smelled like. It was the first dead person she'd ever seen. Her mother hadn't believed in having her held up to kiss her dead grandmother, for which she was thankful because she'd hated to kiss her alive.

They left the house with Gladys holding Aurora's shoulders so tight with her arm that the girl stepped on the side of the older woman's foot. Before they were up the path, the moaning began again.

"Aurora, did you happen to notice that old stove in her kitchen?"

"No, Ma'am," Aurora replied. The only stick of furniture that came to her mind was the cradle with the white rabbits on the side.

"I know we stored it in the smokehouse. It belonged to Hershel's sister B.B. He must have given it to them without telling me."

When they got back to the house, Aurora ran into the room where Tom's son slept. He lay on his side, his body moving up and down with his breath. He was fat and soft. She stooped to look at his shut eyes, the only part of him that had ever been sick.

To heal eyes, her mother taught her, you needed stones

from the sea. She'd walked to the Yellow River for stones, squirted her milk into his eyes and rested a stone on each lid while he slept. When his eyes finally stayed open, black and clear, she believed they had seen that Tom was gone for good.

Hershel stopped his tractor outside the back door, leaving the motor running while he climbed up the back steps with a fresh watermelon, still warm from the field. Aurora took it from his arms as gently as she would a baby.

"Don't know if there's room in the icebox to chill it," Gladys said as she dropped to her knees and began to re-arrange the contents of the refrigerator. "Wash the dirt off of it, Aurora, before I put it in here. You should have done that in the rain barrel before you brought it inside, Hershel."

He reached over her head and took the ice tea jar and drank straight from the container.

"Hershel, I wish you would use a glass. There's people who don't like to drink after other people."

"Yeah, and are any of them living here?" he smiled at Aurora who wiped the dripping melon with her skirt. "You're starting to sound like your daughter Rachel. If I didn't know better, I'd think she had a raccoon for a daddy."

Suddenly a loud noise from outside filled the kitchen, the rattling and crash of metal to the ground.

Gladys sprang to her feet. "Good Lord, Hershel! What was that? Where is the baby? Aurora, where is the baby?"

Aurora looked from side to side, the melon rolling across her knees and onto Gladys' feet, sending the taller woman wobbling like a bowling pin. Hershel was the first outside. He stopped at the top of the steps, and Gladys shoved him out of her way.

"Calm down, woman. Calm down. It was just my mower blade hitting ground like I thought it was."

Aurora ran to the tractor, snatching Tommy from the seat and pounding his rear end twice before she set him on the ground. He cried and ran to Hershel, wrapping his arms around his legs.

"He whip you good now," she screamed after her child.

"My fault, my fault," Hershel replied as he bent to pick up Tommy. "I let him use the hydraulics the other day when he was riding with me." Tommy grabbed the shoulder of Hershel's shirt in both fists. "Just a little fellow telling you he wants to be a farmer, right, Tommy? Farmer like your old grandpa?"

"Drive tractor, fast. Bang, bang." Tommy twisted Hershel's shirt like a steering wheel.

Hershel grunted, then set Tommy down, walking to his tractor without another word.

That night at supper, the family ate some of the same stew they had carried to Aunt Tillie.

"I wish I'd have known there was going to be another baby in this house or I would never have given up that pretty little cradle. Annie slept in it last. Great Uncle Willie made it, but B.B. was barren so he gave it to me for Tom. I bet you would have just loved that cradle, Aurora."

"Tommy's too big for a cradle, Mama," Rachel said.

"I know, dear. But it was such a pretty cradle."

Annie finished her meal and lifted Tommy from his high chair to the floor. While she played pattycake with him, Aurora said to Gladys, "Someone better stay awake to keep the cat from eating the body."

"It's not our concern, dear," Gladys replied. "We'll see to it there's a burying before Saturday. Rachel, if it slips my mind, will you cut a dozen or so of the cape jessamines and take them down? There's a big can under the sink. I put the cloth out on the divan."

Rachel nodded. "It's gardenia, Mama. Cape jessamine sounds kind of country, don't you think?"

"Would you ladies like to tell me what's going on?" Hershel

asked. "Talking gibberish. What's all this cape jessamine and cat and baby talk and who's getting buried?"

"Tillie's newest child died yesterday. Colitis."

Hershel snorted and kept eating.

"They haven't buried it yet. They shouldn't let it wait much longer."

"If you don't mind, Gladys, I'm eating."

"Excuse me," she said, acknowledging her mistake.

Vernon said, "I thought I heard some howling."

"Howling like a wolf," Rachel said. Rachel often heard things that no one else heard: death bells, owls in the night, roosters crowing, even peeps coming from hen eggs. Her mother said it came from her good ear for music.

Hershel said, "Mallard worked all day right beside me and didn't make mention of it. Don't that beat all?"

"What is that?" Gladys asked.

"Man's boy dies and it ain't even worth a mention."

Then Gladys nodded and said, "I guess anybody with that many children doesn't feel that bad about losing one of them."

Aurora looked at Gladys, but there was nothing in her face to tell her any more than her words just said.

Hershel nodded. "One less mouth to feed," he said, and kept eating, lifting his cup for more coffee, which his wife poured.

When they were clearing the dishes, Gladys noticed that Aurora was crying. She put her arm around the girl's shoulders.

"You have a strong, healthy baby, dear," she said. "He's past the danger age."

Aurora nodded, wiping the tears from her cheeks. "Yes, he is strong like his daddy."

Gladys gave her shoulder a quick squeeze and released her; she felt almost as though she'd been struck. Fear shot through Aurora; she had said the wrong thing.

"I think it best not to make mention of the baby's father," Gladys said flatly.

The next day, Aurora saw Mallard carry out the cradle. From where she was, she couldn't see if the little boy was wrapped in the satin pillowslip Rachel had told her to take to Aunt Tillie. Rachel bought the case after she read it made your hair hold curls, but quit using it because it made her sweat.

The rabbits painted on the cradle looked like white spots. The wind was blowing so she couldn't hear if any of the children who stood around Aunt Tillie were crying; Aunt Tillie was not howling now. Mallard lowered the cradle into the ground beside a tall mound of red clay. He stood and looked into the hole.

Aurora closed her eyes tightly and saw Tom on his back asleep, still as death. She shrank him to the size of a doll until he fit inside the cradle, wrapped in the pillowslip. He lay in the hole in the red clay, stones on his shut eyes. She heard Mallard throw in the dirt with the shovel he'd borrowed earlier that day. The white flowers would stay on the mound until the petals turned brown and fell off to get lost in the fall leaves.

16

Tom was in the office sharpening his pencil when he saw the picture on the front page of Ned's newspaper: a man on fire. Allie Burcham had shown him photos of a driver with his back on fire, rolling out of his car at Hickory. But this man was burning all over. When he read the caption, "Monk sets self afire in Vietnam," it was the first time Tom had heard of a country called Vietnam. He had heard the guys gathered in the shop talking about American soldiers marching through the rice paddies.

"Do you think this is the way the big war got started," Zack had asked Cy, "the one your daddy and my uncle were in?"

"Don't know. Somebody got pissed off at somebody and started shooting, I guess."

"You think we're going to end up soldiers?"

"I got a cousin who's a soldier. He signed up hisself. Likes to shoot; he's a champion clay pigeon shooter. That's nothing I wanna do, be a soldier. Drive some damn jeep or get blowed up in a tank. I'd fly a airplane, though."

"My Uncle Vernon's got a bum leg from being a soldier. He figures he got a case of the runs for the rest of his life because he peeled an apple with a knife he took out of a dead man over there. He should have washed the germs off before he used it."

"Was the knife sticking in the dead guy?"

"Don't know."

"Hey, Zack."

Zack walked over to his brother. "Yeah?"

"When are you going to quit sounding like Rachel and Mama?"

"About what?"

"Germs."

"Don't you think there's germs on things? Wouldn't you have washed it off or something?"

"I wouldn't have been there in the first place," Tom answered.

"You'd have been there if the army says you have to be there," Arnold had called from his workbench. "You don't fuck with the army and the U.S. government. You think all you do is go up and say, 'Excuse me, I don't have time to be a soldier'? That's bullshit. They don't care what you're right in the middle of doing. They point at you and you're in the army now."

"Look at that guy burning." Tom showed the newspaper to Richard, the young Negro who part-chased and cleaned up the shop. When Richard saw no one else was listening, he looked over Tom's shoulder, then shook his head. "Who done that to him?" He bent his tall frame over to squint at the print.

"He did it to himself. I think that's the worst way a person can come up with to die."

Richard shivered and straightened up, saying, "Man's crazy," and began to clean out Ned's ashtray. "Going to hell for that," he mumbled.

"Looks like he's already in hell to me."

"Nawp. He ain't seen real hell yet. My mama told me about a woman who threw herself in the river one winter, so she could go see her Jesus. Mama say she mighta set out to die in that cold water, but soon as she choked on the first swallow, God sent her straight to the fires of hell. God done told her the way to see Jesus. And that wont it."

"How's that, Richard? She didn't kill anybody else."

"Because her life ain't hers to do with as she pleases, Mr. Tom. It's God's. He's just letting her use it for a little bit. Same as mine and yours. Ain't ours. It's His'n."

"That's not what I believe, Richard. My life is mine to do with as I please. I could set myself on fire if I wanted to."

"Um-hm." Richard shook his head and walked out with the basket. "You ain't been paying attention to the Lord."

Tom took the paper into the shop. "Look at this guy burning himself up. On purpose. Listen to this." He read aloud to the crew: "Buddha, who was like Christ to the Orientals, was twenty-nine before he saw the real world outside his rich father's house. In the real world he saw a dead man, a sick man, an old man, and a monk who was begging. He decided to be like the begging monk."

"He didn't get a hell of a lot of good choices, did he?" Cy reasoned. "He didn't see no race car drivers or airplane pilots or nothing? Old, sick, and dead. Yeah, I'd probably pick the one he picked. I'd say, okay, I'll be a monk, then I'd slip out the back door when the Pope wasn't looking."

"Here's what he did," Tom went on, "he protested about having too much money and too soft a life."

"Sounds like Buddha was a dumbshit to me," Arnold put in.

"Yeah," Cy added. "What's so hard about burning yourself up? Jump in gasoline and light a match. You get one try and you don't have to do it again better. How hard is that?"

"Buddha wasn't the one who got burned up. It was his disciple here, this monk."

Zack said, "The preacher at the Cedar Grove Baptist Church in Summit told us Buddhist monks were just a bunch of atheists who didn't believe in the divinity of Christ."

"Yeah," Arnold said, "just ask my girlfriend. Not believing in the divinity of Christ is about twice as bad as passing a stopped school bus, which by itself will get you sent to hell."

"Well, that guy must have believed in something pretty much," Tom said, "if he was willing to die just to get his picture on the front page of the newspaper. One time on page one and that's it for him."

Tom carried the paper back to his workbench and spread it out to read while he filed a part. Arnold's head dropped back under the hood of the car.

"Don't you think burning to death is about the worst way to die?" Cy asked Zack. "Did you see them pictures Allie had from Hickory?"

"Yeah, but I don't think there is any *good* way to die," Zack replied.

After Tom saw the burning man, he couldn't put it in words, but he started to feel there was an enemy out there. He learned that Vietnam was in Asia and about the size of North Carolina. The burning man, a Buddhist monk, was protesting the way he was treated in Vietnam. The Americans were going over to help the South keep the North from taking over. There were Communists involved. And young men were having to stop everything they had started and go over there as soldiers.

Yet in the summer of '63 when the guys at Ned's All-American Automotive saw the burning man's picture in the newspaper, Tom believed, like Buddha, the monk, and his younger brother, that he had left his father's house.

After Horace drove the Chevy into the pond outside of Concord, it had spent a week in the police lot where all the wet parts rusted and the seats mildewed. It needed weeks of work. Cy and Zack towed it home behind Ned's pickup. The Chevy looked worse than it had when they had first started work on it.

After drying out in jail for a week, Horace didn't look a sight better than the Chevy. "He's never going to touch those car keys again," Cy said. "I'll fix it so if he hot wires it, it'll fry his balls."

"How do you do that?" Zack asked.

Cy scratched his head and shrugged. "Don't know. Sounded good, though."

The Chevy ate and drank up every cent left over from their paychecks until finally they got it going again. In the meantime, Nadine and Shirley grew tired of competing with the race car for their attention and replaced them with a couple of dayshifters from Graybar. "Oughta paint that car pink," Cy said. "Ain't nothing but a giant piggy bank we pour money in."

"Yeah, except if we smash it with a hammer, all we got is a bunch of busted pieces."

Every day after work, Zack waited for the bus with Richard. Cy stood on the other corner, his bus going to the east side, and Lisa usually picked Tom up, their on-again, off-again relationship now on-again as the time grew near for Tom to race the new car.

Zack didn't know Richard's last name because when he'd asked him his name, he'd just said Richard. Colored guys he had known never said their last name, yet their first names were never nicknames: they were Richard, William, or Ronald, never Dick, Bill, or Ronnie. The white guys in the shop all called each other stupid nicknames, some that lasted only a few days: Zack was Banjo-eyes because of his glasses, Cy was Turnip Seed, Arnold was R.D. for Round Dude, and Tom became Slick. Richard was called names too, but not to his face: Spook, Spade, Shine, and Smoke, names that whistled through the space left by Arnold's missing tooth.

One day, Norma, Arnold's girlfriend, went outside to the stump where Richard sat to eat his lunch. She had her Bible in hand. Richard had his head bowed and she was looking up; it was impossible to tell if he was praying with her, ignoring her, or using prayer as a way to ignore her.

"Norma would take her goddamned Bible in a hog lot if she thought they'd pray with her," Arnold grumbled, his mouth full of hamburger. "She's out there practicing on Richard. Thinks she's going down to Africa and convert them cannibal niggers."

"You better look out, Arnold," Cy kidded. "Old Norma might make a preacher out of you. Ain't much for a mechanic to work on down in them jungles."

Since Arnold started dating Norma, he put JESUS IS THE WAY and MY REAL BOSS IS A CARPENTER stickers on his pickup. "You know, Arnold," Tom added, "I think old Jesus would have better taste than to stick bumperstickers on his camel's ass."

"Hey, Tom," Zack put in. "Remember the one you had on your Chevy about ON THE 7TH DAY, GOD CREATED THE CHEVROLET?"

"That's different," Tom replied.

"Hey, Arnold," Cy pressed on. "You hear the one about the white guy whose wife just loved little colored babies? His wife said, 'Arnold, darling, you go ask that colored race driver Randall Johnson how to make a colored baby so I can have one too.' So old Arnold goes up to Randall and he says, 'Hey, my little woman here wants her a colored baby and I just can't seem to make one. How about you tell me how.' And Randall says, 'No problem, buddy. First off, you got a dick about this long?'" Cy held his hands about a foot apart, "and poor old Arnold darling shook his head." Cy's hands moved in to about four inches and he nodded. "'Well,' Randall said, 'is it about this big around?'" Cy took both hands and made a circle out of both his thumbs and index fingers together. "And poor old Arnold shook his head." Cy made an O with one thumb and index finger and nodded. "Then Randall says, 'Arnold, buddy, I done seen what your problem is. You letting in too much light.'"

Everyone laughed, except Arnold, who threw a piece of metal at the scrap pile, making such a loud noise that Norma, all the way outside, jumped out of her trance and came back in. Richard turned his back to the shop and looked out at the woods.

Zack noticed that Richard spoke only when spoken to, picking something in space to the speaker's side, fixing his eyes so his expression was hidden. When he was sweeping up the shop, every time someone walked by, he pulled the broom out of their way, locating that spot in space to rest his eyes until they were past. When Richard swept near Cy, Cy leapt away as though the bristles would burn his feet. "Nine days of bad luck if a broom touches you," Cy explained, superstitions being one of the few things he always took seriously.

Arnold teased Richard, walking back and forth, getting him to stop and pull back the broom until everyone in the shop was laughing at their little dance. He teased the shop cat with his hamburger, then ate it himself when the cat got near. He treated Richard like that cat, but Richard laughed along, like he enjoyed being part of the act.

Richard was thin, and not just young, unfilled-out thin like Cy. He was so thin there wasn't enough meat on him to hold his pants up; they were strapped around his waist with a belt that had enough slack to go around him twice. He would grin, jump sideways, and draw the belt up tighter, when Arnold pretended he was going to yank down his pants. Arnold never touched Richard, just grabbed at the air around him as part of the game they played.

During break, Richard would go out back to smoke, taking a single cigarette from a flat pack, smoothing it before he lit it up. Even though Richard cleaned the toilet in the shop, he never used it, walking into the woods behind the shop instead. At lunch, he took his usual place by the door, reaching under the bench and taking out his paper sack. Red crayon marks were on it where something had been weighed at the market. As he reopened his half bottle of R.C., a weak hiss sprayed out before he emptied it. On hot days, he went outside to sit on a stump to eat lunch. He never ate close enough for anyone to see what his sandwich was made of.

One day after lunch Ned asked, "Richard, if I give you a quarter, would you go to the lunch counter at Kress and get a hamburger?"

Richard leaned his broom against the wall and approached Ned. "You want me to go get you a hamburger, Mr. Ned?"

"Naw, Richard. I mean if I told you the quarter was for you to buy you a hamburger."

Richard backed up a step, confused. "Naw sir, Mr. Ned, not me." He picked his broom back up.

"What's the matter, Richard? You saying our hamburgers ain't no good?"

"Naw sir. They probably real good."

"Then what if I told you every colored hamburger place in this town gonna be shut down tomorrow?"

Richard hesitated a moment, pushed his broom a few sweeps, then straightened up and said with a grin: "Then I b'lieve yesdity I done et my last hamburger."

Ned laughed all the way into the office. "You're really something, Richard," he said.

Ned repeated his conversation with Richard to everyone who came in. Arnold walked by Richard and said, "Pretty good, Richard. Pretty good."

"Thank you, Mr. Arnold."

Before Richard left for home after work, Ned called him over to his office door and handed him his pay envelope. "Richard, are you gonna get my windows busted out for me?"

Richard backed up, his empty pop bottle and folded paper bag swinging in the side pocket of his baggy pants.

"Naw sir, Mr. Ned. Not me."

"'Night, Richard."

"'Night, Mr. Ned."

When the bus stopped, Richard stepped behind Zack so there would be no question as to who got on first. No matter how empty the bus was, Richard walked to the back. The old sign over the driver reading COLORED SEAT FROM REAR had been painted over, but could still be read as easily as the new one, DON'T VISIT WITH DRIVER WHILE IN MOTION.

Zack waited until Richard passed in the bus, then left his

seat and followed him, sitting beside him in the back. No one was back there but Negroes. Zack asked, "How come you still come back here?"

"Beg pardon?"

"How come you still come back here to sit?" Zack pointed to a seat about halfway back, where a heavy old Negro woman with a child had stopped when the bus started before they got to the back. "That old woman and little kid didn't sit at the back."

Richard made a humming sound. "If I was a old woman or a little kid, I might sit up there too." Richard grinned. It was the most Zack had ever heard him say.

"What do you mean by that?" Zack asked.

"Back gets there soon as the front, is what my mama says."

"Is Arnold's girlfriend trying to make you get religion?"

"I got religion. I just ain't got her kind. She don't bother me none, though."

Zack couldn't think of what to say next. It wasn't easy to carry on a conversation with Richard, but something made him keep the ball rolling. Finally he blurted out, "If the law says you can sit up front, why don't you do it?"

Richard rolled his eyes around, checking to see if anyone else had heard the question. No one met his eyes. He answered finally, "I reckon if it bothers a person to sit back here, he can go up front. It don't bother me none."

Then his eyes closed halfway, as if nothing around him interested him enough to stay awake. Finally he said, "'Scuse me," and got off at his stop. When Zack went back up to the front of the bus, he noticed that the old woman and little kid had moved to the back even though the bus was still half empty.

"Hey, look at this," Tom told Cy and Zack when they came back to help after supper. "We're sponsored. Just like the big teams." Tom had meant to sound sarcastic, but when the words came out, his pleasure overran them.

Ned had talked Maurice Penninger into giving him some more money; in return, he painted over NED'S ALL-AMERICAN AUTOMOTIVE on the door of the race car, then lettered MAURICE'S PURE OIL across a red firebird. Maurice outfitted the team with uniforms. As Cy was trying on the pants in a dressing room at Sears, he lost his balance, falling out into the store with the new pants around his ankles.

"Hey, did you see Roxanne over in the women's department?" Zack teased. "She wanted me to ask you why you mooned her."

Before the Wednesday practice day at the track, Tom was wired with coffee and cigarettes, and hadn't been able to sleep the night before. It was the way he and Zack used to get the night before Christmas; their fear of sleeping past the event made them lose all the sleep time before it got there. When Lisa had phoned him before he left for the track to tell him about winning a match in the country club tennis tournament, he couldn't find anything in his mind to say to her; he just wanted her off the phone so he could leave.

As they rolled the new car off the trailer, Maurice drove up in his tow truck. He climbed out with a helmet in his hand. "Gretchen says I have to wear it," he said, displaying his son's Greenmont High football helmet in front of them before dropping it into the race car seat, "or she'll divorce me."

Tom turned to Ned for an explanation, but he climbed into his pickup without facing him. "Let Maurice run until he wears himself out. It's only a practice day," Ned said to no one in particular. "I got things to do back at the office."

Maurice, the overweight, middle-aged service station owner that no one had imagined had racing aspirations, told them, "I gotta whizz again. Gretchen says you can burst your bladder if you have an accident."

When Maurice returned from the toilet, Tom surprised the crew by saying, "We've got to work on it some more. Need at least thirty minutes."

Arnold faced Tom after Maurice strolled over to look at the other cars that were being unloaded. "Work on what?" he asked.

"Work on keeping that asshole from running my car."

"That asshole's your sponsor."

"He's Ned's sponsor, not mine. I work day and night for a month and he plops down some money on a table and gets to drive it first."

"Money talks, bullshit walks."

"Maurice is the bullshit. You fix it so he can't drive it full throttle."

"He can't drive it full throttle. Maurice will scare himself silly before he puts it in gear."

"You just fix it is what I'm asking."

Arnold crawled under the steering wheel, adjusting the gas pedal so it hit a stop. While he was working, Allie Burcham walked up. Allie's car was at the pit road exit, ready to go as soon as the water truck left the track. Allie noticed Tom's uneasiness.

"What's wrong?"

"Maurice Penninger is getting in. Ned told him he could drive if he'd give him some money."

"Giles did that once. Took some money off a guy and he went out and stuffed it in the wall and cost us twice what he give us."

All the guys stopped working when he said that. Allie began to back down, "Hey, I'm sorry. It was some guy who thought he was going to be a driver. Maurice's old lady won't let him race his motor at a stoplight. That old duffer won't even try to go fast. He just wants something to brag about at Wednesday night poker," he babbled, his voice reaching its high-pitched range. "We'll run together later in the day, Tom.

I'll hang around till he's gone." Then Allie had a thought before returning to his car. "I don't mind if you take a few laps in mine if he don't get out in time to suit you. If Daddy don't mind, I don't mind."

"How 'bout me?" Cy called. "Can I take a few laps?"

Allie shook his head. "You can forget it before you even think about it. I know who it was put that yellow paint on my dog. Coulda give him lead poisoning."

Maurice walked back up and climbed into the car without asking. He started to put on his helmet then stopped. "You got anything to tell me before I put this on?"

Tom froze when he saw Maurice behind the wheel, so Arnold walked to the window: "Yeah, you see that hook on the dash?"

Maurice had pulled on Big Mac work gloves. He stuck his gloved finger on the hook. "Yeah."

"When you get the car up to speed, you put the shifter in there."

"What for?"

"Just do it," Tom interrupted.

"It holds it in gear," Zack explained. Maurice shifted the lever and dropped it into the hook. Without another word, he started the engine and pulled away, brushing Tom's legs with the left rear bodywork.

Later in the afternoon, when Ned returned, Maurice was still circulating. Tom cringed every time Maurice let the revs drop and lugged the engine. Twice he spun halfway around before he caught it. Because he kept forgetting to put the shifter in the hook, the car popped out of gear as he searched for the groove on the bumpy track. His foot stayed down with the engine screaming and the car going nowhere.

"Relax, Tom," Ned consoled. "He isn't going fast enough to hurt anything. I'm surprised he ain't wore out yet."

"You hit that wall at fifty miles an hour and I'll guarantee you'll do some serious hurting."

As he spoke, Maurice leaned against the fence, sending sparks into the air as he scraped the body against the fence bolts.

"Okay, that's it," Ned said before anyone spoke. "Call him in. He's got his money's worth. We want a car to race on Saturday."

Tom ran down beside the track waving him in before Ned had finished talking. When Maurice parked the car and got out, Tom and Cy both ran their fingers over the scrape in the new paint job. Tom had his helmet on when Ned ran a finger under his own throat. The checkered flag was out; Maurice had used up the whole practice day.

After Maurice left, Ned took a pizza he had bought for the crew out of the pickup and sat down to eat with them. He looked over the long faces. "Hey, we got Saturday coming up. And we got enough money out of him to buy a set of tires that I never let him use. They're in the back of the truck."

Tom looked in the truck, not believing Ned until he saw them. He came back and sat down, rolled a slice of pizza and stuffed half of it into his mouth.

"Why is it that everybody who ever wanted to be involved in racing figures that the only good thing is to be the driver?" Ned commented. "Everything else is just something you do until you get enough money or find somebody with money willing to let you drive."

No one answered as they reached for pizza slices and lifted them from the box.

"If I were to go out to a race track," Ned continued, "and say to the guys working on the car, okay, every man working on this car can be a driver right now if he wants to, there would be ten guys jumping in that seat at once. I seen Cy and

Arnold racing just to see who gets to drive the car over to line it up or to load it on the trailer."

"Not me," Arnold defended. "I don't wanna be no driver."

"Take an extra hundred horsepower just to move you, Arnold," Ned said and everyone laughed.

Arnold sneered, "Very funny, Ned."

Then Ned got serious again. "You just remember, Pate, if you don't have a good mechanic, you're a dead man. If that car lets you down in a big way, you got no choice but to go crashing into something with it. Things start bending and twisting around you, a man doesn't seem like much at all. Just some flesh and bones with parts that can't be replaced and take a long time to fix. I felt my own neck many a time and thought how puny it feels next to the pieces of steel I seen get bent double."

"You been listening to your old lady again, Ned," Arnold put in.

Ned smiled slightly.

"A piece of steel doesn't have a head atop it," Tom commented, "that tells it to stay out of places where it might get bent up."

"Amazing how I didn't get a lick of sense in my head until I got too old to be any good," Ned countered. "Now, take your kid brother, here, Tom. He's gonna be somebody. You might think he's just a fifth wheel about half the time, but he'll be a first-class welder someday, make a lot of dough, get married, buy a nice house."

Zack's face began to redden.

"For sure he's saved ninety-five cents out of every dollar he's ever made," Tom commented.

"He's got the patience," Ned went on. "He takes his time doing things. It's the order in which he does things, see? You and Cy there think about getting hurt after you already done something stupid. Take Cy, I've seen him walk the rafters to get to the parts storage instead of using the perfectly good ladder that goes right to it. Not happy unless he's tempting fate. Zack, he would hesitate, think, try to decide whether to do something dangerous; you and Cy just do it."

Cy danced forward to get another slice of pizza, excited to be included in the same group as Tom.

"You got Zack right," Tom said. "Ever since we were little, he never wanted to do anything if he thought he might get hurt. Except he'd bend over to pick up a penny in front of an elephant stampede."

Zack frowned and looked at his food, trying to think of something in his defense, when Ned took up his cause again: "If you worked in a bank, Zack, and told everyone you hesitated to do something dangerous, they'd say, boy, you got good sense and promote you. When you live around race tracks, you gotta go around feeling inferior. Around here they call good sense being chicken."

"Ned, let me tell you about something Lisa read in this class of hers," Tom put in. "In one of those textbooks about how men and women are different."

"You mean you got to go to college to know the difference?" Ned laughed. "Why didn't you ask me? I get reminded every day I got a daughter, not a son."

"I'm serious. Listen at this. It said if you took a red hot coal and tossed it at a woman, she'd take her hands and cover up her eyes. Guess what a guy would cover up, at least according to this book?"

"I wouldn't cover up nothing," Cy answered. "I'd duck quicker than a goose in a shooting gallery."

Tom laughed. "I can't believe it. That's exactly what I told her I'd do. I'd duck."

"Maybe I'm your long lost brother," Cy said, "instead of old Banjo-eyes here. He'd catch it in a bucket of water after it bounced off his glasses."

"Come on, get back on the subject," Arnold insisted. "What did the guy cover up? His dick, right?"

"You got it, Arnold," Tom said, "and all the attachments."

"I oughta be writing those friggin books instead of getting my hands dirty working with you assholes. People pay good money to learn useless shit like that?"

Allie Burcham walked up. "Your timing's off, Burcham," Ned said. "Arnold ate the last two slices in one bite."

"I'm going home to dinner. Mama's got roast beef."

"When you going to get out on your own, Allie? Start batching it like the rest of us."

Allie began to shift his feet. "Mama don't want me moving out. Not till I find a woman to take care of me."

"You mean get married, Allie? You sure don't want that one of mine. She can't even take care of herself."

"I guess I mean get married. But I don't want to do that either, just yet."

"Hey, ask Allie about the hot coal," Cy put in.

"Yeah," Ned responded. "Got a question for you. If I was to throw a red hot coal at you, what would you do?"

"Huh? I'd get pretty pissed, I guess."

"A hot coal. Coming right at you. You better do more than get pissed."

"Why'd you do that to me?"

"It's just a what-if, Allie. I'm not going to do it. What if you saw it coming, falling out of that chimney over there," he pointed at the barbecue pit.

"Try to keep it out of my eyes, I guess. Is that the kind of answer you mean?" Everyone started laughing, so Allie smiled. "Did I say the right thing? Do I win?"

"Uh-uh," Ned said and got up. "That's what I was asking for, only I wasn't planning on getting a daughter-in-law."

"Come on. That's not fair. What's the joke?"

"You are, Allie," Cy replied.

Red Burcham walked up. "Daddy, what would you do if somebody threw a hot coal at you?" Allie asked.

Red grunted. "Spit on it, then beat the shit out of him. Why you asking?"

"Hey, Arnold," Cy called as he climbed into the cab beside Zack. "Guess you're the only man in the lot of us. That Norma is one lucky girl."

17

On race day Saturday, they got to the track early because Tom wanted as much practice as he could get before official runs started. Richard and Zack unloaded the tool boxes and spare wheels mounted with the new tires. The track hadn't been wet down yet. It was so dusty Arnold fretted like a little old lady over the engine he had rebuilt, while Tom circulated slowly to break it in. When Tom pulled back in, Arnold was in a state. "Dammit, I can't believe how careful I was putting this together," he grumbled. "Now look at all this shit in the air!" He waved his arms helplessly then bent back over the motor while it idled.

Tom wasn't listening. He'd gone into his race driver trance where he didn't pay attention to anything else. He watched the water temperature and oil pressure gauges that Arnold had installed to protect his engine. Tom had been driving so slowly for Arnold, he hadn't put on his helmet with the Air Force star in the center that was strapped to the seat beside him. His black hair was covered with a thin layer of dust that made it appear frosted. When he pulled off his goggles and wiped his mouth with the back of his hand, his clean chin looked like raw skin.

"Did someone give Arnold a bum steer?" Cy asked, dancing around Arnold like a featherweight boxer. "I believe Arnold thought he was building a sewing machine for some church ladies. He didn't know he was making something for a bunch of nasty old men to take out and play with in the dirt." Cy had a short memory when it came to Arnold's temper, but he had learned to get more than an arm's length away from him before he spoke.

Randall Johnson, the only Negro driver, drove in with one crew man beside him in his pickup, his race car flat-towed behind. Cy told a story about Randall: "True story. Heard this one over at Burcham's. Randall picks up his crew on the way to the race. Guy's out thumbing, see, and he stops and says, 'You wanna be a pit crew?' and the guy says, 'Sure, man.' So Randall takes him to the race and when he comes in the pits for a stop, this guy shuffles out and says, 'What's the matter, Randall? You wanna cigarette?' That's the gospel truth, I swear it. Tell them it's the truth, Richard."

Richard chuckled. "I reckon it could be the truth. Randall ain't got a dime to pay nobody good."

As the afternoon wore on, the dust got worse. Richard wiped it off the blue paint, taking a wet rag to clean up the red and white lettering for MAURICE'S PURE OIL. As though he were feeling a wound, Zack rubbed his fingertips across the spot where he had spray-painted over Maurice's scrape. When Tom came into the pits, Cy went to the window. "What's the matter, Tom?" he said. "You wanna cigarette?"

"Wash my goggles off. I can't see a damn thing."

Zack took the goggles and dunked them in a bucket of water, then dried them on his T-shirt.

Finally, just before the cars went out to hot lap before qualifying, someone sent out the water truck.

"Wondered when those cheap bastards were going to fix the track decent," Arnold noted. "They just use the drought as an excuse." The clay, already hard-packed from all the running, sent the water down the banked surface to the apron, where it sat in puddles.

When Tom went out, Zack took the stopwatch from Arnold's tool box. The first time the car passed, he thought he had made a mistake so he didn't say anything, but after three more revolutions, he knew it was real.

"What's it say?" Cy asked, looking over his shoulder and squinting at the watch like a man with bad eyesight.

"It's good. It's real good."

The new car was a whole second faster than it had been that afternoon on the dry track. Right then Tom was already faster than the fastest time in the feature the week before. Arnold pulled Zack's hand with the watch over to where he could read it.

"Damn, look at that. We're in there this time. He's already under the record."

The car came off the third turn. Tom tossed it sideways and it crabbed up the banked turn, spurting out straight at the end of the corner like he was driving the only car that knew the way.

Ned had gone home for supper. "I wish Ned would get back out here," Arnold said. "I betcha he's got back with that woman now that he don't drive. He oughtn't be missing this."

Tom saw his crew as he passed. They were giving him thumbs up. He knew the car felt good. He didn't know how good yet. As the flag was given to end the hot lapping, Allie Burcham cut down on the apron to head into the pits. Tom was half a car length behind, still running hard. As he passed Allie's car, a thick spray of mud and water shot off Allie's wheels and through Tom's wire mesh that replaced the windshield, completely sealing him in brown, blinding him to the track and cars while his car shot forward at full speed.

Tom tried to slow it down; he tossed it sideways where memory told him the turn should be. He would have made it if his right front wheel hadn't ridden up on the berm that had built up where the cars had carved a groove into the track. The car rolled over slowly, sliding through the turn on its roof, spinning until the front end bounced off the wall in front of the grandstand. It fell back on its side like a dead animal. His goggles came off, but the world he saw now was inverted, the dirt was the sky.

The crew ran through the infield to the turn, but before they got there, Tom lifted himself out the right side window, his helmet tipped over on the side of his head with the strap broken. The three crew men were joined by a half dozen others who ran to the uphill side and pushed on the car until it fell back and rocked on its wheels. Tom reached through the window to guide the steering wheel as they pushed the car down off the track. By the time Maurice's Pure Oil tow truck got there, they were already examining the damage.

"Hey, Pate, you trying to make me look good," Maurice yelled out the window as he drove the tow truck around to the front of the car and backed up. Tom clawed the mud from his nose. The only clean spot on his face was where his goggles had been and where his left cheek had scraped the ground.

"Yeah, you'd probably drive better if you couldn't see where you were going, asshole," Arnold snapped.

Maurice jabbed the brake on his wrecker, throwing it into first. "You fuckheads figure out how to get your own car outta here," he said and shot away, pulling in beside the tower, where he waited for the next accident. For a change, Zack wished he was like Arnold, big and mean enough to pull Maurice out of his tow truck and bash his face in.

Tom could say nothing. He lifted his helmet off and threw it inside the car. Blood began to surface on the side of his face and the tops of his hands. He squatted beside Arnold, who was examining the front suspension that had hit the wall.

"More than we can fix tonight. We got to get some more pieces," Arnold said.

"I know where we can get a front end," Cy offered. "I seen one over at the West End scrap yard. Guy don't even know what it's worth."

Tom nodded, then shook his head. His body felt numb.

"I'm sorry, guys," he said finally. "It was like the lights went out."

Zack got the pickup and backed the trailer up to the car. They guided the car up the ramp; as they were pushing hard to get the jammed front wheel to slide across the bed, Ned walked up.

"Well, that didn't take long. Didn't even wait for me to get here."

Arnold stuck a brick behind the left front while they took a breather. Cy and Zack watched Tom. There was no doubt that right then, they were glad they weren't him.

"Maurice said you got over your head," Ned spoke into Tom's silence.

Arnold stepped in. "Maurice is full of shit as a Christmas turkey. We had this car hooked up. That dipshit Burcham ran through the mud and threw it up in Tom's eyes. Come right through the wire. It was just one of them things. Wish I'd put in some wire with smaller holes that woulda caught it so he coulda knocked it off."

"Woulda and coulda, Arnold. Wish in one hand and shit in the other and see which one fills up first," Ned snapped. "Guess I've got me a driver who figures he has to win hot laps." He glared at a speechless Tom then went back to his car, leaving without watching the race. The crew stayed on, none of them sure why. Allie Burcham finished dead last. He had apologized to Tom, but Red yelled at him, "Don't go taking the blame for stuff. How much you think he'd give you in a pinch? You go on a race track, you take your chances."

All night Tom was silent, unable to talk. All he could do was pound his fist into his hand as he saw what was in a mind no one else could see.

The week after Tom's crash, everybody worked late every night, trying to get the car ready again by Friday. The race coming up was a bonus money event and Ned didn't want to miss it, but each part they took off the car was another set-back: bent, cracked, or broken.

"You're learning about racing fast," Ned told them bitterly. "An accident is never less bad than it looked. It's always worse because everything that you can see that's busted gets counted in the first look."

On Tuesday night, Richard picked up his cap and started out the door at 5:30 as usual.

"Where you think you're going?" Ned snapped.

Richard stopped and looked at Ned.

"Well, answer me."

"I thought the clock said five-thirty, Mr. Ned."

"It does say five-thirty, but it don't look like nobody around here is done." Richard put his hat back on the shelf. He stood waiting for Ned to give him orders, but Ned wasn't through talking. "You left here last night at five-thirty and we worked half the night with mess up to our knees. If you want to keep working here, you can stay late like the rest of us."

Still Richard didn't say anything: no apology, no excuses, nothing.

"Things don't always go right around a racing shop. You work here because it's a race car shop, right? Not just a car repair shop. *Race car,*" he practically shouted, not expecting an answer. "It's not the same as cleaning up at a office or a school building. Start putting those tools away. Makes a job take twice as long as it should if the last guy don't put the tools away."

Richard bounced around: first Arnold stepped in a drain pan and he had to get the sand, then Arnold said wipe off the tools before you put them up so he went back to the tools.

"Richard, get these shavings off the lathe. I can't see what the heck I'm doing," Cy said, ignoring the fact that Richard was already trying to do two things at once. Richard picked up a brush and headed to the lathe with a cardboard box, then walked outside to take the box full of curled metal shavings to the trash can.

When Richard got back, he looked on the floor, first at the scattered tools, then at the sand that was now blackened. He took two pieces of cardboard and began to scoop up the oil dry, leaving the tools, glancing once at Arnold's back as though he expected him to turn around and scream at him to pick the tools up first. Richard stared at Cy's back, waiting with the box and broom for him to turn off the machine. When he did, he stepped up and swept away the shavings, sitting the box by the lathe. Then he stooped down and started picking up tools again, wiping each one with a rag before he looked at the initials on the handle and put it in the right tool box. Richard never said another word, just picked up his hat before Tom cut the lights off for the night and walked to the bus stop in silence.

Zack and Richard waited a long time for the bus. It was too dark to read the schedule on the post. Richard lit a match and held it up, but it got too hot and he had to blow it out before they could read the times.

"I don't know what time it is anyway," Zack said. His watch had stopped at 12:30 because he usually wound it before he went to bed. "Too damn late, I know that."

"Yeah, It's mighty late. Mama don't wait up this late. I bet I go to bed 'out no supper."

"Me, too. Vienna sausages and crackers. Won't be the first time."

"Naw, me neither. I'm pretty hungry though," Richard offered. "Getting swimmy-headed. Wish I'd knowed Mr. Ned was gon keep us late. Would've saved half my samich for supper."

"We can stop at Auntie's, over near my house."

Richard laughed, a funny nervous laugh. "Naw," he whispered.

Two cars went by, then the square of light of a giant windshield came towards them. The bus hissed to a stop and the door unfolded. It wasn't the regular driver. The bus was empty. Richard sat down only halfway back, dropping into the outside seat.

"Lordy, I'm tired," he said and leaned his head back. "Morning gonna get here too soon tomorrey."

Zack sat across the aisle beside him.

"Where you boys headed?" the driver asked, looking in his rearview mirror.

"Main and Elwood for me," Zack said.

Richard started to speak but the driver said, "Peachwood, right?"

"Yessir."

"Y'all made the last bus. I park it after this run. Half the time, I don't pick up nobody. Don't pay for the gas to make this run."

"I'd buy your gas tonight, just to get home," Zack said, and the driver chuckled.

"Working this late?" he asked, as if there was anything else to do in this part of town at this time of night.

"Yeah, and looks like it's going to be a habit the rest of this week."

"Make lots of overtime."

"Our boss won't give us a dime extra," he said. "He thinks we ought to pay him for the privilege of working there."

Zack looked at Richard. He had said that for his benefit, just to see how he'd respond. First he thought he was asleep but then he opened his eyes and shook his bony body. "Gon sleep right past my stop."

"He knows where we're going. Unless he wants to take us home with him, he better stop at the right place," Zack said, only loud enough for Richard to hear. The driver looked in the mirror again, then back down at the road. He started whistling.

"Why do you work at Ned's, Richard?"

Richard looked like that wasn't a clear enough question for him to answer.

"You know what I mean," Zack went on. "All he lets you do is sweep up shavings and wipe up oil and clean out the toilet and that's all they're ever going to let you do."

Richard made a grunting noise, like he tried to answer, but didn't make it the first try. Then he grinned and said, "I reckon I'm working to be a sixty-five-year-old janitor just like I'm a nineteen-year-old janitor."

That didn't ring true to Zack. For once it sounded like he had forced Richard to lie.

"Why don't you work at a colored garage," he decided to ask, "where coloreds take their cars?"

Richard whistled through his teeth and shook his head, his expression saying this was the dumbest white man he had ever talked to. "Because," he said finally, "I ain't doing this because I like to see pretty clean floors. I do it to make money."

Something happened to Zack that was just as involuntary as sneezing. Heat came into his face. Thoughts raced through his mind, but he couldn't grab onto them. He should be doing or saying something. But what? He had asked for that. The tone. The answer. Richard wouldn't have said that to Ned or Tom or Arnold, just to him. Something about him let Richard know he could get away with it. Because he didn't give him orders in the shop. Because he cleaned up his own mess.

Zack tried to get his thoughts on something else, to name the song the driver was whistling. The driver was mixing two songs up and the sound began to irritate like a spigot dripping. Either whistle "Ebb Tide" or "You'll Never Walk Alone," not both of them, Zack thought.

When the bus stopped, Richard got up and walked to the door, reaching with his thin arms over the seats like a tight-rope walker struggling for his balance. After he went through the door, Zack didn't watch him disappear into the darkness. He stared at the bus driver's bristly neck and felt his daddy rising in his throat like vomit.

After Zack got off the bus, he walked by Auntie's. The open sign still hung on the door that night, but no one had food at any of the tables, just beer. As he walked in, Auntie looked at him like a teacher spotting a favorite student late for class without an excuse.

"You don't look old enough to drink," she said, with a grudging smile.

"Naw, Auntie. But I'm old enough to eat."

"Kitchen's closed."

Suddenly he felt so weak he dropped on one of the stools.

"Oh, all right. But don't say anything about it tasting warmed over, because that's exactly what it is."

She took a cooked hamburger patty with spots of bread clinging to the meat out of a cold bun and threw it on the grill on top of a pat of butter.

"I bet I could eat two of them," he said, "and a cup of coffee."

"Two for the price of one," she replied and put on another one the same way. "And, honey, my coffee at this hour will stand up without the cup."

In a few minutes he left, the two burgers in a paper sack, sipping a thick coffee in a chipped cup he promised to return. "Now get on home before they get cold the second time,"

Auntie scolded. "Then I'll guarantee they won't be fit to eat."

Zack unwrapped one of the burgers on the way up the stairs to his room and ate half of it before he even started digging in his pocket for his key. The second burger went down a little slower.

Did Richard go into a dark house on Peachwood and lie down with no supper, looking at his feet across his rib bones that rose under his T-shirt? Or maybe he had a mother who got out of bed and made him fried eggs with bacon and poured him a glass of cold milk. Then she refilled it for him. The inside of Richard's house was as blank in his mind as the ceiling over his own bed. He cut off the light. Then he cut it back on to set his alarm. Richard was right; morning was going to get there too soon.

Colored lights flashed on Zack's windowsill as Auntie's beer signs flickered, blinking on and off and making a chorus line of dancing colors. A searchlight was beamed across the sky. With each sweep, he waited for its light to flood the room just like he used to wait for the cool air in his bedroom at home from the oscillating fan, an almost painful wait. The coffee buzzed in his ears like mosquitoes.

Before he fell asleep, he remembered a stage show in Durham, the only live one he had ever seen, one that Uncle Vernon had bragged about. One Saturday after they sold the tobacco crop, Uncle Vernon had taken him and Tom to the matinee.

Ten men were in a row on the stage. They all had on tuxedos and top hats, carried canes, and had their faces painted black. They danced in imperfect unison. Cartoons always showed rows of dressed up beetles or pigs, all drawn exactly alike, all doing exactly the same thing, and doing it perfect. These men were trying hard to do the same thing, but one would kick a little higher, then another one would wave his arm a little different.

"The second one from the left keeps messing up," Tom whispered to him.

"I think the third one from the right is worst," he answered.

Someone ran out from backstage to throw cream pies at people. Zack whispered to Tom that he would have liked to have a slice of one instead of seeing them splatter on the stage curtains. Tom said they weren't real, they were made out of soap. People sang songs he didn't know the words to, standing in a circle of light like a moon on the stage.

At the end of the show, the men in the chorus line with the black faces all stopped dancing to take off their gloves. Each man, starting at the left end, pulled off one glove while the others looked at him. Underneath each white glove was a white hand. White glove, white hand, white glove, white hand. Until they got to the last man in the line.

He didn't take off his glove. He put one finger to his lips. Then he put his hands behind him and started backing up. All the other men were moving towards him. Right before the curtain dropped, two of the black-faced men with the white hands grabbed the man on the end of the line. They held him while another man pulled off the glove.

His hand wasn't white.

Before Zack had time to look and see if his face looked real instead of painted, the curtain was down. Those men had been dancing in a row, just alike, and the whole time, the one on the end really was colored.

After the accident, Tom worked even harder on the car, longer hours with no time off at all, often working alone. When Lisa came by the shop now, she wore bright colors instead of tennis whites: shorts, skirts, jeans, like a woman in a fashion show parading everything she had in front of him in hopes that he would see something he liked and be distracted. She began treating Cy and Zack as if they were invisible. Cy began referring to her as "that snotty little rich bitch with the giraffe legs."

One day she walked back into the working area wearing tall black boots and riding pants with leather patches. Arnold had just cranked up his new motor and the air hung with blue smoke. When he went to open the back door and windows to let out the fumes, he spotted Lisa. Tom had warned her to stay outside of the shop, explaining that men in stock car racing considered it bad luck for a woman to be around a car.

"Get that woman out of here," Arnold shouted. "I got a race engine going!"

"What about that Roxanne?" Lisa shrieked back.

"She works here. She's the secretary and the boss's daughter. She don't count," Arnold replied and shooed at Lisa like a chicken.

Lisa went stomping out and drove away. Tom kept working. Then she came back about an hour later and waited for him to come outside. She had changed into a short red dress. Finally Tom walked out, leaned against her Corvette, and lit up a cigarette.

Lisa lifted the red skirt that she wore over her bathing suit. On the outside of her right thigh, there was a small red rose, no larger than a dime. Tom reached over to touch it with his index finger.

"You think that's like one of those decals that you put on an Easter egg?" he shouted at her. She stepped back in surprise. "You think it's something you can scratch off like nail polish?" he pressed.

She didn't answer. She started to cry, and her tall frame began to wilt. Tom didn't reach out to comfort her. She got into her car and started the engine; Tom stepped away. She left, spinning her tires in the loose dirt in the parking lot.

When they started racing again, Tom's finishing positions began to surprise people. The team made the top five three times, placing second twice. Yet Ned never responded with the enthusiasm the crew expected. Roxanne told them he was short of money, that he had taken two bad checks for street work already done that month. And the shop rent had gone up fifty dollars.

The Monday following a third place finish for Tom, the Greenmont Raceway promoter called Ned to say he was putting up some money to bring in a star driver for the Fourth of July. He wanted to put him in Ned's car. Ned stood by the phone so long with a blank look on his face that Tom went in the office and asked him if somebody had died. "Buster Simmons is going to drive my car," Ned said simply.

Ned shut the office door and tried to explain. "I wasn't hurting for a win, Tom," he told him. "That's not why I did it. I never expected us to win the feature. I'm hurting in the pocketbook. I can't afford to turn this down."

Although Tom kept working on the car, he was like a car with a flat engine, still moving but the power was gone. From the moment Buster Simmons said he would drive for Ned, the crew worked even longer hours than they had after Tom's crash. There was extra money from four places in town when people found out about Buster. For Buster, Ned got the car repainted and hired a sign painter to do the lettering.

Ned quit taking in street customers. Roxanne didn't come in to do the receipts because there weren't any. She stopped by one evening and went into the office with her father. The office was just a partition with an open ceiling, so Cy and Zack could hear Ned, but not Roxanne's whispery voice.

"You tell your mother I'm not racing the damn thing, that Buster Simmons is racing my car, not that she has ever bothered to find out who he is, and that, if I play my cards right, he will bring in more money than I can earn in a year doing street work."

When Roxanne opened the door, Cy and Zack heard her response, "Why don't *you* tell her, Daddy? She doesn't believe it."

"Tell her I could play cards and drink liquor and mess around and she might have something to complain about. If she'd come out and watch, she might not be so down on it. You come and watch, baby. Tell her about it. Tell her you like it, okay, baby?"

She didn't answer.

"What's the matter, honey?"

Then she finally broke her long silence. "Tom had his heart set on being the driver."

Cy punched Zack in the arm with a big smile on his face. "Me too," Cy whispered. "Put in a good word for Cy." Then he went back to his workbench.

Arnold said that Buster Simmons was the hot ticket. He was winning nearly every race he entered. If he didn't win, he blew up. He came through crashes, they said, like he was blessed, like the man was so big, nobody had enough of a punch to put him down. Arnold had never met him in person.

They got word that Buster was coming by the shop on the Friday before the race to be sure he fit the seat. Even though they were done with the car, Ned made them all stay late the night before to spruce the shop up.

"This place looks like a pigsty. We got a guy coming who's used to better than this. I want every tool put away and the floor spit-shined and all of you polishing the car when he gets here like the car's so good and ready, there's nothing else left to do. And I want every last one of you in a clean uniform. And that means you too, Cy. And take a bath tomorrow night whether you need one or not."

Tom saw Buster first, through the front window. Buster drove up in the convertible that Ford had given him when he decided to switch from Chevy. He sat in the open car, combing his hair. Then he lit a cigarette and leaned back, smoking like he was waiting in a room. His hair was long, the kind of hair that would've made Hershel Pate ask, "Did your mother want a girl?"

While he watched Buster, Zack remembered waiting with Tom for their mother to finish shopping in Summit, sitting on a bench in the park with his daddy. A guy walked by who could have been Buster Simmons' twin. His sideburns went out on his cheeks and his hair was combed in a ducktail that hit the top of his turned-up collar. His daddy said, almost a whisper, "Skin." His mother would have said, "Hood," because she would think that was the right word. She said things like 'souped-up cars' and 'sorry women'; she got confused and called the twist jitterbugging because she didn't know any better. Zack had watched Buster Simmons' twin that day, knowing every gesture before he made it: he held his cigarette like a hot stick, he sucked on it with a nasty look like he was doing something in public that decent people only do in private, then he spit out the loose tobacco.

Cy, Arnold, and Zack stood behind Tom, watching Buster. He opened the car door and got out, dropping his cigarette butt in front of his feet and grinding it out, not just killing the flame but pulverizing it. All of his moves were so slow and deliberate, it was hard to imagine him going fast in a race car. He stuck his comb in the pocket of his shirt, behind the square bulge of a Lucky pack; the other pocket showed the round bulge of a can of snuff. He wore cowboy boots, a white dress shirt, and tight jeans. His belt buckle had "Buster" written on it, not "Elmer." Elmer was his real name, but he had punched a man from the newspaper for calling him that.

Buster walked as if he had just gotten off a horse instead of out of a convertible, grabbing at his crotch. Before he came through the door, the crew was back at work, polishing. Then they looked up, acting like it was the first time they'd noticed him. Even Ned tried to act cool. He was afraid that Simmons would call his car a shitbox, not necessarily to his face, but behind his back, which was worse.

Buster headed straight to the race car without speaking, singling it out as if it were the prettiest girl in the room and she had been waiting for him. He walked around it, sticking his head in the window. Ned felt jumpy inside, afraid of failing to please Buster, knowing that if you've really tried and it shows, failure is twice as painful.

Buster grabbed the top of the door with both hands. He hadn't spoken one word to anyone; he was just going to climb inside. He lifted his legs up like a monkey, dropping them both through the open window. His fancy white shirt stretched tight over his shoulder muscles, a shirt not meant for action. The crew moved in closer. Buster paused, his ass halfway in the window. Then, while all the guys stood in a circle waiting, Buster farted.

The freshly uniformed crew backed away in unison, like the Temptations doing their moves. Then Buster slid through the window and into the seat.

"Seat's too fucking low," he mumbled as his head dropped below the steering wheel. Buster was shorter than Ned had guessed.

18

Cy asked, "Where can we put her so she don't get dirty?" Everyone looked for a clean place to put Roxanne, who always looked like a doll that was never played with. Zack spread clean shop rags across an area on his workbench; her daddy lifted her up. She sat with her hands crossed in her lap, hands that were tan not from working or playing in the sun, but from smoothing on suntan lotion. Her nails were always colored in pinks or reds, her eyelids in blue or green, colors that were so constant it appeared she must have been born with them. Arnold, whose girlfriend Norma didn't wear makeup for religious reasons, had once offered: "I'll give five dollars to the guy who'll throw a bucket of water in her face so we can see what she really looks like."

Roxanne began picking at a little chip on one of her nails while she waited for her father to finish talking to Tom. Her eyes were rimmed in red. She kept picking at the nail, pulling the color away with her teeth, leaving one flesh-colored half nail. When she saw Zack staring, she balled her hand into a fist, shut it tight as if he had seen something naked that she wasn't going to let him see again. She kept her hand balled up the rest of the afternoon and left with it that way, her fingers clamped shut as Ned put his hands around her waist and lifted her back down to the ground, holding her a moment when her feet touched the floor like he was balancing a small child. "Come on, honey, let's get over to the Burcham's. Seems like a lot to put up with for a home-cooked meal, listening to Red Burcham's mouth all night. What's the matter?"

"I can't stand Allie Burcham."

234

"Oh, he's not that bad. Just a little namby-pamby."

"Well, we're going to eat dinner and come straight home. I'm not going to the movies or anything with him afterwards, and if he says so, you say I'm going with you. He'll try to make me go dancing with him. He thinks he's good and he's just awful. People are laughing at him and he doesn't even know it."

"Whatever you say, sugar. When did you get so out with him? I thought you liked him pretty good."

"He keeps trying to make people think he's my boyfriend. I don't have a boyfriend."

"I thought he was your boyfriend. Talks on the phone all the time to you. Sits with you at church. Looks like a boyfriend to me."

"That's just what I mean about him. He won't leave me alone. I just might not go. You can tell them I'm sick."

"Come on, sweetheart. You're not sick. We won't stay late. I promise."

"Did you hear that?" Cy asked Zack after they left. "Twinkle-Toes Burcham."

"Can you dance?" Zack asked Cy.

"Nawp."

The day the crew went to the track with the car for the big race with Buster, Roxanne rode with Ned in her mother's car.

"Did you see what Roxanne has on today?" Cy exclaimed. "That dress has her whole back out."

"Yeah," Zack replied, "when I saw that I figured she had decided not to go to the race track. She looks like she's going on a date or something. With somebody with a lot of money to spend."

While they rolled the race car off the trailer, Roxanne stepped out of Ned's car and stood to the side, her blond hair caught up under a wide-brimmed hat. Ned turned to Richard. "Richard, you get Roxanne situated while we get registered."

Richard went to the truck and held his arms open for her

things as Ned handed them out: three magazines, a straw bag, a small umbrella, a folding seat cushion with a back. With Roxanne ahead, the two of them started walking away.

"Hey, Roxy. Where you going?" Cy asked.

She looked at Cy as if he were the dumbest creature on earth.

"I'm going to the stands. Where else?"

She turned and walked away.

When they arrived in the infield, Cy looked up to where the wives and girlfriends sat in one place in the stands. They were all wearing pastel dresses and hats perched on varying colors of round puffed hairdos.

"Look up there at all them women. They look like a row of flowers."

"Flowers, my ass," Arnold said. "Them stink weeds is set to spend the day digging in the dirt. I told Norma to stay home and give them something to talk about. Track ain't no place for a woman, if you ask me."

"Only time Mona ever come," Ned put in, "was when somebody told her this little secretary I used to have was hanging around the race track."

"Was it true?" Cy asked.

"Never went to a race. Used to come down on Saturday sometimes in blue jeans and a big old man's shirt and clean up the car. Somebody seen her down there dressed like that and went running home to tell Mona we must be getting into something."

"Did you?" Cy asked.

"Cy, for crissake," Zack said.

"Never did," Ned replied. "Her old man weighed about two-fifty and would have killed the first guy who looked sideways at her. Though I did think she was asking for it, hanging around the cars and a bunch of men like that. Hey, there's Buster," he exclaimed.

While Ned was talking to Buster, Zack said, "Hey, Tom, better go pull his finger."

Tom looked at his brother perplexed. "What are you talking about?"

"Don't you remember? Uncle Vernon would ask us to pull his finger . . ."

Tom walked away without answering and began to unload the extra wheels.

"Did he break wind?" Cy asked.

"Buster?"

"Your uncle Vernon."

"Yeah."

"So did my old man when I pulled his finger. Must run in families."

As soon as everyone saw Buster Simmons was at the Greenmont Raceway, they stared. They stared when Ned's crew went to get tires mounted, they stared when they went to get hot dogs, they stared when they started the motor to warm it up. It was as if everyone quit talking and started staring even though the race car was nothing but a dressed-up version of the same '33 Ford.

Buster, who arrived dressed the same except he had on a blue dress shirt with his jeans instead of a white one, looked like an overripe fruit ready to burst out of its skin, a combination of muscle and good living. He strutted around the pits with his chest stuck out like Charlie, Cy's rooster. Only Buster was more like a fighting cock, the kind that shows up with razor blades on his claws when the bets get high. He had an indifference to the people around him, never speaking unless he was telling them the way he wanted something done. Yet when he got in the car, he came to life. He had one speed and that was fastest.

"Look at that son of a bitch go," Cy exclaimed. "He don't need to warm up for twenty minutes." Tom glanced at Cy.

"Look at him picking them off," Cy went on, "old Burcham didn't even know he was back there."

"You know, Cy," Tom snapped, "if we wanted an announcer, we'd turn on the radio."

Cy grinned and replaced his talk with whistles.

As the afternoon went on, Tom watched Buster's every move. He studied what he was seeing. His anger appeared to melt away because he couldn't hang on to two emotions at the same time. Buster gave him a lesson on driving. When Buster was on the track alone, he seemed slow, almost as if he were drifting by on a cloud, not digging into the dirt. Then, as the proof on the stopwatch began to spread around to the other drivers, they moved around him, trying to imitate his style. But it took more than watching. Allie Burcham moved alongside. When Buster went into the first turn, his car made a gentle move in the direction of the turn. Allie's Ford ripped sideways, dirt flying off his rear wheels and thudding against the board fence, his forward motion stopping.

"Look at that, Zack." Tom took Zack's shoulders to turn him in the right direction. "Buster doesn't pitch the car. He turns it real smooth. I never saw anybody drive like that."

"Allie thought he was hauling the U.S. Mail," Arnold butted in, "until he pulled up beside our car."

"Everybody else loses a lot to wheelspin," Tom added.

By the time they got through qualifying and Buster had the pole by a full second, no one cared what Buster was like as a person.

"I don't care if he beats his mama and farts in church, he can drive a frigging race car," Arnold observed.

When Buster got out of the car, Tom began to ask questions. Buster was a man of few words. "Red Burcham is drilling holes in everything on his car to make it lighter. What do you think?"

Buster grunted and shook his head. "Waste of time. Just drive the motherfucker."

"I seen what he did," Arnold put in. "His motor mounts look like Swiss cheese. He'd save more weight if his fat ass son would learn to push away from the table."

"Don't go drilling motor mounts," Buster said emphatically. "Motor mounts got a job to do and don't need to be flimsy."

When the green flag dropped on the main event, Buster took off from his pole position and never looked back. He lapped every car on the track. Even though it wasn't much of a race, people stood up and yelled. There was just something about seeing Buster go through that traffic: it was like everybody's dream of what it would be like to be a champion. All of their old challenges and measuring sticks were thrown away. The problem was that Buster was on a track full of ordinary men.

It was never quite certain whether Buster punted the car out of his way intentionally, if he did it accidentally, or if Allie just moved down suddenly in Buster's way. Everyone had all been caught up in the magic, thinking the track was parting in front of him like the Red Sea for Moses. Except Allie Burcham didn't part. Allie didn't even know Buster was lapping him again. Buster hit him hard in the left rear. Allie's car didn't spin or slide. It went straight into the wall as though shot out of a cannon.

As the yellow flag came out, the engine noise dropped to a rumble, the other cars still attempting to circulate. Once the cars passed the accident, they started to pull off the track or into the pits. By the time the red flag came out, the drivers had already decided to stop the race. Allie's arm hung out the window, unmoving, his body slumped forward in the seat. He wore the old football helmet he'd used in high school.

His brother Giles ran to the window and looked inside. He turned towards the ambulance and motioned. "Get a stretcher over here, Gordon, quick!" Allie's father was the next to the car. Red began to shake the door as if he were trying to wake up his sleeping son. Gordon, the attendant, opened the back doors of the ambulance and pulled out the stretcher. With no one to help him, he dropped the end of it in the mud. Then he had too many people. They struggled up the track with the stretcher, the mud now slick with gasoline.

"Somebody get a welder. We've got to cut him out!" Giles yelled.

"Horseshit! You'll blow us all sky high. We got gas everywhere," another driver said in frustration, waving his hands at the wet track.

"Ned," Zack said, "what should we do?"

"Just stay back here. There's nothing we can do."

Tom looked around for Buster, and found him leaning against the race car that he had parked on the apron, his back to the accident. He took a pinch of snuff out and stuck it in his mouth, his eyelids drooping sleepily.

Soon there was the sound of saws. "For God's sake, don't make a s-s-spark. Keep pouring on the water where the bl-bl-bla." Giles stopped his sentence when the word wouldn't come out and grabbed his ears as though he had heard a horrible noise.

Allie's crashed car protruded from the board wall like a dog out of a bush. The front of his car had given, not the wall. The drilled-out motor mounts had collapsed and the motor had been shoved back into Allie's stomach. They found no way to lift Allie high enough to pull him out the window the way he had gone in. Red Burcham pushed everyone back and sawed slowly on the bolts that held the door shut. His hands shook, vibrating the saw. "This blade ain't worth a cunt full of cold water. Get a new blade," he ordered. "Get a new blade." People rushed to their tool boxes and came back with blades, mostly old ones that Red threw on the ground.

When the door finally fell off, one man pushed from inside the car while another pulled from the outside.

"Stop that," Red yelled. "You don't know what his insides are like. His neck might be broke. You'll kill him."

Allie still hadn't moved, except for his arms that flopped like a rag doll's. They stopped momentarily, then resumed tugging on Allie. Maurice pulled at the engine with the wrecker cable hook attached to the carburetor. The carburetor broke away, sending the engine back to punch Allie's limp body again.

"Stop it! Stop it," Red insisted. "You're all a bunch of idiots. I'm getting this steering wheel off." His voice began to crack as the saw kept jumping off the twisted steering column. "Motherfucker won't saw through hot butter."

"Let us work on it for a while," Tom said from behind Red. He took the saw from the older man's hands and handed it to Zack, who began to saw, slowly and deliberately, at the base of the column while Tom gripped the wheel. Allie's feet looked like they were sitting at strange angles to Zack; Tom looked only at the steering column. Red finally stepped back, his arms dangling by his sides.

"You should have been driving my car," Red began to babble to Tom. "I wish to fuck you'd been driving my car."

The air was thick with gas fumes. "Cy," Tom called over his shoulder. "Stand here with some water and cool it down when I ask you to."

Cy ran to get a bucket of water from the pits. When he got back, part of the column had broken through and tilted away from Allie's body. Red watched the water Cy poured on the saw blade spill over his son's feet.

"Somebody hold this steady," Tom called. Ned pushed Red aside. Tears streaked the dirt on Red's face. Ned held the wheel while Zack finished sawing. When the wheel was free and Tom lifted it out, Ned said, "Don't let him fall sideways, Cy. Wait till they get the stretcher over here to catch him."

Gordon put the stretcher beside the car and, with Ned's help, pulled Allie's body from the pinched space and lowered him onto the canvas. He came out in one piece; a whole person, but his legs and feet were twisted in the wrong direction. Dark blood spotted his pants. Giles walked beside the stretcher like a pallbearer, carrying his brother's hand to prevent his arm from falling over the edge.

When the sawing was done, music filled the quiet. A car radio. As the men with the stretcher approached the ambulance, the music stopped. Gordon had been listening to the radio. Then they heard the sound of the starter, grinding in slow motion, the battery too dead to crank the engine.

"You dumb sh-sh-sh—" Giles shouted. He dropped Allie's hand and snatched open the door of the ambulance, dragging the driver out. The men set the stretcher down beside the ambulance, the back of Allie's hand lying in the mud. Tom wrapped his arms around Giles, pulling him off the driver.

Suddenly a voice bellowed over the confusion, calling out, "Bubba! Bubba!"

To everyone's surprise, Richard yelled with his hands cupped around his mouth. Then Richard's long thin arm waved and as it did, the colored ambulance began rolling over the bumpy infield towards the track. When the ambulance driver parked beside the stretcher, Tom released Giles. The driver, a short colored man with gray hair, jumped out, opening the back door like he was a chauffeur. Ned ran over and pulled out its empty stretcher while Cy picked up one end of Allie's stretcher. Tom took the other end and they shoved it into the ambulance.

"Tom," Ned ordered, "you go along and make sure everything gets handled at the hospital."

Tom jumped inside and closed the door. Gordon headed towards the driver's set. When Bubba turned to look at Ned, Ned said firmly, "Get your ass out of the way, Gordon. Bubba, take him to City General."

Bubba nodded and climbed back into his ambulance, an old black funeral Cadillac with Hudson Funeral Home lettered on the side. As he pulled out of the pits, Giles and Red ran alongside, Giles banging on the passenger door. Bubba stopped and they jumped inside. The siren blasted as it left the gate, coughing at first, then swelling slow and full until it moved away. Two carloads of men followed it out, one of them stopping near the bleachers for a woman. In the row of women, only two were left. Roxanne was gone, her sweater and purse left behind.

The wrecked car dangled on a hook while men shoveled dirt over the gas that still spilled from the car onto the track. When Gordon tried to jump start the ambulance, he hooked the cables up backwards and sparks flew from under the hood. Maurice grabbed the jumper cables and started the engine for him. Gordon kept the motor running and the radio silent.

Soon race engine sounds broke the silence as the cars lined back up for the restart. The noise seemed out of place, like people talking loud in church. The restart order was sent down, pinned to a clothesline cranked from above by pedals on a tricycle wheel.

Buster began circulating around the track, taking his place at the front of the field. The car colors looked different because the sun was starting to set, the bright blue of Ned's Ford turning to navy, with mud covering most of the lettering on the side.

Before the race was over, Bubba's ambulance came back. Tom got out, trapped on the outside of the track. Everything was subdued now. The field had gotten smaller, making the track noise seem farther away. When Buster took the checkered, more laps ahead than anyone had counted, no one cheered. There were just a few tired sighs, people glad that it was over. Ned was as still as a statue. When the cool-off lap was completed, he headed across the track to Tom. They spoke briefly before Ned left for the trophy stand to wait for Buster.

The crew watched Tom walk across the track, and waited for him to tell them the news.

Tom said, "He didn't die."

When they got back to the shop that night, Ned called the hospital. Allie had broken both legs and he had a concussion. Both wrists and hands had multiple broken bones. His spinal cord was bruised and he was bleeding inside from the engine mashing his guts. When he regained consciousness, Allie had told Tom he still had legs and arms, but couldn't be sure whether he felt them or just saw them still attached. Ned walked out of the shop and said to no one in particular: "We'll give him our share of the prize money for his doctor bills." Then he added, "Tom and Cy, I'll drop you off on my way. Zack, you take the pickup on home tonight. I don't have the energy to go in but one direction. I feel a little sick to my stomach, to tell the truth."

Finally Zack asked what he had hoped someone else would ask, "Where's Roxanne?"

"I told Ralph Bailey to drop her off at her mother's. I haven't got the strength to deal with her or her mother tonight. I've got myself to blame for her coming to this race." Richard stepped from behind the truck. "Drop Richard off if you want to," Ned said. "I'm gone."

When Zack got behind the wheel, Richard climbed into the back.

"Come on up front," he said. Richard opened the passenger

door. "Grab us something to drink." Richard reached into the cooler to fish out the last two beers. He handed Zack the opener and held his beer until Zack's was open. Zack gave him the church key then pulled out, turning in the direction they walked when they rode the bus together.

"You can just put me out at the bus stop." Richard's voice was clear in the night air, deeper-sounding in the small cab. He punched the key into his beer can.

"I don't mind taking you all the way. I got nothing else to do."

Richard laughed. "This time of the night, I got sleeping to do."

"You're right there. You can lose a lot of sleep and miss a lot of meals in this business." No one had mentioned the accident, not even Ned on the way to the shop.

"Pretty bad accident," Zack said finally.

"Yeah, worst I ever seen," Richard responded quickly.

"I thought he might be dead."

Richard didn't answer, but Zack could see him nodding his head after he took a deep swallow of his beer.

"Allie is going to be a long time getting well. If he ever does. Make you think twice about wanting to drive?" Zack asked.

"Not me. I ain't even thought once 'bout it," he laughed. "Turn up yonder. By the light. After that it gets right dark."

After they turned by the streetlight, it was completely dark: no street lights and none of the houses had porch lights burning. Overhead some of the final Fourth of July fireworks were scattering in the sky, the flashes of color over the trees making the street seem even darker. Zack followed Richard's directions, making a complex series of turns between houses on narrow dirt and gravel roads. Richard's nightly walk from the bus stop was longer than he'd ever known about.

"I saw you talking to Randall Johnson today," Zack offered. "You planning on quitting us?" Randall Johnson was the reason Bubba's ambulance had to be there. The track owner told Ned he had to get twenty-five colored people filling their section in the last turn to pay for the ambulance.

"Naw. He ain't got no money. I wasn't talking 'bout no job."

"Would you rather work for him? If he had the money?"

Richard was silent. Finally he answered: "I rather work for somebody gon win races and I don't b'lieve he gon win no races."

"How come?"

"You don't b'lieve he gon win no race, do you?"

Zack thought a moment. He didn't really know. Once they said he had a good car that he was loaned by the promoter to fill up the colored bleachers for a big race in Charlotte. He had placed ninth.

"No," he said. "He doesn't have the equipment or the team."

"We gon win a race. Sooner or later, we gon win."

"Richard, we did win. Today."

"I mean us. Not some man who run our car 'cause you give him a pile of money."

"What'd you think of Buster?"

"Not much."

"How come?"

"He ain't got the time of day for none of us. Mr. Tom 'preciates what we does."

"How do you know that?"

"Bought me a Co-cola day he turnt over. Randall Johnson don't give his men a dime. Begs time off his folks. He ain't got a dime to give is the truth."

"Damn good thing for Allie Burcham that Johnson was there," Zack said.

Richard hummed a yes. Then he chuckled.

"What?" Zack asked.

"Just thinking 'bout old Randall. He say to me, 'Where you reckon Randall Johnson be right now ifin it was the colored ambulance didn't crank? Randall Johnson, he be pushing up white lilies.'"

Before Zack got a chance to ask him another question, Richard said, "Stop here."

Their own dust overtook them, encircling the truck in a white cloud.

"Much obliged." Richard was out the door and up the porch steps. A young girl met him wearing a loose dress made of printed sacks from chicken mash. Oleandra. She spun in the light from the door as she hugged him and Zack saw that the pattern on the back didn't match the front of the dress. A man and a woman sat in porch chairs, out of the light. A white paper fan fell back and forth in the woman's hand.

The next thirty minutes Zack wandered around dirt roads and down dead ends until he finally made it back out to Main Street. Greenmont had never seemed so complicated. He couldn't keep his mind on the streets. He was thinking about a day the week before the race, when Richard had been out back eating his lunch as usual. This time Zack had taken his lunch out and joined him. A giant windup ladybug the size of a melon buzzed around the asphalt at Richard's feet. When the bug ran up against the trash can, it spun its wheels a moment, then backed up, flipped around, and took off in the other direction.

Richard laughed out loud. His teeth spread white in his face when the bug bumped against Zack's foot and backed up. "Don't that beat all?" he said.

"Where in the world did you get that, Richard?"

"Kress. Fifty-nine cents. Give a dollar for batt'ries. Gone wear 'em out 'fore Oleandra get it, ifin I don't mind myself."

Richard showed Zack a School Days snapshot of Oleandra like the ones Annie had got at Goose Bottom Elementary.

When Zack had shown Tom Annie's newest picture, Allie Burcham had said, "Mm, Mm! One more warm summer and that one will be ripe." Zack was so filled with rage, he couldn't respond. Tom had said, "If I see anything that looks like you near her, I'll shoot it."

Now he took Annie's picture out to share with Richard. "How old is she?" Richard asked. "Ten," Zack replied.

"Oleandra just turned thirteen. She's right small for her age."

Zack began to eat his lunch that Auntie had packed for fifty-nine cents, the same price as the bug. Richard picked up the toy, lifting the switch on the bottom that disconnected the batteries.

"Is it her birthday?" Zack asked.

Richard looked down and the fun seemed to drain out of him. His long hands set the bug down as gently as a living thing.

"Naw. She real down in the dumps. Sick to her stomach."

"What's the matter?"

"She gon have a baby. She just a baby herself. Make me want to do bad to the man done it to her."

"You know who it was?"

"Mama's friend done it. She thought it was herself he was stuck on. Eat at our table. Mama say she take care of it, so I guess it be all right." Up close, Richard had the look of a man taken care of by a woman, his shirts smooth and clean. Richard's lunch sandwich was neatly packaged, with the tomatoes in a separate wrapper to keep the bread from getting soggy.

Richard bent over and lifted the ladybug back into its box. The box was painted like its contents. "I never had no use for that man," he said.

Arnold walked out of the shop, throwing out a box of metal shavings that clattered against the sides of the dumpster. He looked hard at Richard as he wiped his hands on his pants. Richard and the bug were gone as quickly as a breeze whipping away two leaves.

Zack had figured out that being around Richard was like watching a dog twitch when he was asleep: you knew he was having a dream or nightmare, but you had no idea what he was seeing. Zack caught Arnold's look that said, See, I had to clean up my own mess, which you're supposed to do, while you were out back playing with a toy—and for an instant, Zack intercepted Richard's fear.

When Zack got to his own house the night following Allie's accident, he parked Ned's truck in the driveway. The house was dark. As he reached behind the seat for his hat, he felt Roxanne's purse that Richard had gone up into the stands to retrieve before they left.

Without a thought he gathered all of her things into his arms and took them up to his room: the magazines, lipsticks, nail polish, perfume. He spread it all out on his bed, touching each item, spraying his pillow with her perfume. He looked through the photos in her wallet; there were two of Allie beside her, taken at a school dance where she wore flowers on her wrist. Allie didn't have a belly then; he had a waist cinched with a rented cummerbund. There was a younger Ned beside Mona. When he took out Ned's picture from the clouded plastic, behind it was a photo of Tom. Zack recognized the shot; it had been cut from their group photo beside the car that Ned had taken. Zack's severed hand lay on Tom's left shoulder, Cy's long fingers grasped his right. Suddenly the feeling came over Zack that he was doing something wrong. He packed her things back up quickly and used his shirttail to wipe his fingerprints off her pink wallet. He carried her belongings back out to the truck.

When he cut off the light in his room, the smell of her perfume was so strong that he turned his pillow over. But instead of dreaming of Roxanne, he spent the rest of the night climbing over boulders back home on the farm, his hands bruised and bleeding as he struggled with the underbrush. He was trying to find Annie before Allie Burcham did.

Tom stepped back slightly from his front window to watch a blue Chevy Nomad pull up to the curb. The car belonged to Mona Morris, Ned's wife. Roxanne got out, her face repainted with colors from the collection on her mother's dresser, shrouding her face in a doll's mask.

Roxanne stopped on the sidewalk. She'd had to wear her mother's perfume and catching a whiff made her feel for a quick moment that she wasn't really alone. Her hands felt empty, her purse lost. She glanced back at her mother's empty car before picking her way as carefully as a girl on her first high heels to the stairs to Tom's apartment.

He waited for a knock at his door. Roxanne's heels scraped up the stairs with the same tired cadence as the woman in the overhead apartment coming home. She stopped outside his door and then clicked down again like his neighbor did every morning, late for work. The Nomad revved up—the engine that Tom had tuned for Ned—and left hurriedly, jammed into gear like a getaway car.

Tom opened the door, looking for something tangible, a note or a package in the hall, but meeting only the thin scent of unfamiliar perfume.

One Saturday in the summer after both of her big brothers were gone, ten-year-old Annie Pate walked down the road alone. Her mama had sent her to remind Mallard to haul off their dead mule and her daddy had told her, "You watch out for the coloreds that Kennedy has made so uppity." Mallard's latest uppity act had been to tell her daddy he thought a white Leghorn was a sorry excuse for a hen and, if it was his place, he'd order a box of Rhode Island reds out of this catalog he saw.

Her mama had said she could go to town if Aurora or Rachel went with her, then her daddy sent them to pick beans. She wished her parents could make up their minds.

Annie was barefooted and barelegged, stepping from hot sand to puddles that still held the cool night rain. She had pulled her hair up into a ponytail tied with a pink ribbon and dabbed her lips to match with Rachel's Snow Pink lipstick. She sang the little rhyme that Aurora had taught her, "Red next to yellow will kill a fellow; red next to black a friend of Jack," its meaning skipping across the surface of her mind the way Tom would skip a pebble across the pond. Finally it fell through and got lost.

Tommy Jr. picked up a corncob and flung it at her as she left the yard, heaving his body so hard he fell down, but the cob didn't travel half the distance to her. She trotted out of his range as he scrambled to retrieve the cob for another throw. She didn't want to take him with her because she knew he wouldn't mind her.

Annie decided to go see the fallen John Mule, whose nose was already full of white whiskers the day she was born. She climbed over his body that was wet with dew and cold, still smelling like a mule instead of like dead. Suddenly she froze, the only sound her blood pumping through her heart, while her mind reached for ditties: Thirty days have September; spruce up, fir down; his wife could eat no lean. A snake lay in the corn furrow, seemingly as frozen as she, the mouse in its belly holding it like a ball and chain. Its colored stripes were as alive as could be, but it didn't seem to know she was there.

Annie heard a wagon coming up the road behind a live mule, its jingles and squeaks sure to wake the sleeping snake. The driver was Mallard come to take John Mule to the glue factory. Mallard pulled the wagon up in front of Annie and climbed down. He looked at the young girl, who was shivering on a hot, humid morning. He tipped an imaginary hat and stood a moment before he spoke.

"What you scared of me for, Miss Annie?"

While he looked at her, Annie rolled her eyes back towards the ground, fearing the snake could see the blue orb moving in her eye. Suddenly the ditty came to her, a voice loud and clear inside her head, not Aurora, who had taught her the words, but of both her big brothers come back to protect her, calling in unison: "Red next to yellow, Annie!"

At just that moment, Mallard saw the snake.

Moving towards her as fluid as a lizard after a grasshopper, Mallard reached to the ground and cracked the variegated ribbon down the furrow like a whip, a black-skinned Lash LaRue in a corn row.

"Mallard! That was a good snake," Annie shrieked, "red next to black!" Too late. Her brothers had told her wrong.

"A good snake, Miss Annie, be a dead snake," Mallard said clearly. "'Scuse me, Mr. Snake, I begs your pardon," he said. As he lifted it up with a stick and slung it into the woods, the link between its head and twitching red and black body severed.

Then Mallard used the live mule to drag the dead mule, which had dropped in its traces, off the bank into his wagon bed. John Mule's nose and the top of Mallard's head looked the same to Annie: a hair brush with lint caught in the bristles. Mallard drove back down the road with the dead mule rocking in his wagon as though it were scratching its back.

Annie walked back up the path to her house, singing Aurora's ditty in the daylight, until it was a song she danced to, and the words were lost behind the music. She would never forget it again. She wasn't going to run. She walked slowly so she wouldn't be noticed, like a pill bug unrolling when the danger was past, but when she got to the kitchen door, she ran and wrapped her arms around her mother's hips.

"Annie! What makes you give me a fright like that?"

She recoiled, back to the pill bug.

"Go pick up your room. You know better than to go out to play with such a mess on the floor. Cut up paper and cloth and I don't know what-all that doesn't belong there, and Eunice Treckler stopping by and sticking her big nose right in to take a look. 'My mama would have tanned my bottom for such doings,' she tells me, so I told her I was going to tan yours, which is just exactly what I should do . . ."

"I was working on my postmark collection." Annie collected city postmarks from envelopes, searching through the trash at the church and at school, looking for places she wanted to go, trying to guess which city held her brothers. "You let Tommy make messes," she retorted.

Her mother stopped talking and looked her hard in the eyes.

"Tommy. Tommy?" she repeated as if she had never heard the name. Gladys searched for somewhere to fix the anger spinning in her head like a dust devil. "Tommy's a child," she said, then, "Who told you you could wear lipstick?"

"It's Saturday."

"All the more reason not to go acting grownup. I don't want to see a speck of it left on your mouth tomorrow morning when you're out in public."

Annie ran to her room and slammed the door. She wadded the paper and cloth from the floor and threw it around the room, saying the name that seemed like using the Lord's name in vain: "Tom, Tom, Tom, Tom." Annie was twice as old as she'd been when Tom left home; she'd been on earth without him for half her life. She'd never be that old again.

That Saturday afternoon, Annie dressed in her Sunday dress and patent leather shoes and packed a sack. She didn't have her own suitcase, so she emptied out Aunt B.B.'s old carpetbag that smelled like snuff and filled it with her own things: her nicest underwear, her pajamas and toothbrush, and two pairs of corduroy pants. She decided to take her jacket because she might be gone until winter. She wanted all the money in her glass bank, and didn't have time to fish it out on a knife, so when her mother went out to the clothesline, she put the bank in a pan and broke it with a tack hammer. Red dots appeard on the glass bits as she picked out the coins and put them into a sock.

Before she left the house, she coated her fingertips with soap to stop the bleeding. She decided to take off her dress and pulled one of the corduroy pants from her bag. Her shiny black shoes looked silly to her then, but, after putting on the ugly oxfords she wore to school and taking them off again, she decided to wear them anyway. She put on the T-shirt with her name on it that Zack bought her at the state fair the fall before. It was too small and her swelling nipples showed through like mattress buttons. She pulled an undershirt on top of it, then buttoned up a plaid shirt to hide her sprouting breasts behind the pockets.

When her mother left to feed the hogs and chickens, Annie went out the back door. She had to put the bag down twice to change hands before she got to the cover of the woods.

Mallard, who had brought the now-empty wagon to a stop under the big persimmon tree to unhitch, watched her stop both times and rub her hand before disappearing into the green of the woods. As he led the mule back to its pen, he fretted over what he now knew, one minute wishing he hadn't seen it, the other relieved that the little girl hadn't gotten away like her two brothers with no one's eyes on her.

Annie would call him a tattletale. Maybe he'd be the cause of a whipping and she would hate him. He couldn't keep his mind on his work, letting the bullheaded old mule get away from him and duck its nose in the bathtub of water with its sweaty sides still heaving from their trip. Aurora put down a bushel of beans on the porch and ran to help him tug the hot mule from its drinking.

"Miss Aurora!" The words burst from him as slime fell from the mule's lips onto their feet. "I fear that Miss Annie is being a bad girl."

20

Tom, Zack, and Cy stopped for gas on their first trip in the Chevy since Horace's plunge. There was a twisted wreck of a car behind the station. The crash had a fresh look; the grass clumps wedged in it weren't dead yet and it smelled of leaking fluids. They walked around it; it was too far gone to make a race car. Except for an identifiable piece of chrome—the slab of silver on one rear fender that marked the car as a '58 Buick—it could have been anything. Cy looked inside, trying to see if there were blood stains on the upholstery and trying to imagine how the human bodies had ended up positioned in the twisted space. The gas station attendant walked up.

"How many people got it in this one?" Cy asked.

"You can't kill a drunk," the man said flatly, as if he'd said it to everyone who asked.

"There's nowhere for them to have been," Zack said. "How could they have lived?"

"Like I said. Look in the backseat. One of them didn't even bust his bottle." A mason jar with the lid still on was a quarter full of a stringy, milky fluid.

"Did they get thrown out?" Tom asked.

"Two of them did, but the other two rode it out."

Cy shook his head. "Like slugs," he mused. "Like there's not a bone in their bodies."

"You think that guy was lying?" Cy asked Tom as they drove away.

"About what?"

"About them dying."

"They love to tell you how many people died," Tom answered. "Couple on their honeymoon. High school sweethearts on their way to Myrtle Beach hit by a tractor trailer, their heads end up in the back seat. That's why most people go to races, to see the wrecks. People talk that way, until it happens to somebody they know. Giles and Allie used to talk about bad wrecks all the time."

"Yeah," Cy said, "now all they want to find out is that it happened to Buster Simmons."

Allie Burcham hadn't come by Ned's shop until a month after the crash, three days after he got out of the hospital. Giles brought him over in his pickup. He had made a ramp so he could roll him in and out of the truckbed. Allie sat slumped like a dead man in the wheelchair seat. Both of his legs were solid plaster, sticking straight out on a foot rest. One smudged arm cast lay in his lap. Names and dirty pictures were drawn on his plaster like it was a bathroom wall.

As soon as he arrived, Roxanne asked her daddy if she could leave.

"Honey, just say hello to him. You don't have to look at him long."

Roxanne walked across the shop like an obedient child. She didn't let her eyes rest on him; they darted trying to find something to fix on. "Hello, Allie," she recited, then went into the office, dropping her face over the giant ledger.

Allie had difficulty holding his head up. His eyes rolled around, wiggling in the socket even after he had located his subject. He didn't appear to be aware that Roxanne was no longer in front of him. In the part of him that didn't get broken, his chest and upper arms, the muscles had drained away, making him look like a skinny twelve-year-old with an old man's face. His stomach rested in his lap like a deflated basketball. Suddenly his head jerked up. "I see where that cocksucker Simmons got his ass blown off at Martinsville," Allie snarled, his voice the same but rolling over a bottom lip that moved like a chewing cow.

Giles sputtered, "F-F-Fireball put him in the w-w-weeds."

"He'll get his," Allie hissed, as though nothing were inside his body but venom.

Tom kept working, nodding his head at the Burcham brothers. Tom was trying to look at Allie, but not see him.

"Pretty grim," Zack muttered to Cy over by the vise after the Burchams left. "Tom didn't say anything about him the last time he went to the hospital."

"Yeah. I didn't know he was still that messed up. He acts like part of what he had between his ears got dumped out.' Poor dumb sonavabitch."

"You mean dumb now or dumb then?" Zack asked. "I don't see what being dumb had to do with it. Buster would have run a smart guy in the wall too, if he was in his way."

"He wouldn't have run me in the wall."

"Sure he would have."

"You can't run somebody in the wall if they're right on your bumper."

"Oh, I thought you'd be beating him."

Cy laughed. "Right. I don't know what got into me. Buster wouldn't get close enough to me to hit me."

Ned interrupted them. "What all of you need to take a long look at is that people get hurt racing cars. And sometimes they get killed. And it can happen to anybody. Even Allie, who nobody thought was going fast enough to get hurt."

"Allie getting hurt doesn't have a thing to do with me," Tom put in quickly. "He didn't even want to do it. His old man wanted him to do it."

"That's not the point. The point is that racing is dangerous."

"No, Ned, the point is that racing is hard to do because it's dangerous."

"I suppose you think Allie could have got hurt that bad playing baseball. Or how about golf? You don't think golf is hard, you oughta try it."

"I think Allie would have made a fool of himself playing baseball and golf just like he did racing cars. He just wouldn't have gotten hurt. Allie was like a record on the wrong speed; somebody left him on the thirty-three switch and everybody else was on forty-five. But he never knew the difference."

"He knows it now. He hurts all over."

"I'll tell you what it is, Ned. Nobody wants to have to look at him, because he's messed up for good. He could have gotten that messed up fighting in a war and nobody would have wanted to look at him, either. They just don't have a special hospital for guys who get messed up in race cars because there aren't enough of them."

"A hell of a lot of guys have gotten messed up in race cars. You just wait until you've been around as long as I have."

"That's not what I mean. I think it's because people just have this thing about cars. They think when they teach you how to drive at school, they have to show you a bunch of pictures of people torn up in a wreck. They want to scare you out of using a car for what it was made for—for going fast. They don't show a soldier a bunch of pictures of guys all blown up, because they don't want him to think about that. It keeps him from being a good soldier. That's the way I am. I don't want to have to look at Allie all the time because it might keep me from being a good race driver."

Tom looked at Ned, waiting for an answer. But the older man shook his head and went back into the office. As soon as he was gone, Tom said, to no one in particular, "See, Ned didn't quit driving because he got old. He quit because he got chicken."

On Friday night, the crew took off to go to the county fair. Arnold was the only one with a date, his steady girlfriend, Norma. Arnold spent eight dollars throwing baseballs at the wooden milk bottles to win her a Jesus clock that he could have bought for a buck-fifty. As buxom Norma clutched it to her chest, Cy remarked, "Look out, Norma, you're going to smother Jesus." She curled her upper lip, revealing teeth that were off center as though they should be clicked around on a dial.

After watching the Dome of Death motorcycle show three times, they ran out of money and headed towards the exit, but Arnold insisted on doing a new ride no one had been on: Climbing the Bavarian Alps. Unlike the other rides that spun and jerked, this one had an uphill treadmill that pulled the riders to the top of the mountain; it was like climbing an escalator with no steps. If they fell down, they were helped up by Negro boys dressed in suspender shorts and green hats with feathers.

"Didn't know there were niggers in the Alps," Arnold said. "Swiss niggers."

"Are the Alps in North Carolina?" Cy asked.

"Look at their butts in them little suits," Arnold went on. "Nigger asses really stick up in the air." Arnold pulled Norma towards the ticket line, reaching for his wallet that swung in the loose seat of his pants.

"Old Norma don't look too eager," Cy said.

Arnold stepped on the treadmill, but when he reached for Norma, she jerked back her hand, and he was sucked away from her. Arnold tried walking fast backwards, but he couldn't make it back to Norma. He reached for her hand again, but she didn't reach for him because both of her hands were clutching her Jesus clock.

"Get on the goddamn thing, Norma. I can't keep this shit up forever," Arnold panted, his stomach erupting from the bottom of his shirt as he was swept towards the peak of the mountain.

Suddenly, like a little kid who finally got the nerve by ignoring her brain, Norma jumped on the treadmill. When her top-heavy body swung over backwards, her arms flew out, and her Jesus clock popped away like a spring and crashed to the ground below. An attendant stepped in behind her, attempting to shove her forward to keep her on her feet, but he was too small. He tried turning around backwards, pressing his back against her backside with all his might, trying to keep her upright, but it didn't work. Norma flailed her arms and screamed.

"If he ain't Joe Louis, he better step aside," somebody yelled behind them.

"Calm down, Norma. Calm down," Arnold yelled uselessly from the top.

Norma lost her balance. As she toppled towards the railing, the attendant grabbed her around the waist from behind. She pounded on him like a drowning person, her arms turning like a windmill. People lined up below to watch. She screamed above the sounds of the midway while Arnold kept trying to jump on the treadmill to save her, but each time the moving walkway flung him off.

Finally the attendant got a grip around Norma's shoulders and steadied her for a moment, one arm across her chest. But Norma found it in herself for one last lunge. When she did, her blouse stayed under his arm and her huge breasts dropped out the bottom, swinging down like two water-filled flour sacks.

"Zack, her boobies fell out!" Cy grabbed Zack's arm just as a whoop went through the crowd. "Jesus Christ. Her nipples are so big it looks like her tits are wearing hats."

Tom said, "Zack, pinch me. I can't believe we're seeing this."

Norma fell to her knees and was carried by the treadmill to Arnold's feet. But Arnold ignored his fallen Norma, grabbing past her for the attendant. He tripped over Norma, and landed facedown on the ramp. Two white men suddenly appeared, but Norma jumped up and butted past them with her head, both her hands holding her blouse down as if it might spring back up again on its own. The attendant vanished, and when Arnold turned around, Norma was gone too. He glared at the crowd, searching for his opponent, his fists clenched like a boxer's, ready to take them all on. The crowd was whistling and chanting: "Show us your tits, show us your tits."

"Hey, man, bring back the free strip show," one man hollered.

"We've got an escapee from the cow barn," another shouted.

Tom put a hand on Zack's shoulder. "Hey guys," he said, "we've got a problem here."

"Yeah, you're right," Zack agreed. "We better get old Arnold out of here before he decides to take on the whole mob."

"And gets hisself killed," Cy added, still laughing.

They headed up the ramp, but Arnold had disappeared.

On the way back to town, they found Norma walking beside the road and gave her a ride home. No one saw Arnold until he arrived at work on Monday, his face swollen, one eye almost shut. The knuckles on his left hand were covered with scabs. Cy watched him trying to break a nut loose. He pressed on stubbornly, stopping to spread his stiff fingers, but the nut didn't budge.

"So who redid your pretty face?" Cy finally asked, curiosity getting the best of him.

Arnold dropped the connecting rod he was holding and glared at Cy. He hadn't talked to anyone all day. "I got that nigger son of a bitch," he snorted.

"Looks like to me he got you, Arnold," Cy replied.

Arnold, who usually treated his engine parts as if he were handling a baby, began banging the rod on his work bench.

"Hey, Arnold, cool it," Tom said. "You're dinging it all up."

"Forget I mentioned it, okay?" Cy said.

Arnold threw the rod across the bench and rushed out the back door.

"Old Arnold's hell-bent on fighting the Civil War again," Cy said.

"I think you better lay off of him," Tom cautioned. "He slipped a cog in his brain on Friday night."

Tom turned to Cy. "What do you know about the Civil War, anyway?"

"That was the one where we beat the coloreds."

"Oh, yeah, right. The day they studied the Civil War must have been the day you went fishing."

"Yeah, you're so smart. What was it about?" Tom didn't bother to answer, so Zack tried.

"We fought the Yankees, Cy, so we wouldn't have to turn the colored people loose. You remember Miss Wilson, Tom?" he asked.

"Sure, I remember her."

"When I was in sixth grade, she told us how the South had lost the Civil War. So I went up to her after school, asking if we would ever get a chance to fight them again. I thought it was supposed to be like a ball game where you got another shot at them the next season . . ."

Loud profanity came from outside the shop.

"Out back, where Arnold went," Tom said, and headed towards the door. Cy and Zack followed.

Richard had been walking up from the woods when Arnold saw him. By the time they got outside, Richard was down on his knees with his arms folded over the back of his head.

"Get up and fight, you sorry nigger," Arnold screamed. "Get up before I kick your goddamn guts out."

Richard didn't move. Arnold was dancing around like a prizefighter, the scabs from his Friday night bout already knocked off, blood running between his fingers down to his elbows.

"Fight, goddamn you." Still Richard didn't move, just stayed in that kneeling position with his head down.

"Why don't you cut it out, Arnold?" Tom walked towards Arnold. "What the hell did Richard do to you?"

Arnold turned and looked at Tom. For a moment the anger left his twisted face and he looked confused, like an old man halfway through a sentence who forgot what he was talking about. Arnold looked from face to face, as if searching for a clue as to what he was doing. Then, when he saw his bloody hand, his meanness rushed back. He swung around and kicked Richard in the side before Tom could grab hold of him. Richard balled up on the ground like a caterpillar while Tom twisted Arnold's left arm behind his back.

"Jesus Christ, Arnold," Cy said. "You bastard. That must have hurt like hell." Cy grabbed Arnold's other arm, and he and Tom held the man between them. Still Arnold moved towards Richard, as if Cy and Tom were just two weights he had to tug along. Zack was helping Richard up when Ned came out.

"What the hell is going on out here?"

Ned's anger instantly sapped Arnold's strength. Cy and Tom released him. "Arnold, get your ass in my office," Ned ordered. "The rest of you get back to work." Arnold walked towards the door like a scolded dog. "You okay, Richard?" Ned inquired.

Richard's chin and lips were shiny with blood.

"Yessir, Mr. Ned."

"You can clean up in the washroom. Did you say something to Arnold?"

"Nawsir, Mr. Ned. I was just coming up out of the bushes and he come after me like a crazy man."

"What the hell has gotten into Arnold?" Ned asked. No one answered. No one had told Ned about the fair, but he knew Arnold was late for work and had noticed his face when he came in. "You should have seen the other sumbitch when I finished with him," Arnold had grumbled to Ned that morning. "Three of them jumped me at once."

Ned went back inside, pushing Arnold into the office and shutting the door. Richard examined his body, lifting his shirt to see what damage was done.

"You get a busted rib?" Cy asked.

"I don't b'lieve so," Richard said and jabbed gently at his protruding ribs. "Ouch. I ain't never broke no ribs to know what they hurt like."

"They hurt when you take a deep breath," Tom said and straightened up, drawing in his chest.

Richard drew in his breath and grimaced. "Maybe I ain't broke no ribs," he said hopefully. He walked over to the hose and turned it on his face, washing the blood away.

"Ned said you could do that in the washroom," Zack said.

Richard ignored him. Cy and Tom went back in the shop.

Zack walked over to Richard. "Why didn't you beat the hell out of him?" he asked. "He just thinks he's tough because he's big."

Richard picked up the bottom of his undershirt and wiped his face. As he looked at the blood-smudged cloth, he shook his head. "Mama gonna get me for doing that." As another drop of blood slowly oozed out of his nose, he wiped it onto the shoulder of his shirt. "Ruint now."

"Did you hit him back a single time?" Zack kept on. "I don't think you touched him. How can you let somebody beat on you like that?"

Richard looked at his shirt for a few seconds longer, then he closed his eyes. He sniffed the blood up his nose, spit, then spoke almost in a whisper, though there was no one anywhere nearby who could have heard him: "I want to tell you something. I want to tell you something." He struggled and then he stopped talking.

"Well, tell me then."

Richard didn't shake his head like he usually did as if that were his way to silently throw away all his words. He wiped his nose again and this time the blood didn't reappear. He took one step closer to Zack and resumed talking in that same quiet voice.

"I want to tell you that you don't have to tell me to get mad. I don't need you telling me I'm mad." He tried to look Zack in the eye when he talked, but his head turned involuntarily to the side. His eyes kept flickering like an out-of-control child that won't mind, but he kept talking, even slower and quieter, the words struggling to come out. "Don't go telling me to do what a white man does when he gets mad, 'cause I ain't no white man." Richard breathed loudly, the air going through his bloody nose as though he had a cold. "I seen my bottle there. You see my bottle there?" Zack looked where he was pointing. Richard's half-empty R.C. bottle sat beside the stump where he ate lunch. "'Fore he come back at me," Richard went on, "I coulda had my bottle by the neck busted and stuck in his gut."

Richard's mouth twisted and his chin lifted up as though he'd been hit by an invisible fist. Zack looked up at the blood rimming the taller man's nostril. Richard sniffed it away and began coughing, then turned and spit again.

The door to the office opened. When Zack looked up, Richard darted back inside the shop like a wild animal escaping from a captor. He picked up his brush and began cleaning off Tom's workbench.

Before they left for home, Zack asked Tom, "You remember that weasel we caught in our rabbit gum?"

Tom thought a minute. "Yeah, I remember it. Why?"

They'd kept the weasel in a chicken cage for a day. They dragged a stick up and down the bars, trying to make it grab at it, but the weasel just went to the middle of the cage and relieved itself. It hunched its back towards them from the corner and went to sleep. They put food and water in, but it left it untouched. It grew so listless they thought it was dying so they took it down by the road to turn it out. When they put the cage down, opened the door, and jumped back from its sharp teeth, nothing happened. The weasel waited inside the cage until they backed up, but it didn't leave cautiously. It took off suddenly, streaking across the highway into the brush on the other side before they could blink. No matter what, they hadn't been able to make that weasel do what they wanted it to.

"What do you remember about it, Tom? Did you think it was too chicken to fight us?"

"Chicken? It didn't act chicken. It acted like we weren't even there. Like it had just as soon die as be in that cage."

21

When Roxanne Morris had gone with her Sunday school class up to Spruce Pine with the choir for the living Christmas tree at the First Baptist, she'd seen Priscilla Partin, the 1963 Apple Blossom Queen, who not only was the most beautiful girl in Madison County but also sang first soprano. Supposed to be the most beautiful. To Roxanne's mind, that could certainly be a matter of taste. The same went for her soprano voice, which had the kind of shrill pitch that gave you chill bumps for the wrong reason.

Priscilla had been the master of ceremonies; they kept calling her that because they probably thought mistress sounded a bit risqué. But what Roxanne couldn't stand was the way she kept saying, "When I got my great honor." It just seemed so conceited or something. Roxanne thought when you were chosen queen of anything at all that you should just act like it was your normal job, like being a person's wife or secretary, and not keep trying to draw attention to yourself about your great honor.

That was certainly the way she planned to regard her own great honor. That afternoon, going to the track for the Labor Day Classic at Greenmont, Roxanne didn't step into her role like the Apple Blossom queen, feeling that since she had achieved what God had put her on the earth for, now she could settle down, get married, have children, a lovely home, and feel fulfilled. Roxanne had never campaigned for the job; it came to her because she was the kind of girl who would act right when everyone's eyes were on her, a sparkly little crown sitting in her hair and a satin ribbon over one shoulder—Miss Greenmont Raceway.

Her daddy kept kidding her about it. He said things that were supposed to make her feel good but that did just the opposite.

"Did you hear what Tim Flock said when he saw your picture, honey?"

"Who in the world is Tim Flock?"

"Baby, he's just about the hottest thing going."

"Not in my book."

"He said, 'I can't wait to meet that little doll baby from Greenmont. She's got eyes like a doe and a figure like an angel.'"

"They shoot does, don't they, Daddy?" Roxanne snapped.

"Only in season," he replied with a smile. "When you going to learn to take a compliment, sugar?"

"Honey, sugar, baby. You shouldn't call me those things in front of people. You were the one who named me Roxanne."

"Foxy Roxy."

"I wish you'd seen fit to make it just plain Anne."

"Not a plain bone in your body, sweetie pie."

Roxanne sighed. She never won a talking contest with her daddy. Those queens at the track: they were supposed to just emerge from nowhere, walk out and hand a cup to the winner, and then disappear like Cinderella. It never crossed anyone's mind that one of them might have to ride out to the track like she did with a bunch of smelly mechanics in a pickup.

That bag of bones Cy was driving, Zack was in the middle with the gear shifter between his legs, leaning back and snorting at the smell of her perfume and hair spray and wiping his nose on his sleeve like he had an allergy or something, while she sat in her daddy's lap by the window. Her mother just had to have the car so she would be able to come out and see her right at the end when she gave out the trophy. Her own MG was broken down as usual, and just try to get anybody to lift a finger for Roxanne when they were getting a race car ready.

And Tom had gone down to the radio station to do some advertising for Greenmont in exchange for a free entry fee. She didn't know how he was getting there, but she had her suspicions. He was still seeing that Lisa. Little rich bitch with her fancy car. Flat as a board. The truth was she wouldn't mind being stuffed in the trunk with Tom. Not really; she was just trying to make herself smile with her secret. She turned the radio to the station he was supposed to be on.

"Honey, don't you think you got fixed up a little soon?" her daddy asked.

Her bottom lip went out and her nylon-covered leg rasped against the side of Zack's jeans as she attempted to cross it, but banged it into the dashboard instead. She let her leg fall next to the other one. She had on pink satin shorts that her mother had taken in so carefully that they fit her bottom like skin.

"Just where do you think I could go to get fixed up after I got there, Daddy? There isn't even a mirror in that filthy ladies room." She couldn't stand the way his words "fixed up" came out, although she had spent three hours tending to every square inch of flesh down to the tips of her pink nails—toe *and* finger; and her hair had been doctored in every direction like a wedding cake on a rotisserie. Her mother had packed a picnic basket with food for the guys that she would be expected to serve.

"I mean I don't know where we're going to be able to put you until it's time to do your thing."

"I'll just sit in the truck."

"It's going to get pretty hot and miserable in here."

"I brought a magazine. I'll go sit under a tree."

"Aren't any trees."

"Well, what do you want me to do, Daddy?" The back of her neck got hot and her voice got higher.

Her daddy touched his finger on her neck. "Look. My finger made a white spot on you."

Roxanne hated it when he noticed things she couldn't control. One day he playfully pinched her cheeks when she was chewing him out for writing three checks and not putting down the amount. He'd said, "If she stayed mad, she wouldn't even need to rouge her cheeks." And if she'd been born a boy, she thought, she'd have punched him in the nose.

Ned wheezed and reached across his chest for his cigarettes in the narrow space behind her back. When she turned to glare at him, he patted his pocket, telling his cigarettes he was sorry he'd disturbed them, that he should have remembered that smoking in that tight truck would make her eyes water and her hair smell like smoke. It was all his fault she started smoking anyway, giving her a puff of his.

"I just want you to be the prettiest little queen that Greenmont Raceway has ever had." He smiled. "You'd be that if you'd just gotten up out of bed and scrubbed your face," he added.

"That's what you think," Roxanne said bitterly.

Ned reached around to take her left hand and held it until she quit tapping her nails on the shift knob and the color faded from her neck.

Cy obviously hadn't been paying attention to them. "This guy was telling me a funny story," he related. "Want to hear it?"

"I guess," Zack said into the awkward silence.

"There was these two guys riding to the track up at Bristol with their rig. They'd done an all-nighter and neither one of them could stay awake. The guy on the right side notices the guy driving is nodding out, so he hollers, 'Wake up, you idiot,' and the guy driving opens his eyes and sees the headlights of this tractor trailer dead ahead, right on his nose, so he swerves off the road, rolls the whole thing up in a ball, dumps the race car . . ."

"What's so damn funny about that, Cy?" Ned interrupted.

"I'm getting to it. See, this tractor trailer he thought was about to get him head on was really a wrecker towing a tractor. See, they were both going the same direction."

"Real funny. I would think that was really funny if that happened to you towing my rig."

Cy grinned and started whistling "Only Love Can Break a Heart." There was something about Cy, Roxanne thought. Nothing seemed to bother him. Lord, Zack had about as much sex appeal as a turnip.

"Stop, stop!" Roxanne shouted. Her words slipped out before she thought. Cy hit the brakes and looked from side to side for the danger. Richard bumped his head against the back window, then stood to squint over the top of the truck, his jaw puffed out of line from Arnold's pounding. She flopped back against her daddy. "I didn't mean stop the truck," she blurted. "I meant stop whistling and talking. . . . Tom's coming on the radio."

Cy shifted slowly with only the sound of cars passing in their ears. Roxanne fiddled with the volume. There were engine sounds on the radio, old canned sounds from Darlington or Charlotte.

"Thrills, chills, and spills. Greenmont Speedway tonight. Fifty-lap Labor Day Classic. Listen here, racing fans. Tom Pate, alias Pole Cat, is here in the studio. He'll be there tonight in Maurice's Pure Oil Special, the very same car Buster Simmons drove to victory on the Fourth. Tom's been gunning for Simmons for putting our old buddy, Allie Burcham, in the wall. What have you got to say about that, Tom, alias Pole Cat, Pate?"

There was a silent moment, another rush of engine sounds, the tape slipping and sputtering, then: "I'd like to say hey to

Allie and get well soon and tell him I'm gonna dedicate this win to him and for all the guys over at Ned's Auto Repair, Ned Morris, our boss, and Arnold, Cy, and Zack."

"You heard it here, folks, Pate is out to avenge his good buddy, Allie. Get well wishes to Allie from all the folks at the station who hope to see you back racing soon. Don't miss the big race. Tonight, Greenmont Raceway at eight. Get out there early before the good seats get took."

When the engine sounds came back, Cy pounded his chest: "You hear that, Zack? We got our names on the radio. We're famous!"

"That guy made it sound like Buster Simmons was going to be there," Zack answered. "How can you avenge someone when they're not even there?"

"I hope my old man heard that," Cy went on. "I was on the radio."

"I hope mine didn't," Zack said quietly.

When they turned into the track, Cy sped up. He drove over a pothole so hard, Roxanne bounced up and hit the roof, jamming the rhinestone crown into her scalp. She worked her finger down through her hair to see if she was bleeding.

"Oops," Cy said. He slowed the truck and checked to see how the race car had fared over the same bump. "Sorry, Roxanne," he said, his eyes fixed on the rearview mirror.

Now the crown was crooked, so she sighed and snatched it from her hair. The curls piled on top of her head were so stiff they bobbled like fishing corks on water. One curl stuck to the crown until she gave it a final tug, leaving a blond, uncoiled spring suspended over her head.

Her daddy had quit noticing her. Something happened to all of them as soon as they saw the sign to the track, the M in GREENMONT painted like two faded green mountains.

22

At that time of the year in Greenmont, the disappearance of the sun was the only relief the night offered. The ground was so dry that the mosquitoes didn't have puddles to breed in and the air lay so still that a person felt his sweat cool his body only when he was standing near a fan. When a stoplight changed and the driver in front didn't respond, the next driver was so slow to blow the horn, the front car was already going by the time he did. That was the late summer pace in Greenmont, North Carolina.

The race track was a world to itself. When a race car passed on the track, it sucked a man's sweat-soaked clothes away from his body. Dust filled his eyes and ground between his teeth, even if he couldn't see it in the air. Everything he touched burned his hands, holding the day's heat and the new heat generated from within. After he got to the track, he became as much a moving part as the inside of an engine; heat was just something he slung off his hands or wiped on his shirttail.

After they drove into the infield, and Cy and Zack had climbed out, Ned shifted Roxanne over to the seat, the center of his attention for the last twenty minutes suddenly as interesting to him as a sack of potatoes. The boys unloaded the car and tools. Except for her hand slowly turning a page in *Photoplay* or reaching up to punch her hair, Roxanne didn't look alive. She didn't feel alive either. It was supposed to feel special today, not like all those other times when she had to go up to the stands or wait at the office to see if she could figure how they did by seeing Tom's face, or the size of the little piece of golden plastic her daddy brought in to catch dust

274

on his trophy shelf. Her daddy was right; the pits were the pits, and no place for a woman.

All of her excitement at getting ready had tumbled down out of her head and twisted into a knot in her stomach. After she had taken off her crown, she'd dropped it down into the dark insides of her open purse. It snagged her finger when she reached inside for her mirror, making a little bloody spot. She looked at her face, tipping it around so all of it would fit the small oval, and poked twice at her hair that moved as a solid arc. Then she made a circle of little blood spots on the mirror until it quit coming.

She put on her new sunglasses that wouldn't let people look in at her eyes; instead they would see their own reflections. She wanted to find out how conceited people were, to watch them looking at themselves, to be, herself, the mirror, mirror on the wall. Her daddy accused her of never passing a mirror without looking at herself and that wasn't true. Sometimes she didn't want to see herself; she would rather sit there and pretend she looked like Priscilla Partin, not Roxanne Morris. And Priscilla Partin wasn't all that perfect, either; her nose was too pointy and one side of her upper lip puffed out more than the other, like a bee had stung her or something.

Roxanne climbed out of the truck, took her lawn chair, and dragged it to the shade made by the qualifying board. The backs of her legs, where she had sweated on the truck seat, felt cool. Norma, who had ridden out with Arnold, waited in the shade too before she had to go up into the bleachers.

Zack had never witnessed Roxanne around another woman. It was a surprise. Words ran out of her mouth like a radio disc jockey who was afraid of a moment of silence: "I don't know what it is about me, but some days I can't seem to hold on to anything," she was saying to Norma when Zack took Cokes to them from the ice chest. "This morning," she went on, "I knocked over my best perfume and spilled half the bottle and so's not to waste it, put it all over me, even though I knew I smelled too high, then Daddy had to go and say I smelled like a French you-know-what. I ought to know better than to keep anything in the big bottle it comes in. Ever since I was a little girl, Mother had to pour out a little nail polish or a little bubble stuff in another bottle for me, because I'm just a born spiller."

Norma, who wore no nail polish or perfume, nodded slowly, but didn't answer.

"Then it wasn't five minutes before I broke my beautiful shell ashtray," Roxanne continued, "and I thought if I could just go back three minutes, it would be sitting there perfect and I could tell myself, 'Now, be careful, Roxanne; you have just put cold cream on your hands and they are slick and that smooth shell just might slip out of your fingers, and be extra careful because you are standing in the hall and there's no scatter rug to break its fall.' Then I wouldn't have to look down at my beautiful shell, broken in pieces mixed up with the cigarette butts that are so nasty. Don't you sometimes wish that was the way life was?"

Norma searched her brain for the appropriate Bible verse, but only "Waste not, want not" came fast enough before Roxanne's mouth was going again.

"I know how much the guy I used to go out with sometimes, Allie, said he hated those rings of lipstick on my cigarettes just like the ones I left on the glasses at his house and his mother fussed about having to pay special attention when she washed them. If I had not gotten so mad at him, I would never have even started using that shell as an ashtray."

Zack stepped a few feet away, but found himself frozen, listening. "I think he's jealous of all those men looking at me. Now, just look at him. I can thank my lucky stars I wasn't married to him, or I'd have to spend the rest of my days looking after him like his mother does. They don't ever consider that when they get in those cars, do they? Like going off the end of the diving board. I have nothing against just turning right around and going back and saying, 'I'm not going to bust myself wide open hitting that water.' You can knock your eyeballs out of their sockets, you know what I mean?"

Roxanne stopped to breathe and looked at Norma. Norma nodded, but didn't contribute. Zack shook his head. Usually Roxanne was so quiet. But as queen for a day, she ran her mouth like a broken record. Neither Zack nor Norma had ever seen her smoke one of those lipstick-smeared cigarettes, either.

"Allie was with me at Topsail Beach when I found my ashtray," she went on. "I could just picture drilling my hot cigarette right down in his navel hole instead of that mother of pearl with him laying on his back in the sun with his face under his hat. He started into teasing me again, knowing it made me mad as fire, saying that nigra man was going to win the race when I was queen and that I'd have to kiss him right in front of everybody."

Norma gasped. "Nobody in this world would make you do that," she said. "Allie ought to be ashamed for teasing you. You do mean Allie Burcham, don't you?"

"Yes," Roxanne stumbled. "Allie Burcham, yes, but we've broken up now anyway. I mean we did before his wreck."

On the far side of the pits, Tom had arrived, pulling up in Lisa's red Corvette. Roxanne was about to get a sick headache. But he was alone.

"You ever get that mad?" she asked Norma, her voice shrill and her nose pinched. "So mad you wish all of a sudden you were twice as big as a man and could hurt him real bad if you felt like it, go right for his weak spot and get him?"

"I get that mad at Arnold sometimes," Norma offered. "That's the Devil telling you that," she added. "The Devil gives you the guilt, too, now that Allie's laid up for life."

"I'm not guilty," Roxanne said loudly as Tom walked across the pit, not looking in her direction. "Not one little bit. It wasn't me who had a thing to do with him getting in that car. I know where he is, sitting up there in that wheelchair," she turned sideways and pointed so only Norma could see her. "He's not right in the head. All he does is talk about killing that man my daddy hired. And he can't kill a fly. Besides, I'm not talking about getting mad at a man so much as I am . . . as I am . . ." Roxanne's record stuck. "Oh, you know, flustrated with them," she said to Norma and glanced at Zack as if she were hiding her answer, not losing it in a dark corner of her mind. "A man should make a woman feel all safe and protected, not the other way around. They do anything they please. Men do. And women have to sweep up the pieces."

"I know just what you mean," Norma said, then stepped away. "I better be getting up yonder, before Arnold gets peeved at me. I reckon you don't have to leave today." There was a touch of jealousy in Norma's voice.

"I reckon not," Roxanne answered and shrugged. She stood and lifted a hand to wave as though Norma were a child.

Roxanne sat back down in her lawn chair. Zack found himself unable to quit looking at her, watching her talk, thinking how pretty all her expressions were, even when she frowned and pinched up her nose. Beads of sweat sat like pearls trimming her red upper lip.

"Quit worrying about her," she heard her daddy say to Zack. "She don't need much to occupy her. Never has."

She moved her chair when the sun shifted, slipping her feet from her sandals to prevent a strap mark, leaving just her legs in the sun. Why had she worn those nylons? Well, they did make her legs look perfect with the white three-inch spikes she planned to wear tonight, as far as she could tell, except for that one little blue vein behind her left knee that happened when they'd made her play volleyball on that hard floor at

Greenmont High. And the stockings did cover the place on her right knee where she got cut on the jagged fender of her daddy's race car when she was five years old. She ought to hate race cars. She'd put pancake over it and that blue vein too.

She felt Zack's eyes. He never could take them off her until it got bothersome. She pulled down her shorts in back when she stood up, but she had bent over enough times in front of the mirror to know she couldn't make her underpants show if she tried. And neither them nor her panty hose had any seams to show through her shorts.

She backed into the shade. The sun felt sticky coming through her nylons. Zack was getting burned already. His face never saw the light of day except on weekends. She reached down and pinched the nylon away from her skin.

"Did you know my brother, Tom, invented panty hose?" Zack said. "He should have been a millionaire. You know what I started thinking, Roxanne?" he went on, now that he had her attention. "I started imagining you were made of ice and we should have found somewhere to put you where you wouldn't melt."

Roxanne gave him a puzzled look. What happened to Tom and the panty hose? She didn't even know Tom noticed such things. But what he must think of her. She'd walked into their garage at home without a speck of makeup on and there he was working on her mother's car. He'd stared at her like she was a freak and said her name like he wasn't even sure she was her. "Roxanne?" he asked. "Where are your eyes?" She could have died.

She could tell Zack wasn't looking in her glasses to see himself. He was looking lower. Zack didn't have anything to be conceited about. One of their parents must have been homely and that's the one he took after.

"Like the time Mama told me to unload the groceries," he

went on, "and I forgot and the store-bought ice cream melted and ran out of the bag onto the truck seat. This thing in my brain ate away at me the whole time that ice cream was melting, but it wasn't enough to make me remember what I was supposed to do. You ever have that happen?"

"Yes," she said, even though she hadn't, because that was the only way to get him to stop talking about it. About half of what he wanted to talk about sounded too complicated to think about. "Why did your brother decide to become a race car driver instead of an inventor?"

Zack grinned. "Which one would you rather marry?"

"I wouldn't marry a race car driver if hell froze over," she snapped. He looked out to see who had caught her eye: his brother, Arnold, or any of a dozen other men in her sight. "Look at half of them's wives," she went on, "come into town wearing a feed sack special and rolling their hair with bobby pins. Look like they come in sitting on top of tobacco in the backs of wagons, I mean, just like it isn't the modern age. Mother says they still boil their clothes in a pot and put spiderwebs on cuts and wash with lye soap. And those men are wearing bib overalls. Nobody I know wears bib overalls."

A moth fluttered in Roxanne's face. When she swatted at it, it left yellow dust beside her lips like a spot of mustard. She looked vulnerable, like a little girl with a dirty face, and no mother to wipe it clean.

"I guess you don't have a very high opinion of country people," Zack remarked.

Roxanne tipped her head sideways, suddenly aware that she had talked too much. "You don't look that backward, I didn't mean that," she apologized. "You dress real modern, I mean what I've seen you wear, which is mostly what every guy in that shop wears, which is Levi's and a T-shirt. That's not what I meant. I do pay attention to the way a man dresses and that is not what made me like you the first time. I think you have about the prettiest eyes I have ever seen, and some people might not even notice because you wear glasses." That should do it, she thought, to keep his feelings from being hurt. Sometimes she went too far.

Zack felt his face heat up. No sooner did she give him her attention than her daddy called him back to work. "Zack, get over here. Tom's back and we gotta get this thing running."

"I better get back to work. Can I get you anything to eat? A hot dog?"

"No, thank you. I brought supper for all of us, so don't spoil your appetite," she said softly, suddenly subdued. He glanced back at her flipping through her magazine, a stranger to the babbling woman of a very few moments ago.

Ned walked over to them. "You've got mustard on your face, sugar."

Roxanne grabbed into her purse for her mirror, nicking her hand again on the crown. "I do not. I haven't eaten a thing."

She dampened a tissue with her tongue and began dabbing at the moth dust, then she held it on the new bloody spot on her finger.

"You better get on out of here now, honey. Things are about ready to start up."

Roxanne stood quickly and walked away, dragging her lawn chair, her head high, a queen banished from her kingdom. Ned put his hand on Zack's shoulder and shook his head. "My little girl's wound up like a spring today. Poor little thing is scared to death somebody's going to say she's not perfect. That's her mother in her."

"She's the most perfect-looking woman in the world," Zack said without shame.

Ned chuckled. "Don't let her hear you say that. Her head's already too big for that skinny neck."

When Zack got back to the race car, Tom and Cy were working frantically, trying to remove a broken spring that they had missed. Now they had to waste time on a repair when they should be rolling the car out for practice. Zack squatted down to hand them tools as they tugged and grunted. He hoped they hadn't noticed he'd been missing.

Tom yelled at Zack, as he often did when things were going wrong. Even though his anger appeared out of control, he was careful to direct it safely. It was always at Zack or Cy or Richard, never Ned or Arnold. And Tom never threw a valuable part the way Arnold did.

Soon they were all struggling with the repair, working up until the time for qualifying to start. Cy watched Tom crawl out from under the front and stare into the tool box, his hands and mind jammed. Cy shoved him aside to get the tools and complete the repair himself. Tom didn't resist. On race days, he became clumsy and forgetful, the mechanic's ability he showed in the shop replaced by a racer's concentration.

Before they could get the car on the track, the practice time was over. Tom would have to take his qualifying laps with no practice. His frustration channeled into the intensity that he always got before he drove. It looked like anger to some people, but it was different. He just didn't want anyone to bother him. He stayed in his own world, one where he might not even hear what someone said to him, a state that eliminated everything but driving the car. It was important to give it everything he had.

Cy swung out from under the car and motioned to Tom. "Get in. We'll roll you to the back of the line. The motor's plenty warm." Arnold had adjusted it three times while Cy worked on the front end.

Tom jumped into the car, as obedient as a child, and cranked the steering wheel towards the qualifying line.

"Go check the board, Zack."

No one had paid any attention to the board while they were fixing the car. Zack grabbed a pencil stub out of the top of

Tom's tool box and ran over to write down the times. When he got back, Cy asked, "What's fast time?"

He started to hand the sheet to him, then he caught himself. He pulled it back and read the times out loud. Tom nodded from within the car.

"About what I'd expected," he said.

Tom started the motor. Arnold lifted the hood and revved the engine. Tom pulled on his helmet and a pair of heavy leather work gloves. As he drove away, Arnold was smiling. "Sounds good. Damn good."

Tom headed around the track on the low side, stabbing at the throttle as he felt the surface, trying to educate himself as quickly as possible on the conditions. The car danced sideways like a crab, then darted in a straight line past the grandstands. When he took the green flag, the engine responded smoothly. His first run was a good one, enough to put him fifth in the standings.

"Damn good for no practice, Tom," Ned said as though Tom could hear him. "Now don't press your luck." But he did, getting a little too sideways, but bringing it under control without hitting the fence. He backed off, heading for the pit entrance. The second lap had been slower.

When he pulled into their area and lifted himself out through the window, everyone slapped him on the back. It was a good show, to start in the third row after no practice. Even Tom was smiling when he climbed out of the car. "Overcooked the second one," he said to Ned.

"I noticed," Ned replied, and shook his hand with a smile.

They left the pit area to eat the food that Mona had packed. Roxanne had arranged the supper on an oilcloth that she spread on a picnic table near the stable area. The barns where the horses were kept were in much better shape than the buildings in the car racing area—all freshly painted with the grass cut. When they first saw her from the gate, she was like a cat after a flock of birds, chasing after the empty paper plates that kept blowing off the covered dishes. She had put on a skirt over her pink shorts and with the crown out of her hair, appeared ready to go to the office.

"Well, you all look hungry," she said enthusiastically. She pointed them towards the food, putting plates and cutlery in their hands and instructing which spot on the bench to take, until they were all sitting around the table with food in front of them. "Please excuse all the flies, but they must be drawn to the horses. I did my best to keep them away from the food."

Everyone began to eat but Tom, who hardly touched his food. Roxanne noticed.

"Didn't I fix what you like, Tom?" she asked.

"Oh, yeah. Yeah, you did. I just have trouble eating sometimes when I'm going to race. Nerves, I guess."

"Did I ever tell you about the time I puked in the car?" Ned asked.

"Daddy, not at the table. For goodness sake."

"Sorry, sugar."

When they were finished eating, Cy, Arnold, and Tom started walking back towards the gate, Arnold calling back over his shoulder to thank Roxanne for the meal. Cy and Tom thanked her too, and Ned gave her a quick hug. "Got to get back to work, honey. You did a real nice job of fixing. Wish we could keep you company awhile but we've got to get going." Then he looked at Zack. "You, too, Pate Junior. We didn't bring you out here to entertain the women."

"Real good food, Roxanne," Zack said. "We aren't used to such."

She smiled a little and began to clear off the table. "Just a minute," she said. He stopped. "Take this to Richard." She took the plastic fork off Arnold's plate and jabbed it into a mound of potato salad and the baked beans she had scraped from the serving dish. Then she laid the ham from Tom's plate across the top.

"That was a terrific supper she fixed for us," Zack said as he caught up to Ned.

"Roxanne? She can't boil water without burning it. I had to repaint our kitchen ceiling once after I scraped off her attempt at hard-boiled eggs. Her mother fixed that food."

Thirty minutes later, Tom's car was rolled out to the line, Cy hopping inside to steer it around the cars already there, up to the third row position. They all felt good about where he was starting. If anything went wrong up front in the first turn, Tom wouldn't get hooked into it like the tail end of a train. After he'd seen Buster drive, Tom had bought a used racing helmet to replace the old Air Force helmet he'd been wearing, and Zack had spray painted it red. He carried it to the car.

Tom lit a cigarette, looking around to see if anyone else had climbed in yet. He began to fidget. When anyone got close to him, he backed away and began looking at things, something inside the car, the wheels; he reached through the window and felt the slack in the steering wheel.

"What are you looking for?" Zack asked.

"Nothing," he answered.

"There goes Roxanne." A Ford convertible moved slowly onto the track with Roxanne perched atop the back seat, her Miss Greenmont Raceway ribbon draped diagonally across her chest. The sun had set, the overhead lights sparkling on the sequins her mother had stitched on her ribbon. Tom looked away as soon as Zack spoke and began rechecking the slack in the wheel.

When the other drivers started climbing inside, Tom lifted himself through the window hole. Zack held the helmet out to him; he took it and placed it on the seat beside him like it just might be in there for the ride. Suddenly a big grin spread across his face. He hit the steering wheel with both fists, picked up his helmet, and strapped it on.

"All right," Ned said and banged the metal over his door.

"Crank it up," Arnold called, but Tom had beat him to it.

As his engine sound was lost among the others, his crew trotted back to get the tools sorted out in case he came in. Richard was placing two spare wheels against the inside wall. He'd been working without catching anyone's eyes, except when Zack had handed him the food from Roxanne, which he'd carried away somewhere to eat like a dog hiding with a bone. The bottom half of his face was darker and puffed so far out that it looked like a fat boy's face on Richard's skinny body.

The race started smoothly, running without incident for twenty-five laps, until the air filled with fumes and dust too heavy to be moved by the slight breeze. Tom settled into third with the second qualifier, Ernest Jenkins, and the first, Leland Cummings, both comfortably in sight. Then, as the visibility got worse, Tom's speed seemed to pick up.

"Ernest is used up and the race is just half done," Ned commented. "That was the smart thing to do, just keep the pressure on him. He's too damn old to run hard for fifty laps." Zack knew Ernest was younger than Ned.

Tom passed Jenkins' '34 on the inside, and left him wobbling in the turn as he chased after first.

"Listen at Cummings' engine, Ned," Arnold urged. "I swear to you it's getting rough. I seen it smoke when he backed off."

Tom moved behind Cummings, testing him on the high side, then the low, looking for a hole to pass.

"He'll get him," Cy said. "Next lap."

Cy was right. Tom took the lead with a high side pass then stretched out a gap.

"See!" Cy shouted. "Told you they were holding him up. He's on his way now."

It seemed like a short time before Tom was passing them again, going a lap up. Then on lap twenty-five, their hopes fell. As the sound of a tire exploding bounced off the backside fence, Tom's car dropped down on one side. The tire shredded into black strips that flapped against the car, hammering on the sheet metal as Tom slowed to enter the pits. He struggled with the steering, trying to keep it pointed straight as he headed for the crew. Arnold was over the wall with the floor jack and Cy grabbed the spare wheel. Zack poured water over the radiator while they changed the tire, Cy knocking the lugs off with his foot on the wrench.

Ned yelled, "Let it down!" and they all jumped back as Arnold released the jack. Tom's wheels spun and he was at the pit lane exit before they were back over the wall. They stood in silence as they waited for him to appear. When he did, it seemed as if nothing had happened as he sped past.

Ned slapped Arnold on the back. "Good show. He's on the tail end of the lead lap with Cummings and Jenkins. He had a lap on both of them. We're still in there."

"Is that right, Richard?" Zack asked.

Richard was holding the clipboard Zack had handed him. In the confusion, Zack hadn't given him his wristwatch so he could use the sweep hand to keep track.

Richard kept his eyes to the side of Zack's face as he handed him the clipboard. He didn't answer.

"You were watching, right?"

"Yeah, I was watching real careful. Since you was busy and all."

Tom passed again, the gap closing on Cummings and Jenkins.

"Well, is he on the lead lap?" he pressed.

"I b'lieve he's on the lap with Cummings and Jenkins."

Tom appeared again and Cy let out a whoop. Tom was diving to the inside on Cummings and before he was through the first turn, had a wheel under him. They turned with the cars to see if the pass would hold and watched Tom spurt out of the second turn ahead. In two more laps he was hammering on Jenkins again.

Finally Richard spoke, so only Zack could hear it. "I don't b'lieve he's ahead of Randall Johnson."

Zack looked at the track, trying to find Johnson's car. The robin's egg blue car had been invisible until Richard spoke. Tom passed. Cy beat on his shoulder to watch Tom's progress, while Zack followed Johnson's car as it moved through turn one. If Richard was right, then Johnson was ahead of Jenkins.

"He's been right there the whole time," Richard went on. "He ain't had no trouble at all today. He been doing every thing Mr. Tom do. Staying right behind him till the tire blew."

Zack looked down the pit lane at Johnson's crew. They were easy to spot because, except for Richard and the one other Negro who helped change flats, they were the only coloreds there. They were jumping up and down and cheering.

"He got him," Cy shouted. "Block that son. . . . He's got him!" Tom passed Jenkins and dropped down low on the track about fifty feet behind Johnson. Cy was shaking Zack now, trying to get him to respond. "Look at him go, Zack. Look at him go!"

Johnson had qualified well that day, in seventh place. They heard he had gotten some money from the track owner so he could make the race and they could fill up the colored section at the end of the third turn. People said Johnson hauled liquor at night and put the profits back into the engine. In the third-turn grandstand, the bleachers were filled with colored men and boys who held up their arms to stop the flying dust clods. Zack didn't know what to do. He felt helpless. In the box over the grandstand the people who counted the cars were talking to each other instead of watching the race. A man had placed Tom's number in the lead on the scoreboard of three cars; Johnson's number eleven wasn't there.

"Three more laps," Ned shouted. "Look, there goes Roxanne."

Ned pointed at the victory platform, where Roxanne was climbing the stairs, carefully placing her white spike heels on the wooden steps. She had stripped back down to the pink shorts and the little crown glistened under the lights. The men in the grandstand started whistling. Roxanne turned and waved to the crowd. As her hand dropped she straightened the wide white ribbon over her shoulder. The announcer stood beside her and the track owner, carrying the trophy. Roxanne's long legs came up higher than the stubby track owner's waist.

Zack couldn't keep his mind off Johnson's car. It was true that he hadn't lost any ground since Richard pointed him out. He was going as fast as Tom because he was still fifty feet ahead.

"They give him the white flag," Arnold called.

The white flag was waving. The starter turned to take the checkered flag from the flag stand. He rolled it up around the stick and looked down at the track. The nose of Johnson's blue car came off the third turn like a giant Easter egg. Tom entered the turn as Johnson exited. Johnson took the last turn, spurting towards the finish line. The man with the flag tightened his grip around the shaft as the blue car approached. The car passed. Zack felt his heart begin to race. The checkered flag began to wave. They gave the checkered to his brother.

Johnson's crew—his two sons—just stared as their father passed without getting the flag. Then the smaller one slammed a tire iron to the ground and shook his head. He shook his fist at the starter until his brother pulled him back, putting his arm across his shoulders and talking to calm him. Richard stepped back away from the pits and began to load the truck.

Tom parked in front of the victory stand and climbed up to the platform. Roxanne put the wreath around his neck and handed him the trophy, which he held high with one arm. Tom took his victory kiss, putting both arms around her. The ribbon fell off her shoulder. She reached up with one hand to catch the crown as she tipped her head sideways and her other hand caught the ribbon before it passed her waist.

Arnold and Cy ran to the victory stand behind Ned. Ned kissed his daughter on the cheek and took the trophy from Tom, sitting it on his head. Zack stood frozen in place in the empty pit.

Richard climbed into the back of the pickup, dragging Arnold's tool box onto the bed. Zack helped him load. There seemed to be no noise anywhere, behind him or from Richard. He couldn't go up there to the victory stand: the happiest moment in his brother's life; him up there, believing it was real.

When Richard finished loading, he crouched in the corner of the pickup bed, his long hands hanging over his knees.

Everyone was heading back now to the truck. Ned had scooped up Roxanne to carry her across the track that had dried like a baked crust. Her crown dropped off the back of her head and Cy caught it in his palm like a falling star. He placed it on his own head. Zack saw Tom, the flash of his teeth, but he couldn't look at him. He looked down at Richard who rolled his eyes up.

"I told you Randall Johnson wont gonna win no race, didn't I?" he said, then looked back at his knees as though he had never spoken.

Arnold took one of the beers that Ned was pulling from the cooler. Just then Norma walked into the pit area, and the beer quickly left his hand and went into Cy's.

"Why, thank you very much, Arnold, for giving me your beer," Cy said loudly.

"Wasn't my beer. I was just getting it out for you. I got to be going. See you Monday, Ned. Why don't you fire that queer wearing that crown?"

As Arnold headed towards his truck with Norma, Cy made a chicken sound, tipping Roxanne's crown. Arnold stopped for a moment, his back flexing like that of a bull readying to spin and charge, but he shuffled away instead with Norma tugging at his arm.

"Tell Lisa to come down and have a beer with us," Ned said to Tom.

"She's not here. She's at a tennis tournament in Southern Pines."

Roxanne held the truck door handle with one hand and with the other took off her high heels, sliding her feet into her sandals. She lifted the Miss Greenmont Raceway ribbon over her head, rolled it up and dropped it into a large straw bag from which she pulled her wraparound skirt. Cy handed her the crown which she also tossed into the bag before snapping it shut. She then looked up to find everyone's eyes on her.

"Why are you looking at me now?" she asked.

"You look like you're ready to go work in the office, honey," Ned commented.

"So do you think I should dress up like a race queen forever? I'm not a race queen anymore. Stop looking at me."

"That's asking a lot of a man, sweetheart. Maybe I'm prejudiced, but I don't think Miss Southern 500 can hold a candle to my little girl," Ned replied. "Well, Tom, what do you say?"

Tom drained his beer can and sat it on the tailgate of the pickup. "About what?"

"About winning. About having a little celebration for what we've been working our butts off for all summer long. About having your own personal queen here."

"Daddy, stop it. When can I go home?"

"I'd like to thank everybody who worked on my car," Tom started to say slowly.

"You already said that. Up there to the microphone," Ned answered.

Tom took another beer from the ice and opened it. He thought a moment then held the can out for a toast. "Here's to the day when we're loading up after a win at that other race that happens today."

Cy drank a long swallow and said, "Oh yeah, Darlington. So that's why Fireball and Freddie didn't show up at Greenmont."

Ned put his hands on his hips. "That's about what I'd expect you to say," he wheezed and looked around. "I guess we got everything loaded. Why don't you drop Roxanne off at her mother's, Tom. The atmosphere in that truck cab is going to be a little riper than it was when we came out this afternoon. And you, Miss Queen, don't leave any of those cigarettes with the lipstick on them in the ashtray in that Corvette. I don't want my driver wearing a tennis racket around his neck."

Roxanne let out a quick gasp as Tom picked up her straw bag and started walking towards the red Corvette. She followed like a puppy on a leash, looking back once over her shoulder. Zack was silent as he watched them leave, but he told Roxanne good-bye.

That evening, rolling down Highway 70 towards home in Summit, Claiborne Pernell, Rachel Pate's fiancé and an elastic sock salesman for Carmichael Yarn and Hosiery, listened to the radio in his Plymouth station wagon. When he tuned in the "Speed Show News," hoping to pick up the results of Darlington, he caught the tail end of the North Carolina dirt track racing news:

"Tom Pate, a constant front-runner this summer, has won the Greenmont Labor Day Classic in the Ned's All-American Automotive Ford sponsored by Maurice's Pure Oil."

Claiborne put his foot on the gas as hard as he dared, racing to get home to tell the news to Rachel. Hershel Pate, his soon-to-be father-in-law, who had given Claiborne back the three pairs of sample socks he brought him because the elastic pulled the hairs on his legs, had no idea where his sorry son was. Tom had sat behind Claiborne in fourth grade and made Woody Woodpecker noises because of his red hair. Thanks to Tom Pate, he never could shake the name Peckerwood Pernell.

People get found out, sooner or later, Claiborne thought, people who think it's smart putting "Get thee behind me, Satan" on the back of their jackets. Sooner or later, somebody blows the whistle on a showoff like Tom Pate.

23

Hershel Pate fell in his lower field late in the afternoon of November 23, 1963, sixty-two years after he was born, and sixty-two years after President William McKinley had been felled by a man with a gun in his rag-bound hand. The assassin, a poor farmer, had been electrocuted and thrown in an acid-lined casket.

A strand of electric fencing, the boundary of his ever-shrinking land, had tangled around his tractor disk; Hershel tugged at it but it yanked back. Aurora ran to his side, struggling like a little mule hooked to a post to set him back on his feet. While Hershel heard words over him in a language he didn't know, he couldn't force the language he did know to pass through his own lips. Then the dark girl was gone. He cried like a baby, his face towards the ground. Now he'd lost her too and she was the best kid he ever had.

When he finally reached the back field near sundown, moving on his hands and knees like a giant terrapin, he stopped. His women were coming to meet him. His women were four different sizes: Aurora, firm, rounded, and dressed like a man in her bib overalls; Gladys, gaunt as a scarecrow; Rachel, wide as a barnyard animal with Tommy riding her shoulders; and Annie, like a little puppy leaping over the barren rows. At that moment, his body flooded with love for his women.

He pulled upright using a fence post, heavy, wet mud hanging off his overalls. But as he went to lift his arm in greeting, a terrible helplessness came over him: his head had told his arm to do something and it might as well have been talking to a cat. He wanted to grab all four women and squeeze them

294

till they squealed, but half of him wasn't there after he stood upright. His right arm hung like a busted limb.

Annie reached him first. Just as he was about to drop back down to his knees to tell her she was the best thing his old eyes had ever seen, out of her mouth came words that he never got quite straight: "Daddy, Daddy," she whimpered. "President Kennedy is dead."

Hershel cocked his head to her and replied, "Annie, I think your old daddy may be too," but he stood tall and walked back towards the farmhouse, a woman at every corner of his body.

Arnold ran into the shop, his wide face flushed. He'd heard it on his car radio when he went to buy parts at Burcham's.

"They think somebody shot Kennedy."

"Kennedy who?" Cy asked.

Zack did the same thing Cy did: when he heard the name Kennedy, he tried to think who it might be: someone they knew who owned a restaurant or filling station, or a guy everybody hated, somebody shot by his wife or the police. A bootlegger, maybe. Those were the only people who got shot.

"The president. They think somebody shot the president."

President. President Kennedy. The news didn't penetrate anyone's mind easily.

Tom was the first to speak. "Is he dead?"

"I don't know. They don't know yet. Him and another guy, the governor of somewhere."

"Was it the Russians?" Cy asked.

"I don't know. Turn on the radio. He was riding in a car in a parade."

The radio stayed on until Ned went home and got his television set, putting it on top of the file cabinet, twisting foil on the rabbit ears. Everyone quit work and came into the office. The announcer said a priest had been called for.

"That's bad," Ned remarked. "Real bad. They do that when they think you're gonna die. Could be for the other guy. He might be Catholic too. You'd think they'd tell us if he was okay." He paused. "Or he'd tell us himself he was okay."

Then they heard the newscaster say: "Ladies and gentlemen, the President of the United States is dead."

It became more real each time it was talked about by people they didn't know. Everyone stayed close together in the shop, not because they wanted to talk, but because they felt afraid, even afraid to go outside where the whole world might be collapsing. When Richard left to go to the woods, Zack watched through the window until he saw him return safely. They felt confused. No one knew how you were supposed to feel when a president got killed. It wasn't like it was somebody they knew.

People kept coming into the shop to tell them what they already knew. Some of them stayed because Ned had a television. Then, early in the evening, Roxanne arrived. Her eyes were wide open and staring, like a person in shock. No one had to ask her if she had heard. Before Zack left to go home, he passed by Roxanne in the office with the ledgers open under her elbows. She had been staring into space for a long time and hadn't picked up a pen to work.

"What in the world will happen to her?" she asked.

He didn't know who she was talking about, but he was the only person she could be talking to.

"What will happen to Jackie Kennedy?" she insisted.

"She's real rich. She'll be taken care of," he told Roxanne what she ought to know.

"But she can't just marry a man who will be president. They said that other woman is First Lady already. Jackie didn't do anything wrong but now she won't get to be there anymore. In the White House. She was so pretty she ought to be able to keep on doing it without him. That other lady isn't even pretty. She's old."

He didn't know how to respond, or if he should respond at all. He wished Norma were there.

"Jackie will have to pack her things," Roxanne went on, "so that other woman can move in. She won't get to travel with the president because the new one isn't her husband. And have her picture in magazines and have everybody copy her clothes . . ."

Cy came in; he'd been listening. "She's lucky she didn't get hit," he said. "Getting her would have been a lot better for us because she's not that important . . ."

"Can't you understand?" Roxanne interrupted. "Why are both of you so stupid?"

A newscaster began to talk about Jackie, which caught Roxanne's attention. Zack backed out the door as Walter Cronkite described how Mrs. Kennedy had had a priest perform the last rites, how Jack's strong body had continued to breathe even though his head was mortally wounded. They showed Jackie Kennedy being led away. Roxanne clutched the edge of the ledger and moaned.

"She has his blood on her skirt. Look. Look!" she insisted.

"Could be dirt or coffee," Cy remarked stupidly.

"It's blood!" she shrieked.

"Bad luck," Cy said weakly. "She's doomed too."

Roxanne began to sob, dropping her head face down on the open book. While Zack went to get Ned, Cy shrugged and walked back to his workbench.

Ned hurried into the office. "Honey, why don't you cut this off?" he said, snapping off the television. "You don't need to keep watching it and getting all worked up. What's done is done. There is no reason in the world for you to do the books tonight anyway. Let me take you over to your mother's."

Ned led Roxanne outside to his pickup, his arm around her shoulders. He called back to Zack, who stood in the doorway, "Why don't you guys just go on home, okay? You lock up for me, Zack."

After Arnold left, Tom said, "We might as well go home. Nobody's got their minds on working anyway."

"We'll give you and Richard a ride in the Chevy," Cy offered. They climbed into the car that still smelled like a musty closet.

Main Street was empty except for a beat-up old Plymouth that went past with a deer strapped to the fender.

"I bet that guy don't even know yet," Cy said.

"He's probably got a radio," Tom told him.

"The president's just like that deer on the fender, you know?" Cy continued.

"You mean dead."

"I mean he got up and ate breakfast this morning and didn't know he'd be dead before dark."

"I think he might have had a good idea it could happen someday," Tom said.

"The deer or the president?"

"Both of them, if a deer is that smart."

"That's a pretty creepy way to feel."

Tom answered, "Seems to me it'd be that way if you took the chance of being president. Same as if you decide to be a race car driver. You don't figure you're going your whole life without having any bad wrecks. Or a space man. You could get lost out there. It's not like the president's somebody innocent getting it who just happened to be riding by in a car in the wrong place. Nobody made him be president."

"I tried to tell Roxanne it would be better if he'd shot Jackie," Cy said, "and she acted like Jackie was her sister or something."

"You mean she acted like Jackie was her," Tom replied.

"That guy who done it was a hell of a good shot," Cy said. "Think how hard it is to hit one of them ducks on that moving thing at the fair."

"That's not hard," Tom said.

"Not for you," Zack put in. "You should have seen what a shot Tom was when we were little. Remember that wildcat, Tom?"

"Yeah, I remember it. Our old man would rather have shot me than that wildcat."

When they stopped at a stoplight, Richard spoke up from the backseat beside Tom, "Much obliged if you'd let me out here." He had been so quiet they'd forgotten he was in there. Zack jumped out and folded the seat forward, then watched him walk away as he settled back in. Richard made it to the sidewalk before the light changed. He had said nothing about Kennedy dying.

"Why don't you guys keep the car tonight?" Cy said as he made a U-turn on Main. "We're closer to my place than yours. I ain't got nowhere to go. Nothing's going to be open anyway."

When Cy stopped beside the curb in front of his house, Charlie the rooster came running to the edge of the porch like a dog. He glistened under the porch bulb, catching the only light.

"Look at that stupid chicken," Cy said. "He ain't got any idea in the world that somebody just shot the president."

Charlie jumped off the porch and flapped into the bushes when Horace came out the door. The old man's arms were pressed tightly against his chest, holding a blanket over his shoulders. He wore no shoes though it was cold; his bare big toe came through his black sock, as red as his nose. When he stopped in the doorway, he looked like a person who had to tell everyone some bad news.

"What's she burning tonight?" Cy called.

Horace made a loud sniffing sound. "Believe it's meatloaf."

On the next corner in front of the post office, the flag hung at half-staff in the dark. "Look at that flag, Zack. It's half down." Ned always asked them to quit work at the track while they ran up the flag, not to be disrespectful like some of the guys and start the motor during the national anthem. "This whole town is shut down."

"It isn't going to be like normal for a long time, Tom. You want to go back to the shop or home?" Zack asked. "You can have the car if you want to go back to work later on tonight."

"Home, I guess," Tom answered. "There's no reason to work any more anyway." When Tom spoke, the weight of his own words appeared to overcome him. He didn't speak again until they got to his apartment. "Don't you know what this means?" Tom asked.

Zack shook his head.

"It means they cancel Turkey Night."

Turkey Night. The Thanksgiving race, the last event of the season. A week after the race Tom won, the organizers had come for his trophy, because there was a dispute with Randall Johnson. Nothing was written about the controversy anywhere, but people were talking about it. Tom knew a lot of them believed Johnson had won, yet no one would say that to him. No one except his own brother.

"I guess it does," Zack said quietly.

"I worked all summer long to win this one."

"It's not going to bring him back to cancel a race," Zack replied, "but I don't think Turkey Night will seem very important to people after this."

Tom pounded the dash, at first with no real fury, just something to do with the hands that he couldn't use, but as his temper began to build, he hit harder. Zack sat still beside him. Tears came into Tom's eyes. He turned to look at Zack and when their eyes met straight on, Tom got out of the car and slammed the door.

Zack drove around a while, turning on the radio, but nothing was playing but sad songs and the same news. He went to his boarding house. When he walked into the living room, the landlady invited him to watch her color TV with her. Jackie stood with the blood on her skirt, a pink skirt. It was the same picture he'd seen in black and white at the shop. Roxanne hadn't known it was pink with red on it.

The brother, Robert Kennedy, came on. It was strange; everyone in the country was hearing the same information, only that man was the dead man's brother. They showed Jackie again. Zack didn't hear the words anymore because he was trying to think. Real people didn't die the way they did in the movies, a small red hole in their bodies. Cy was right. When she put her clothes on that morning, she didn't know she'd take them off that night, smeared with her dead husband's blood.

His landlady sent him into her kitchen, insisting that he not try to go out to find somewhere to eat. She acted like it was a death in his family. "I've got yams and fried chicken left over. And Veda can warm up some biscuits. You know you can't get a meal good as that, wherever it is you go. If you'd eat decent, your face wouldn't break out so. And you shouldn't have to go out, not tonight. I insist, Zachary."

He didn't fight back. In the kitchen, Veda Washington, the colored cook who wore a white ruffled cap and hummed and rocked around the kitchen like a windup toy, began to dish up a plate of food. He said thank you and sat down and ate like a starving man while she hummed "Rock of Ages," washing a mountain of dishes. After he finished, he walked up behind Veda with his dishes. She spun around, took them and dropped them into the suds. She smiled the only smile he'd seen all day, but she had tears in her eyes. Before he left to go upstairs, he hugged her. He thought it would be a quick hug, but he pressed himself into her as though she were a bed pillow. She patted him on the cheek, leaving suds that turned into a cold, wet spot on his face before he made it up to his room.

In bed that night, Zack tried to imagine which man he might be someday: the president or the man who killed the president. He couldn't fit either man into his fantasies. But his brother took both parts with ease. The man with the gun and the man in the limousine.

Tom was a good shot. They'd had only one shotgun, an old double-barreled one. It kicked so hard it turned Zack's shoulder blue, sending most of his shot straight up when he went over backwards.

"Press the butt against your shoulder," Tom instructed. "If you hold it away from you like it's going to hurt you, that's exactly what happens."

Zack never took his second shot. Tom sighted the wildcat that had eaten their daddy's mouser. When he fired into the tree, the leaves exploded.

"I got him!" Tom yelled.

Zack thought, Are you sure you hit him?, but by that age he had learned the value of silence around his brother. It was time for Tonto to serve his friend, the Lone Ranger. He crawled on the ground under the tree.

Picking up a batch of leaves, Zack found blood on his fingers: dark on the green leaves, but bright red on his skin. He held his hand up for Tom, who sniffed his cold fingers as if he knew what blood smelled like. In the woods, Zack found more splashes. Each time he pointed, Tom touched the spot then wiped his fingers on his pants. Soon the side of his jeans was stained dark.

Suddenly they heard a sound.

Tom lifted the gun. "Zack," he whispered, "I hear him."

Zack froze. A crunching sound on dead leaves got closer.

Tom spun with the gun. "Zack," he whispered, softer now, "you look this way and I'll look the other. As soon as you see him, holler 'shoot.'" Instead, Zack kept looking at Tom, who had one eye closed with the other so wide it was rimmed in white. Suddenly the crunching stopped. Zack felt the wildcat's haunches tighten as it prepared to jump. He dropped to his knees and put his arms over his head.

When he was waiting for the claws to dig into his back, Tom hissed and kicked him in the side. "Look, you bastard! Look for him, you chickenshit bastard." Zack bounded to his feet and began to spin with nothing focusing in front of his eyes, not even up close. His feet danced to keep Tom from shooting him, the coward dancing for the gunslinger.

Zack didn't know who saw him first, he or Tom. But if Zack had been the one with the gun, he'd have shot his own daddy.

Hershel stopped suddenly, popping out of the trees. He lifted his hands in front of his face as if all he had to stop was a paper airplane.

"Daddy!" Tom gasped, dropping the gun barrel to point at the ground. He talked fast. "It was a big wildcat, Daddy, and he was coming after us and I shot him, but I think I just winged him . . ."

"What the hell you doing shooting a wildcat?" Hershel's voice boomed over Tom's. "You planning on eating wildcat for dinner?"

"No," Tom said weakly.

Hershel found the wildcat for them, remembering a hollow tree in the woods as if it was a closet or a cabinet. "I wish you hadn't done that, Tom," he said simply.

"Daddy," Tom pleaded, "scare him back in if he tries to get out. I'm going home for my rifle."

As Hershel stood up, a rustle inside the tree caught their attention.

"What the hell you talking about?" Hershel's voice cracked a little.

"I want to shoot him with my rifle. I don't want to mess up his head."

Hershel swung his hand back, hitting Tom hard, as hard as he would hit a mule on the rump. Then Hershel leveled the shotgun into the log, took aim and fired, the gun kicking him back a little. When the noise of the explosion passed, shot rattled inside the log. Then there was silence.

Hershel rose up, opened the gun, and flicked out the empty red shell. Then he held two empty barrels towards the sky before he dropped the gun at Tom's feet. "Before dark I want to see that wildcat skint and up to the house so Mama can cook it." He turned and walked away.

Tom snatched the gun off the ground. He was crying. Crying mad. He pointed the gun at the spot in the trees where his father had disappeared. Without thinking, Zack tackled him from behind. They rolled down the creek bank, then slugged at each other for a while, mostly missing because the ground was too wet to stand up. They fought until fatigue made them both sit down.

At supper while everyone including Zack got chicken, Hershel made Tom eat wildcat, every bite he made his wife put on the boy's plate. The house reeked from the cat cooking; Rachel opened all of the windows and turned on the oscillating fan.

Before Tom fell asleep, he threw up five times. His mother brought him a bowl of ice cream to settle his stomach, but after she left, Zack ate it instead while Tom buried his face into his pillow.

The taxidermist had a mailbox with a stuffed deer head coming out. He didn't want to mount the cat. He stitched on a piece of fur from the rump to patch the face. Tom told him to leave the teeth showing, the scattered ones Hershel hadn't blown out with the shotgun. When Tom went to pick up the stuffed head, the cat looked more like a werewolf. He still wanted to hang his trophy up because it had cost him ten dollars, but Gladys put it under the bed every time she cleaned the boys' room.

"Tom, did you remember that the shotgun was empty when you pointed it at Daddy?" Zack had to ask.

"Sure I knew it was empty. You think I don't know how many shells a double-barrel shotgun holds?" Then he laughed a phony laugh. "Mark my words, little brother, if killing was my job, I'd of killed him dead."

Zack tried to remember which movie Tom got that line from.

"You're a lying dog," he told Tom, who pulled the thunder jug from under his bed to throw up again.

Zack never saw another wildcat on their farm. The truth was he would never have seen that one if it hadn't been dead. On the day Kennedy died, he thought about that wildcat; how easy it was to kill a sparrow or step on a bug, but a wildcat was hard to kill. Would they hunt it at all if it caught starlings and mice in the open fields like his daddy's mouser, drank cow's milk from a bucket and let you pat it on the head if you talked sweet to it? Tom wouldn't have, he was pretty sure of that. A president was supposed to be hard to kill, too. If Zack had been the one doing the hunting, that wildcat and President Kennedy both would have gotten to die of old age.

Tom believed that their daddy would rather have shot him than that wildcat. But it seemed to Zack like something else was going on, that his daddy was trying to make them love what he loved. And it didn't work. Hershel said you should work so hard you don't have time or energy to get in trouble. Or to stop and think you might be bored. They did that, Tom and Zack, working on the race car so hard that nothing else existed. But the only kind of working their daddy thought earned you a place in heaven was farming. If you raise enough food to keep your body going and wood and cotton to keep it warm, then when you lie down to sleep, you know all your needs are taken care of. For Tom that was the same thing as lying down and dying. Zack wasn't sure. Zack didn't know if his daddy ever had nights when he couldn't sleep, when his mind kept him awake. His daddy had to know that things weren't that simple even if he didn't have the words to say so.

But things did seem that simple to Tom. He knew where he was going, how to become his own daydream. A broken tooth in the wheel that rolled him towards that goal—even if it was the death of a president that jammed the wheel for everyone else—didn't stop him. Tom would butt against the wheel until it rolled again.

With Tom, action wasn't a momentary thing, gone in a split second. It was a state of mind that he could sustain for a whole performance. Zack could go to the end of a diving board and, for that one split second, find something within himself that would hurl his body into the water. It was different for Tom; action wasn't one seemingly fearless act that resembled the way a man commits suicide.

"Doesn't it ever bother you that you might get killed doing one of these dangerous things, Tom?" Zack had asked him ten years ago.

"Doesn't bother me," Tom answered flippantly, "because I won't be around to be sad about it." As far as Zack could tell, Tom's feelings hadn't changed.

On November 23, 1963, Zack was sure his brother's heart and his brain were barreling full speed in one direction like a train through a tunnel. But he wasn't sure anymore if he was riding on the train with him.

24

Turkey Night was rescheduled for the following Saturday. The name was changed because Thanksgiving was past; it became the Santa Claus Classic, but everyone still called it Turkey Night.

The week following the assassination, everyone came back to work at Ned's as usual. Tom had been in the shop alone, working every day, going through the car again even though it had been ready to run the previous week. He whipped the enthusiasm back up, and soon Cy and Arnold were back working overtime again. Zack had grown melancholy as the first signs of Christmas began to appear, and spent most of his time practicing his welding, making and remaking parts. By race day, the car was the best it had ever been.

Buster Simmons' picture still hung upside down in Ned's office, a position Cy insisted was necessary to place a hex on him so they could beat him in the final race. Buster's hot streak had continued. As a novelty for the fans on his hometown track at Rougemont, Buster had started at the back of the field. On Bust Buster Night, he had taken the green backwards, doing a bootleg turn before he was facing the right way. He still won. He won all the races except three: one when he lost his motor; one when the rear end seized; and one when a tire blew and sent him into the wall.

The Santa Claus Classic organizers were hoping for a dry day because it was too late in the year to try again before winter set in. The promoter told Ned that Buster had driven in with his rig to an empty track on the original Turkey Night date, wondering where every one was. Tom took pleasure in that.

They were eating pizza in the office, with Roxanne picking the pepperoni and green peppers off her slice. "You know one of the main reasons I can't stand racing?" Roxanne said.

Ned chuckled and decided to humor her. "No, honey, why?"

"You don't even care what I think. Quit making fun of me. Mother agrees with me."

Ned's mood changed. "I don't need for you to tell me her opinion. I heard it more times than I wanted to for twenty years. Okay, two reasons: because I spent every dime I made on something that I could wreck in a second, instead of on her. And because I loved it better than her. I know it wasn't because she gave a damn if I got hurt, right?"

"Wrong," Roxanne snapped. "Besides, I have my own opinions."

There was an awkward silence.

"Are we going to hear them?" Cy asked. Everyone looked at him, including Ned.

"We don't need to butt into a family argument," Zack said awkwardly.

"It isn't a family argument." Roxanne's eyes darted for a moment, then they found Tom's. "Is it, Tom?"

He looked away, then he answered, "She already told me. The reason she hates racing is because the only way we're ever happy is when we've beat somebody else."

"That's not the way I said it."

"But it's what you meant. Don't ask me to say something if you aren't going to like the way I put it."

"What I meant is that's all you've got to look forward to," she blurted out, "making somebody else feel bad or get hurt. You let all the beautiful things in life pass right by you while you're out there trying to make someone else feel miserable. How can that make a person happy for long? It shouldn't make a nice person happy."

"Come on, Roxanne," Ned reasoned. "The guy losing was trying to be a winner as much as you were. He's not some little innocent lamb. Besides, a driver could win a bunch of money. He's got that to look forward to. Your mother certainly enjoyed spending it when I won it."

"Well, if you insist on bringing her into this, she told *me* that if you'd brought her one bunch of flowers for no other reason than to say you loved her, she'd have been happier."

"Oh, bullshit. She spent enough money to buy a florist."

"Why can't you want to do something that makes everybody happy?" she asked.

Ned stood up to walk to the door, the signal that the lunch break was over. "That's the job we save for you women, honey." He smiled and patted her on the head. "You make love and we make war. Right now the guy we don't love and are gonna make war on is Buster Simmons. World War III, right here on Greenmont Raceway."

After Ned left, Arnold turned to Roxanne and pointed to her picked-clean slice of pizza. "You eating the rest of that?"

She shook her head so he folded it up and stuffed it into his mouth as he walked out. The others followed Arnold, like Snow White's troupe of dwarfs with Cy singing, "Hi-ho, Hi-ho, it's off to work we go." Roxanne slammed the door to the office so hard the wall partitions rocked.

It had rained all week, saturating the track, so the water trucks sat idle in the infield. Pickup trucks circulated on the oval, trying to pack the wet clay, their tires like giant black doughnuts iced in orange. A mild odor of decay hung in the air mingled with the scent of cured tobacco stacked in the warehouses in town. During the night, the temperature had dropped, giving the ground a crunchy feeling underfoot. The stands were almost empty, though a few loyal spectators huddled in blankets.

"Look up there, Tom. People act like they're freezing," Cy said.

"Send them down here," Arnold put in. "Get their butts moving and they'll warm up."

Allie Burcham sat by the announcer's booth in his wheelchair, wrapped in an Indian blanket. Red deposited him there, while he went back into the pits. Tom had heard Red was building another car and might need a driver for the spring season. Tom told the crew that this time he would let Red ask him; maybe he would tell him he would consider it, but that he had other offers.

Tom picked up a list of entrants. "Randall Johnson isn't entered," he told the crew. They had let Tom keep the winning money from the last race, but they hadn't given him back the trophy. No one knew if they had given it to Johnson. Tom told Zack he went over and over the race in his mind. It was true; he didn't recall lapping Johnson. But he thought he could have caught him, if anyone on his crew had told him he was behind.

Giles Burcham crossed the pit towards them. "B-B-B-Buster is here. I seen him signing in," he spit out. "He brought his old car. Daddy says he didn't figure anyone around here could beat him even in that piece of shit. He tore up his good car at Hickory three weeks ago." Then Giles added a surprise. "Daddy says if you p-p-put his ass in the fence, Tom, you can drive our car next year."

"How about I just beat him?"

"Daddy says crash him."

"That isn't how I beat people. I want to outrun him. If you want him in the fence, you do it."

"Get out of here, Burcham," Arnold snapped. "We're here to race, not crash people. You're a goddamned busted record. If your brother hadn't been so fucking slow, he wouldn't have gotten hit."

Giles balled his fists, his face glowing red. Arnold went back to work on his engine, leaving Giles nothing to do but pound on Arnold's backside if he chose to attack.

"Hey, Useless," Arnold called.

Both Cy and Zack walked over to him. "I meant you, Useless," he said, nodding at Zack, "not you, Useless." He shooed Cy away. "Get in the car and do what I tell you to."

Zack climbed in the window, slowly dragging his short legs through the opening. Arnold's gauges stared at him, twitching as the engine warmed up. He slumped in the seat like a sack of feed, pumping the pedal when Arnold told him to.

Tom drew the twenty-third qualifying attempt. Buster was sixteenth. After Buster's run, Tom would know what time he had to set. "Buster won't push too hard because he don't expect nobody to beat him," Arnold commented. Buster sat on a stack of mounted wheels in the pits. They belonged to Homer Foushee, who was so shamefaced he ran on his old practice tires rather than ask Buster to give up his seat so he could put on his better rubber. Buster lit up a cigarette and squinted at the numbers as they went up on the chalkboard. The track was getting faster.

He jumped down off the tires and headed towards his car, nodding at Tom as he passed. Tom watched him talk to his mechanics, who crawled under the car to adjust the suspension.

"What's he doing?" Tom asked Arnold.

"Shit if I know. Send Cy over to look."

"Yeah, get my head bashed in."

"You're too fucking stupid to know what you're looking at anyway," Arnold replied. "Maybe he's loosening it up. Yeah, that's it. The track is sliding better."

"Then loosen up mine," Tom said.

Arnold lifted an eyebrow at Tom. "You think you want something changed you ain't run?"

Tom shrugged his shoulders. "I guess not. I-I don't know," he stammered. He opened and closed his fists.

"Maybe you want to put a turd in your pocket," Cy mimicked Horace. "I hear Buster has one in his."

Zack thought of the story their mother used to read them when they were little, about Little Reddy Fox. The fox piled up his turds to build a fire. Tom made his mother read that part over and over because he couldn't believe they would say turd in a book. Zack knew better than to mention the story as he watched Tom pull out the drawers in his tool box and order the tools according to size. When Buster climbed into his car, Tom slammed the drawers and hurried down beside the track.

"Your brother's a fly on a horse pile today," Arnold told Zack, loud enough for Tom to hear. "Nobody gives a shit who wins this race. Even Buster's mother wouldn't come to sit out in this rotten cold if you give her a free ticket."

Buster went onto the track, sampling the corners with his warmup run. Tom watched on his wristwatch. Buster's warmup lap would have put him on the pole. He took the green. Tom glanced up and down from his watch to the track after each turn, watching Buster's technique. It was a fast one. As Buster set up for the last turn, Tom's eyes stayed on the track. He was on the throttle hard. Too hard. Even Buster couldn't make it that fast. The rear end broke loose and he slid up against the wall, cutting a rear tire and dumping the car down on one side. Buster's run ended as he shot across the track into the pits, the tire unrolling from the wheel.

"Still want me to make that suspension change?" Arnold laughed. "Looks like Superman took a shit."

"He's still got a lap coming. Damn, I bet he waits till the end to take it after he knows how fast I've gone."

"You think he knows you from Adam's house cat, Pate?" Arnold asked.

"Yeah, I do."

On his warmup lap, Tom saw Buster standing beside the first turn to watch him. By the time he took the green, Buster was gone from his mind. He put together two laps that felt like the best he had turned all season. He saw Cy jumping up and down as he passed the pits on the cool-off lap; Zack's face had no expression.

When Tom got out of the car and went to check the qualifying board, he was two-tenths of a second under quick time on his final lap, putting him on pole.

Buster stared at the qualifying board. Then he turned to look at Tom and his car as if it were the first time he was really seeing them. Buster's mechanics rolled his car to the back of the line for his one remaining qualifying lap. The rear body-work had been pulled back out where he'd brushed the wall, the paint cracking around the bent metal.

Tom's whole crew walked down to the first turn to watch. Buster had more spectators in the infield than he did in the stands as a chilly wind swept across the open track.

"Getting windy," Cy said, pulling on a dirty sweatshirt that hiked up in the back. "Maybe that'll mess him up."

"You think I can't beat Buster unless something gets screwed up for him?" Tom snapped. Buster passed and the mud drilled at the fence behind him. The track was in good condition, better than when Tom had run.

Cy ignored Tom's question and commented instead, "Track's coming in now. Wish we'd got a higher number."

Their eyes followed Buster around. No one spoke as he went through the turns. Unlike in his earlier run, his car was handling now. As soon as he took the checkered, Tom went to the qualifying board, waiting for the time to be posted.

The man who tended the board had a big grin on his face when he walked out. He chalked in the time beside Buster's number. Tom didn't take his eyes away. Cy tugged at his sleeve like a child, waiting to be told what it said.

"Son of a bitch, we got it!" Arnold shouted. "We're on pole, Pate."

When Tom turned to shake hands with his crew—Ned wasn't there yet—Zack went back to their area to gather up tools. Arnold slapped Cy so hard on the back he almost knocked him down.

"You want to put on your new tires now, Mr. Tom?" Richard asked.

"Yeah, sure. Why not? No use saving them until spring. Who knows where any of us will be by then."

As they spoke, Ned arrived. Roxanne wasn't with him.

"Where's Roxanne?" Cy asked. "She said she was coming."

"She didn't feel so good. Got a sick headache," Ned replied. "Said she didn't want to stand out in the cold."

"I can't believe she's missing our last race," Cy said. "I guess she really means she doesn't care about all of this."

"She doesn't care," Ned answered. "I can guarantee that. Just like her mother. When she's not going to be the center of attention, she'd just as soon sit home and pout. Where'd you qualify?"

"Pole," Tom answered.

"Pole! Why didn't you say so?"

"I just did."

"Serves her right, missing that. Serves me right too. I ought to have gotten out on time. Mona says hop and I ask how high. Where's Buster?"

"Second. He's going to be tough, though."

"That ought to turn some heads. Outqualified Buster. What'd Red say?"

"Nothing. Nothing except he wants me to put Buster in the wall."

Ned shook his head and carried two bags of burgers and

fries that bled grease spots through the brown paper to the tailgate. Zack didn't look up from scrubbing dirt off the car.

"Zack, come on over here," Tom called. "Let's eat our food now before it gets cold." Ned tore open the bag and dealt out the burgers. One was left over.

"Richard!" Ned yelled. "Get on over here if you're hungry."

Richard hurried over, took his burger, and went off to find a place to eat it. Zack's eyes followed him until he disappeared around the corner of one of the stables.

"Well, are we ready for him?" Ned asked.

"Damn right," Arnold replied quickly. "Buster's going to find out it was the team he was on that put him in the front before." He grinned at Tom.

"Hey, don't give me so much credit, Arnold," Tom said.

"Wouldn't want your head to get any bigger, Pole Cat. Might not be able to get your helmet on."

When the cars were in place on the grid, the national anthem began to play over the P.A. system. The flag still flew at half-staff, snapping in the cold wind that rolled shop rags around the pit area. When the song ended, Zack ran around with a bucket, scooping up the orange cloths.

"What's the matter with you?" Tom asked Zack while the announcer was introducing the drivers, going through the list in reverse order.

"Me?" Zack looked around. "I guess you mean me. Nothing that I know of. What did I do wrong?"

"Nothing that I know of," Tom mocked with a laugh. "You're acting funny, is why I asked."

When they reached Buster's name, he acknowledged the introduction with a quick wave to the stands that had filled to half capacity for the feature. When the cheers died down, there was a lingering boo from the man in the wheelchair beside the announcer's stand. The announcer waited until Allie's voice grew hoarse before he introduced Tom.

"And tonight's pole-sitter, for the first time this season, is Tom Pate from right here in Greenmont, driving the blue and white number seven out of Ned's All-American Automotive. Let's hear it for Tom."

Allie waved his arms like a drunken fighter as his cheers were lost behind the whistles from the stands. People stood up and lifted their fists. Tom Pate had fans he didn't even know. They wanted him to beat Buster bad. He felt a shot of electricity go through his body before he climbed through the window. His engine, already warmed up by Arnold, ticked in the cold air, sitting in line waiting to be rolled out. Tom's brain was empty of everything but the race ahead of him; it was nothing he had to try to do, it just happened.

"Crank her up," Arnold called. The engine hopped back to life quickly.

The pace car pulled onto the track, a 1964 Chevy Impala off the showroom floor from Compton's Chevy downtown. Buster began to inch forward. Tom got on the throttle, feeling a touch of anger that Buster moved first. He was the pole-sitter, not Buster. He got to lead off. As they moved slowly around the track, mud flew off the spinning wheels of the pace car and rattled under the front of his car. Tom reached up to tap the wire in front of his face, knocking off a wet clod that rolled off the hood.

He tried the throttle with the brake on, feeling out the surface. It was slicker than when he'd qualified. They had wet it down while the crew was eating. He should have gone over to look at it. Buster probably had. It felt strange, seeing the back of the pace car like that with no cars in between, knowing everyone was behind him except Buster, who rode up on his right side. Usually his wire windshield was clogged with mud by now. He faced the track like an animal with the cage door left open.

The pace car pulled off, heading into the pit entrance. One more time around. Buster spurted ahead, biting at the track, teasing him. He had to get his mind off Buster, on his own car. You can't drive just looking out the window, he told himself.

As they came off the third turn, Tom glanced up for the starter. He saw the stand, the new wood where Termite Bivens' flipping car had ripped the bottom out, dumping the starter on the ground three weeks ago. The starter's left arm was in a cast now. He held the furled flag stuffed in his left arm pit. Tom couldn't see how they were lined up behind, or if he had paced them too fast. He couldn't hold his eyes on the wobbling rearview mirror. He thought the starter's eyes were on him and Buster, making sure he was the first off. He began to gas it in the third turn. He felt a tap. Buster had moved over into his lane, trying to shove him low and take his place in the fast groove. When Tom got on the gas, Buster moved as though he was glued to his door. The starter snapped out the green, sending them both forward like bulls.

As they reached the first turn, Tom held the inside. Buster didn't move in behind, accepting second position, but chose to go high instead, trying to take him. When Buster didn't back off, Tom stayed on the throttle too long, getting into the corner a little too hot. Buster moved over quickly, catching his chance to nose ahead while Tom stabilized his car, but Buster's car bobbled too because he also had come in too hot. Tom had sucked him into the corner too fast.

Tom recovered first, coming out of the second turn ahead, and spurting onto the straight. He lost sight of Buster. He went four laps before he spotted Ned standing in the third turn, his hands pressed together like book ends. He didn't have to look to know Buster was right there, waiting like a cat for him to lose his concentration. In the next turn, he felt another tap, Buster reminding him where he was.

On the next lap, Buster dove low. He got underneath Tom and shoved him high into the loose dirt. Tom felt his front end get light as the car moved up. Buster's car moved half a length ahead of him. Instinctively he backed off then came back hard on the throttle as he went low under Buster in turn two. The pass worked both ways as Tom came out ahead and on the gas with his wheels pointed down the straight before Buster had recovered. By three he was tapping Tom again, all the way through the turn almost politely as though Tom were blocking his passage down a hallway.

When they began to overtake lapped cars, their driving styles changed as they both moved through traffic, trying to set up the slower cars as blocks. Tom stayed in front, so he did the picking and choosing, but a slow car in turn three on the fourteenth lap let Buster move high and pass them both on the outside. Heavy clods off Buster's wheels hit the wire in front of his face as Buster drove down off the loose wet dirt on the berm. Tom saw a slow car in the turn ahead sending off blue spirals of oil smoke each time it decelerated. He went deep to the inside, startling its driver, who moved up, tapping the rear of Buster's car. When they reached the short straight, they were in a dead heat to the next turn. Overhead in the starter's stand Tom caught a quick glimpse of the crossed flags—the race was half over.

Through turns one and two, they stayed even, Buster on the high side. As they exited two, Tom gained a few feet. He lost sight of Buster out the side. He glanced at Ned, who stood on the inside of three. His hands were spaced a few inches apart and he pointed to the inside. Buster was going to the inside again to pass. Tom moved down lower into a defensive position, to shut the door if Buster was coming through. Just as he moved, he felt a sharp jolt in his left rear. Buster was further up than he had realized. His own car leapt forward, shoved off the ground by Buster's momentum, then it dropped and he steered it into the groove. The hit was hard, hard enough to damage a tire, but he couldn't let that fill his mind.

On the next approach to three, he saw Red standing beside Ned. Ned was still signaling that Buster was closing while Red slammed his fist into his palm. Red knew only one command: crush him. It might be the easy way to get a ride for next year; move into him and shove him into the wall. But there was no guarantee that he wouldn't crash at the same time. And he wanted to beat Buster racing.

As he drove past Ned on the next lap, Tom shut Red from his vision. Ned was giving him a countdown. Two hands. Ten laps. Each time he glanced at Ned, Buster moved alongside. He couldn't tell if he lost his concentration on his driving then, or if Buster thought he did, or if he was just weak in that turn. Then he had to struggle until turn two when he was able to pull Buster onto the straight.

The clay was getting too dry, with rubber and oil pounded into the groove until it glistened black like pavement. The lower groove became the racing groove and the lapped cars moved up high into the loose dirt. Tom still maintained his lead as passing grew difficult to impossible on the one-lane track. Then, as the two front-runners moved into the second turn four laps from the end, a lapped car moved into the loose clay too abruptly, lost it, and hit the wall, bouncing back into the traffic lane. The yellow flag came out, but not before the third and fifth place cars had collected him.

When Tom passed under the starter's stand, he saw the yellow flag hung limply from the official's good arm. Tom slowed and moved into the first turn. To his surprise, Buster darted past. The corner flagman wasn't waving his flag, he had turned to look at the pileup. As he exited the second turn, the yellow flag was out. Buster let up and squeezed through the slot between the three tangled cars and the edge of the road. Tom followed him through, expecting Buster to slow and let him move back into his front position.

Red was jumping up and down in the third turn, waving his fists. Ned looked disturbed. They didn't see how Buster got ahead. He passed under yellow. Why didn't they know that? He had to go back to second position. When they went under the starter's stand, Buster moved over into the groove, blocking Tom. The starter held the flag unfurled now, but he didn't motion for Buster to drop back. Tom moved up on his rear, tapping him lightly as they went into two to get his attention. Buster gassed it, moving through two and back through the slot between the crash. One wrecker had crossed the track and was tugging at the front car.

When Tom passed by, he saw Ned hold up three fingers. Red still waved his fist. As Buster passed under the starter's stand, the green was waving and no one had made him get back into position. Tom jumped on the gas and nudged him in the first turn. When they reached the crash area, a second wrecker moved across. They had given the green too soon. Tom butted the rear of Buster's car and they both went sideways. Buster accelerated when the wrecker was clear, racing toward the last turn. Tom got on the gas, charging in behind Buster. He tried to move inside, but was blocked. Tom forgot to look at Ned. His eyes were on Buster, searching for a hole on the one-lane track. His anger propelled him. The surface was starting to get slick, pounded as hard as black ice.

Every time he tried to get around him, Buster moved over in his path. Tom saw the white flag. One lap. He followed Buster into turn one, leaning on him until he heard their sides meet. He had to get him this lap. He kept his foot down, forcing Buster's right front wheel into the loose clay. They came out of two, then three, side by side. He knew Buster would move to the inside and block him out of four. As they went into the last turn before the flag, Tom dove for the high side, up into the loose clay. The car had no bite, but he stood on it anyway, racing across the hard center groove until he was up beside Buster. The steering wheel vibrated violently in his grip as he leaned against Buster's door, pushing him lower on the apron. The checkered waved overhead, but Tom didn't look up or let up. He pressed down harder on Buster until he felt him give, his left front fender reaching ahead of Buster's right by inches.

Before he reached the first turn, he backed off. The race was over. The engine noise died and he could hear people, whistles and yells. He hadn't looked into the pit area to see his crew; his vision had gone no farther than the side of Buster's car. He knew he had beat Buster across the line, though he'd refused to yield, even after the race was over. Buster stubbornly took the cool-off lap ahead of Tom.

Ned was gone. No one was on the third corner. Tom had a terrible sinking feeling. He drove down the pit lane. Cy and Arnold came over the wall and pounded on the car.

He shut down the engine.

"You beat the motherfucker," he heard Arnold say.

Tom's whole body began to tingle.

"Yeah? Yeah, I did, didn't I?"

"Sonavabitching right, you did."

Cy pounded Tom on his back as he climbed out the window. Zack came up to shake his hand. Red was behind him. He was agitated.

"Why didn't you crash him out, you chickenshit?" he asked.

Tom was taken aback.

"You had him right th-there," Giles added. "Acted like you were scared to death of him."

"You guys are nuts," Tom said as he climbed from the car.

"What's that?" Red snapped.

"You guys are *nuts!*" Tom shouted from beneath his helmet, loud enough for men to hear for fifty yards. "We were racing, not having a fight!" He pointed across the pit area. "Look over there. There's Buster getting in that white-top Ford. Just take your pickup and crash the hell out of him yourself."

"He ain't racing now," Giles said, perplexed. "Get in t-t-trouble with the law for doing that."

Tom turned away from them. "Where's Ned?"

"I don't know," Arnold answered. "I thought he was on the third turn."

"He was gone the last time I came by."

"There's Mr. Ned," Richard pointed. "Going up them steps."

They turned to see Ned as he climbed the stairs to the scoreboard. First and second had been taken down. The man stood holding both numbers, waiting for instructions. Ned walked across the platform, taking Tom's number 7 from the man's hands. He moved across the scaffolding, holding it high over his head. When he dropped it into the slot, a cheer went up from the pits and a few isolated claps came from the nearly deserted stands. When Ned left to climb back down, the scoreboard keeper stared at his back, still holding Buster's number.

While Ned waited at the payoff window, Tom and Richard lifted the last tool box into the truck. Cy, Zack, and Arnold had left for the shop in Arnold's pickup as a light snow began to fall. Tom reached into his pocket for a cigarette, pulling out an empty pack.

Richard took out the Lucky Strike pack he kept in his T-shirt pocket. He slowly removed a Pall Mall, slightly bent because it was too long for the pack, handing it to Tom.

"You're running on empty too," Tom said. "I'm not going to take your last smoke."

Richard straightened the cigarette gently, holding it it front of his face, doing a mental measurement before carefully breaking it in two, then handing Tom half. Richard tapped the loose tobacco back against his thumbnail, then struck a match between his fingernails, holding the flame to Tom first, the heat and sulfur smell so close to his face it made him recoil for an instant. Tom leaned his face back towards the flame.

Richard's cigarette was almost gone after two long deep drags. His fingers, dry and creased from washing parts barehanded in the solvent tank, had a white ash as though they had been dusted with flour.

"Thanks," Tom said, drawing on the cigarette and spitting the loose tobacco off his tongue.

Richard nodded, then shivered. He stuck his head through the neck of an oversized sweatshirt with the short cigarette still lit between his teeth.

"Guess our racing's done for sure now," Tom said. "Just when we get going good, then it's over with. We've really got the car working now."

Richard took the butt between two fingers and sucked on it with his eyes closed.

"I don't 'spect to race no more."

"How's that?" Tom asked. "You quitting Ned?"

"Naw, sir. I b'lieve Mr. Ned be quitting us."

Richard climbed up between the tool boxes and huddled into a ball in the darkness.

25

"See this picture, Tom," Arnold waved the photo under Tom's nose. Tom looked at the 1963 racing review in *Southern Motoracing* so Arnold wouldn't accuse him of turning away.

"Half the car is here," Arnold pointed, "and the other half is clean over there. This half's where the driver got it. See his leg out there?"

Then Arnold stuck his face in front of Tom, waiting for a response like a bulldog with a rag in his mouth. "That ain't what I call racing," he insisted. "Guy screws up and smacks the wall, okay, that's his fault. This guy blowed a tire and it kilt him. That's murder."

"Okay, Arnold. Let me ask you this," Tom replied. "Would you go to watch a circus act, a man on the flying trapeze, if the guy was using a net?"

Arnold stepped back and thought. "I thought they just used a net when they were practicing."

"If they put up a net," Cy broke in, "I'd climb up there and do it myself."

"See," Tom countered. "That's exactly what I meant. Taking the net down keeps any idiot from doing it."

"So?" Arnold questioned.

"So some drivers want to race on the big tracks and some don't. The ones who don't can slide around Greenmont Raceway in a bunch of junkers for nickels and dimes the rest of their lives. I'm not scared of going that fast, if that's what you're asking, Arnold."

"Yeah, well, that's kind of what I'm asking. Looks like to me if you got that fast then it's the car driving you instead of the other way around."

"If everybody is out there going three hundred miles an hour in motorized bathtubs, I'd do it. And I'd be the fastest. They just need to get better tires for those cars. And until they do, then that's the chance you take. Any of those guys starts to feel chicken, I'm ready to take his place. Like those guys who won't drive unless they've got a fireproof suit."

"I'd drive in my birthday suit," Cy put in.

Roxanne listened to all the talk through the office wall. She said to her daddy one evening as he closed the shop, "If Tom gets hurt in those cars, who's going to look after him? He never thinks about that and it happens all the time. And not just to drivers who aren't any good, like Allie."

"What are you getting at, sugar?" Ned asked with a smile.

"Where would he go?"

"Why don't you just bring him home?" Ned laughed. "Just like you did that kitten you found out back and give your mama something else to have to look after."

"I would look after him. I'd nurse him back to health."

"Sure you would. You still can't even stand to look at Allie.'

"That's not the same," she snapped.

"You don't want to nurse him back to health, honey. You're just trying to come up with a way to hold onto him. Once a guy like Tom thinks he's well, he's off looking for another car to take the place of the one he busted up. You might as well leave that thorn in his paw and be done with him."

"I don't know what you're talking about, Daddy."

"I didn't figure you did."

And so it went. The race car rolled to the corner of the shop, the street work came in steadily, and the 1963 season became nothing but the fodder of bench sessions at Ned's All-American Automotive. After Tom beat Buster on Santa Claus/Turkey Night, he was able to talk about the race against Randall Johnson. He asked Richard, "What you think of me going over to Randall's shop and telling him when I win one next season, I'll split the money with him? I'd do it now but I spent it already."

"The law got Randall. Tuesday night week ago," Richard answered. "Took his car and locked him up."

"What for?" Zack asked.

"Hauling, I reckon. It's what he's always done. Santa Claus going past Randall's house this Christmas."

It was mid December, and Zack was at Cy's house watching a Christmas tree descend through an attic door. The base appeared first, then the dark green lower branches. The top branches were covered in a year's worth of dust that had seeped through the attic roof and coated the top like artificial snow. The tree's perfectly proportioned sections stood like a cardboard cutout with branches as stiff as bottle brushes. Glass balls swung on the limbs, a red one losing its grip and bouncing to its death down the ladder staircase. Cords from the lights hung in a tangle.

"Stop laughing, motherfucker, and help me," Horace yelled at Cy, his voice muffled above the tree. When it was finally in place in the living room, the four of them encircled it: Mrs. Thomas, Cy, Zack, and Horace.

"See what I told you about leaving the shit on it?" Horace told his wife. "Now I don't have to decorate the damn thing again this year."

"You proved your point," Mrs. Thomas grunted, leaving the room. "Wouldn't want to cut into your sleeping time."

Horace rolled his lip up at her as she left and balled his fist. "The Bitch of Christmas Past and Future." Then he attempted to stoop, reaching towards the electrical cords, but changed his mind and pointed to Cy. "On with the lights, boy."

Cy plugged in the tangle. Nothing.

Zack's memory was suddenly filled with strings of lights that didn't work, screwing and unscrewing bulbs to locate the guilty one, lost in the decorated branches. Last Christmas, before he left home, he had helped his girlfriend, Laurie, decorate her tree; she had the kind of lights where a dead bulb didn't kill the whole string, a miracle his family was too cheap ever to experience.

Horace regarded the dark tree, saying, "Crap. Just put it in my box when you plant me, son. Here lies two burnt-out old carcasses." He crossed the room to his couch and curled up, his back to the tree. Then he popped back up and started towards the door.

"Where're you going, Pop?"

"To my milk truck."

"The door won't stay shut from the inside anymore."

"Why not?"

"Because I busted the lock."

"Why'd you do that?"

Cy stopped clowning, for once. "You know good and well why. Because I don't want to find you in there turned blue."

"You don't know how warm it is in my truck. It ain't like no refrigerator. Come out and try it." He scratched his side, his stubby fingers like a paw.

"Yeah, I know a guy is supposed to feel real hot all over right before he croaks, too."

Horace grunted and went back to the couch. "In here's too close to her," he mumbled and started snoring.

Cy asked Zack if he'd like a beer.

"Aren't you going to make the lights work?" Zack asked.

"Naw."

In the shop the next day while they ate their lunches, Zack told Tom about the dead lights on Cy's tree, "Imagine going all the way through Christmas with a dark tree."

"Cy's like me there," Tom replied. "I wouldn't fix them either if somebody didn't make me do it."

"How about Christmas?" Zack asked. "Don't you kind of

want to go home? Annie would be pretty excited about your trophy. Remember when that weed roller you invented got stuck and Annie fell off and got skint up."

"I've been gone a bunch of Christmases."

"I mean, Annie really liked us. We shouldn't have gone off and left her like that. Wouldn't you like to be there to give her a present and tell her you're sorry?"

Tom didn't answer. Zack waited for Tom to change the subject the way he always did when he'd try to pry into his thinking. Finally Tom asked, "Do you know why you're here, Zack?"

"Huh?"

"You heard me. Why are you here instead of there? Why did you come after me? You don't seem that happy working on cars anymore. You don't want to drive a race car."

"No, I wouldn't be good enough," he answered lamely. "I don't mind riding in a car going fast, but I don't want to be the driver."

"Then what's the point? I don't know what you want."

Zack dropped his face and shook his head. "I just wanted to know if you still thought about being at home at Christmas. I didn't mean to make you mad."

"I'm not mad. I'm sorry. I guess I am mad. I'm something. I'm irritated. And worried. Yeah, and mad." Then he paused. "But I'm not mad at you. And I don't worry about something dumb like not giving Annie a present and skinning her knee five years ago. Someday I'll see her and she'll be grown up and smart and pretty and I'll be proud she's my sister. And when I make a lot of money, I can buy her nice things." Tom took out his wallet, pulling out Annie's old school picture. "I sure hope she stays pretty."

"She doesn't look at all like that old picture anymore." Zack took the newer picture from his own wallet.

"I know that. You showed me that picture. You didn't offer to give it to me."

"It's the only one I've got."

Tom took the photo from Zack's hand. He looked at it for a moment, then put it over the other picture of Annie in his wallet. Zack watched Tom fold the wallet slowly, putting it back into his hip pocket. Zack's hands dropped to his sides for a moment before he put his own wallet away. He began to pick up his hamburger wrappings, wadding them up. He stood up slowly and walked towards his workbench.

"What are you doing?" Tom asked.

"Going back to work, I guess."

"Just like that, huh?"

"I guess."

"How come you let me do that?" Tom reached for his wallet, taking the picture out and handing it back to Zack.

"You can have it. I'll get another one."

"Take the picture back, Zack."

Zack took the photo and put it back in his wallet. "You just did that to see if you could get away with it?"

"No, dammit. I did it to get a reaction out of you. You've been hanging around Richard too much or something. You let people walk all over you."

"I was always like that. You just never noticed before."

"You weren't like that when you were a little kid."

Zack didn't answer.

"It's just a day," Tom said suddenly. "Like Thanksgiving. Nothing has to be a big deal if you don't have somebody making it into one." Then he paused. "You know what I think of Christmas? It means another year is gone and I'm one year older and I'm not even close to where I want to be yet. Look where Richard Petty is. He's only three years older than me, and you think when I'm twenty-six, I'm going to be where he is? I've got to put together a better team and find an owner willing to spend some money."

"I don't know, Tom. I think Ned has spent all he's got."

"No way. Think about it. He built two rooms on his house this year, bought Roxanne that MG, gives Mona money every time she squeaks. Roxanne has been Christmas shopping every day this week. He's not committed, is what I mean. He doesn't put it first." Zack shrugged. "What about you? If I leave Ned's, are you coming with me?"

"You mean you'd drive for Red?"

"Screw him and his two-bit team. I mean leave, really leave. Go to Charlotte, where the big teams are."

"I don't know if I'd want to leave. It's sort of like family here, everybody working together. Wouldn't seem right doing a car without Ned and Cy. And Arnold and Richard."

Tom shook his head. "You still don't get it, Zack. Things change. In two years I might have forgotten Arnold's last name even. You know what the big teams are doing now? Getting ready for next season. They went to Detroit and picked up new cars at the factory."

They both looked at number seven when he said that, the Ford pushed over to the side to make room for customer work, still dirty from the last race.

"You can get too used to having a steady paycheck," Tom went on. "This is the longest I've been working in one place since I left home. You have to keep asking yourself if you're losing sight of the big picture, starting to get too caught up in what's under your nose."

Ned called Tom away. Zack rushed back to his workbench without answering his brother's question. An old woman had driven in with a '61 Falcon that needed a tuneup.

Before the shop closed that evening, while Tom was out taking the Falcon on a test run, Maurice's wrecker pulled into the drive, the shell of a '40 Ford hanging from the hook. The engine compartment was empty and the front wheels were missing.

"Where you want it?" Maurice called.

"Drop it out back where you can't see it," Ned replied.

Zack and Cy followed the car around. Ned answered without being asked, "Don't nobody go getting excited. Guy owed me forty bucks. That's the only reason I got it."

During the two weeks before Christmas, Cy and Zack worked at odd jobs, loading and unloading trucks and starting cars with dead batteries for Maurice's Pure Oil. Arnold and Tom tuned up street cars for Ned. Richard had started working nights cleaning at the city hall. Ned put everyone but Arnold on part-time salary, while he spent his own days on the telephone or meeting people in the office. At first Tom thought he was trying to get financing for the next season. The '40 Ford still sat where Maurice had left it and Ned hadn't mentioned it. He called Tom into his office.

"Red called me again. I think he means it about letting you drive his car next season. Maybe you ought to butter him up a little. At least try being civil."

"Yeah, sure. All I have to do is shove Buster in the wall and hurt him worse than Allie, and it's all mine. You ever see what Arnold does to that old cat that hangs around out back? He sticks out his hamburger till old Dead Eye gets right up close enough to bite it, then yanks it back and stuffs it in his own big mouth. That's what Red has in mind for me. Like I'm some dumb animal."

"I don't think so this time. He's getting pretty bored. You know why I don't think so?"

Tom sighed. "Okay, why?"

"Because Red primed his son's pump for five years and he never pissed a drop. And never would have, even if he hadn't gotten messed up. So now Red wants somebody driving his car that goes fast and can win races. And he wants somebody he don't give a damn about. You're just what the doctor ordered."

Tom let Ned's words flow over him then stood up, driving his fist into his open palm with a loud pop. "Well, I care about my own ass and I'm not sitting around on it waiting for him to offer me a ride. He had his chance to let me drive it and didn't. To hell with him."

"Damn choosy beggar, you are. You young guys are all alike. Think you got it so hard. Got all kinds of people putting money up for grabs now. Factories giving stuff away. Wouldn't none of this be here if guys like me and Red hadn't put every dime we had on the line to go racing."

"First time I ever heard you and Red come out in the same breath."

"We worked side by side down at Shaw's, cutting out gears for airplanes during the war when we both had families to take care of. Never even seen what we were making parts for go together, much less fly. You're not even listening to me."

"I am. Gears. Airplane gears," he said, then brought Ned back to his subject. "If I get anywhere, it will be because I went out and found somebody to back me. Nobody's going to come to me offering the world. I don't care what anybody wants to dream about, you can't tell how good somebody really is until he's in a good car." Ned went silent. Tom read his silence wrong. "I'm not ungrateful. I know it was the best car you could afford."

"I've been meaning to talk to you about that. We've got some changes to make. I want you to get the new Ford in here in place of the race car. You and Arnold get the motor and rear end out of the race car and push it out back. Then put the wheels on the 'forty and roll her in here."

Tom didn't understand.

"Come on out in the shop," Ned said. Tom followed him

to where the new Ford sat. "Zack can cut the car out for me with the torch. We need to get as much space in the back as we can before we put in this wooden framework." He pointed to a stack of wood by the wall. "Use the trunk area and into the back seat. Keep it down low so it isn't so obvious. And pull out the springs. I got some heavy ones to go back there."

"Looks like you're going into the hauling business," Tom said. "You ever done this before?"

"Not built my own car. But I been around enough of them. I've done some driving. There's not a guy over fifty out at Greenmont who won't admit to some driving. You can pick up quite a bit of change around Christmas time. Nobody wants to spend a dime keeping their car running good, but they'll empty their pockets partying."

"I thought you might be saving that car for next season."

"I told you. Guy owed me some money." Ned shook his head. "You've got a lot to learn, Tom, about hard times. What you young guys have got to learn is how much it takes out of your pocket to make a little money at racing. Somebody has to spend a lot for you to make a little and I spent a lot. I should have quit after Buster drove my car. We got to get a hundred and eighty gallons in here to make it worth our while. I'll get Zack down here to chop all this out in here."

"I don't think we should cut out anything we can't put back. We can work around it. I looked at that car. It's not bad. I could run in the Late Models with it. I sure hate to use up our race motor. That was the best one Arnold ever built."

"Tom."

"Yeah."

"The season's done. Every car in the world's not a race car, okay?"

26

A few days later Zack and Cy saw Roxanne in the office. Torn-open letters lay all over her desk, not neatly cut with her white pearl letter knife, but violently jerked from the perfumed, pink, flower-lined envelopes bearing upside-down stamps. Her black eyeliner melted beneath her red eyes. "Look at these," she wept. "Look at the things these girls say! They're disgusting! Look at what they offer him. They don't even know him."

Zack read one of them aloud to Cy while Roxanne stomped to the rest room: "I can't get you off my mind, Tom Pate. You are the man of my dreams. If you ever come to Martinsville, just call 289-2312 and ask for Candy. Make three wishes and tell them to me, and I'll make every one of them come true."

"Woo-ee!" Cy exclaimed. "Three wishes. I'll give her three wishes."

"I didn't hear her ask you," Zack said as he thumbed through the letters. The letters were addressed to Tom in round letters that all looked similar, one with a happy face in the *o* in Tom.

At the bottom of the stack, Zack found a different letter, business-sized with no upside-down stamp. No stamp at all. "Route 2, Box 14 Summit" had been crossed out and "Ned's All-American Automotive, Greenmont" was penciled beside it. The handwriting wasn't flowery.

"This went to Summit first," he said. "It looks like Rachel's writing over to the side. It got here without the street on it."

Ned looked over his shoulder. "Uh-oh. That's from the government."

Zack turned it over. There was a note on the envelope: "If

this doesn't reach my brother, Tom Pate, and is returned to sender, then his family has no further information on his whereabouts. P.S. to Tom. My fiancé, Claiborne, heard your name on the radio when he was traveling. Daddy had a stroke the day President Kennedy died. No connection of course. Daddy talks funny now and has trouble with his right hand and remembering things more than five minutes. Rachel."

Ned went into the shop and called Tom, who rolled out from under a '58 Ford. Tom glanced at the envelope, then opened and read the letter. He leaned back against the rear tire when he was through.

"Army?" Ned asked.

"Yeah. Says report to my draft board for my preinduction physical."

"When?"

"A month ago. In Summit."

"They're getting more people now," Arnold put in. "A guy that goes to church with me and Norma got his a few weeks ago. Him and his girlfriend is getting married because that gets you out."

Tom folded the notice and put it in his pocket before shoving back underneath the car. The others went back to work. All except Zack. "Maybe Rachel didn't tell them where you were. Maybe she just put it on the letter. Maybe we better go back home."

Tom didn't answer.

When Zack got back to the shop that evening, Tom was inside. From outside it sounded like a fight, but Tom was alone, throwing pieces of metal at the scrap pile and cussing. The welding tanks stood beside the '40 Ford and the engine and rear end from the race car were on the floor.

Tom spotted him. "What did I do wrong this time, goddammit!" Tom yelled. "I worked my tail off on that car and

Ned just shoved it out in the weeds like it was junk. I didn't hang around bars and girls all the time. Lisa and I busted up over racing because I didn't have as much time for her as she thought she ought to get." Tom threw another piece of metal and it rattled over the top of the stack. "I did pretty damn good in that car. I beat Buster Simmons fair and square. A lot of people have heard of me now. So what do I get for it? I get a boss who's so broke, he's hauling liquor. I'm broke. I had to sell my TV to pay my rent. I get my draft notice saying the government gets to take a big hunk out of my life right when I need it the most to get sent to a war that isn't any of my business and I don't give a shit about. Ned made me pull all the good stuff off my race car. Now he's going to hack the new one all up."

Zack couldn't move. He was supposed to be the one who cut up the new car.

"I never bitched about working on it," Tom continued. "And I let Ned keep all my extra money to keep it running. I hear people bitch all the time, drivers bitching about not having this new and that new. Then they stand up there and lie about how they won for Ford or Plymouth or some dumbshit oil company. That's not who they won for. Why don't they just say they won for themselves? Let them be Tom Pate. Then they'd have something to bitch about.

"Some swimmer was bitching on the radio today, a goddamn swimmer saying the water in the pool was too hot. That was why he was so slow and if they don't make it cooler, he's not going to race," Tom mocked. "Let him run about fifty laps in that race car in August. He'd sweat enough to swim his fucking race in."

Tom yanked the welding glasses from the top of the tank and the elastic popped him on the wrist. "Son of a bitch." He threw them on the floor. The glass broke on one lens.

"Why doesn't the army draft those rich bastards like Harris

Carmichael? They're the ones who get rich when they have a damn war. Let them go fight it. I'm so goddamn poor I have to let an asshole like Red dangle his car under my nose and I have to stand there and take it. I worked my ass off to drive that car."

As Tom began to pace, Zack moved backwards, keeping his distance. "These goddamn baseball players," Tom went on, "who make so damn much money they don't know what to do with it, they got this big deal about making an error. They count them. Got nothing better to do than count errors, baseball's so boring. This guy dropped a ball he should have caught. This shithead let a ball roll between his legs. Count your errors in my game, asshole. Make an error and it damn well might be your last."

Tom threw another piece of metal, this one hitting the office partition and knocking something off the wall inside that fell to the floor. Zack wondered if it was Tom's Victory Circle picture, the one that had replaced the upside-down shot of Buster. Zack was immobilized in the center of a battlefield with his brother's temper exploding all around him.

"I don't have time to go in the army now. I've lost too much time already. All those years before you got here. I didn't get anything going. Nobody even knew I existed."

Tom quit talking and began to breathe loudly. It felt strangely familiar to Zack. He knew that now it was safe to walk across the floor, something he learned a long time ago in a corn crib. He picked up the welding glasses and shook out the broken lens. He heard Tom's breath begin to slow, become more evenly spaced.

"I didn't mean to break your glasses," Tom said.

"There's another pair on Arnold's torch." Zack looked at his brother. "I don't have to do it tonight."

Tom stooped and began to gather up the glass slivers with his fingers.

"You'll cut yourself." Zack saw Tom's shoulders start to tremble. "I'll get a broom," he offered. His big brother dropped to his knees. His fingers reached around his head and dug into his own scalp. There was already blood on his fingertips. Zack turned and ran to the door and outside. He huddled beside the garbage cans, arms wrapped around his knees, and sat there for a long time.

Tom finally came out, locked the door, and left. Zack stood and waited until he had walked out of sight down the sidewalk, then he unlocked the door and went back inside. The glass still lay on the floor. He checked inside the car; nothing had been done. He hoped, momentarily, that he wouldn't be able to find Arnold's welding glasses, but there they were, hanging in place on the other welder. He pulled them on, adjusted the loose strap to his head, and lifted the trunk lid. He screwed on the cutting torch and hit the striker, sending out a long blue flame. Then, engulfed by flecks of molten metal, he started cutting out the car, just the way Ned had told him to.

One morning the next week Cy picked Zack up for work, and as he opened the door to hop in, Cy warned, "Careful! Don't kick over the flowers."

On the floorboard sat a round cluster of pink flowers bought from a florist.

"Oh, Romeo," Zack said. "For me?" He slid his feet around the pot as they took off, water splashing on his shoe.

"Watch my style," Cy replied.

He left the flowers in the car until Arnold and Tom went to lunch. Then Cy carried them in behind his back, setting them inside the cabinet where Roxanne kept the ledgers. He handed Zack a card to write her name on the envelope.

Zack printed it carefully, then asked, "Did you do the inside?"

Cy yanked the card back. "I can write my own damn name, for crissake. It ain't but two letters." He shoved the envelope under the pot, smudging the white paper with his fingers.

That afternoon when Roxanne came in, Cy kept strolling by the office and looking in. At first he was doing it jokingly, glancing over at Zack. But later he came over to Zack's bench with a worried look on his face. "Zack. She's in there crying."

"Tears of joy, Romeo. Women are like that."

"Asshole." He walked away, then came back. "You go in there. Ask her what's the matter."

"Me? Why me?"

"Well, I can't do it."

Zack picked up his pencil and walked into the office, heading for the sharpener. Roxanne turned her back to him; she was sniffing and the blond curls piled on top of her head bobbed. Cy's flowers were on the desk. Zack could see the card was out of the envelope. In the center of a circle of flowers, a stork carried a bundle with a banner that read CONGRATULATIONS ON YOUR NEW ARRIVAL!

Zack hurried back into the shop.

"Cy, did you look at the card you gave her?"

"Sure, I looked at it. It had a bunch of flowers and a bird. The woman at the flower shop picked it out."

"What did you tell her?"

"She asked me what color flowers and I said pink and she said a girl, right, and I said yeah. What are you laughing at, dammit? What's wrong with the card?"

"You nitwit, Cy. You gave her a card you give a woman when she just had a baby."

His mouth dropped open. "I did?"

Before Zack could stop him, Cy went into the office to explain things to Roxanne. Only she spoke before he could.

"How could you be so mean!" she shrieked. "You, of all people."

"I thought you said you liked flowers. Or you said your mama did, so I thought . . ."

"That wasn't very funny, Cy. In fact that was the meanest thing anybody has ever done to me in my whole life."

"Mean." Zack came to the door. "Mean?" Cy repeated and turned to look at Zack. Roxanne pushed past both of them and stomped across the shop to the bathroom. It was quitting time before she came out, her face completely repainted, but her eyes rimmed in red. Arnold had been beating on the door, threatening to use the floor if she didn't come out. When Roxanne walked out, she shoved past Norma without speaking and walked straight to her car, leaving the flowers on the desk. Norma went into the office to wait for Arnold. Cy followed Norma in.

"Norma. Tell me something," he said.

"Tell you what? You tell me why Roxanne is being so nasty. Because she didn't get her way? One day she talks my ear off and the next she won't even speak to me. Oh, what pretty flowers." She sniffed them. "Who are they for?"

"For Roxanne."

Norma picked up the card. A smile spread across her face. "Ah-ha! I told Arnold she was p.g."

"What?"

"She better hurry up and get married. They say she got pretty thick with Giles Burcham after Allie got hurt. Or Arnold thinks it could be Ralph over in the parts department. I think she's already starting to show." Arnold appeared at the door. "I told you so, Arnold." Norma dangled the card between her fat fingers.

He looked at the card and grunted, not interested. "Let's get out of here. I'm tired."

"What did you want to ask me, Cy?" Norma asked from the door.

Cy shrugged and walked back to his workbench.

Finally he turned to Zack and said, "If I inherited a punkin patch, good buddy, they'd cancel Halloween."

27

After they installed the heavy springs in the rear of the Ford, the back end stuck up when it was empty.

"Looks like a stink bug," Cy remarked, "like it's asking to get its ass kicked."

"Is it scary, Tom?" Zack had asked the previous afternoon. Tom had quit working days in the shop, making three night runs that week.

"Is what scary? Nevermind. I know what you're asking. Yeah, a little, because it's illegal and I might go to jail and because it's so obvious-looking. I feel better when I've got a load in the trunk than when it's empty." Then he added, "They'll never catch me, though. Nobody in the county can catch me."

After an afternoon of filling cars with antifreeze, Zack and Cy stopped by after supper to see if Ned had their paychecks. Zack was down to three dollars, with his rent overdue by two days. Tom had borrowed his last twenty. Ned was in the office and he was mad. "Have you seen Tom?"

"No, not since yesterday."

"He was supposed to be here an hour ago."

Ned had them wait another thirty minutes, but Tom didn't show up.

"You two are going to have to do his pickup and delivery for him. I'll draw you a map. I can't be two places at once. My mother fell today on the ice and Roxanne is sick as a dog."

"All right!" Cy said. "Finally going to let me drive the race car."

"This is serious business, Cy, and don't forget it."

"Yes, sir!" he replied, without a change of attitude. "Tell Roxanne I hope she feels better. I'd send her a get well card, but it'd probably say I was sorry her grandma died."

"What?" Ned asked, confused.

"He was saying," Zack interrupted, "that he hopes Roxanne and her grandma feel better." Zack took Cy by the sleeve and dragged him into the shop. Richard had dumped out the dead pink flowers and left the pink ribbon on her desk.

They met at the shop at two in the morning. The temperature dropped fast, the first snow of the winter predicted that night. The moon was still clear, captured in a white ring. Cy started the engine on the '40 Ford. The big V-8 warmed up slowly, then blasted the inside with heat that sucked away and was replaced with cold air as soon as they started moving. Using the map Ned had given him, Zack directed Cy to a side road about ten miles outside of town.

"Damn, it's cold. Arnold can build a engine, but he ain't much with heaters," Cy said. "Did you bring a bottle of whiskey?" Cy laughed at his own joke, but Zack could tell he was nervous. "I wonder what Ned would do if we got caught?" Cy continued. "Any idiot can tell what this stink bug is for."

"Let us rot in jail," Zack answered quickly.

"Do you mean that, really? I mean, we're doing it for him."

"Why do you think *he* isn't doing it? What did he tell us when we left: if you get stopped by the sheriff, don't give any names, don't tell anybody where you work or who the car belongs to. We get caught and he doesn't know us, you can count on it."

"They can figure out who the car belongs to. All they got to do is look at the tag, right?"

"You must not of looked at the tag."

"Just a bunch of numbers," Cy mumbled.

"That's not what I mean," Zack said. "I put brown paint

on the tag for Ned to make it look like mud. The year isn't even right."

They drove for a while longer in silence before Zack asked, "Have you ever gotten caught for anything before?"

"Naw. Well, I got caught taking hubcaps for a guy, but they let me off because I was a little kid. My old man beat my ass for it. Not 'cause I stole. 'Cause I didn't get enough money for doing it and got caught to boot. How about you?"

"Not that I remember. Just speeding once, fifty-five in a thirty-five. Cost me fifty-four dollars."

"I don't believe this is like doing anything crooked, anyway," Cy said.

"How's that?"

"Because it's hard work making the stuff, that's why. Just the gov'ment trying to horn in. That's what my old man says. That it's a lot easier to haul a few jars to market than a hundred bushels of corn. It's okay to squash up tomatoes and apples and make juice. I just don't see it."

"Because tomato and apple juice don't make you drunk."

"Pop says you put them people up there in Washington to work for you and then they get uppity and start working for theirselves. Reason a pint cost so much more over at the ABC is you got to pay the politicians. Pop drinks enough rotgut by hisself to float a boat. He oughta know."

They reached the bottom of the mountain. "What next?" Cy asked. Zack showed him the map, holding a flashlight on it. Cy took it and turned it around. "I can't figure which way is up. Here, I rather you figure it out and tell me. It's just a bunch of squiggly lines to me."

By then Zack had taught Cy his left from his right by telling him to think which hand he used to pick up a wrench. He would take his left hand off the wheel and say "Wrench," then yank the wheel and the car would go squealing to the left.

They went through a series of narrow dirt roads before they

344

reached a section of blacktop with no center line. "This thing don't handle worth pea turkey when it's empty," Cy said as they roared through a series of switchbacks. "Pushing like a pig."

As they crested the hill, Zack spotted the three oak trees where they were supposed to stop, but before he could get the words out, they had shot past them. Cy was overjoyed because, for the first time, his bootleg turn wasn't just for practice. They parked and began their wait. The colder air on the mountain quickly filled the car.

"Hey, good buddy, did you hear what Norma said today?" Cy said.

"No," Zack replied.

"She said Roxanne is getting married."

"Who to?"

"Giles Burcham. Or Ralph down at Burcham's. She's not sure which one."

"Ralph? I never even knew she liked him," Zack said.

"Well, anyway. Norma said she was engaged or something. Guess we better mark her off our list."

"Yeah, list of one. She sure seemed upset today. I guess she's too emotional or something. I thought she was in a bad mood because Tom got drafted. She's got a crush on him anyway. Maybe she's trying to make him jealous saying she's getting married . . ."

Zack heard a pinging sound and jerked in his seat. The sound multiplied, and he saw white dots bouncing on the hood. "Starting to sleet," he said.

"Yeah, wish they'd hurry up. Road is going to turn to junk before long."

"You think they changed their minds when the weather got bad?"

Cy shrugged and beat his hands together.

The moonlit sky had fuzzed over with clouds as they came

up the mountain. Now the clouds moved closer to the car as a heavy cover dropped over the mountain. The windshield began to ice over, making what moonlight was left bounce over them in crazy patterns. Cy jumped out.

"Woo-ee," he said, grabbing the door as his feet slid out from under him. "Slicker than a skeeter's peter. How about I let you drive us home?" he said with a laugh. "And I ride in the back with the bottles?"

"Hey, get back in here and get quiet," Zack whispered. "I hear somebody." Cy jumped back inside and locked the door. Zack locked his side. Three dark figures came out of the woods with wheelbarrows and stopped at the back of the car.

"Don't look like the sheriff and two deputies to me," Cy said softly. Zack noticed a tremble in his voice.

Ned told them not to help load; if anything happened, he wanted them to be able to say they didn't know what they were putting back there. The back of the car settled like a seesaw with a fat kid sitting on the end.

"Oughta pour a gallon of this poison in the radiator tonight," Zack heard one of the men say in a slurred voice.

"You done got a gallon in your radiator," said a deeper voice.

"Not me. A pint maybe, but not a gallon. Ain't the best . . ."

"They ain't deaf and dumb."

Somebody said "Shhhh," probably the third man. A limb cracked in the woods and banged to the ground, followed by a thumping sound.

"Owl," one of them said.

"If that hoot owl had hollered," Cy whispered, "one of them would have woke up dead tomorrow."

The trunk lid slammed and the men disappeared between the trees.

"That's it," Cy said, confidence back in his voice as he

flexed his grip on the steering wheel to warm his hands. As Cy started the engine, Zack cracked the door to see the sleet hitting the ground like pebbles.

"The road looks real bad, Cy."

"Rats," he said.

"What?"

"Crummy wiper's stuck," he answered, pulling on the button. "It's froze up good." The windshield looked like the frosted window glass in the restroom at the shop. Zack got out, holding the door frame to keep from falling. The sleet pelted his back as he tugged at the wiper; it was frozen stuck. The metal bent a little in his hand as the ice held it firm.

"Wait a second," he heard Cy yell. "Don't bend it up."

As he got back in, Cy climbed out and went to the front of the car. His form was dark with the faint moonlight behind it; his face had no features through the rippled glass. Cy scraped his feet on the gravelly ice like a bull getting ready to charge. Then he stepped on the bumper and up to the hood. He danced for a moment, like a skater getting his balance, on the wet metal where the warmth from the idling engine had melted the ice.

"Okay," he called to Zack, "now, when I tell you to, turn on the wipers and give it some gas."

Zack slid into the driver's seat. The image of Cy started to get clearer because the frozen rain on the windshield had turned into a stream of water.

"Now. Hit it!" Cy called. When Zack pulled the knob and pressed the gas, the blade broke free with a groan and began to flap back and forth. Between the sweeps of the blade, the moon was clear, but Cy was gone.

"Move over," Cy said as he appeared suddenly at the window. Zack slid across the seat as he jumped in. Cy revved the engine and pulled up his fly before he shoved the car in gear.

"You peed on the windshield!" Zack exclaimed.

"Only hot water I could find, good buddy."

The wheels spun a second while Cy tested the traction. The tires grabbed at the loose ice balls. "Feel that grip," Cy kidded. "This old car feels like a thousand-legged worm."

"Feels like an eel in a bucket of snot, if you ask me."

"Hang on!"

They took off like a sled down a frozen waterfall. As they whipped through the curves on the white road, Cy's fingers let the steering wheel slip through, then tightened at just the right moment after every bend. When he let off the gas, the bottles clinked together in the truck like chimes. He shifted down instead of using the brake, pitching the car sideways and catching it. The Ford stayed on the path between the trees as sure as the little magnet car Zack had gotten for Christmas when he was eight, sliding down the refrigerator. Cy was giving a performance on a stage with no audience; it was like singing a perfect "Heartbreak Hotel" in the shower.

When they reached flat land again, Cy was still high, sliding through the mud where the sleet had melted. "Damn, this old car feels good with a load in it." They passed a car going the other way and Zack felt his heart tighten. He watched the car turn down a side road then back up and turn around.

"Cy, that car's following us."

Cy looked in the mirror, dropping one hand off the steering wheel and onto the emergency brake.

"He's getting closer."

"Just relax, good buddy. I see him. I'm letting him get closer."

The car continued to close the gap. Its headlights began to flash, lighting the inside of their car.

"Hold on to your seat!" Cy yelled. As Zack dug his nails into the upholstery, their car reversed directions. Zack saw writing on the door of the other car as Cy floored the pedal, but they were going too fast to read it. Cy was laughing.

"What makes you think he won't turn around too?"

"There ain't anywhere to turn around in that direction until he gets near 'bout to the city limits." Zack looked in the rearview mirror. The car was turning around. Suddenly he saw the car's headlights shoot upwards and flash through the tops of the trees. Then they receded into the distance.

Cy checked the mirror again. "Sonavabitch's in the ditch now. Shoulda listened to me. Ain't no where to turn around on this road. All right!"

After a series of switchbacks on roads that Cy knew, they drove up to Apex Road, where they would make the dropoff.

"How'd you know where to go?" Zack asked. "You never even looked at the map."

"I been here a million times. I musta bought my old man a swimming-pool-full of bootleg up here. Might even save him a couple of bottles out of this load for Christmas. They'll never miss it."

They drove to the back of a dark building where two men emerged. Cy got out and opened the trunk.

"Mind if I get my old man a couple of bottles?"

"Cy Thomas! What in the world? Give the old bastard three of them. Tell him I said merry Christmas and happy New Year. And happy Valentine's Day to the old SOB. Tell him I 'spect it to last till Valentine's Day."

"Yeah. He'll be lucky if it lasts till Sunday."

Cy jumped back in and placed three cold mason jars in Zack's lap.

"He's going to be tickled pink at this. Won't feel no pain for a week."

When they parked Ned's car at the shop, the sun was starting to come up. Cy stumbled into the side of the building, carrying his bottles. He handed Zack the keys to the Chevy. "You drive," he said. "I'm getting sleepy. Past my bedtime." He laughed.

Zack dropped Cy off and watched him weave up his porch

steps with the three bottles clutched against his chest. Charlie stood on the railing crowing.

Before going home, Zack decided to drive to Tom's. At first it felt like a long way over there. But when he got there, he was surprised the street appeared so quickly. His mind seemed to go in and out of focus. It was six-thirty in the morning; Tom should be up. He wanted to ask him why he hadn't shown up. They needed to talk about how he was going to get out of going to the army. Maybe he could change his name. Zack wanted to tell him about Cy peeing on the windshield to melt the ice. He wanted to ask Tom if he got paid. Then he would go back to Ned's to see if he had his own pay yet so he could pay his overdue rent.

When he climbed the steps to Tom's apartment, he picked up a sock that was caught in the railing. A clean sock; Tom must have dropped it coming from the laundromat. He knocked. Tom didn't answer.

As Zack went back outside, he saw a sign that he hadn't noticed going in: APARTMENT #3 FOR RENT. He ran to the side of the building. The stained glass Ferrari Lisa had bought Tom in Italy no longer hung in the window. Zack dropped the sock in the yard.

He began to circle the building, picking up and dropping the sock twice on his revolutions. He stopped at Tom's trash can. When he lifted the lid, he saw unopened cans, a half loaf of bread, and jars half-full of mayonnaise and mustard, cool as though still in the refrigerator. There were two frozen beef pot pies and three beers. He began taking the food out, stuffing it into the paper bags he found under it. At the bottom of the trash can was B.B.'s globe and a Maurice's Pure Oil racing shirt. He shook the shirt out because it was covered with cigarette butts smudged with lipstick. He spread the shirt on the ground, folding it carefully before bagging it with the globe.

He hauled all of Tom's discarded things to the trunk of the Chevy, returning to put the lid back on the trash can. While he was hurrying back to the car, an old man started moving up the alley, lifting the lids off the cans.

Zack drove slowly back to his rooming house, Tom's things rattling in the trunk. It grew harder to do things. He shifted gears slowly and had to look for the switch to turn off the engine. He carried two bags of food to his room and locked the door. He put his head under the pillow and ignored his landlady when she knocked.

Zack fought sleep, imagining he might never wake up. The old man across the hall had died in his sleep a month ago; he'd had a heart attack while passing a kidney stone. Zack didn't know him; the man had always growled when Zack said hello. His kidney stones must have been hurting him. Or else he was just a nasty guy. Maybe they would carry Zack out like they did the old man. "Zack Pate? He had a brother, but he left town. No one knows his next of kin. All he has is a cheap watch he got for his high school graduation. No one knows where to send his body. There is a big stone in his bed. He passed a kidney stone."

There was a lump in his bed. He was getting a bruise, tossing on the kidney stone. He couldn't let himself sleep. He had to figure out what had happened. The kidney stone crumbled into dust.

Somebody had to tell Roxanne. She wouldn't understand. She'd never had Tom up and leave her before. He should tell her. "Roxanne, I'm afraid I have some bad news." She would look up from the ledger, the pencil going between her teeth like a beaver with a stick. That was the wrong way to tell her. "Roxanne!" She sat in her broken MG in the shop, tying her curls into a checkered scarf. "Yes, Zack. What can I do for you?" No.

The old dog who followed his master across the country: If

Zack could sing the story, he could stay awake. He could always stay awake if he was singing. He walked across the desert after his master, dragging his bum leg. He was getting very tired. He was very tired of following Tom. The old dog turned around and headed back where he came from. He didn't stop to see if the man followed him now.

Zack finally slept soundly. At midnight he woke up in his dark room, wide awake when the rest of the world was going to sleep. He stayed in bed, not even walking across the room for the peanut butter and jelly. He ate the half loaf of bread and got crumbs between the sheets.

A square of paper lay on the floor by his door. Maybe Tom had come by while he slept. He grabbed the note with his toes. It was a note from his landlady: "Call Cy. His father is missing. Did you forget your rent?"

After he read the note, he wished he'd never found it. The note made the earth start turning again. Cy. Horace. Horace must be on foot because the Chevy was parked out front. His mind was too full to think about them. Things had to stop moving long enough for him to figure out what had happened to Tom. Tom was on the run, trying to hide from the government. He was bouncing away from Zack again like the ball of lightning that he'd once seen, ricocheting down the railroad tracks from the rails to the wires above in a terrible pattern of its own, controlled by no one. Even Tom accused him of imagining it. He could see that lightning ball right then, even clearer than he could see Tom's face.

Zack felt his way down the dark hall to the phone. He dialed Cy's number; it rang a long time before he heard a muffled hello.

"Cy? It's Zack. Did you find him yet?"

"Yeah. I found him."

"Where was he?"

"In his milk truck."

Zack couldn't find any more words. He had asked too much. "Cy. I'm sorry. Is he dead?"

"Naw. He ain't dead. Like the guy said, you can't kill a drunk. He was near 'bout blue though. Now he's in there sucking on them bottles I brung him like he's afraid somebody's gonna take them away. I shouldna got them for him. I don't know what I was thinking about. He won't even know it's Christmas when it gets here. Do you know what time it is?"

"No. Did I wake you up?"

"Yeah. Are we supposed to be at work?"

"I don't know. Cy, he's gone."

"I told you I found him."

"Not him. Tom. Tom's gone." When he said it out loud, it finally became real.

"Gone where?" Cy asked.

"I don't know. Dammit, I don't know." Zack's voice broke.

"Maybe he went to the army."

"Why didn't he say that? He could have told me."

Cy didn't answer.

"Why aren't you answering me?"

"Maybe he don't need us no more, Zack."

28

Tom Pate rode the local bus to the main Trailways station in Greenmont, dragging his clothes along in one large suitcase he had bought at the Salvation Army thrift store. He'd left his tools at the shop for Zack. When he bought his ticket, the agent said he had thirty minutes before the bus to Raleigh arrived. He bought a Coke and sat outside on one of the green benches.

The station was under construction; they were tearing out the wall between the old colored section and the white section. A rosy-cheeked Santa was taped to the glass of a door that leaned against the wall. All the benches were shoved at odd angles, the seats covered with white plaster powder except for two large heart-shaped clean spots and two smaller ones. The women and children whose rear ends matched the spots now stood in front of the magazines, one of the women beating the dust away from her behind and yanking back the cloth that kept grabbing her crotch.

An older bus belched out a thick black cloud as it climbed the hill to its slot. It was a local bus. As soon as the door opened, two old farmers got out and trotted towards the men's room.

A new crowd started arriving. They came in taxicabs. They were young, laughed a lot and made a lot of noise. They wore expensive clothes. All of them were colored, but some were as light as polished wood. A girl passed him whose face was so light that he could see she had reddened her cheeks and painted her eyelids blue like Roxanne. Some of them had on blazers from E.T.C., the Negro college in Greenmont.

"Maxwell. Come here. Show them your mouth," one of the colored girls called.

Maxwell began to spin and dance towards her.

"Look at him!" she shrieked. "Metal mouth."

Maxwell grinned widely to show the silver braces on his teeth.

"Just in case I don't pass Chemistry," he said.

"Braces?" a low-voiced male asked.

"Orthodontic appliances. Four-F."

"Better than having to puke up pig blood."

One of the girls hit him in the arm. "You're gross, Henry."

"That's because my old man isn't a lawyer like Maxwell's. They won't let me out so easy."

"I could get married," Maxwell said. "LBJ says married men don't have to go. Will you marry me, Althea?"

"You hush, Maxwell."

Tom tried not to let it go through his mind again. He had taken himself through a way of thinking that week for the first time in his life; he repeated it over again to be sure. It started with Ned understanding his side of the story. Tom would tell her daddy how she came to his door the night Ned thought she spent at her mother's, the same night Zack told him Randall Johnson had won the Labor Day Classic, not him. She had baked him chocolate chip cookies to cheer him up. And it wasn't the first time she had stopped by. She'd come the night Allie was hurt, too, but she'd never even knocked on the door. The bottoms of the cookies she brought had been burned to a charcoally taste. She would have done them over, she'd said, but she'd run out of chocolate chips. He ate them anyway and said they were burned just like his mother's. She laughed at him, telling him bachelors would eat anything. She didn't laugh much. It was nice when she did. She got tickled once. He was rinsing the soap off the MG and she walked right into the stream of water from the hose. He'd expected her to be mad because her hair fell down like a yellow rag mop, but she wasn't. They laughed. It wasn't totally his fault. It wouldn't have happened if she hadn't come to his apartment. Ned would understand and they would be friends again.

It was useless. Ned would never see it that way.

Tom had tried a fantasy: He asked her to be his wife. She said yes. Ned said that made everything okay and slapped him on the back. He could drive Ned's Sportsman at Greenmont the rest of his life. After their wedding, Tom woke up before she did and saw her sleeping there, her golden hair loose on the pillow. She fixed his breakfast while he showered.

But she disappeared, like the dew after a few minutes of full sun. He knew what he was leaving out of the story, but it was there anyway, making him run. There was no use trying to make a place for Roxanne in his life. It was hard for him to hold on to fantasies of anything but racing cars.

When the bus to Raleigh pulled into its slot, all the farmers on the first bench got up and crowded the bus door. The driver cracked the door, yelling at them to stand back until the passengers got off. The fancy Negroes stood over by the station chattering away like they were continuing a party they had started before they arrived.

Tom boarded the bus, went midway back to an empty pair of seats and took the one by the window, stuffing his bag overhead. The Negro kids outside loaded their luggage underneath. Tom wanted his things to be with him. They were all he had left.

All the empty double seats up front filled up with the Negroes who shifted around, joining and leaving each other as in a game of musical chairs. Tom felt hunger rush through his body. Outside the window a man sold crackers and candy from a pushcart. Tom tried to open the window, but it was sealed. He remembered slamming the door to his emptied refrigerator; he'd forgotten to make a sandwich before he threw everything into the trash. But when he'd stepped onto the bus, he'd left Greenmont for good. To go outside the bus to buy something to eat would feel like coming back.

He sensed someone standing near him. He looked up into the face of the girl with the blue eyelids and red cheeks. She was very tall with shiny brown eyes and hair set stiffly around her face. Her hair was as rigid as Nancy's in the comic strip. She wore a short fur coat instead of a blazer. Under the short coat, her full, firm hips were wrapped in a green dress that moved with her like feathers on a parrot. One hand pressed a large shoulderbag against her stomach. His eyes fixed on a ring on her middle finger with a green stone in a setting that seemed to move, like a flower opening and closing. He glanced at her face again; unlike the ring, it didn't move. In the large group of students, she was the lightest-skinned by far. But if he had taken her home, there would have been no doubt in anybody's mind that she was colored. She had been shut out of the musical chairs game with the other Negroes and she stood over him, without a seat. She looked down at him like an African queen waiting to give the order to have him taken away and thrown in a pot so that she could have his seat.

The driver got on and looked in his rearview mirror, saying, "Be seated please and we're on our way." She sat down quickly, holding her purse in her lap as if it were a part of her that had become disconnected, and she didn't want to drop it. If he'd been a thief, he would have figured there was a bunch of money and jewelry in that purse.

Tom studied that strange ring. It did move. When she had tension on her fingers, the setting quivered around the stone. She had a lot of tension. He guessed that the stone was real, whatever you called real green stones. When he saw her perfect round nails, his arms crossed and his hands slid under his armpits before his brain had told them what to do. She had probably already noticed his dirty, split fingernails. And that he hadn't shaved that morning. His tattoo creeped out beneath his rolled up sleeve like a lizard trying to escape. Her skin was light enough for a tattoo to show, but he figured Maxwell with the braces could only get one if they could use white ink.

Tom felt the soft fur of her coat against his skin. She was aware she was touching him, she had to be. It was too hot on the bus to be wearing a fur coat, but if she took it off it would be one more valuable thing she would have to clutch. She looked straight ahead, as though her neck was so stiff her head wouldn't turn. She couldn't ride all the way to Raleigh sitting that stiffly. The other Negroes on the bus were laughing and talking with each other, turning around in their seats and discussing teachers and ball games. Maxwell, the draft dodger, was obviously the comedian. She wasn't a part of it.

Tom felt uncomfortable; it was as if he and this woman were mad at each other. But they didn't even know each other. It was as if they needed to talk things out, and he was waiting for her to give a hint to what was wrong.

Finally he couldn't stand it anymore. "Going to Burlington?" he said.

He thought she wasn't going to answer because she waited so long before she did. When she finally said, "Yes," it was the kind of yes Tom thought a cartoon character would say, with icicles hanging off the word in a cloud over her head.

"Live there?"

The same thing happened again. The long delay, then the "yes." She waited so long it seemed more like a slap than an answer. But afterward nothing changed. As if he'd never said anything. All he knew was she was going home to Burlington.

He could only assume she went to school in Greenmont and figure which one it had to be because there was only one college for Negroes there.

Her arm moved slightly and the fur tickled his skin as she tightened the grip on her purse. Then she pulled her arm away. To Tom, it felt like having the cat jump down out of your lap when you wanted to keep petting it.

She had to be roasting inside that coat. Tom leaned forward to see if her face shone with sweat, but her skin looked as cool as her voice. Those long fingers with the dancing ring must have smoothed the red paint onto her cheek, onto her warm skin over that curved bone.

He tried to think of something else to ask her. It didn't make any sense to ask her where in Burlington she lived because he had never been there. There was no reason for him to want to know because, like Greenmont, there was probably only one place where rich Negroes lived.

That's what she was, rich. Roxanne could have smelled her perfume and told him how much it cost. To him it just smelled good, like it came out of a girl's pores, not out of a bottle. She had on fur that had once been worn by an animal, lots of animals put together. Her shoes were leather and made with little stitches so they must have cost a lot. And she was going to college. He could ask her what her daddy did. Uncle Vernon said there were only three ways that Negroes got rich: sold dope, sold caskets, and sold insurance.

"What are you going to college for?"

"What?" she snapped. He thought a minute and realized his mistake.

"I mean, what are you studying?"

"Political Science."

That answer was quick—not like the two yesses that had taken forever—as though she wanted to hit him with it fast and knock him over. Maybe she thought he was too damn stupid to even know what it was. He was smart enough not to ask and prove it. Then she really surprised him. She swiveled to look at him as if her neck were a frozen bolt that suddenly turned free. At first he didn't understand what the look meant, not until she turned back around and laughed, kind of a snicker.

"What's so damn funny?"

She kept laughing. He would be embarrassed, laughing by himself. But it was more like little puffs, just for herself.

"Nothing," she replied. The snicker quit, but the smile stayed on her face. To his mind, it wasn't a nice smile.

"I know what you think," he blurted out. "You're thinking that stupid redneck doesn't even know what political sociology or whatever you said is. Well, I do. I used to date a girl who took classes like that. My girlfriend was a college girl. She went to Rosemount."

Her body returned to the stiff pose, with her face turned a little farther away from him. When he looked at her profile this time, it seemed he had imagined the laughter. That cold, stiff girl couldn't laugh if she wanted to. He couldn't think of anything else to ask, so he tried to figure out what somebody else he knew might say. Arnold. That was easy. Arnold would say, I may be stupid, bitch, but I ain't a nigger. Richard. He would say, Yes, ma'am, to her like she was a white girl; he'd be scared to death of her. Cy. He would ask her if she was just half-colored and which parent was white. Zack. Zack probably had enough sense to talk to her like she was anybody else. Zack would get along with her just fine. She might even like him. Write him a letter on stationery that smelled like she did. They could be friends.

Tom looked out the window; it was getting dark. Soon there was nothing outside he could identify, just dark, round shapes: trees; and dark, square shapes: buildings. He looked at his watch, the one that Lisa had given him because he was always late. She'd brought it to him from Switzerland when she went skiing with her family. It said four o'clock; he had forgotten to wind it. He could ask her what time it was and set his watch. He couldn't see if she had a watch on because the fur reached over the backs of her hands.

As it got darker inside the bus, he became more aware of her perfume. He tried to imagine her as just any girl. He looked to see if there was anything about her in the thin light that would make you sure she was a Negro: her nose, her hair, her cheekbones. He didn't see anything. She was starting to feel him looking at her because she turned her face so far away, he could only look at the back of her head.

"Okay, tell me about that stuff you're studying in college?" he asked finally.

He got the long silence, then: "I beg your pardon?" She didn't look at him when she spoke.

"Hey, you don't have to beg." She tightened up inside the fur. "Just kidding. I mean what is that political stuff you're studying, what is it really?"

She sighed softly as though she were tired. "Political science. It is a science dealing with the political rather than the social, ethical, or economic relations of man."

"Oh. Thanks." He could have looked it up himself in the dictionary.

"What kind of job do you get from that?"

"I'll probably go to graduate school. Maybe into law."

"A lawyer. What kind of customers would you get?"

Then she turned and looked at him straight on for the first time. Her wide-set brown eyes glistened. "Just what do you mean by that?"

He felt the heat from her voice. "I mean what I said, who would come to you to be their lawyer?"

"Do you mean who would hire a Negro except other Negroes?" She was talking louder than he'd thought she was capable of. She didn't turn away when she spoke; she gave him her anger full face.

"Naw, I mean who would hire a woman." This time Tom laughed. But his laugh didn't sound like he wanted it to. It sounded forced, like he was putting on. Her silence returned and he found himself looking at that stiff profile again. There was nothing for her to be looking at but the back of the seat in front of them.

"Pissed you off, huh? Excuse me, made you mad?"

She didn't answer. She must be mad at herself for letting him know he'd made her mad. Or for even talking to him.

"I was just kidding. Can't you take a little kidding? I was trying to get your goat. You ever heard that saying? I did, too, huh?"

"I have no idea what you're talking about."

"Why not?"

Suddenly the lights overhead popped on. The bus hissed to a stop.

"Gibsonville," the driver turned and called. "Stay on board if you're not getting off for good. We are leaving in five minutes."

The bus was noisy with people getting off. A girl stopped next to their seat, trapped in the aisle while the boy in front of her got his tennis racket out of the overhead rack. She turned to the girl beside Tom.

"Bye, Valerie," the girl said to his stone-faced seatmate. "See you Sunday night."

She got the silence too. Finally Valerie answered, "Bye," but it was too quiet and too late for the other girl to hear, because she had moved away down the aisle.

Valerie. Valerie was snooty with everybody. Maybe that was why nobody sat beside her. She didn't know his name, but he knew hers.

The bus driver got back in, hopping over into his seat with the sureness of a movie cowboy hopping into the saddle. Looking so cool, Tom thought, and his hemorrhoids are probably killing him. Two new people got on and walked past Tom. When the driver shut the door, the inside lights went out. Just before the engine restarted, Valerie jumped up with an energy Tom didn't know she had and moved into the empty seat across the aisle. She sat in the aisle seat even though the window seat was empty, keeping the purse in her lap.

The lights of the station faded away and they were back out on the road, darker now as the bus groaned through the gears back up to speed. Valerie's perfume left with her, and the space filled with the diesel odor that sucked inside at the station, making Tom's empty stomach a little queasy. His cheeks burned as though someone had thrown hot water in his face. He sat there dumbly for a minute before his hot face told him how goddamn mad he was. Bitch.

He moved over into the seat she had left empty, closer to her. If she had left any warmth behind, he couldn't feel it. She took her big purse and lifted it into the empty seat on her other side.

"Saving that seat for somebody?" he sneered.

She didn't answer.

"You don't need to do that to keep me from sitting in it."

She left the purse there and ignored him.

"I'm sorry I made that crack about women, okay? Most women are smarter than me. In school, anyway."

Still no response.

"I didn't go to college. I could have. I was smart enough, but my family didn't have enough money. My sister was the second smartest in her class."

He wanted to ask her if she was married, if any of those rings on her hand meant that. "What would you rather do," he asked instead, "take a chance on getting killed, but know your time for getting shot at was up in a year? Or do something that kept you from getting shot at for the rest of your life, but, uh, it lasted as long as your life?"

The girl's face didn't budge, as if she didn't know he was talking to her.

"Why won't you talk to me?"

Her face snapped towards him. Anger was the only way to get her to talk. "Because I don't know you and I don't have anything to say to you."

"Well, you could still talk. You could ask me what I do, like I did you. I'm a stock car driver. My name is Tom Pate. They call me Pole Cat. You might have heard of me. I won the last two races at Greenmont Raceway. Maybe you've heard of Randall Johnson. He's the only Negro I know of who races. I beat him." She was still silent, but the silence was hot. "You could tell me your name. I know your first name is Valerie. People can make conversation with each other if they have to sit beside each other to make the time pass faster."

"I don't care what you do."

"I think I'm going to Vietnam."

When he said that, he heard it like it came from someone else's mouth. If he could have killed himself right then and had it called murder instead of suicide, he believed he could have done it. Set himself on fire like the monk and burned up in front of her.

When the bus pulled into Burlington, he didn't even hear what the driver said. She must have gotten off because when he felt a draft from the open door, he saw that her seat was empty. He looked out the window one last time to see if he saw her in a group of her friends, laughing and pointing at him in the bus.

He saw her. His heart began to beat faster. It wasn't Valerie's style to laugh or point at anyone. She wasn't standing with anyone. She looked shorter, standing on the ground.

She was staring blankly forward, looking sad. She could have been looking at anything, the bus, the night, him. She could have been thinking about anything. That was the only look she had when she wasn't angry. Three colored guys walked by and stopped, blocking her from his view.

The next thing he knew, he was off the bus in Burlington, dragging his old suitcase down the steps, watching the bus pull away and head towards Raleigh without him.

Tom saw Valerie only once more. She was no longer staring off into space by herself. She was being hugged by a Negro man who was about ten feet tall, her daddy, not her boyfriend, by the way he hugged her and kissed her on the cheek instead of the mouth. And there was a woman with him who was as light as Valerie and two little girls exactly the same size. Twins. They were dressed alike. She could have told him about her little sisters. That would have been something to talk about. He heard her laugh. Her father picked up her two heavy suitcases while Valerie walked towards the car, a twin holding each hand. The three of them got into the backseat of a black Lincoln Continental. He watched her father lift her luggage into the trunk. On each suitcase there was a Rosemount College sticker like the one Lisa put in the back window of her Corvette.

He had told Valerie a lie, but he'd thought it was the truth when he said it. He wasn't a stock car driver anymore and he wasn't going to be for a long, long time.

29

"You know what I been thinking?" Vernon Pate said to his older brother one evening near Christmas. "I reckon there is something the Devil put into dark people that makes them sneaky."

"Who you talking about, Vernon?" Hershel asked, attempting a smile. In the silence that followed, he puffed on his pipe, sucking and grunting, touching his lips with his fingertips because, since his fall, he couldn't be sure what his face was doing. The right side of his lip hung like a leather flap over his mouth.

Vernon rested in the cane rocker in the front room at his brother's house. He had taken to smoking a pipe of late, too. The spot where his cigar used to rest on his lip had grown sore, swollen with a blister that never seemed to heal. When he'd tried to kiss Aurora, she had turned her face to the side. When he went to slap her, her face had stared straight forward, those black eyes set like a batter waiting for a pitch. She'd caught his arm in midstroke, hacking it away, bruising the fair skin on the side of his arms.

"I mean that Mexican woman. You know who I mean."

"I ain't never seen her go nowhere," Hershel said. He touched his lip, checking to see if it swung back and forth after he stopped talking. "'Cept when she went out looking for Annie, she sticks real close to home."

"She don't have to go nowhere to be sneaky."

"Found her, too. Went right out and found her curled up by the river. Burned a dozen ticks off that child," he recollected. "I think she's pretty as a picture, myself. Looks like them Indian women in the books Rachel brought."

"Maybe I don't want no young'un by her. Maybe something the wrong color would come out of her. Or it'd have horns and a tail. That Columbus who made this country, he was from Spain and he might have been a sight dark to suit most people. That Tommy is a sight dark to suit me."

Hershel turned towards the fireplace so no one could stare at him; he soon forgot about his lip. Once he got going, the words rolled out easily. He could tell that Vernon didn't like him taking up for Aurora. "I don't find no fault with her at all. She's a good worker. She works like a man, sticks right by me. 'Cept sometime I think it's a youngun helping me. Not knowing a word for everything keeps a person from appearing grownup."

"She can talk good. She just don't talk good English."

"Other morning she saw a robin redbreast and she says to me, 'That bird scorched its belly carrying dew to the sinners in hell.' Now, if you ask me, that's a funny way of seeing things. That girl's got some stories. Had an uncle who would be planning to take his old turkey to the chop block, but he'd get him drunk first so he wouldn't feel no pain."

"That don't sound like a Spaniard to me. I seen them Spaniards during the war. Little children even, no bigger than Tommy, throwing rocks at a rabbit they got all tied up. They hung up a live goose and rode by on a horse to pull her head off. Now, they want to eat something, why don't they just chop its head off and get it over with? You gotta think twice about having somebody come from that kind of raising around your house."

"What I'm saying, Vernon, is if you're planning on taking a wife, this one's a bit too young for you." Hershel chuckled. "B.B. always said you were too lazy to go looking, but you'd take the first one come up to your doorstep. 'If your eyebrows meet across your nose, you'll never wear your wedding clothes,'" he teased.

Vernon reached up and felt the ridge of hair that grew between his eyes.

"'Dimple on the chin, the Devil within.' B.B. said that too," Vernon retorted, referring to the large dimple in Aurora's chin.

"Aw, she ain't no devil. Just a girl don't know how to act sometimes. Had that foreign raising."

"You don't know the half of the hobgoblins and devils in that woman's head."

"I know one thing she's scared to death of. Ghosts. Ain't that something? Took her down to B.B.'s house and told her I'd fix it up for her to set up housekeeping and her eyes got big as saucers. She thinks B.B.'s ghost is still in there. And she's scared to death of my tractor, but I reckon that's the girl in her. Tried my best to teach her to drive it.

"I was standing square on top of a stump the other day," Hershel went on. "Told her to get up there and give it a little bit of gas to take the slack out of the rope. She let that clutch out all of a sudden and I took off like I'd got shot out of a cannon. She cried like a baby when she thought she'd hurt me."

Hershel stopped talking; his right shoulder rolled forward and the loose flesh on his face dropped. He looked down at his hand like it was a misbehaving puppy he didn't have the heart to smack. Then he spoke softer, "Now I got Gladys harping on me about getting pitched off that stump. It's hard to make it clear to her, but it was the day I caught that wire up in my bush and bog, I got hurt. I remember the date, November twenty-third, the day they shot Kennedy. Done it to myself. Fell and twisted it and that was when the hurting started, when I crawled up past the mule spring. That's when the pain set in and my breath wouldn't come. But you know how Gladys is. She gets her mind made up."

Suddenly Vernon got up from his rocker so fast it thumped

over sideways. His whole body began to shake as he slung open the front door, walked to the edge of the porch, grabbing the corner post.

"Cat walk over your grave, Vernon?" Hershel called after him.

Vernon didn't answer. Hershel shuffled slowly out beside his brother, looking out into the light that filtered through the persimmon tree. He squinted, then reached up to rub his bad eye, but his good eye had already seen Zack walking up into his yard.

Gladys answers the phone on the first ring. She'd already heard the news on the radio. Another accident at Martinsville. There was a fire and Tom had been taken to the hospital.

"Hey, Mama. It's me."

"Tom. You've hurt yourself again. We heard it on the radio."

"Yeah, Mama. I'm going to be okay, though, don't worry."

"Oh, thank the Lord. Did you break your arm again?"

The year before at Martinsville, Tom had broken his left arm. At first she couldn't picture it. Her boy who'd been swept eight miles down the Yellow River and come home with only a skinned knee, her boy who'd gone through Vietnam without a scratch, that same boy had his arm snapped like a matchstick in one of those cars. Now this.

"No, Mama. Just got a little hot in there is all . . ."

Gladys drops into the chair by the phone, her legs gone weak. It is a sign. The Good Lord is warning him again.

Hershel sits across the room from her as she talks and appears to be laughing. "His mind isn't all there anymore," she hears herself telling Tom when he asks her to leave home to come care for him. Tom's hands are burned and bandaged and he has to go to the bathroom. She sees him holding the phone with a giant white clown hand.

The operator interrupts. Tom is talking fast. He is out of money. Then the line goes dead. Gladys holds the dead receiver as if the buzzing might go away and Tom will come back. She hadn't asked Tom if his face was spared. She shivers and Hershel sees her.

"What's the matter, woman," Hershel calls then chuckles. "Cat walk over your grave?"

Gladys hangs up the phone and walks to the window. She doesn't want to look at Hershel. "No, Hershel. Not *my* grave." She watches out the window until her family returns from the beach—Rachel, Annie, Aurora, Tommy and Zack. Tom's son jumps from the car, his skin dark as a shadow and runs through the broomsage below her. He is searching for straight sticks for the kite she promised to help him make tomorrow. Everyone else is rushing to the house. They have heard it on the radio too.

No one else is watching Zack as he struggles to get his injured leg out of the car.

"I won a Grand National, Zack. At Waverly," Tom writes. "Maybe you read about it. I beat Petty and the rest of them. Well, to be honest, Petty broke. But I'm going to get him. Maynard Peyton, you probably heard of him. He was racing on Daytona Beach before I was born. Maynard's my crew chief. I got a team with some money now, Zack. Bullfrog Embers owns it. He made a lot of money selling used cars in Fuquay-Varina and now he's got the biggest Chevrolet dealership in Charlotte. It's not like it was when we were busting our asses at Ned's for peanuts.

"Next month I'll come get you on my way to Raleigh," he adds. "I'm going to be signing autographs at Capital City GM and you can watch." He adds a PS: "You can tell that guy at Cut-Rate Used Cars where I'll be. Tell that bastard who repossessed my Bel Air what Tom Pate is driving now."

This is the most Tom has ever written in a letter to anyone. Zack imagines how he must have looked when he was done putting down all those words, panting like a dog who's treed a raccoon. Tom encloses a picture of himself, squatting beside his Chevrolet race car with number 7 on the door. His black hair is cut short and he wears a neat white uniform with his name embroidered between the sponsor patches on the left side of his chest.

Annie finds the same photo reprinted in the Summit News. "My big brother is handsomer than Elvis. He's a movie star," she brags to her friends, but Zack tells her he is better than that—he is a stock car driver. He gets paid for driving fast.

In late September, the squealing tires of a convertible announce Tom's arrival at the home place as he turns off Highway 43. Some of his family stands on the porch, as still as statues in a model train setting: his mother, his little sister Annie, and his son Tommy. His father bends over in the garden beside Aurora, who stands firmly planted with her feet wide, her skin dark as a cigar store Indian. Only Zack is missing, the one he has come to see.

When the Chevy stops rolling in front of the farmhouse, Tommy wrestles away from Annie's grip then runs from the porch to his mother in the garden. Hershel Pate keeps searching through the vines, never looking up, while Aurora watches Tom step from the car. Clutching the bottom of her apron that sags with tomatoes, her other hand wrapping the back of her child's head, she appears as much the country woman now as she had seemed the French maid in her black and white waitress costume when they'd met eight years before.

Gladys speaks his name from the porch, "Tom?" and he answers, "It's me, Mama."

Annie runs to meet Tom, and as he puts his arm around her, she stiffens at first as though allowing a stranger to touch her. Then as he says her name, she relaxes. "Tom, guess what? In thirty-three days, I'll be old enough to get my learner's permit."

"My baby sister's going to be driving a car. I'll teach you how."

"Zack promised to teach me, but he had to go back to the hospital."

Tom drops his arm off her shoulder.

"Zack's gone?"

"Yes, last week. To Washington."

Tom shakes his head slowly. Annie tugs him towards the steps. His mother doesn't move, her hands wind into her apron.

"Welcome home, Tom," she says finally, her voice barely a whisper.

"Zack had to go back to Walter Reed, Mama?"

"Yes," she replies. "He has a lot of pain." She pauses a moment, then asks, "Won't you have a glass of iced tea?"

"To wet my whistle?" he asks with a smile.

"Yes," she answers, hugging a body that she can no longer remember ever feeling in her arms. Gladys doesn't tell him, but she can see the marks the flames left on his face, a white mask etched around his eyes. And those hands, the skin drawn so tight from the burns. He'll never be able to do the fine work that Zack can do. But he has chosen to play with fire. Tom comes back into her life like a picture postcard from hell.

"So you near 'bout got burnt up," his daddy comments when Tom sits down for supper in Zack's empty seat. "Do you ever win?" he asked with a chuckle.

"Don't you keep up with anything?" Tom answered. "I won the Grand National at Waverly."

"To save my life, I don't know how we raised a gambler, Gladys," Hershel needles.

"I'm not a gambler," Tom snaps. "A gambler wins for doing nothing."

"You risk your life. That's gambling in my book."

"It's not fair to call it gambling. You don't have any idea

how hard I've worked to get a chance with a good team. I'm doing good now."

"Tom," his mother says softly. "Don't get so upset. Your daddy was just teasing you. You must have forgotten his sense of humor. We believe the Good Lord chose to spare you again that day, Tom."

"That's complete baloney, Mama," Tom replies, his agitation growing. "I saw on TV the next day that five miners died in a cave-in in West Virginia. There were all these women and children crying their hearts out. Why didn't your Good Lord spare them? They were probably a lot better men than I am. And don't tell me He works in mysterious ways." Gladys looks down at her plate. Tom turns to his father. "You come watch me run," Tom insists. "I'll get you tickets. You'll see I don't gamble. I play it smart. Ask anybody. They'll tell you Bullfrog hired me because I use my head. A good driver doesn't take a chance without a good reason. The biggest chance you ever took was switching brands of fertilizer."

Hershel nods his head, looking at his right hand where the fingers are drawn into a claw.

"Switching fertilizer is a hell of a gamble to a farmer," Hershel answers, his voice falling. He no longer has the energy to argue long. "How come he got so mad at me?" he asks Gladys as though Tom has already left. She pats his shoulder.

After supper, Gladys waits until the others go up for bed, first Aurora and the child, then Hershel, and finally Annie, who leaves reluctantly under her mother's orders. "I want to talk to Tom alone, dear."

When the last door upstairs clicks shut, Gladys levels her stare at Tom.

"Have you come back to marry Aurora this time?" she asks bluntly.

"Mama, don't start into me on that again. I've come to sign autographs in Raleigh tomorrow. The only reason I came is to see Zack and now he's gone. I can't believe I came all this way and missed him."

"And what about your son?" she presses.

"He's too bashful or something. It takes too long to make friends with him. That's probably her fault. Maybe when he gets a little older we'll have something to talk about."

Gladys shuts her eyes and begins to rock, her chair squeaking into their silence until Tom says, "I've got a girlfriend, Mama. I already told you. I can't help it. I just don't have any interest in Aurora. If she'd walk by me and I didn't know her, I'd never look twice. Her figure's gone. Men used to stop everything just to look at her."

"Well, we happen to think she's pretty as a picture since she filled out," Gladys defends. "And don't you believe for a minute that men don't notice her. Your brother is proud to walk beside her to church. She's the biggest help to us you've ever seen. We've come to count on her as part of our family. But you don't understand, do you? What it's like to count on other people?"

"Sure I do, Mama. I count on the guys who do my car to do it right. When I'm going a hundred and seventy, I don't have on my mind that somebody on the crew is going to let me down. I have me on my mind. Not messing up. So I have to count on people and they count on me to get the job done." Tom looks around the room and says absently, "You got a TV. Is it color?"

"No. We've had it for a long time. All they seem to have on it now is that war. I'd just as soon leave it turned off."

"Yeah, it's getting a lot worse over there. I sure wish they'd missed Zack's name." Tom's face brightens suddenly as he says, "I just had a funny thought, Mama. Aurora's like when you tried to make me wear those pants with the heiny binders, two years after everybody else quit wearing them. Just because they weren't worn out yet." Then he adds, "If Aurora was those pants, I'd give her to the Salvation Army." Tom laughs by himself. "I sure wish Zack was here. He would get a kick out of that. Sounded like something he would have come up with."

Gladys stands up slowly. "I wish Zack was here too. I'm going to bed, Tom. You know where the light for the attic room is. Just screw the bulb in tight. Your daddy still hasn't found the time to put in a switch. Use the green towel with the pink flowers."

At daybreak the next morning when Tommy runs off to go fishing, Gladys feels a little sting that Tom won't be going with him, then admits a pleasure to match the pain when the boy digs his worms and leaves before Tom gets up, saying, "Tell Grandpa to meet me down on the Indian Rock and I got both our poles."

31

Zack drives into the parking lot of the North Carolina Motor Speedway in Rockingham. Tom has invited him to a test session there, about an hour's drive from Summit. Zack drives his own car now, a '64 Ford Fairlane with an automatic transmission. Tom has offered to get him a deal on a new Chevy with his factory connections, but Zack doesn't take him up on it. He would feel awkward collecting a government check and owning a flashy car.

Zack has spent the past six months in the Walter Reed Army Hospital undergoing repairs to his right leg. He hasn't seen Tom since he got his own draft notice, four years after Tom's. In his four seasons of active racing since he got out of the service unscathed, Tom has broken his arm and badly burned his hands and foot. Tom still believes that nothing really bad will ever happen to him. Zack knew something bad would happen to him and it had.

Near the closed concession booth at Rockingham is a red '69 Chevrolet SS 396; Zack doesn't have to ask who it belongs to. He parks his Fairlane beside Tom's SS and begins the arduous task of getting out of his car. He moves the seat back, drops his left leg outside and, with his hands, lifts his right leg from under the steering wheel. His leg is now an appendage that he drags along with the dead weight of a ball and chain. He plants his cane between his legs, slowly pulling his body upright.

In the hospital, after they put the pins in his leg, Zack had joked with his doctors about trying to sneak past a magnet; but in his dreams on morphine, he stuck to a steel door like a fly on wet paint. The morphine eased his pain, but he ceased to walk into the wild scenes in his mind with pleasure. The doctors had given him a built-up shoe for his short leg.

Aurora had clapped her hands and laughed when she saw how the shoe repaired his leg. He wore it the evening that his old girlfriend Laurie Collins visited, walking level across the porch to meet her. Later Aurora frowned when his mother said how pretty Laurie had gotten since she filled out, so, to make Aurora laugh, Zack replied, "She always looked like a pond fish to me, Mama. Her skin is so thin, you can see her veins running under it. I bet if she stood in front of a light naked, you could see the food in her stomach." His mother scolded him and laughed at the same time like she always did.

Now he tiptoes on the right side, his heel off the ground like a child with a thorn in his foot because he's left the special shoe at home. He jabs his way across the lot at Rockingham, walking in his own dust cloud towards the gate, wishing he hadn't been so vain about wearing the shoe. When he stops moving, his dust cloud passes him. He sees a man he recognizes right away; he can tell the man is having trouble recognizing him.

"Zack, is that you? Hey, buddy!"

"Hey, Tom."

Zack pinches his clothes away from his damp backside, the top of his head stinging in the sun. Tom wears a white polo shirt and jeans and is deeply tanned, his tattoo almost lost in his brownness. Zack squints at the white shirt as Tom gets closer, the glare blackening his brother's face.

"Hey, buddy. You don't look so good. You better get over to the shade."

"Look like I just stepped out of a closet, huh?" It's his own voice, but Zack isn't sure where the words come from.

"How long have you been out of the hospital? You didn't tell me that you got that messed up." Zack considers pulling up his pants leg to show his brother what it really looks like and to watch him cringe.

Instead, Zack jokes brightly. "But my wee-wee still works. That's always the big question at the Vet's hospital. They bring in a guy with no arms and legs and somebody asks, but does his wee-wee still work?" When Tom shivers, Zack quickly switches the subject. "Look at the lumps on that hood," pointing his cane at the twin dome hood on Tom's car and relieving his brother's eyes of viewing his short leg. Zack ambles towards the new Chevy SS convertible. "Air conditioned. Guess you need it with that black interior when the top's up. Wow, three-hundred-ninety-six cubic inches," he read off the side.

"Yeah. This one's got a special-built engine with three-hundred-seventy-five horsepower."

"Can anybody get one?"

Tom stares at his car like a salesman without a script. "I d-don't know," he stammered. "I don't think so. I think they're only going to make a few of them. Five hundred maybe. Bullfrog ordered it special."

"Four-speed on the floor."

"Yeah, want to give her a try?"

Zack shakes his head, looking at his right foot, which has dropped his hip like a car with a flat.

"Your clutch leg is okay, isn't it?"

"It's fine, but I have to use it on the brake and the gas. The right one is useful when you need an anchor."

"That leg is short now, huh?"

"Yeah, broke it too many times. Just like an old piece of tubing with too many welds."

"You're not old, Zack. You're younger than me. I wish I was still twenty-four."

"I'm twenty-five. On a cold, damp morning, I'm an old

man." Zack swings his face from his brother's stare. Some things he doesn't mean to say, but they come out on their own. Tom was halfway around the world from Zack when he'd been hurt, but it sounds like he blames him. Just like with his daddy, when every missing tool was Tom's fault though he hadn't touched them for years. Zack tells people who don't know him that he got hurt falling off the hood of Tom's race car when he took too long to clean the windshield. That is a funny story. And he can be a hero—a stupid hero—but a hero.

"Come on inside," Tom offers. "I want you to meet my team."

Tom takes the race car out for a few warmup laps before bringing it in and giving a list of responses to Maynard Peyton, his crew chief, a gray-haired man with a clipboard. Tom has written to Zack about Maynard. The air fills with hot smells when the car comes into the pits: burning paint, burning oil, burning fuel. Tom has always said there are no bad smells at a race track.

A crew man yells as he brushes his shoulder on a hot pipe reaching for a dropped tool. While Zack holds ice cubes wrapped in a rag to the man's hairy back, he remembers the smell of hair and flesh burning when they used to brand calves. It was the end of innocence in those calves' eyes, when their hair caught fire and had to be doused with water for the stinging to stop. Aurora had told him of her Uncle Marcos, how he would stick a poisonous flower under the calf's nose when the brand was applied so it would never eat the bad flower. Would this man remember getting burned every time he reached under the engine for a dropped wrench?

Tom's spirits are high when he sees his times.

"Yeah, ain't it amazing how fast you can go," Maynard

comments, "when you ain't got all those other nasty cars out there in your way?"

Tom laughs and shoves the older man's chest. "Doing just like you told me, Maynard. Using up all the road."

"It belongs to you in qualifying, too, you know. All that empty road. We pay them to let you use it."

"You set it up right, I'll put it on the pole for you."

"It'll be loose as a goose eating blackberries, hotshot. I promise you."

Tom's team is dressed in the same red as Tom's new street car, with the race car sporting a red stripe around the lettering down the side. Zack is taken by how nice the car looks, no dents in the sheet metal, nice smooth paint, no mud. It seems like too nice a car to risk on the race track. On the nose is a red flame rising from the words EMBERS CHEVROLET, CHARLOTTE, N.C. Tom is still number 7, a crisp white numeral against a black background. A small blue bullfrog squats at the bottom of the flame, there for its namesake, the team owner, Bullfrog Embers. Zack wants to ask if it's blue because green is bad luck on a race car, but he doesn't.

He sits in a folding chair that Tom has opened for him, holding in the stories of Tom's old team that he has garnered from a trip to Greenmont to visit their old crew at Ned's. Tom has it all now: a good crew, good car, good sponsor. That's what Ned had said he needed, the combination to go with being a good driver. If one of them was missing, you'd lose. Nothing seems to be missing now.

Ned's old shop had changed to Across the Pond, a foreign car repair garage with only Arnold left from the original crew. He sported a new Chevy pickup with a double gun rack and a bumper sticker that read: GET A GOOK FOR GOD. Arnold's engine talents would stay in Greenmont because Norma, now a mother of two, won't let him go on the road, her payment for keeping him out of Vietnam by marrying him the first time his name came up, then having a child when his name came up again. Arnold had filled in the blanks of the past six years for Zack.

First he told him what Zack already knew. "Everybody thinks it's just going to be some nobody-never-was who can't drive who gets it. I heard Fireball in there screaming when he was burning. I ain't never going to Charlotte again." Next he told Zack what he hadn't known. Giles Burcham got his deferment by marrying Roxanne, who had miscarried right after they married, but went on to have two little girls before they separated. No one knew where Ned had gone; some kind of trouble with the law. Roxanne worked in a beauty shop. Outsiders were winning all the races at Greenmont. They were talking about paving the track.

"No place for the little man in racing anymore," Arnold tells Zack. "Just big money and fancy talk. People used to take care of one another, help a guy out when he was down. It's all cutthroat now, sink or swim, and you ain't using my life preserver. Truck breaks down on the highway and them guys driving the big semis don't even stop to give you a hand. Guys in coats and ties at the races, giving and taking all the money. They don't care about dirt tracks. I think dirt tracks is finished, if you ask me."

There are no men in coats and ties at Tom's test session; even Bullfrog, who leaves early for a business appointment, wears a golf shirt like Tom's that stretches to cover his belly, a dark spot in the center from his navel crater.

Tom still drives the dirt tracks because the points there count just like the ones on the superspeedways. But he's made the transition to pavement and high speeds, leaving behind most of the Greenmont dirt racers. The speeds have doubled. After a pavement race, fatigue doesn't flood his arms and shoulders like it did when he spent an evening sawing at the steering wheel on a fairgrounds track. Now his chest burns before and after the race and food doesn't taste good again until Tuesday. He takes aspirin to kill the pain between his eyes while he opens and closes his hands, each fingertip feeling like the recipient of a hammer blow. It's not physical fatigue but mental tension that wears him down. The high speeds mean a man's brain has to concentrate farther down the track, never an easy task in life for Tom Pate.

He circulates in the race car, faster than Zack has ever seen him run, the car hugging the turns on the smooth pavement like a slot car. The paint job glistens in the sun, no dirt to dull its finish.

"Every old beat-up gray-haired fellow like me you see around a car put down a little of that pavement your brother's rolling on," Maynard tells Zack while Tom is on the track. "We done it just so these young fellows could come along after us and make all the money."

Tom's success hadn't escaped Arnold. "Your brother'd drive through hell on a ice cube if they give him enough money," he told Zack. "He got hisself a good middle-of-the-field ride with Embers. But if he's gonna make the big time, he better hurry his ass up. There's guys out there younger than him already winning. You get racked up and you ain't made a bunch of money, you're really shit out of luck."

Tom looks older, his skin more weathered and more tightly stretched over his cheekbones. He wears the goggle image permanently on his face from his burns at Martinsville. Each time the crew chief tells him the change is going to take a few minutes, Tom climbs out and pulls off his helmet and gloves. There are white spots that won't tan on the backs of his hands. He reaches into a pocket on his chest for his cigarettes; his name is embroidered in script on the pocket. His firesuit sticks to his skin and his hair is soaked, pressed into the shape of the inside of the helmet until his fingers comb through it. When the engine shuts down, the silence sweeps over them. Zack notices his brother's hearing is starting to go. "Hit him up side the head to get his attention," Maynard calls with a laugh. On the back of Tom's head, hidden from his own eyes, are white hairs scattered in the black.

"Your brother ain't had the shit knocked out of him real good yet," Arnold had told Zack. "He ain't been stung good. But he'll get it. They all do, sooner or later. And he can count on one finger the people who'll wait till he mends."

After the test is over, Zack goes to Tom's motel room and waits while he showers before dinner. He follows Tom's red Chevy to a steak house near the track. When the brothers walk in, the team is already seated at a large table drinking a round of beers before dinner. Two cold ones await Tom and Zack in front of two vacant seats.

"Hey," one of them calls. "Didn't I tell you I smelled Pate? You can always tell an Aqua Velva man."

"They ought to sponsor him. He uses their stuff like a cattle dip. And wouldn't you know it. He went to all that trouble and it's Nora's night off."

Tom glances towards the kitchen just as an older woman pushes through the door backwards with a tray. He turns to Zack. "I guess I should have come to supper smelling like I did when I got out of that steam box they built me."

"You think you worked up a sweat today, wait till this weekend," Maynard puts in.

After they order, Tom asks Zack, "Are you still in touch with Cy? We've got an opening for a mechanic because one of our crew got drafted. He was pretty good as I remember. Kind of a natural."

Zack shakes his head. "Cy's in Vietnam. Horace told me he signed up for extra time."

Tom tips his head and frowns. "I never could figure where that guy was coming from. I always halfway figured he was after my ride."

"He wanted it, but Cy would have stolen the preacher's car before he'd have gone after your ride."

"You guys oughta meet this Cy," Tom says to his crew. "He was just like Bobby Isaac about black cats and peanuts. He'd go back to bed on race day if a peanut rolled under his car."

"But Cy wasn't scared of anything real," Zack says. "He told me once, 'It don't matter if I never get to race cars. Just so I get to drive them. Take my Chevy away from me for good and tell me I'll never have enough to buy another one, I'll steal the next Chevy I find with the door unlocked.'"

"He's like a little kid or something, isn't he?" Tom says. "What's the point of driving if you can't race? Ned would probably have let him drive my car after I left if he'd played his cards right."

"Yeah, Ned did offer him the chance to race a little the next season, but two days before his first race, Cy was joyriding with Arnold and Giles Burcham. They drove up beside this fat woman," Zack relates the story according to Horace, "and Cy yelled, 'Lady, your ass is so wide, you need turn signals!' Just as Cy slapped her on the butt, Giles gunned it, and Cy broke his arm in three places."

Tom's crew laughs at the story. "Tom, remember that Albert Peachtree guy?" Otis, the truck driver, asks. "The night before he was supposed to get a tryout in Bullfrog's car, he rode his Harley into a bar and broke both hands on the door frame."

"Lucky for me, huh?" Tom replies. "I was scared to cross the street the day before my tryout." Tom winks at the waitress and points at his glass. As he watches it fill, he says to Zack, "If Cy comes back, tell him where to find me. Maybe they taught him to read and write."

"I don't think so," Zack replies. "Not the way Horace talked."

Horace had told Zack that after Cy lost his chance to drive, he'd got so down in the dumps that he went to the draft board to sign up before the cast came off. They turned him down twice, but the second time he promised them that when his arm got well he would show them he knew how to write. By then they were running out of warm bodies and took him anyway. Cy sent one letter home that someone had written for him: "Tell Ma and Pop I was looking through my rifle and saw a tiger. Tell them it's real crazy over here but I'm still alive."

Horace's eyes had begun to tear when he talked to Zack, running his hand over a faded Charlie the rooster who was shedding feathers like an overripe flower. "You oughta get you an animal, son," Horace sputtered. "They get old real fast. Everybody oughta see something get old faster than they do. I'm not much to look at, but Cy seemed to listen to me when I had him right here in front of me. I want to tell him he's got no business over there. He'd be too proud to ask anybody to read a letter to him." Horace blew his nose on the bottom of his T-shirt before a glint of the old Horace came back. "Even a busted clock is right twice a day."

"I remember that old bum," Tom tells Zack. "Got drunk and thought he was a race car driver. Taught you how to weld."

"You remember that?" Zack says. "Horace didn't even remember it. I told him I was going back to my job at Carmichael's now that I was out, restoring cars, using the welding he taught me, and he said, 'I did?' I reminded him of something he said, that a fabricator is like God, that a butcher can cut up a cow, but only God can make one, and he said, 'Don't remember saying that. But if I did, I was full of shit. A fabricator is just as big a asshole as the rest of us.'"

Tom's crew begins to laugh. Zack's face reddens with the attention; the last six months he has had only hospital people around him who knew his body better than he did. He had made them laugh sometimes, because there sure wasn't much to cheer you up in that place. They had been impressed that his brother drove race cars and one of the orderlies had even heard of Tom.

"How about old Holly Lee? Does anybody ever see her around town?"

Zack chuckles. "All around town."

"How's that?" Tom is puzzled.

"She's a hooker."

Tom leans back in his chair. "Well, I'll be damned. I guess that's kind of a shame. She's damn good-looking though. I bet she makes a lot more than she did roller-skating."

Zack smiles as he butters a roll. "Probably does. Six years ago she got twenty bucks a throw."

Their eyes meet briefly and Tom is the first to turn away.

"I told these guys that you work for a rich guy, Zack, who's got a bunch of fancy foreign cars that you look after," Tom goes on. "They know the type, the sporty car types who say, 'I just took that corner at nine-tenths, by jove,'" he mocks in a British accent. "Speaking of sporty car types, what's old Harris Carmichael driving these days? Let me guess. He's got a GT-40 for the street."

"Harris is dead."

The table goes quiet. Zack attempts to cut his steak up into bite-sized pieces, examining the red meat in the center.

"I can send that back for you if you want it cooked more," Tom offers. "Most people don't get their steaks well done anymore." He signals to the waitress, who takes Zack's steak.

"Take mine, too," Maynard says, handing her his plate. "If you rush this one over to the vet, honey, I think he can save it."

Zack stares at the empty placemat where his plate has been; there is a semicircle of blood stains.

"How did it happen," Tom goes on. "The Porsche? Last time I saw Harris he was driving that silver Speedster down Flycatcher Road with a blond beside him. I figured he was practicing so he could beat me . . ."

"He died in Vietnam," Zack replies.

Tom is silent for a moment, then he said, "His old man didn't fix it so he got out of going?"

"He graduated from West Point. He had to go. He got shot by mistake, by his own men."

"That is what happened to one of the finest generals in the Confederacy," Maynard puts in, "Stonewall Jackson. Lee would have won that war if he hadn't lost Stonewall."

"Harris got shot in the back," Zack says.

"I almost got shot by my own man," Tom comments. "Well, not exactly a man, but he had a gun. I never even told you about this one, Zack. Want to hear it?"

"I guess I do. You're still here."

"Tell us, Pate." Maynard's eyes light up; he loves talking war. "I didn't think you wore a uniform long enough to get shot at."

"Maynard's a war nut, Zack; we're used to him. Anyway, there was this guy in my company who had this monkey for a pet. It was really a nasty little bastard, crapped all down his back when it rode on his shoulders. And it had a rotten temper. One day it jumped on my back and I hadn't even been teasing it and bit me on the shoulder."

"You're lucky you didn't get rabies," Maynard breaks in.

"Funny you should mention that," Tom laughs. "See, one of the ways to get off duty in Vietnam was to say a rat bit you, but when I got to thinking about telling them about the monkey, I decided that thirteen rabies shots were a pretty bad tradeoff. Anyway, a few days later, I happened to be guarding this bridge with this guy who had the monkey. So the guy decides to go relieve himself and he leaves the monkey and his rifle behind. And I'm sitting there, trying to keep from falling asleep, when I see that damn monkey has picked up this guy's gun."

"This is my rifle, this is my gun," Maynard mocks, pointing between his legs.

"Rifle," Tom corrects and pushes back in his chair to imitate the monkey. "He's fingering it and looking at it and next thing I know, he's got it pointed at me."

"Great," one of the other guys says. "Can't you see the telegram? We regret to inform you, Mr. and Mrs. Pate, but your son was shot by a monkey in Vietnam. And even more regrettably, it wasn't even an enemy monkey."

The waitress brings back the two steaks, charred black and shrunken.

"What happens is," Tom continues, "well, you know how much it costs to replace a rifle?"

"Ninety-eight dollars if you lose it," Zack answers.

"It was eighty-seven when I was there. Anyway, I'm feeling pretty desperate, like this is going to be it for me. So I get this flash in my brain: monkey see, monkey do. I take my rifle and lift it over my head. The monkey does the same thing. Then I made like I was tossing it and the monkey did it too. Only he let go of it. I mean, I was ready to pay the money for mine if I had to let go for him to get the idea. That gun went flying all the way down and splashed in the water."

"What'd you say to the guy when he got back?" the crew chief says, laughing.

"I said your little son of a bitch monkey just threw your weapon off the bridge. Well, the monkey knew he was pissed so he took off up in a tree and wouldn't come down. I went around for weeks waiting for that rotten monkey to bite me again."

"Why the hell didn't you just shoot the little SOB?" Maynard asks. "I'd have blasted him in two."

"I couldn't just shoot this guy's pet. Besides," he adds, "that would have been too easy."

"What happened to the monkey?"

"Disappeared. Some Viet Cong probably ate it." Tom looks around. "Hey, Maynard," he says, "how's Cheeta there?"

"Little tough," he replies, "but well done."

"Hard to believe Harris is dead," Tom says to Zack. This surprises Zack; he thought Tom told the monkey story to change the subject. "Some guys got it when I was over there, but not many. Nobody I knew well. Harris's the only person I know who's been killed and if you'd told me to pick one, I'd never have picked him."

"You know another one, Tom. You just don't know you know him."

"Who?"

"Richard."

"Richard who worked for Ned?"

"Yeah. MIA."

Tom looks at his plate then shoves his potato skin around. "I hate to hear that. He was a good guy. Richard wasn't cut out to have to kill people."

"I went by to see his mother. She took it pretty hard."

Zack had gone to see her in his uniform, not knowing Richard was dead. She was hostile, remembering the two soldiers who'd come to say Richard was missing. " 'How come you can't find him?' I ask them. 'You lost him. My boy don't know his way around that Vietnam. You find him and bring him back.' I know what they saying. They ain't even tried to find my Richard. White men spend my chil'ren like pennies. When they get dropped, they ain't worth bending to pick up."

As Zack walked away from Richard's house, he saw a photo of Richard had been set on the ground in a round gold frame;

pieces of silverware, a peeling candlestick holder, and other shiny pieces of metal were stabbed into the earth around it to mark off a small square no larger than a sleeping dog. In the photo, Richard was wearing a coat and tie.

Zack had heard it often in Vietnam: "Same mud, same blood." But when Martin Luther King, Jr., was shot, someone ran a Confederate flag up the pole at their camp. A cross was burned at Cam Ranh Bay. That night it had been quieter than usual. When the faces and plants and huts melted into the night and he saw only the stars arranged in familiar patterns, he hadn't felt so far from home.

"Did you know Buster got hurt over there?" Tom says finally.

"Arnold mentioned him," Zack replies. "Said he was a hero. Got a medal for killing more Commies than ten men put together is what Arnold said, and that he lost his hand."

"Lost his right hand," Tom replies, holding up his own right hand and examining it.

"Part of it," Maynard adds, "but it wouldn't hold a steering wheel so he got the rest cut off by a doctor. Got fitted with a special-made hook that fits a special-made steering wheel."

"He's not half as good, though, Maynard, do you think?" Tom asks.

"I don't know. His car ain't as good as it used to be. Hard to get the sponsors. They give you all this hero business in the newspapers, but try and get them to put their money where their mouths is. Got real short memories."

"That's what Arnold said," Zack replies. "He said if Buster had as good a car as the other guys, he could still blow their fucking doors off."

"I can hear him saying that," Tom laughs. "Old hot air Arnold. He'd get married and have ten kids to stay out of the war then talk about killing Commies. Did you see Allie?"

"No. He got a motorized wheelchair, but Arnold says he walks when nobody is looking. His brother married Roxanne," he says without a pause and looks hard at Tom.

"Boy, you got all the gossip, didn't you? Like reading the newspaper. Is she fat yet?"

"I didn't see her."

"I bet she's fat. She had that kind of figure. Girl like that has a couple of kids and she's broad as a barn."

"She didn't have your kid."

Tom's face reddens. He glances at his team, but they have missed the remark. "How's Mama?" he asks quickly.

"Okay." Zack continues to stare at his brother, but his remark has zinged past Tom like a bird hitting a windshield, the quick bad feeling gone as soon as you see the glass isn't broken.

"Tell her I'll call her and Tommy and Annie. Rachel still married to Peckerwood?"

"Yeah, she'll always be married to him."

"How about Annie? I told her if she wanted to go to college, I'd help her out, but she never asked."

"She's going to East Carolina. Mama got some money from selling part of the back field to some computer company."

"That's good. Tell Annie I'm proud of her. Maybe she'll leave that place and never come back."

The waitress comes for dessert orders. While she is at the other end of the table, Tom says to Zack, "Holly Lee is something else, isn't she?"

"I don't know," Zack answers. "At the time I didn't have any means of comparison."

Tom laughs and turns to the waitress. "We'd like the strawberry shortcake. You'll love it, Zack. Fresh strawberries and real whipped cream and the cake is still hot."

Tom doesn't ask about Aurora. They both know she has filled out like a pony who has adjusted to pulling a horse-sized plow, but Zack thinks it suits her. She's stayed light on her feet, generating enough horsepower to use her weight. She arrived at Sunday dinner on Zack's first week back home with her long hair braided with colored ribbons, Annie's handiwork, wearing the white skirt she had worn to church. As he hobbled behind her on the path to B.B.'s old house that Aurora was repainting, she looked like a creature from a magic lamp, the skirt blowing between her legs like pantaloons. "The gravestone of the old lady is here," she insisted after a dinner table argument. "I am sure of it." When she led him to the back step of the old house, he laughed, marveling at how she knew the farm better than his father now, how the locations of stumps and rocks were as familiar as furniture inside a house. B.B. had had the stone carved for herself when her husband died, but the family couldn't find it after her death. B.B. had been stepping on her own name for forty years as she left her back porch.

"You've found the stone, Aurora," he explained, "not the body."

"She is not buried there?"

"No. The body is at the churchyard. I'll take the stone over there and put it where it belongs." When Aurora smiled and walked inside where she had transformed the drab walls into Easter egg colors, he knew the ghost had left the little house for good.

Tom interrupted his thoughts. "We're going to Talladega. Did you know that? Talladega looks just like Daytona but it's got a steeper banking and it's a bit longer so it's faster. Have you heard all the mess about it?"

"Not much," he admits. He struggles to follow the racing talk, the names familiar now only from the newspapers and what Arnold had told him.

"Petty is the one causing all the trouble," Maynard puts in. "He's getting just like his old man used to be."

"Yeah, guys like Petty don't know what it's like to be Tom Pate," Tom says. "He's had it made from day one. All his life his daddy's been building race cars right in his own yard. In 'sixty-four, Petty ran sixty-one races. I haven't run that many in my whole life."

"Yeah, that's what Pearson says," Maynard replies. "All you bellyachers are alike. Pearson says if he run as much as Petty, he'd beat him more. Don't work that way. You run more, you use up your car more, so you're not as prepared."

"So you're saying Petty's crew has to work twice as hard as mine," Tom says with a smile.

"I'll work twice as hard if you pay me twice as much," Otis chimes in.

"Mention that to Bullfrog. Anyway, I'm serious about this," Tom goes on. "That's why it's so easy for Petty to boycott a race. He's got money coming out the ears and everybody in his family behind him. Nobody in my family ever gave me the time of day."

"I thought you said Zack here was on your first crew," Maynard comments.

"I don't mean Zack. I mean the rest of them."

"We could put them two sisters of yours to work rolling tires," one of the younger crew members jokes. "'Cept with that pretty one around, it'd be hard to keep my mind on my work."

"Cold day in hell when I let my little sister get messed up with a racing mechanic," Tom replies, staring briefly at the mechanic.

"Arnold says a driver might as well be a trained monkey," Zack says, pressing on with the Talladega question. "That it's all cars and tracks now."

"Arnold still knows everything, doesn't he?"

"Yeah. He says a driver's brain will blow up at those speeds."

Maynard laughs loudly. "Shows you what that guy Arnold knows. He thinks a race driver has a brain."

"Arnold says the drivers are just scared to go that fast."

"I wish that son of a bitch was here to do his own arguing. I don't like arguing with my little brother when I don't see him but about twice a year."

"I'm not arguing."

"Okay. Petty thinks the drivers will black out. It isn't just the speed. It's g-forces. 'Pogo Effect,' they call it. I don't happen to think it will be that way. If you're getting ready to black out, you'll know it, and you can slow down."

"You ever black out from going too fast, Pate?" one of the crew asks jokingly.

"No," Tom answers seriously. "Well, yes. If you mean getting knocked out. I think I got knocked out for a little while when we crashed at Martinsville. But I wasn't moving by then."

"You drivers get me. How come it's always 'we crashed,' but it's 'I won'?" Maynard cuts in. "You just think you weren't moving. That car took you for a hell of a ride that you missed," he says.

"How are you so sure that I got knocked out?" Tom asks Maynard. "You weren't in there."

"I know it because this guy named Tom Pate told me. When you were on the stretcher by the track, you saw a bunch of wrecked cars and asked me, 'Who had that wreck?' and I said, 'You did, you dumb fuck.' Looks like to me," Maynard winked at Zack, "all you know how to do at Martinsville is hit the wall. Two years in a row. Bust up your arm, then you get that pretty suntan." The crew laughs.

"You think you can spook me about Martinsville, don't you, Maynard? Not on your life," Tom came back. Tom grins at Zack. "These guys don't give me much slack."

Zack stares at his food, his meal hardly touched.

"What's the matter, Zack?" Tom asks. "Don't feel too good?"

Zack picks up his utensils and begins to eat like a child who has been scolded for not eating his supper.

"Zack got banged up in Vietnam," Tom says to the crew. "That's how he tore up his leg. He hasn't been out of the hospital for long."

"Yeah, you told us," Maynard says. "Chopper crash, didn't you say, Tom?" he asks as though Zack can't answer his own questions.

"Yeah, got shot down picking up wounded guys," Tom answers. "Only survivor. Viet Cong took his graduation watch. Guy thought he was dead meat and just picked up his arm and yanked off his watch. Damn nice watch," Tom says with a laugh. "Uncle Vernon got it in Simon's basement for five ninety-eight. Shows you what kind of taste those Viet Cong have."

When Zack looks up at Tom, his big brother stops talking suddenly as though the look demands his silence.

32

As they walk across the parking lot to their cars, it's beginning to rain. Tom asks, "What did you think of my team?"

"Seem like a nice bunch of guys. Real smart and experienced. Older than I thought they'd be."

"Yeah, they know a lot. They know how to bend the rules a little. They don't cheat, though. Maynard might have it a little light or a little short, but if he thought somebody was using a big motor, he'd break his head. He ratted on a guy once for a locked rear end. Maynard knows the guys building the cars are smarter than the ones inspecting them. My crew's not the best though. Best I ever had, but we don't always do the right things in race strategy."

Tom speaks to Zack with a looseness he didn't have when his team was present. "Until Maynard came along to coach me, I couldn't see what I looked like. He's good at setting up for the short tracks; my car handles as good as anybody's. And he's real good at setup for qualifying and making the tires last in a race, but there's a bunch of guys who pull me on the straight and I know it's not just money holding me back. I'm worried about Talladega because you need an extra-strong engine and he's not paying enough attention to that. Maynard's good, but he's kind of stubborn. Ned got like that. A lot of the old stock car guys get like that. You know what I mean. They're phasing out the dirt tracks and Maynard's too bullheaded to admit it."

"Yeah, Maynard told me he paved the road for you."

"He tells everybody that. He's been good to me, though. I moved in with him and his wife, Ethel, the first season and she used to get jealous, we talked cars and strategy so much.

He's just mad because he got old before things really started happening. But you don't want to get Maynard talking about Indy. The Indianapolis cars are faster than stock cars and anybody who says they aren't is ignorant as hell. I told Maynard once I would like to work my way up to them and he got all insulted. Then he gave me this lecture about apples and oranges and that it wasn't racing if all you had to do was build a little four-wheeled coffin and put a motor and a man in it. He says I don't know there's not enough metal between me and the wall until I hit it. He saw Marshal Teague die at Daytona in 'fifty-nine doing a demonstration drive in an Indy car. So I keep it to myself, but that's where I'm going if I get the chance. Indy is where the big money is."

"Seems like I'm hearing a lot more money talk than I used to. Is that what you like most about competing, Tom? The money?"

"No, no, not really. That's good. It's real good. If you're broke, you can't drive hard 'cause you have to pay for what you break. I like having money and having somebody else paying the bills and having people know me and ask for autographs and send me letters. I got girls offering me things that would shock the pants off of Arnold. I mean I like that side of it, but don't get me wrong. That's not what is important. What's good is the good feeling you get when you win. Nobody gets to win all the time. Not even Lorenzen did. When you get so you don't want to compete, then you're an old man. If I get to race these guys at Talladega from now on, I'll get better because they're the best. You get satisfied with middle of the road and your body starts to sag and there's nothing to live for, you know what I mean? I betcha that's how Lorenzen feels right now. He quit too soon. He thought he was big enough, but he wasn't. A lot of people will forget about him."

"You lose a lot more than you win."

"Yeah, and I've got good at bouncing back for the next one. I could always do that."

Zack moves slowly towards his car, opening the trunk for his umbrella. He holds it over his head, leaving Tom in the rain. Tom looks like he doesn't notice the rain. He's never had an umbrella and always got mad if you asked him to carry one.

"You can stick around a day or two, if you like, Zack. We oughta talk more often. I get kind of tired of the same company all the time. I know the other guys do too. They wouldn't mind a bit having you stick around for a few days."

"I've got to get back. Mama's expecting me. And Daddy, he's in pretty bad shape." Zack hears his own words, but knows they are rolling off Tom like the raindrops. He doesn't go on.

"So what else is new," Tom shrugs. "Before you go, I've got something I want you to do for me. I just don't have the time. You can see that." He gestures as if the parking lot is filled with unfinished chores. Tom opens the trunk of the Chevy SS. Zack moves closer. Lying on its side is a Fox mini-bike, bright red with a black seat, with the cardboard packing still around the chain. Tom runs his fingers around the handlebars and his face brightens like it's Christmas morning and the scooter is for him.

"I was dying to crank it up myself," he says, "but I didn't want him to think it wasn't brand new. Wouldn't you have loved one of these when you were ten, Zack? That would have been the happiest day of my life, seeing it was for me."

Zack doesn't answer. Aurora had led Zack out to watch Tommy handle the tractor, sitting forward on the seat to reach the pedals. The little boy spun it around at the end of the rows, mashing one brake to pivot a giant back wheel, lifting the hydraulics carefully so the dirt and grass didn't drop from the blade onto the road surface. Aurora's pride was in Tommy, Zack reminded himself, not how his coordination and mechanical ability compared to Tom's because she had never seen Tom perform in a car. Gladys had told Hershel not to worry, that all little boys like going fast but they outgrow it, then realized her mistake and wound her hands into her apron. Hershel went out to slow the boy down although he had done nothing wrong. "It could get away from him going so fast," he explained to Aurora. She frowned and with his good hand, Hershel patted her cheek to make her smile. Nobody liked to make Aurora frown. "Children are just like race car drivers," Hershel added with a smile, "They don't worry about what's going to happen to them. That's our job."

"Can you help me put it in your trunk, or should I get one of the guys?" Tom gestures towards the scooter. "I don't know when I'll have time to take it to him."

Finally Zack speaks. "To Tommy," he says, no question in his voice. He has a photo in his pocket that he intended to give Tom. It was taken on Zack's twenty-fifth birthday, when he pretended not to have enough air for the last candle and Tommy ran and blew it out for him.

"What's the matter? Mama will have a fit, huh? Afraid he'll get hurt."

"Who are you, Tom?" Zack asks.

Tom tips his head sideways. "Huh?" His hair is wet and sticks to his face. The rain has slowed to a drizzle and steams off the hot pavement around them.

"Who are you to him?"

"He knows. I don't know. You can tell him about me, Zack. You can figure out what to say. Explain it, okay?"

"What do you want me to tell him?"

"I wanted to leave that up to you. You're better at that sort of thing. Show him my name in the newspaper when I run at Talladega. Can't you tell him I'm a famous race car driver so

I don't have a lot of time to come see him? And if he asks you why he's never heard of me yet, tell him that he will real soon. Something like that. That's okay, isn't it? That kind of thing. I don't know what she's telling him."

"I know you don't."

"I mean she doesn't fit in with my life. I just made a mistake. I needed somewhere to live. I didn't have a dime. I don't ever think about her anymore. I've got a great girlfriend now. Miss Charlotte Motor Speedway. She gives me all the rope I need. You know I don't want to talk about this, Zack."

"I had this thought driving up here," Zack says. "It was about something you told me about racing. You said you could hit something going as fast as you and be okay. It was when you hit something standing still that it got you. Remember that?"

Tom turns his head; Zack sees that the white hairs have melted into the black ones as though they held ink. "I remember saying that about racing, but if you're trying to make it mean something else, then I didn't say it. Open your trunk, okay?"

Zack reaches slowly into his pocket and pulls out his keys. Tom struggles alone with the scooter. When it's finally inside Zack's trunk, he lowers the lid to check the clearance, then presses it shut.

"I better let you get on the road," he says, his eyes not meeting Zack's. He rubs his hands together. "I guess I better go wash my hands."

Zack holds out his hand. Tom wipes his hands on the sides of his jeans before he shakes his brother's hand.

"I guess I'll see you one of these days," Tom says. "Anytime you want passes to a race, just let me know. Bring Tommy. Or Annie, okay?"

"Okay," Zack replies. Then he moves towards the car door, closes the umbrella, and begins the slow procedure of lowering himself into the seat. It starts to shower hard again and wets his pants before he can get his legs inside. "North Carolina is the same as always," he jokes, "forty percent chance of rain means forty percent of your body is going to get wet."

Tom smiles faintly. "We're lucky we got our session in today." He pauses. "Wish me luck at Talladega," he adds, then waits a moment for Zack to respond.

Finally Zack answers with Tom's old words instead of his own: "Don't back off," he smiles. Tom once told Zack if the driver beside you went into a turn too fast, taking a chance, then you had to take the same chance. If you backed off, you were finished.

"I won't buddy, I promise," Tom replies. "And if I collect the wall, I'll tell Maynard my brother told me how to do it."

Tom doesn't run to shelter, but turns slowly towards the restaurant, his back hunched and hands in his pockets as though he has a long walk ahead.

Zack stops on the outskirts of Rockingham, pulling off onto the shoulder. The rainstorm has passed and the air feels washed clean. He repeats his leg procedure getting out of the car, then edges his way back to the trunk without his cane. Only an occasional car passes. He studies the hillside, strewn with rock and paper. An old stove sits in a willow like a treehouse. He can't help but smile at that; an old stove had gotten his guitar.

He hears a voice behind him, a child. "I help you change your tire, Mister. Only fifty cents."

Zack turns to face a small black boy. The knees of his jeans gape like mouths. He lays down a pink bicycle that is too small for him and has no rubber on the wheel rims. Zack opens the trunk.

"How 'bout a quarter?" the boy asks.

"Don't have a flat," Zack replies. "But give me a hand with this."

The boy stands on his tiptoes and looks at the scooter.

"You gon ride that home?" he asks with a smile.

Zack doesn't answer.

"I ride that a hundred miles an hour, easy," the boy continues, excitedly.

"You ever hear of Randall Johnson?" Zack asks.

The boy squints. "Who he?"

"Ask your daddy." The child shrugs. "Ask your big brother. You got one?"

"I got four."

They both tug on the scooter, the boy pinching his finger once, howling then stopping to suck on it. They manage to tear the rug mat and put a long scratch under the trunk lid before the scooter finally sits on the ground. Zack shoves down the kick stand with his good leg before releasing the handlebars. The child never takes his eyes off the scooter or asks for money again. "You gimme a ride?" he asks brightly.

"Where's your house?" Zack questions.

The child points behind himself without turning. Zack sees a woman on the porch throw out a pan of water that hits with more a thud than a splash on the saturated ground. Her eyes are on them. She doesn't break her gaze as a dog runs from under her house to sniff the spot where the water struck, then slinks back beneath the house.

"You can push it that far. It won't run without gas. Tell your big brothers that Randall Johnson gave it to you. If you remember to do that, you can keep it."

Zack ambles back to the driver's side and gets in, holding his right leg in both hands and banging it against the car to get the mud off, like a man cleaning a shovel. He drives away slowly, glancing twice in the mirror. On the second look, the child grabs the handlebars and begins to push the scooter towards his house. The boy's pink bicycle is gone; Zack missed its tumble down the hill.

Before he reaches the main highway, he sees a boy pretend to throw a stick, and a dog run and look into the empty sky, waiting for it to drop. He slows the car, thinking he will go tell the boy never to do that again. He hates to see people tease animals. The boy is about the same size as Tommy.

No, he will wait and tell Tommy never to do that. Tommy is starting to get a mind of his own and needs someone to tell him things. That morning Tommy had headed down the trail to the woods carrying Uncle Vernon's old Winchester .22, the sky above cackling with black birds, flashing back the same glint as the boy's own hair.

"Are you going hunting, Tommy?" Zack asked before he drove away.

"No, Uncle Zack," he answered, "you don't hunt blackbirds. You just shoot them."

Zack's left foot presses the throttle and he accelerates past the speed limit on the road to Summit. By the time he reaches the city limits, the sky is dark, balls of mistletoe hanging uncollected from last season making black dots in front of the full moon. The scenery around him begins to fall into place like the world of a blind man who taps familiar objects with his cane: the Time to Retire boy, his hair white with pigeon droppings, still holding his tire; the old Blue Moon building that has become a real estate office with too much parking; the Burma Shave signs on the old Summit Highway, two of them fallen over, their lettering worn away and unreadable, except to people like Zack who knew what they had said when they were new: PAST SCHOOLHOUSES / TAKE IT SLOW / LET THE LITTLE / SHAVERS GROW; then the SLOW CHILDREN sign at Goose Bottom Elementary where Tommy went now.

His left foot drops down harder on the throttle, the awkwardness of the angle fading now as he speeds through the familiar turns, eager to get back home. As he approaches the farm, he smiles when he sees B.B.'s old house where Aurora and Tommy stay now; the light is still on in the living room. He is sure now. He will walk down to ask her tonight before she goes to bed and she will say yes.

33

At the first race on the Talladega superspeedway, the big-name NASCAR drivers go through with their boycott, but Tom Pate and the rest of the unknowns take a shot at glory. The only well-known driver who chooses to run, Bobby Isaac, a superstitious man of humble beginnings said to have been born in a sawmill, stands looking at the expanse of Bill France, Sr.'s dream, the biggest superspeedway in the world. Tom walks to within speaking distance of him and comments, "I don't see what they're all afraid of."

Isaac doesn't answer, staring at Tom with eyes more like a man who has spectated races than one who has driven close to two hundred miles an hour. Isaac's heart will give up eight years later while he smothers in the fumes from his own race car at Hickory, the track where he'd run his first race. A man dogged by bad luck and haunted by demons, Isaac is determined to defeat his fear at Talladega. He walks away from Tom Pate without an answer.

Tom doesn't win. Bobby Isaac doesn't win either. The driver who wins, Richard Brickhouse, will have to settle for Talladega 500, 1969, as the high point of his life. But for Tom Pate, a different story begins. Although his engine lets go on the high banks sending out the yellow flag for the oil-slicked track, he runs long enough to turn the right heads.

Max Owens, a team owner with a big shop in Dover, Delaware, comes up to him after the race, saying the words he has dreamed of hearing: "You've gotten all you can get out of the car you're running. No offense to Maynard Peyton and Bullfrog Embers. I've got the highest respect for them. They do the best they can with the equipment they've got, but if they can't run all the races, then you can't go for the championship. With the right car and the right team, I think you can run up front." With those words ahead of him, Tom has no reason to look behind.

For Tom's last night with them, Maynard's wife Ethel fixes Tom's favorite meal, roast beef, fried okra, creamed corn, with biscuits big as a man's fist.

"Bet they don't know how to make biscuits like this up in Delaware," Maynard comments as he pours thick gravy over two of them before chopping them with his knife. "Sure you don't want to change your mind?" he asks.

"I hear you've already replaced me," Tom answers. "Dewey Warren."

"Hum," Maynard muses, "I heard he had a big mouth. I see he went and proved it. That's a kid for you."

"He's no kid. He's twenty-two. He's married, too."

"I bet you're glad to hear that, Ethel. At least you won't have to wash his underwear. I thought you got to be called a kid in this business till you hit thirty," Maynard chides. "I was kind of hoping this one was young enough to learn something."

"You're a good teacher, Maynard, I'll give you that any day. I learned a lot from you."

"Yeah, but you must have been playing hooky the day I taught you about them little coffins with wheels. Owens ain't got his heart in Grand National racing is what I hear. Indy has killed the best of them. Stay with stock cars, boy. They'll take a lot better care of you when you run two hundred."

Tom excuses himself to go pack, thanking Ethel for her meal and hugging her though he half believes she is glad to see him go. When he shakes hands with Maynard, the older man can't let pass his last chance to lecture. "You know, I've decided I'm not going to worry about you. Race drivers don't ever get lost out in the big, bad world, Pate. It's part of the deal. That's 'cause race tracks end where they begin." Then he adds, "In case you ever want me to introduce you, I know the one fellow real well that all you fearless drivers is scared of. His name is old Father Time. No matter how fast you go, old man Time's always a little bit faster."

Tom stops in the doorway before heading out back to his room. He doesn't have a reply for Maynard.

That night, the night before he will leave for Daytona to practice with his new team, Tom has a dream that wakes him up. He looks for windows in the room the way he always does when startled from sleep, trying to place himself without having to turn on the light and search for something with the name of the motel and the town he is racing in. The window beside his bed is open and he can smell the paper mill on the Catawba River. He knows then he's still at Maynard's house, in the garage apartment where he stays when they aren't on the road.

He reaches for his cigarettes and the blue flame from his lighter erases the stench from the mill. His dream hasn't left him yet, but he is not sure he wants to hold onto it.

He was down on all fours, his hands and knees hurting him bad like when he was burned at Martinsville. He was the old lame dog in Zack's story, trekking across the desert, following his master who had left him behind. But when he reached his master's street, holding that uneasy feeling that he'd been there before and knowing that the garbage truck was going to get him, he looked for the new doghouse. Only it was a race car. And the puppy in it was a young driver who had got there before him.

The hands of his alarm clock across the room form a lighted sideways V; it's 2:15 A.M. He reaches for the phone in the dark and dials Zack's number.

Tom hears the sound of the phone receiver being dropped, then a muffled hello.

"Zack, it's Tom."

Zack's answer isn't clear. It sounds like a question, but the words don't fit together. That's the way Zack is when he's not awake yet.

"Zack, wake up. I've got something to tell you."

"It isn't morning yet."

"I know that. Wake up. I know you're not awake yet. You're still goofy. I'm not telling you until you wake up. I've got to tell you about my dream. It was the old dog story you told, the one you said made me cry."

"You did cry." Zack is awake now.

"Okay, I did. I admit it. But not for the reason you thought all these years, not because some old dog got run over. Zack, it was because this young guy was in my race car. I know him. It was Dewey Warren."

"Who's Dewey Warren?"

"He's this young kid from Hickory who's been winning all the Modified Sportsman races this season. Maynard's hiring him to take my place and there he was in my dream, sitting in my new race car. I quit Maynard to go there and he beat me to it." Tom's voice breaks.

"Tom," Zack says clearly. "You didn't even have a race car back when I told you that dog story."

"But I wanted you to know why I cried," Tom insists. "It wasn't because of the dog."

"Okay, Tom. It wasn't the dog. It was the guy in your race car."

"Yeah, that's it."

"And when you wake up tomorrow, everything will be back like it was and your race car will be empty."

"I don't know. It seemed awful real."

"It's not real." Zack is quiet a moment. "You know what the real thing is, Tom?"

"No, what?"

"You really cried."

Tom didn't answer.

"Goodnight, Tom."

"Goodnight."

Tom hangs up the phone and looks out the window where the night bugs squeal, their bodies bouncing against the screen when his cigarette lighter flares again. The insects quiet as though Tom's voice had stirred them up and his silence now has lulled them back to sleep. Maynard and Ethel's snores come from their room across the backyard, a gurgling duet. He recognizes Maynard's snore from all those nights on the road. His bluster fades into a squeak, higher pitched than Ethel's, as sleep takes over.

Tom knows Zack is next to Aurora, still awake, thinking about the dream. Maybe not.

They are married now. Zack changed the wedding date twice, hoping Tom would come, then gave up on him. "I let you pick my women," Zack joked. "I don't guess I have to let you pick my wedding date too." Tom can't remember how she sleeps, maybe face down like a baby. He does remember that her sleep was so silent that at night the tiny space they'd lived in seemed empty.

By the time Zack wakes up to his alarm clock next morning, maybe he won't even remember Tom called.

Tom decides to fall back asleep, and this time he plans to dream about riding down the river to Raleigh in his tractor tube, or maybe he'll try for the race he won with the devil after Soho the palmist told him his life line ran out. But when sleep comes, his mind is as empty as the desert the old dog has already passed through.